The Rock'N'The Roll.
'N That

Steven J. Gill

Clink Street

London | New York

Published by Clink Street Publishing 2018

Copyright © 2018

First edition.

The author asserts the moral right under the Copyright, Designs and Patents Act 1988 to be identified as the author of this work.

All rights reserved. No part of this publication may be reproduced, stored in a retrieval system or transmitted, in any form or by any means without the prior consent of the author, nor be otherwise circulated in any form of binding or cover other than that with which it is published and without a similar condition being imposed on the subsequent purchaser.

ISBN:
978-1-912562-55-8 - paperback
978-1-912562-56-5 - ebook

Dedicated to

Darren Clarke and John McBeath. Both are much missed.

And the twenty-two innocent lives lost on 22nd May 2017.

Manchester will never forget you.

Don't Look Back in Anger...

Chapter 1

Low-key.

He'd insisted on low-key.

Low-key. It's unambiguous.

Without fuss.

No surprise parties.

Resolutely no fucking surprise party.

No '*see them once in a blue moon*' friends making up the numbers.

No debauched weekend in Eastern Europe being rinsed by preternaturally attractive girls.

And resolutely no navel-gazing or 'what if' recriminations.

At least not outside the confines of his inner narrative…

Male pattern baldness. Erectile dysfunction. Pension shortfalls. Prostate checks. Taking up the saxophone. The fucking saxophone. Earhole, eyebrow & nostril hair sprouting overnight. Middle aged spread. Just for fucking Men hair dye. Fuck me. Buying a bike worth twice your first car and dressing up in lycra like a Poundland Bradley Wiggins. Fucking Lycra. Prozac. Viagra. Vitamin supplements. Anti-wrinkle moisturisers at 30 quid a pop. Getting your five-a-day every day. And your once a month bedroom treat. If you're really lucky. Stop wearing trainers. Christ. Health MOTs. National Trust membership. Three-day hangovers. Dinner parties. Stroking you chin in Real Ales Pubs and Ministry of turn the Sound down please. Going. Fucking. Bald. And so on…

It'd better be fucking low key, Johnny thought to himself as he idly peeled at the dampened label on his bottle of lager.

Johnny Harrison.

Thirty-nine years and 364 days old.

Or young. Whichever way you want to wrap it up.

He had begun to warm to the vagaries of thirty-something…

But forty.

Fucking forty.

Middle-aged.

Proper middle aged.

How the fuck had that crept up on him?

4-0. That was a whole new demographic. The 39–45 bracket on applications. And that's nearly 50.

He had been fifteen when his dad hit the two-score milestone. The half century eluding him as he dropped dead of a stroke at 48. Congenital heart condition. Long odds of it being hereditary. But still…

It was to be a drink or two with his closest friends in Manchester's burgeoning Northern Quarter.

Dressed for the occasion in his immaculate, but seldom worn, Navy Stripe Boating Blazer, green gingham checked shirt and jeans – the same brand and fit for the past fifteen years. A pair of new brown Desert Boots completed the outfit. A present from his long-term partner, Claire. Complete with a card saying that it should really have been comfy slippers. Drum roll please.

"There's just no place for the balds in rock 'n' roll," said Johnny

"Elton John," Mark replied, with a self-satisfied look on his face.

"He's not a bald! Proper head of hair on him," Johnny replied.

"Fuck off. He's bald as a coot! He wears a wig. I'm sure of it," said Mark with an exasperated tone.

"AHH!" Johnny said as he held an index finger to his nose and pointed at Mark with his other hand.

"You're such a sarky twat," Mark grumbled.

"Look. For every bald you can think of, I can name a dozen that are hirsute in the extreme. Ozzy. All The Beatles. Bowie. Zep. Let's not start on The Stones. Clapton. Duran Du-fucking-ran. The Gallaghers. Him out of Depeche Mode. The Roses. Pete Doherty. But I wouldn't encourage his narcotic intake."

"Yeah, yeah alright," Mark ceded.

"I'm right. A healthy diet of drugs gives you a great fucking head of hair. For life. So, shut the fuck up and tuck in," Johnny said as he nodded in the direction of the mound of cocaine that sat centre stage on his finger-marked glass dining room table.

"FLEETWOOD MAC! They took loads. Legendary for it," he shouted smugly.

"Behave. Stevie Nicks has got a lovely head of hair. She wouldn't thank you for that," Johnny retorted.

"Always the smartarse," Mark said.

"Always. But you still love me. Now get that polished off. Taxi will be here soon. Give Chris a shout. Chain-smoking like a lab monkey out there."

"Anyway. Don't change the subject. That's it. All downhill from here," Mark said pithily.

"Fuck off. I've still got my hair. Bit greyer. Well, a lot greyer," he said shrugging, "and my eyesight's only just giving up the ghost. And I won't be shopping for Blue Harbour's finest elasticated jeans like you. That bay window above your belt," Johnny said as he reached across to pat Mark roughly on his receding pate.

Mark recoiled, slapping Johnny's hand away.

"Look at the fucking state of you man. You've given up. Five years ago, you'd have never been seen dead in them shoe trainers or whatever the fuck they are. They look like someone dropped two pies and you've stepped in them"

"Given up? You've not got a fucking clue mate. Given up. Fuck me," Mark said with a weary shake of his head. "I'd love to drop a week's wages on clobber. But the last time I looked at something smart, it didn't come in a wipe down from baby puke range."

"Come on mate, I'm only messing. I'm 40. What changes? It's only a number. I'll be right. Something'll happen for me…"

"Do you mean you're actually going to grow up and face up to your responsibilities?" Mark asked. "It's not too late for you to become a dad or make an honest woman of Claire. Decide what you want from your career!" His tone becoming serious as he attempted to add gravitas to his advice

"Haha! I'd love to take you seriously mate! I'm hanging on your every word. But I cannot take life coaching from a man with a lump of coke hanging from his nose."

Rubbing his nostrils furiously, "You could at least start with a proper haircut," Mark said.

Chris returned from the backyard, having just extinguished his fifth cigarette of the afternoon. "But it's not *just a number* is it. You'll look at what you've achieved or in your case…"

"Balls," Johnny said, a little too defensively.

An angular chin away from being classed as classically good looking. Just under six foot, with an athletic build he had somehow retained despite a lack of any meaningful exercise over the last decade. A thick head of hair that had seen teenage attempts at a Morrissey quiff – lamentably limp – '90s rave 'curtains' which morphed into an indie bowl cut and was now worn in an unkempt fringe that he felt was an act of rebellion towards his corporate paymasters. And in his vainer moments, made him look like Richard Ashcroft.

Decent enough house. Money wasn't that much of an issue. His job as an HR manager at a large IT company paid well, but it wasn't exactly what he had planned. Claire was a good partner. Although she was not behind the door at reminding him what a catch she was. He missed her more free-spirited days. Sort of. She was seemingly now far happier planning interior design makeovers, with hours spent slavishly pouring over aspirational magazines.

This can't be it.

There must be more to the conundrum of life. There's got to be more than sitting on a sofa and asking each other what you want to eat before you die.

The front door to the terraced house opened and Claire walked in, dumping her neon striped sports bag at the foot of the stairs.

Claire Cooper – who went by the moniker of CC in her clubbing days. A natural blonde with a dancer's body. Upon the closure of her beloved Hacienda, she'd switched overnight from pill popping to detoxing. This epiphany resulted in her looking a good ten years younger than her 38 years.

Standing and hugging her, Johnny kissed her warmly on the neck. "Careful now. You don't want to get sweat on your best jacket, do we?"

"I was just going to say how nice you smelt," Johnny smiled.

"Don't creep. Doesn't suit you. And I know you're only coming out with the charm to make up for the shit state you'll be in tomorrow," Claire retorted.

"Hiya Claire," Mark said with a surreptitious rub of his nose.

"Hello boys," Claire purred, well aware of the effect that her Lycra-clad figure would have on her partner's drinking buddies.

With a polite peck on her cheek, Chris returned the flirtatious comment with interest. "Hiya gorgeous. You look great. As always. Way too good for this deadbeat!"

Mark smiled back, discreetly trying to wipe the stream of coke induced dribble that had leaked from his right nostril.

"Lucy and the twins doing well?" Claire asked.

"Great ta. She said to say hello," Chris replied as he studiously tried to stop eyeing her up and down.

And failing.

Checking his chunky stainless-steel watch, Johnny sighed at the platitudes.

"Won't be a massive one. Just town for a few and that. Maybe a curry."

Making finger quotes, she said, "A 'quiet one'. Hmmm. You'll tell me anything. Come on, it's your big 4-0. I'd be disappointed if you didn't make a tit of yourself somewhere along the line. No pun intended," Claire laughed as she tapped the tiny silver stud on her nose. A throwback to her wilder days.

Spreading his arms wide, feigning innocence, Johnny looked at his two friends for moral support.

"And if you low-rent Scarfaces could tidy up the evidence before you run along. My mum's coming around tonight and even she's not daft enough to think that I've gone all 'Bake Off'."

Again, she made finger quotes with her salon painted nails.

Decanting the gak back into a '*here's one I prepared earlier*' wrap, Johnny pulled out a hankie and wiped down the table, dabbing a rogue grain on his gums.

"You don't get any more house-trained with age. A snotty hankie! I'll clean up after you all. Disgrace. The lot of you," Claire said with a smile.

Hearing the parp of their taxi, Johnny said, "Right, that's us honey. Ta for the boots, dead comfy and look the business."

In a mock condescending voice, Claire replied, "Now you be careful, and don't drink too much."

"Yes Mum," said Johnny, playing out the threadbare routine.

"And look after Mark. You know he can't hack it these days," Claire added sympathetically.

"We'll be fine and he's a big boy..."

Blowing a departing Pepe le Pew-like kiss, Johnny did the obligatory keys, wallet & phone check and slammed the wooden front door shut and in three strides was in the front seat of the waiting cab.

"Hiya mate. Northern Quarter please, and we'll need a cashie so if you could just stop off on the way. Nice one."

Pulling the seatbelt across him, Mark said, "I knew I should have had a piss before we left."

"Christ. We've not even pulled away yet," laughed Chris.

"You know what I'm like once the seal's broken," sighed Mark, lamenting his thimble-sized bladder. A gift seemingly bestowed on all middle-aged men to quell their drinking valour.

They headed straight to The Crown & Anchor – a quiet backstreet pub that served a decent pint, with a secret smoking terrace on the rooftop providing great views across the city's constantly evolving skyline.

As they entered the pub Johnny sidestepped to let his friends to go in first, enabling him to confirm that there was no *'surprise, surprise'* party awaiting him.

They spotted a table equidistant for the bar, toilets and the well-primed jukebox – which was easing the evening in with something pleasant by Crowded House which Johnny just couldn't quite name.

"My shout," said Johnny to the back of Mark's head as he made a beeline straight for the gents'. "Three lager flavoured drinks?"

Taking their seats. "That laser eye treatment has knocked years off you man. Can't get used to you without your Ryans," Johnny said. "You're now more Game of Thrones than geography supply teacher."

Rubbing a hand across his salt and pepper beard, "I do love your backhanded compliments," Chris said, aiming a playful punch at Johnny's clean-shaven chin. "Save me a fortune in the long run, the number of pairs I've lost or sat on."

"Claire keeps telling me I need to get mine tested. Either that or get my arms stretched. And buying a whole new wardrobe would be way too expensive," Johnny quipped. "Mind you. If it stops her with the Specsavers gags it'd be worth it."

"I think you could pull that look off. Might even make you look intelligent. Anyhow. Big one tonight Johnny. I've not been out in ages. Work and the wife and twins and that."

"Christopher," Johnny placed his hand on his heart, "I can honestly. Sincerely. Wholeheartedly. Without doubt. Guarantee that we will get totally and utterly pissed tonight."

They laughed and chinked pints.

Three swift pints. A line each. And a collective five pisses. Three of which were on Mark's scorecard.

"Right," said Mark, standing and smacking his thighs. "A quick JD and we'll scoot to somewhere a bit livelier. I just need a quick piss."

"FOUR!" chimed Johnny & Chris with drunken sniggers.

As Mark returned carrying the three whiskies, Johnny held up his phone towards him. "Some bloke from Guinness for you. Wants you to call him when you've broken the world record for pisses in one evening."

Clocking the grave look on Mark's face, Johnny put the phone down. "Only joking mate. We're all as bad as each other."

Inhaling deeply and then knocking his drink back in one, Mark lowered his voice. "Look. Don't go off on one. But I've had a bit of an accident. I. I've dr—"

Leaning over the table, Chris looked at Mark's crotch, turned to Johnny. "Nope, he's not pissed himself!"

"Quit it," snapped Mark, pushing Chris back down into his seat. "Right. Some fucking idiot banged on the toilet door and I—"

"AND WHAT?" snapped Johnny.

"Shhh," gestured Mark. "Keep your voice down. Look. I've dropped the Charlie down the toilet. I'll pay. Fuck. I'm sorry fellas. I'm really, really sorry. I said I'll pay."

"Oh, that's okay," Johnny growled, "just toddle off to the bar and ask for three pints and a couple of grams of coke. And make sure it's not fucking diet!" slamming his hand on the table top.

"It was an accident. I'm as gutted as you are," Mark said as he kneaded his temples.

"My first night out in fucking ages and you flush the drugs down the fucking bog. Fuck me," Chris said with a slow shake of his head.

"Hundred and fifty quid. Fuck me. Hundred and fifty notes down the pan. Literally," hissed Johnny.

"I said I'm sorry," whispered Mark.

"Right. Fuck it. I need some fresh air. Let's move on. I can't stay in here," Johnny said.

Chapter 2

An hour had passed. Punctuated with awkward silences and sardonic grunts – principally from Johnny.

"It's not like we need drugs to have a laugh," Mark said. Much more of a question than a statement.

Johnny looked at him, wide eyed. "I'm not even answering that." Drumming his fingers on the table. "I'll remind you of that in a couple of hours when you've lost the power of speech and need helping into a taxi."

Chris returned from the bar with three extravagant cocktails. "Here you go birthday boy. That'll put a smile on your face."

Grimacing, Johnny stared at the ceiling. "Right. 'Cos a vase of alcoholic slush will make everything fine." Picking out the brolly, he snapped it between his fingers.

"Let it go man," said Chris. "He's apologised. Could have happened to any of us."

"Exactly," Mark said. "C'mon mate. Don't let it spoil your birthday."

Draining his cocktail with one slurp, Johnny stood and buttoned his blazer. "I'm just gonna grab a burger from the top of the road. Gimme ten minutes. Fresh air and some scran and I'll be right."

Raising his 'Frog in a Blender' cocktail, Mark said, "Grab me one mate."

"Shall I drop it down the toilet first?" Johnny said, before kissing Mark on the top of his head. "You daft twat."

As Johnny exited, Chris patted Mark on the arm. "Give him ten minutes and he'll be right. Let him chunner on to himself and we can forget all about it."

"Thanks mate. Another cocktail? My shout."

"Don't push it. A pint. And no umbrella!"

Leaving the warmth of the bar, Johnny hunched his shoulders against the cold. Pulling his blazer around him and rueing the decision not to wear his trusty Parka.

"Fuck, it's cold," he hissed to himself as the wind picked his pockets. Sidestepping a pouch of pavement smokers outside The Millstone, he headed for the takeaway on the corner of Thomas Street.

A screech of 'hens', goosebump-prickled arms linked, teetered towards him on skyscraper heels. Swathes of exposed flesh the hue of a freshly painted fence. Cheaply printed T-shirts bore hashtags indicating their respective roles in the upcoming nuptials.

"HELLO SAILOR!" giggled #Bridetobe, exposing a hunk of well chewed gum.

Stifling a grimace, Johnny smiled and proffered a half-hearted salute. A smorgasbord of mononymous celebrity perfumes assaulted him, and he gave an exaggerated cough as payback for the nautical quip.

Pushing the plate glass door open, he was met with a fat saturated warm blast. Picking his way across the tiled floor, slick with smeared rainy footprints. A couple sat at a Formica table that was cracked into grease-engrained fractals. They made gooey eyes at each other as they fed each other fried chicken.

Who said romance is dead, thought Johnny.

With a cursory glance of the backlit menu. "Cheeseburger please boss. No ketchup ta."

"You want drink with that? Chips?" asked the burly proprietor as he busied himself at the skillet.

"No. I'm fine ta," Johnny said.

Johnny leant against the tiled wall and then thought better of it, rubbing the back of his precious jacket. Glancing across, the deep-fried lovebirds were now attempting to eat their last piece of chicken a la *Lady and the Tramp*.

He busied himself with nothing on his iPhone. Skimming through a few blasts from the past birthday greetings on Facebook.

"You want ketchup on your burger?"

"No ta," Johnny said, smirking to himself.

Inadvertently catching McRomeo's eye, Johnny nodded. "Alright mate. She's a keeper."

"Fuck off yer dick. Only a first date innit. Why do you think we're eating in this shithole?" Turning to face the counter. "No offence mate. And you look a right cunt in that jacket! I didn't know they were doing boating on the Ship Canal."

"A cunt on a punt," his date sniggered as she wiped greasy fingers on an already soiled serviette.

"CUNT ON A PUNT! OH YEAH! I told yer that youse was funny for a girl." He snorted as he snapped his fingers.

"Hilarious," Jonny muttered under his breath, regretting his intervention into their culinary experience.

He nodded his thanks as he took the warm carton, electing to eat on the go rather than endure anymore of the gastronomic floorshow that had now moved on to a one cup/two straws finale.

Heading over the road towards Stephenson Square, Johnny wolfed down the burger in four bites and headed towards an 'open all hours' to pick up some chewing gum.

As he surveyed the 'ghost buildings' – awaiting the inevitable hoovering up by avaricious developers for yet more rabbit-hutch-sized aspirational lifestyles – he saw a sticker on a lamppost advertising a gig that evening. Roadhouse. Two minutes around the corner. Bound to be someone in there I can pick up a couple of grams from and get the night back on track…

***

The Roadhouse. Newton Street. Manchester.

A subterranean club, hidden by two huge black metal doors. It had been doing shabby chic since way before shabby chic was a thing.

A for once fully functioning neon sign cast a garish halo over the bouncer as he multi-tasked cupping a cigarette whilst drinking from a small Thermos.

Johnny skipped up the three oh so familiar stone steps.

"Hiya pal," Johnny offered breezily. He never failed to be shocked by the facial tattoos sported by the behemoth of the door.

He reached to his back pocket for a couple of pound coins to cover the early evening entrance fee but the booth cum cloakroom was unmanned. A promotional poster on the wall indicated that there were three bands playing that night under the imaginative banner of 'Soundclash'. The typeface done in a punk styling even down to the 'Anarchy A'. *Somebody being oh so retro*, Johnny smiled to himself.

A headline band going by the name of Kaspar, with support from The Salvo and Lonely Souls. With the promise of 'Classic Indie Bangers' from DJ Sirus the Stylus. All for three quid. Not the usual cringeworthy band names, mused Johnny as he stepped into the veiled darkness.

The smell of bleach hung heavy. The freshly swabbed floor anticipating the evening's spillages. The air was begging for the heady cocktail of booze to eliminate the sterile, just-cleaned odour. Frustrated ambitions hung thick – the attendant bands myopically challenged by their own musical shortcomings.

The Rock 'N' The Roll. 'N That

The club's patrons would have filled two Hackney cabs. Just. Two small groups stood on opposite sides of the dimly lit room, resembling hormonally frustrated teenagers at a local youth club.

Johnny headed straight to the bar which was staffed by a skinny indie boy with a wince inducing collection of piercings and tattoos and a petite redhead who seemed to be skipping to be seen over the high wood panelled bar.

Spoilt for choice of server, Johnny nodded to the diminutive girl, who was wearing some seriously elaborate Cleopatra style make-up. The walking piercing busied himself stocking the fridges for the evenings demands. Slabs of Red Stripe, Breaker & Bulmers were stacked high awaiting a cursory chill before consumption.

Just as he was about to order, his phone pinged. Phone reception was more than a little hit and miss below street level.

'Don't forget my burger? x'

Mark. Predictably getting the burger hunger after his toilet mishap.

Johnny nodded for his fellow patron to go ahead of him.

The skipping redhead's eyes widened at the new arrival. "Anything I can get you?" she offered flirtatiously, leaning her head coquettishly to the side.

Glancing into the large mirror behind the bar, Johnny saw what had flipped her attentions up a couple of gears. A lad with thick brown hair worn in an outgrown crop, having ordered a half pint of Guinness was now counting out loose change onto the bar.

Wearing a black denim jacket buttoned to the neck, with a blood red cotton scarf worn muffler fashion, he glanced up nervously as his limited shrapnel seemed to be adding up to not an awful lot. Just as he reached for his back pocket for further funds, Johnny interjected – an act of half generosity and half to impress the barmaid who was rapt by her financially challenged customer.

"Make it a pint and I'll have a Red Stripe please. And your own," said Johnny, nodding across to the flustered customer.

"Thanks man," he said quietly, glancing in Johnny's direction.

Johnny's glance to his left was met by the most arresting petrol blue eyes. "Gonna be a short night for you if you're struggling for your first beer," he offered sympathetically. Dabbing slightly at the corner of his mouth, Johnny indicated that there was something on the lad's face.

Rubbing at the corner of his mouth self-consciously, he said, "Thanks man. Pre-gig nerves." Taking a small sip, "There's no Guinness on the rider and I've spent up on guitar strings."

"You're playing tonight? Which band are you in?"

He pulled slightly at his scarf. "Lonely Souls. We're on in 15 minutes. Reckon the crowd must have got lost," he said before laughing self-deprecatingly. "Thanks for the drink, man. And nice jacket."

Johnny soaked up the compliment. "My pleasure man. It's my birthday. Enjoy the drink. And have a good gig."

"It's the first gig we've played...." were the last words he said as he walked towards the not so salubrious dressing room situated to the right of the cramped stage.

The barmaid, leaning against the bar and stood on tip-toes followed his exit until he was out of sight, shaking her head slightly to herself before ringing the order through the till.

"You know if Phil the pow—" He corrected himself, "Phil Taylor will be in tonight?"

She looked up at him blankly. "He's not been in yet. Probably in later as a rule," the barmaid replied in a surly monotone. Looking disdainfully at yet another weekend Rock 'n' Roller looking to be taken to his dealer…

Turning his back to the bar, Johnny looked over at the stage as a skinny black clad figure with a cigarette behind his ear and a can of cheap lager clutched between his teeth hastily gaffer taped a hand-sprayed bedsheet behind the drum kit, walking with an awkward gait as if his bottom and top halves were in some coordination based disagreement. Stage adornment complete, the figure skulked back to the dressing room.

In large capital letters that had bled into each other, the sheet read, "LONELY SOULS. PROPER FUCKING SONGS".

Johnny rolled his eyes in a seen-it-all-before way at the self-aggrandising slogan.

As the stage lights snapped on, projecting stark white light from erratically situated floor and ceiling lighting rigs, four silhouettes became discernible. A small pocket of cheers was audible from a group who had made their way to stand equidistant between the bar and the stage.

The drummer looked too big for the stage, never mind the undersized kit he was uncomfortably wriggling his way behind. Built like a modern-day rugby prop forward, he spun a pair of drumsticks adroitly between his fingers.

The bass player – who Johnny had clocked whilst he dressed the stage – was now sporting black wraparound shades and a black bandanna pulled over his nose. Standing stage right, he plugged his black bass into an amp

The Rock 'N' The Roll. 'N That

and then placed a can to the right of him, rubbed at his forehead and then nodded at the drummer. The guitar seemed to earth him as he now moved with a fluid confidence.

Johnny's eyes were again drawn to the lead singer. The lad with the red scarf was now looking intently at the fretboard of his champagne coloured Fender Stratocaster. Nodding at the guitarist to his left, and with a 1-2-3 jut of his chin, the band roared into action.

A bottom of the bill band would never usually command much attention – aside from the obligatory rent-a-crowd of friends and family.

However, as the beneficiary of his early kindness set about their first song, Johnny was transfixed. With a Strummeresque vocal, the lead singer was a captivating presence. As the lead guitarist picked away at an angry rising guitar line, the singer held the neck of his guitar in one hand and the mic with the other in a white-knuckle grip.

Lost in song. "*You started the fire, but I stood by and watched it burn...*" he sang with eyes tight shut. The chorus was slightly muffled, but it hung anthemically over the rhythm section's precision.

Grabbing a bottle of water between songs, the lead singer introduced themselves. "We're Lonely Souls. For those that are down tonight, I'll stick you on the guest list when we play the Arena..."

The band were dressed in uniform blue or black denim jeans, Converse with either a black T-shirt or black denim jacket, the only concession to on-stage colour being the lead singer's red scarf. Pushing a hand through his hair, the lead singer announced, "This one's called 'Opaque'." A loquacious bassline threatened to distort the sound but dropped perfectly to let a cascading, spiralling guitar line chop out a staccato opening verse. A chorus of "*nature or nurture, I didn't mean to hurt yer…*" was coupled to an irresistible hook

Johnny looked around the room. Was it only him that was seeing something very special here? His heart rate had upped a notch. Not drug induced. The earlier cocaine toilet mishap had seen to that.

Glancing towards the bar, he saw the redhead barmaid point in his direction.

Phil 'The Powder' Taylor was in the house. Bowing theatrically towards Johnny and tipping an imaginary hat. Johnny flashed a two-finger peace sign and turned straight back to the stage.

Mancunian psychedelia all underpinned with a drumbeat firmly rooted on the dancefloor. The dreaded rock dance hybrid that could easily go oh so horribly wrong.

Spellbound, Johnny knocked back a large gulp of lager, wandering over to the back of the room and standing centrally in front of the sound booth.

Appearing like a genie in Johnny's peripheral vision, "I believe you require my bespoke services," Phil said as he made his way to the kitchens situated to the back of the club.

"Yeah, cheers man. I'll be through in a bit," Johnny said, not taking his eyes off the performance.

"Suit yourself. Good to see you as well," Phil said with a shrug.

"Nice one. Two if you've got 'em," Johnny said to no-one as Phil was already through the door that led to the back of the club.

At this the band kicked into their next song, a pealing guitar riff roared the song on, rawer and more urgent; the lead singer had slung his own guitar behind his back, the classic guitar gunslinger stance and was, eyes closed, snarling the lines "*the city looks pretty as the flames rise high. Burn the streets, burn the sky...*"

Closing his eyes, Johnny found himself holding his breath as the song unleashed its killer chorus. He imagined an arena full of bodies moving en masse.

He checked his wallet to see he had a 'business card' within, like a lustful teenage boy stashing a condom within the confines of his wallet. The crumpled card read 'TCB Management' – a lame Elvis/Colonel Tom Parker reference – with just his name, mobile and email address.

During his mid-twenties Johnny had managed a couple of Britpop style bands which were ten a penny at the time. Any scally that could afford a guitar and a Berghaus cagoule thought that they could be the next Noel Gallagher.

Neither band had achieved much success although Epiphany – dreadful name he had always thought, which sounded even worse when the North Manchester Herberts pronounced it with a crass exaggerated emphasis they thought made them sound 'real'. They had released a self-financed EP which had been played heavily on local radio and secured them a tour support with an equally doomed to failure band. Johnny had never given up the hope of finding the next big thing and the card was a constant reminder of this.

Great chorus, but the verse needed a little spice in the soup. But this was a band that had something. A decent producer would sort them right out. Feeling exhilarated, Johnny started to plan his post-set chat with them. *Nice and laid back, not giving it the big one*, he thought. Considering what would impress without promising them the moon on a stick.

Next, a gentler number, all downbeat chords and metronomic drumming married to a euphoric chorus.

Throughout the set, the band had stood stock still as if in front of a firing squad – the perpetual-motion drummer aside.

The lead singer then announced in time honoured fashion, "This is our last song. It's called Salvation. Thanks for coming." With a gentle laugh to himself, "Remember the name. LONELY SOULS!"

Then that moment.

The band 'locked'.

Everything was right. Striking a squealing series of major chords, the song careered off at breakneck speed. The rhythm section pounding down an incessant groove which just about managed to hold the song down as the two guitarists now faced each other, chords exploding.

Mesmerising. Utterly fucking mesmerising. Open-mouthed, Johnny felt dizzy on pure adrenalin. Astonishing. Bands like this don't play bottom of the bill to less than you could get in the back of a cab.

But they fucking do. His mind raced. Compose yourself. Get a grip. Fuck me. They are the gold nugget in a parched riverbed.

The chorus opined that the singer could be '*Your salvation*' and seemed to be working on the level of both a lost love and 'the people' in general. A roaring anthemic chorus insisted that "*I'm your salvation, you're my salvation, we're your salvation*". A neat backing vocal of 'ahh's completed the irresistible nature of the track.

The last chorus finished, the singer pulling at the blood red scarf still tight round his neck and the band hit top gear, clattering into a final flourish, as controlled feedback squealed, the guitars soloed to dizzying effect, with the huge drummer throwing in perfect fills at sweat inducing speed. The bassist, with his guitar held at textbook 'Sid' height, powered the song to its conclusion as he continued to stare down an imaginary packed crowd. The band finished as one, looking at each other and exchanging barely noticeable nods.

An understated smatter of applause rattled round the sparsely populated venue. Equipment was quickly and silently packed away as the next band stood stage right waiting to load on.

With his opening gambit planned, Johnny made his way across to the bar and nodded at the barmaid for another Red Stripe. After ten minutes and a half drained can, the lead singer and the lead guitarist made their way over to the bar, the cramped dressing room which would be being shared by all three bands not affording them any post-gig pleasure now their paltry rider had disappeared.

Nodding at Johnny, the lead singer ordered two half-pints of lager from the still admiring barmaid. Okay. *No time like the present*, he thought, and stepping over to the two musicians, Johnny offered the threadbare opening platitude of, "Great set lads." Instantly regretting the mundane nature of this, he then followed this up with the equally clichéd, "You lads have really got something. Certainly did what the sign said!'"

The lead singer laughed softly at this.

Noticing that the guitarist had the identical blue eyes as the singer. And with them also sharing the same cheekbones and hairlines – although the blond guitarist sported some faint scarring on his cheeks – they had to be brothers, possibly twins, he thought.

"We have. A proper fucking thirst," offered up the guitarist.

Seeing that both pint glasses were already drained, Johnny attempted to redeem his earlier opening clumsiness and offered up the next round. Once the two pints had settled, Johnny struck. "I really enjoyed that. It was fucking superb. I've looked after bands in the past. Not for a while, but I want to get back into it. And I thought you were fucking brilliant. Have you got a manager?" It all came out far quicker and sounded far more rehearsed than he had intended.

Pausing. He offered his hand out to them. "I'm Johnny. Johnny Harrison."

Glancing at each other they both returned the handshake, gig sweat still making the guitarists' hands overly warm to the touch.

"I'm Jamie. And this is my brother, Dom."

Pulling out the time worn card, Johnny half mumbled, "I'd love to have a sit-down with you sometime. You'll be wanting to have your night out now and catch up with your mates, so no point talking now."

"Which was your favourite song?" Jamie asked probingly.

Without missing a beat, Johnny replied, "The last one. Salvation? Great chorus and the middle eight was fucking top."

Taking the business card from him and putting it in the sweat stained pocket of his black Levi's denim jacket, Jamie then said, "Pass me your phone."

Without hesitation, Johnny unlocked his iPhone and handed it over. Going straight to the iTunes icon, Jamie held the phone between him and his brother and started to scroll through the music library contained within the phone's vast memory. With muted nods and approving pulling of their mouths, the seeming initiation process was over, and the now sweaty phone passed back. "Some decent tunes on there, you clearly love your music."

Johnny glowed inwardly at the platitude.

"But that jacket!" proffered Dom.

"Nah, nah, that's cool man. Nothing wrong with a Mod blazer," laughed Jamie warmly. "Pass me the phone back." Smiling at them both and slightly lost for words, Johnny frowned and handed the phone back to Jamie. Tapping at the smudged screen, Jamie entered the numbers to his own phone into the handset, rang it once to store the number before handing the phone back.

"We've both got each other's digits now. Let's see who blinks first."

"Cheers. I'm serious about this. Dead serious," Johnny said.

"I know," Jamie said quietly. "Here's Mikee and Danny. I'll introduce you."

"Alright man," Mikee said, offering out a paw. "Smart jacket. Bit fucking cold out for strawberries and cream though."

A brusque nod and a surprisingly firm handshake was proffered from the bass player, who now had his shades on top of his head and was flicking a lighter on off in anticipation of a post-gig smoke.

"This is Johnny, we're going to meet him next week and have a chat about stuff. Used to manage bands."

"Looking forward to it! And you lads enjoy the rest of your night. I've got to dash. Meeting my mates and I'm late after watching you lot. Enjoyed it though!" Johnny added as a parting flourish.

Heading into the kitchen discreetly, Johnny saw Phil hunched over his phone, stabbing at it with a bony finger.

Phil Taylor – nee Phil the Pill. He had been dealing since the early '90s. The then burgeoning dance scene having made him a hectic but lucrative living. Since the demise of club culture, he had moved onto dealing high quality cocaine. This had earned him the beautifully crafted moniker of Phil 'The Powder' Taylor. A wonderful borrow from the current World Darts Champion. Although to Phil's disappointment, he was a terrible darts player…

"Come into my office," he said as he looked up from his phone. Phil had special privileges afforded to him as he supplied the club's seldom seen owner with his South American merch. "Right then birthday boy, what we looking at? Blow job? Full Sex? Anal?"

"Did you see that band? Un-fucking real. Best band I've heard in years. Fucking brilliant. That last song!"

"When have I ever been arsed about bands? Not bought an album since Beefheart were in their prime. Anyway. Calm down. Getting all excited at your age isn't good for you."

"How did you know? I've not been shouting about it."

"Ah, the wonders of social media. I'm always looking at pictures of your Mrs on there. Way too good for you," Phil said with a throaty laugh.

"In that case, two grams and a blow job," Johnny deadpanned back. "And I'd have paid more if you had actually had a shave."

"Ooh, ya bitch," Phil replied, cod cattily. "Getting fussy in your old age?"

Pulling out a large plastic click lock plastic bag from within the lining of his brown overcoat, Phil dug out the wraps and handed them to Johnny with all the subterfuge of a magician's sleight of hand. "There you go, Jonathan. And smart blazer. D'yer leave the straw hat on the bar?"

"Not fucking you as well! Has no-one got any idea of style? Do you want paying or not?" he grinned, counting out £120 in tens, lining them all Queen's head face-up in a vaguely OCD manner.

"And now my present for you." Phil hunched over the kitchen work surface and chalked up two chunky parallel lines.

Ever the master craftsman, the lines were both perfectly symmetrical and resembled bookies' biros in thickness and length. Assuming the manner of a wine sommelier, Phil deftly rolled a twenty and proffered it with an affected bow. "I hope this is to your palate, Sir. It's from a very well-tended crop in deepest darkest Bolivia. Not far from the sea, which gives it its fragrant salty and bitter undertones."

Clearing his nose in readiness, Johnny laughed at the routine he had heard many times before.

"Bottoms up," Johnny said as he ducked down, imbibing the choke inducing line in one. He swept a few stray grains on the end of his damp index finger and wiping it, as tradition dictates, on to his gums. "Fuck, that's good gear," Johnny said, already feeling the numbing affect hitting his front teeth.

"You're a good 'un. Let's grab a beer and I'll go about my business," said Phil, ever the entrepreneur.

"Love to, mate. But I've left Larry & Moe on their own. Best catch up with them or they'll send out a search party."

"Suit yourself. But don't be a stranger. And say hiya to the lovely CC for me."

The Rock 'N' The Roll. 'N That

Johnny winced at the mention of Claire's former moniker. "Yeah. I will. Nice one man."

With a clumsy urban handshake all fingers and thumbs, Johnny made for the stairwell, noticing that the redhead was busying herself talking to Jamie. Maybe she had taken his advice after all….

Leaving the club, Johnny had to check himself from bounding up the stairs, *Rocky* style. As he made his ascent, he laughed to himself and clapped his hands together just as a vintage shop vision of gold lame and leather navigated the perennially sticky stairs.

"Fuckin' hell. How long have you been on it?" asked Denise, a friend from back in the day.

"Just seen the future of rock 'n' roll!" Johnny replied as he planted a kiss on both her cheeks.

"Have you balls! At half eight in here. I don't think so mister. You need to ease up on the party powders!"

"You'll see," said Johnny over his shoulder as he passed the catatonically bored doorman and reacquainted himself with the chill February night air….

***

"Where the fuck have you been?" snapped Chris, animatedly pointing at the flotilla of pint glasses that adorned the ring-marked wooden table. Glancing down at the dark beer stain on Chris's check shirt, Johnny counted six empty glasses. A decent effort in just over an hour, but it hardly constituted Withnailian proportions.

Impatiently throwing his black leather wallet on to the table, Johnny sarcastically shot back, "It's in there if that's all you're arsed about!"

Grabbing the wallet, and checking behind the credit card flap, Chris marched – *more of a flounce*, Johnny thought to himself – across to the gents' toilet, indicated by a stab at Euro bar culture with a marker pen italic scrawl of 'Hommes'.

"But where the fuck have you been?" asked Mark in conciliatory tones.

Seizing his friend's verbal olive branch, Johnny shrugged his shoulders apologetically. "I met The Powder and then started watching a band."

His barely concealed excitement then gushed to the surface. "I saw a band. And they were fucking brilliant, man. And the music, fuck! It was like The Clash and The Roses, bit raw here and there but you'd expect that. Man, they are fucking...." Pausing as he struggled to articulate his excitement, Johnny's hand waved up and down like a linesman unsure of a borderline offside decision. "...Fucking hell. They are. They could be brilliant."

Mark nodded in an exaggeratedly sage manner. "That's alright then. You've been doing your Simon Cowell bit in a shit club on local band night." Then assuming a very poor 'Del Trotter' voice – "This time next year you'll be a millionaire."

Not rising to the withering tones of his friend's comments, Johnny said, "I'm serious. They could be the next big Manchester band. You didn't see them. They look great. Top musicians and they've got songs. They've got the fucking songs that you need. That people will want to hear." Johnny's eyes had widened as he waxed lyrical about his find.

"I'm going to meet them and ask..."

Smack. Just as he was about to finish his sentence, his wallet landed in front of him, just missing a small collected pool of lager that had formed in one of the scars running across the table's grain.

Chris nodded a sort of acknowledgment to Johnny. "Right. Where have you been then knobhead?"

Misreading his now drug sated friend's interest, he said, "I was just saying to Mark, I've seen a band that are fucking ace and I'm going to meet up with them and see if they want to work with me."

Chris laughed in a way that bordered on an unpleasant sneer. "You are fucking kidding me!" He reached for a glass and then embarrassingly slammed it down when he realised it was empty. Wagging his index finger towards Johnny's face, he said, "We're out for your birthday and you stand around watching some shit band that gives you a hard on."

Johnny grabbed at the accusing digit. "You don't get it, they were superb and..."

Cutting him off sharply, Chris said, "Superb my arse, you don't 'find'" – performing annoying finger punctuation marks in front of Johnny's face – "bands just like that these days. And what the fuck are these band of undiscovered geniuses called?"

Snapping back at his friend's dismissiveness. "And what the fuck do you know? You buy your half dozen a year or so albums from fucking Tesco. If it doesn't have 'Greatest' in the album title, you wouldn't know a decent album if it got stuck in the stereo of your shite green Ford Mondeo. You fucking dick. And you thought that Keane were the future of rock 'n' roll!" He paused momentarily to compose himself. "And for your information they are called Lonely Souls."

The Rock 'N' The Roll. 'N That

As the conversation started to become more barbed and personal, Mark stood up and leant between his two sparring friends, and said in calming tones, "Right, he was a tit for not letting us know what he was doing but we were fine having a beer. It's only just gone half nine. Plenty of time to enjoy ourselves. And we can all agree that Keane are a big moist bag of posh toss." He laughed at his little joke. "My round. Whilst you two kiss and make up."

Chris rubbed at his nose in typical coke user fashion. "You should have just let us know. We were sat here like a right pair of twats waiting for you. And this band, come on mate…" Tutting at Johnny, Chris fortunately ran out of steam.

"I couldn't get a decent signal in The Roadhouse and the band are the business. You'll fucking see." Adding in an unnecessarily high-handed way, "I know" – emphasising the next part – "'*a good band.*' I've always been looking for someone like this. I'd do it all again, but way better than I did the first-time round. Honestly mate, I was only in it for a laugh and to stand a better chance with the birds then, but I could do it again and get it right this time. With the right band.…"

Just as Chris was about to dismiss Johnny's heartfelt sentiment, Mark intervened with three fully charged pint glasses and a packet of dry roasted peanuts between his teeth. "Here you are then children, we friends again?"

Reaching for the pint glass and gulping a third of it down, letting out an overly loud satisfied 'ahhh', Chris looked over the table to Johnny. "We're fine. Brian Epstein here is convinced he's found the future of rock 'n' roll, The Lonely Arseholes or whatever they are called, but we've kissed and made up and now we've got the bugle, the night is young."

Far from letting it go, and as always wanting the last word, Johnny said, "They are going to be something, you fucking wait. I'm going to manage them, if they want me to and I'm going to make them big."

Spotting Johnny's bullishness, Mark put a hand on both his friend's shoulders. "No more talk of bands then, eh. Let's crack on and go and find a decent bar and let's make a proper night of it."

Glowering over the top of his pint glass and with thoughts far away from the night ahead, Johnny drank deeply, stood up and said as convincingly as he could muster, "Deffo. Let's go and make twats of ourselves and work on tomorrow's shitty hangovers!"

Winking at Mark, he handed over the drugs-packed wallet. "And your turn on the tackle next mate. That'll get you sorted."

Leaving the bar and letting his two friends through the frosted glass door ahead of him, Johnny felt a tightening feeling in his stomach and played over the 'what ifs' of the potential meeting with the band…

Chapter 3

"So then. How was it? You were quiet when you got in. Not like you after a big one. You're normally like a one man wrecking ball," Claire said, not looking up from the screen of her laptop which flickered in her glasses as she trawled through the latest essential eBay offerings.

"New found maturity now I've hit forty," Johnny replied sarcastically. "Anyhow. I never make a mess. I'm not one of those daft twats that pisses in wardrobes or drawers and that."

Still not visibly acknowledging him. "Charming as ever though I see."

"It's true! You don't know how lucky you are."

Finally looking up from the laptop and blew an insincere kiss across the room. "No Johnny. I count my lucky stars every day."

Running the cold tap for a hangover stabilising drink, Johnny rolled his eyes and muttered crudely under his breath. Assuming a confrontation free air. "Yeah it was a good un ta. Mark and Chris can't hack it these days. Pair of lightweights. Both flagging by midnight."

Not missing the open goal that his last comment presented, Claire looked over the top of her designer tortoiseshell glasses, "I didn't think that'd be a problem with you and your little bag of magic powders."

Bristling at the pointed but pointless barb. "You never used to say no when you liked to party," Johnny batted back.

She rose to the occasion with consummately practised ease. "I grew out of that sort of thing though. I don't need to waste money on drugs to make me popular."

"You never paid for it anyhow!" Backing down to avoid an argument which would be levelled at his hungover/coke crankiness, Johnny softly offered up, "It's only now and then that I bother, I'm hardly Scarface am I?"

"I know. But you should knock it on the head. You don't want to be the oldest swinger in town now do you?"

"Haha. I'm definitely planning on a massive cake made of smack for my 50th, so think on." Tapping his forearm for added comedic effect, Johnny peered into the graphite humming behemoth that was the Smeg fridge/freezer that stood in the centre of the kitchen wall. "Want anything for breakfast?"

"You mean lunch. It's gone 12 now, lazyarse. And I'll have a bacon butty on brown if you're offering."

He put on a mock addict voice. "Don't mention 'brown'. you'll set me off wanting more drugs." Laughing at his own joke, "No brown bread. Will white do you?"

"That'll be fine, grumpy drawers."

Johnny winced at the triteness of the comment and busied himself at the frying pan.

"And don't leave the cooker in a mess, my mum's coming around later with a present for you, so I don't want the place looking like a greasy spoon."

Assuming a world weary accepting tone, he said, "No dear, I'll clean up after me. Promise."

"If you could. So where did you middle aged disgraces get to then last night?"

Pleased at the feigned interest but without wishing to divulge too much about the highlight of his evening, he said, "Just the usual. Northern Quarter. Saw a couple of bands in The Roadhouse. One of them was great. For a change." He deadpanned to deflect any hint of excitement over the band. "And then off to lap-dancing bars. Those two must have dropped a couple of hundred quid."

"I know you don't like that sort of place. If only because you say the music's rubbish, so don't try and be clever. Mind you'd all fit in nicely now with all the other greying middle aged saddoes."

Running a hand through his thick but unkempt hair, Johnny ruefully thought of the carbon dating grey flashes at his temples. Having polished off his late breakfast with the gusto of a condemned man, he ensured the cooker hob was fat free, then made his way past Claire and headed to the bathroom for a much-needed shower.

Unable to let even this innocuous activity pass by without comment, she said, "If you're having a shower, don't leave the bathroom like a swimming pool, and open the window so it doesn't get all steamed up."

Tensing his fists at the banality of the comment, Johnny lifted the ecru coloured blind up slightly and opened the double-glazed window sufficiently. He stripped out of his red and cream check boxer shirts and love worn Nirvana *'Nevermind'* T-shirt – still a staple of his bed attire after 15 years' wear.

Stepping under the power shower's scalding hot needles, adjusting the temperature slightly, he selected his favourite Black Pepper recharge shower gel. Bowing his head under the showers watering can head, his thoughts turned to the band and when he would contact them. It almost felt like chasing a girl – if he could remember that far back – too soon and you looked too eager. Leave it too long and it and you look like you're not bothered….

Chapter 4

"Sick night! Loved playing live at last and that barmaid had it bad for you bro!" said an exuberant Dominic. The brothers sat across from each other at a small, round, wooden kitchen table. Two cups of brick coloured sweet tea had been dutifully served up by their ever-doting mum.

Jamie looked up and winked as he idly flicked through his mobile phone internet browser.

"So then, my two rock stars. How did your first gig go?" she asked, adjusting her brown wavy shoulder length hair within the cerise pink hairband.

Jamie pushed both hands back through his hair and exhaled noisily. "Went well Mum, sound could have been a bit better and there weren't many people there."

"And a few of them were right dicks. Talking through the songs!" interjected Dominic.

Turning around and tutting at the colourful language, she asked, "How many songs did you play? You did 'Salvation' didn't you? That's definitely your best song."

"Yes, we played it Mum. Course we did." Jamie smiled warmly across at his mum as she wiped her wet hands on the back of her snug fitting navy blue jog pants. He loved the way she cared about their music. "Bit of an odd one as well, there were only a dozen or so people there, but this guy said he'd be interested in managing us. He seemed pretty cool, and sounded like he knew what he was talking about. He bought us a beer, so he can't be all bad."

"And Jamie pulled," laughed Dominic as he gave his brother a playful kick under the table.

Wiping her hands on to a red gingham checked tea towel, the boys' Mum became instantly defensive. "Who was he? What did he say? What—"

Cutting her off with a whoah-whoah-hands-up gesture, Jamie laughed at his mum's concern. "Don't worry. We've not signed our souls away."

"Pun intended," Dominic snorted.

"We're going to chat with Mikee and Dan and meet up with him. Doesn't do any harm and it'd be good to get a bit of guidance."

"Well just be careful, you're really good boys and I don't want you getting involved with some..." She struggled for the suitable noun, "...shark."

Dominic cackled and started beating out the Jaws theme on the table top, singing out the unmistakable string driven 'der der der der' as loud as he could. His table-top percussion causing the tea to splash up and down.

Blue eyes sparkling and laughing along with his brother's cinematic comedy turn, Jamie turned to his mum and smiled. "Take no notice. He's just winding you up. He was alright, and we won't make any daft decisions."

Leaving the two brothers to conduct their gig post-mortem, she kissed them both on the top of their heads. She left the dimly-lit kitchen, feeling proud that someone had spotted her offspring's obvious talents.

"Yeah, it went well didn't it. For a first gig," Jamie said emphatically, rubbing a finger across a thick brown eyebrow then wiping a trace of sleep from the corner of his eye.

Agreeing with his brother, Dominic changed tack. "Look at the way that cute barmaid was with you. She couldn't get enough of you. Now that I could get used to!"

Smiling at the thought of the lingering kiss he had shared with said barmaid as they had gone halves on a cigarette - huddled in a fire exit at the side of the club - Jamie nodded wholeheartedly.

"From a serious point of view, Mikee needs a new kit. Which won't come cheap. He looks ridiculous behind his. It's like a kid's set! And we haven't got time or contacts to sort gigs and shit out."

Draining the last dregs of tea from his 'I heart Manchester' mug, Dominic agreed with Jamie's sentiments, adding, "He seemed decent enough. Let's give him a listen. What's the worst that could happen?"

"Alright Dr Pepper. I'll text him. We owe him that. I mean he enjoyed the gig and bought us a beer."

Grabbing his mobile, Jamie smiled to himself when the SnapChat icon flashed up on the screen –

U BETTER CALL ME! KATIE xx

He didn't even remember giving out his number, but liked the tones of the sweetly succinct message.

"Right then! What shall I say to him then bro?" Jamie asked out loud but was already mid-message. A slightly calloused thumb – the faintest of indentations left from a plectrum – flew over the phones keypad with a second nature the digital generation seemed blessed with.

Knowing that the message was almost complete, Dominic still offered up some brotherly advice. "Just keep it short, and tell him we'll all meet for drink and a chat. All it needs. Yeah."

"Yeah, yeah. Done it. I've asked him to come and watch us rehearse. He should get to see us playing again and it'll be good to get another set of ears down."

"Your shout J. We know we're fucking good. And it'll mean we're on our toes," said Dominic

Offering across an upheld right hand, Jamie clasped his brother's hand tightly, gloving it with his left. Jamie patted their two adjoined hands. "You're right! WE ARE FUCKING GOOD…"

***

Stepping out of the bathroom, having ensured that he had fully complied with 'His Mistress's Voice', Johnny stood in front of the full-length mirror mounted on the wall adjacent to the bathroom door. The aquamarine coloured towel was tied round his waist. Looking in the mirror, he pushed his wet hair back, looking intently at his reflected hairline, moving his head from side to side and looking at any possible signs of receding. Satisfied that the tide wasn't going out, Johnny then turned attention to his midriff. Patting his stomach for tell-tale signs of the dreaded middle-aged spread, Johnny pursed his lips and deemed the slight gatherings of fat at his sides as manageable for a man of his age. The self-conducted personal MOT was concluded with a grimace to reveal his teeth; rubbing at his top gum, he made a mental note to himself that a trip to the dentist wouldn't go amiss.

Hearing the familiar 'ping' announcing that he had received a text message, Johnny finished his vanity routine and padded to the bedroom to retrieve his phone.

Good meeting you last night. We should meet. 8pm Tuesday. Beehive Studios. You won't regret it…

Johnny's pulse quickened; they'd got in touch with him before he had made a first move – and no shitty text speak either! Grabbing a pair of grey trunk style boxer shorts, a red Lacoste polo T-shirt from the second drawer of the dresser and picking up last night's jeans, he dressed with a veritable spring in his step, any lingering traces of the previous night excesses evaporating with an all-consuming air of expectation…

Chapter 5

"Should have booked today off. Schoolboy error. I'm shagged," Johnny replied wearily as he tabbed through his email inbox. "I was alright yesterday."

"You look how I feel mate. Big birthday weekend?" asked Paul as he busied himself transferring paperwork from one side of his desk to the other with a half-arsed nonchalance. Leaning back in his swivel chair and looking out of their fifth-floor corner office window across the Salford Quays canal basin, Paul stretched his arms out wide and yawned noisily. "'I'm sure it was better than mine mate. DIY hell. Kids running ring rounds me. Couldn't even find the time, energy or privacy for a quick wank!"

Scratching at an ear, Johnny said, "Ta for that, mate. I'll mark that down on my spreadsheet of your masturbatory habits. Hang on." Making exaggerated stabs at his desktop computer keyboard, he added, "Your weekly average is dropping, with a typical 0.54 wanks per day. A spike seems to occur on a Wednesday evening when you peak with a massive two wanks in three hours." Nodding studiously, Johnny beamed across at his colleague.

"Funny fucker," Paul laughed. "I'll order some breakfast," he said, perusing the dogeared café menu. "So, tell me more about your weekend then Mr Harrison. Thrill me with some vicarious debauchery!"

"Yes, all that," said Johnny, winking back. "We had a good 'un. Out in town. Northern Quarter. Usual places. Saw a great band though," he added enthusiastically. "I'm going to meet up with them tomorrow."

"Bit old to be a groupie, aren't we?"

A little more irritably then he intended, he said, "Not like that you dick. I mean I saw a new band that I want to work with."

With deserved sarcasm, Paul raised his hands up. "Of course. Why didn't I realise straight away?"

"Sorry mate. But you know I've always wanted to get back into doing a bit of the showbusiness stuff."

"Yeah, yeah, I know you did some managing stuff in your younger days. But…"

The Rock 'N' The Roll. 'N That

Cutting him off abruptly, "But nothing! I'm smarter and wiser these days, and I've got a few quid behind me as well."

Picking up the phone distractedly and starting to dial his breakfast order through, mouthing 'do you want anything?' just as the phone was answered. Shaking his head, Johnny pursed his lips in frustration at his colleague's perceived lack of interest.

Retrieving the situation neatly, Paul said, "Sorry Mr H, they answered quicker than usual. What were they like? What are they called?"

Johnny smiled at having caught Paul's attention. "They're called Lonely Souls. Cool name. They were bottom of the bill at The Roadhouse. You know it. Bit of a dive but I fucking love it." Lowering his voice at the dropped expletive and to avoid prying ears.

"Anyway. They were unbelievable. Sort of a dancey rock psychedelic sound. Bit raw, but the songs were brilliant. A couple of them sounded amazing. They looked good as well. The lead singer's cool as fuck and the drummer plays like a fucking dream," he gabbled excitedly.

"Bloody hell mate, I've not seen you this excited since…" Stumbling for an apt analogy, Paul stuttered, "since, well never!" Laughing at his own linguistic ineptitude, Paul asked, "What are you going to do then? Jack your job in and go and hit the road with a rock 'n' roll band?"

He put his finger to his lips. "Shhh! I'm going to meet them after work tomorrow at their rehearsal room. See what they're about and then who knows."

Paul nodded in approval. "You are serious!"

"C'mon. I know you hate this place more than I do. Why wouldn't I blow it off for something, well y'know, a bit more exciting."

"Amen brother Harrison."

"If I hear another cock in a shiny suit trot out the 'work hard, play hard' bullshit. By which they mean doing a load of shots in an All Bar One whilst ranking the girls in the office in terms of fuckablity!" Johnny hissed.

"If you bring the matches, I'll bring the petrol," Paul said. A little too manically.

"You know what I mean though?"

Tapping on his desk excitedly, Paul laughed, "Remember me when they hit the big time and you're dating a supermodel."

"All that," Johnny smiled back. "First name on the guestlist at any gig. And I'll make sure there's a quiet room so you can have a wank in peace."

"I'll hold you to that, Mr Harrison," Paul said, extending his hand over to him, "Deal!" He got up and hungrily rubbed his paunch.

Just before he made the office door, Johnny shouted after him, "Grab us a bottle of sparkling water."

Feigning diligence, Johnny busied himself with the slew of emails that he had amassed, but his focus was unwaveringly on his meeting with Lonely Souls…

***

"What time will yer new mate be here then?" Danny asked as he idly tuned his bass and checked the levels on his Fender amp.

Jamie frowned in the bass player's direction, putting extra emphasis on the name. "*Johnny* said he'd be here about 7ish which gives us an hour to set up and get things sounding nice and tight."

Strumming a few minor chords to make sure his guitar sound was just as he liked it, Dominic offered dup a new song that he'd been working on.

"Not tonight bro, let's keep it nice and simple for now. Play what we know. Get it right and if things are going well, we can always jam it out towards the end of the session. You know I love it when you bring something new to us." Smiling warmly at his brother, Jamie knew his placating words would not fall on deaf ears with his brother and two closest friends in the world.

Mikee finished putting a tartan car rug inside his bass drum to deaden the volume, and lazily struck a cymbal, instantly grabbing it in his paw like right hand. "He seems sound enough, only met him for a minute, but let's see what he's got to say for himself."

A heady combination of taskmaster and perfectionist, Jamie removed the packet of Marlboro Lights from his black denim jacket pocket and tossed them to the floor of the rehearsal room. The packet landed perfectly upright against his battered Marshall amp, looking like a dodgy attempt at an album sleeve. "Right, 'Is What It Is' needs a bit of work. Let's run through that and get it right…"

***

Leaving work on the dot of 5.30, Johnny reckoned forty minutes door to door would give him time to grab a quick pint at The Kings Arms – the nearest decent boozer to Beehive Studios – and still be there on time. He felt that was important today. His timekeeping bordered on the shambolic, which was made more pitiful given his penchant for a nice timepiece.

Checking that he had his ubiquitous packet of chewing gum, he entered the pub past a peeling CAMRA sticker that wafted every time a punter used the door. It was a proper boozer that attracted a mixed but resolutely trouble-free clientele. This masked the fact that the landlord was a miserable twat of the highest order. Ordering a Guinness and a packet of salt & vinegar crisps, Johnny selected a table as far away from any other customers as possible and tried to play out all possible scenarios.

Did he show his hand about money straight away? Should he exaggerate his experience and contacts? Or confess to being a chancer who wanted out of the rat race? he thought.

He swore to himself. He'd not felt this nervous in ages. Taking a sizeable gulp to drown the self-doubting butterflies, he exhaled and looked around the bar, hoping that tonight really could be the start of something…

***

The band had played three songs repeatedly – each time noticeably tighter and sharper than the last. Like all great bands, a symbiotic relationship forged a greater than the sum of the parts dynamic. Not that the individual components were too shabby…

"Let's go again with 'Salvation'," Jamie encouraged. "But let's nail the middle eight this time. It's loose when the guitars kick in."

As Jamie struck the first chord, there was a sharp double-knock on the studio room door and all four bandmates exchanged glances, willing each other to be the first one to break the silence.

The door opened ajar, and with the demeanour of a nervous interviewee, Johnny stepped into the band's inner sanctum.

Before he could mumble his introductions, Mikee shouted, "HERE'S JOHHHNNNYYYY!"

As icebreakers go, it was perfect.

Blinking to acclimatise himself to the starkly light room, Johnny was momentarily lost for words.

Striving to make the right first impression, he inhaled deeply. "Never fails that one. Always grateful that my mum picked the name. Once I'd seen the film." Clapping his hands together loudly, he said, "Right then, good to see you again…"

Nods and mumbled 'alrights' were forthcoming before Jamie assumed control. "We've just been going over a few tracks. Just to get them right. Sit yourself down over there." He pointed at an upturned beer crate positioned in the right-hand corner of the room. "You'll be as far away as possible from Mikee's kit as well."

As if marking his territory, Mikee struck his bass pedal twice and *Fight Club*-nodded in Johnny's direction.

Perching on the uncomfortable makeshift chair, Johnny sat upright, leaning against the wall, with his hands on his knees, looking like a footballer posing for a team photograph.

The band, counted in by three juts of Jamie's clean-shaven chin, kicked in as one. The sound roaring through the compact white-washed room.

Feeling a pounding in his chest - part adrenaline, part amplification of the bass drum - Johnny relaxed his pose and leant forward, cupping his chin between the thumb and finger of his right hand. He was certainly right about the drummer who was capable of rocking out, grooving and holding a tight but simple drum pattern down.

The two brothers who he now was convinced were twins – exchanged vocal harmonies and guitar lines symbiotically. Dominic taking the more liquid lead with Jamie holding down the rhythm parts. The vocals were far better than at the gig and Jamie's Northern Strummeresque snarl was also capable of a softer, more delicate falsetto when sharing vocals with his brother.

They are fucking good. No, they are fucking great, thought Johnny. Choking back a dry swallow he rued not having bottle of water with him to quench his thirst and to busy his fidgeting hands.

Bringing the song to a conclusion, Dominic placed his gold Les Paul into its stand and rolled his shoulders and bobbed his head from side to side loosening up any kinks and knots. Stretching his fingers out and then clasping them behind his head, his attentions turned to Johnny, who was now sat with his legs crossed, one arm folded across his chest and the other stroking the five o'clock shadow on his chin.

"Well?" he asked succinctly.

At a loss for superlatives, Johnny blew between his lips, and shrugged his shoulders. *Come on*, he thought, *this is your moment*. "I wouldn't be here if I hadn't loved what I heard on Saturday. And you sounded even better just then. The sound system did you no favours at the weekend, did it?"

The Rock'N'The Roll. 'N That

"You mean the lazy cunt of a sound engineer did us no favours," snapped Danny, clearly still harbouring a grudge with the apathetic performance they had been served up by the venue's resident sound man.

"Forget that," interjected Jamie, "that's history now. Go on then Johnny, tell us what you think."

It almost felt like a challenge. Like one of those naff magazine caption competitions whereby you could win a holiday if you described the utopian destination in suitably hyperbolic prose in less than twenty words.

Inhaling deeply, Johnny composed himself and launched into as spontaneous appraisal as he could. "I think you're as good a band as I have seen in fucking ages and I include a shit load of signed bands in that. You've got some great songs, that believe me, are not a million miles off the finished item. You can all play, fuck me, you can all play. I think your image is cool as well, nice and simple. You look like a gang, which all the best bands always are. And you all love playing, that's really fucking apparent. Oh, and I wouldn't fuck with Mikee…"

Smiling at the staring faces and wanting, no, craving, instant gratification at his little speech, Johnny held his breath.

"Can't argue with that," chirped up Dominic. "And wh…"

Before Dominic could finish, Danny butted in, direct as ever, "So what about you? What can you offer us?"

Sensing a little unnecessary hostility, Jamie said, "Let's pack up our gear and lock up here and go for a pint. We can talk then. And I'm dying for drink and a cig."

Nodding in agreement, the band set to packing away their instruments. Flight cases were snapped open and guitars laid to rest with a practiced tenderness. Glancing over at Jamie as he crouched over his battered black case, he noticed the red scarf that he had been wearing at the gig was folded neatly ready for the champagne coloured Fender to be placed over it. It almost looked like a prayer ritual as the three musicians bent over, clasping the cases shut almost in tandem.

Stepping into a now empty bar – hardly surprising for a wet Tuesday evening in February – Johnny asked his potential protégés what they would like.

"Two Guinness and two lagers. Cold Guinness," requested the affable drummer, not able to resist temptation at the hovering punchline, "and I don't know what these lightweights will have!" Beaming a big toothy smile, Mikee headed for the gents whilst Jamie, Dominic and Danny sat at the same table Johnny had occupied earlier in the evening.

Fetching the drinks, Johnny sat down on a threadbare red velvet upholstered stool between Jamie and Danny. Dominic and Mikee, who was wiping his hands on the seat of his jeans, sat against the wall on an uncomfortable looking red sofa – the springs groaning their resistance every time the huge drummer reached for his glass.

Deciding that he needed to take control of the situation, Johnny put his glass down and pulled at the collar of his blue houndstooth checked shirt.

"Okay. I've been more than impressed with what I've heard – and seen. I used to look after a couple of bands, so I know what's involved. It was a while ago, but…" pausing for dramatic effect, "I've got a few quid in the bank and I'd put my money where my mouth is. You'd get my time and enthusiasm. Financial support and my worldly wisdom!" Proffering up a final flourish," and we don't need to fuck about with contracts at this stage…"

Johnny waited for the reaction. He'd decided that he would show his hand over the finances but not talk specifics until he knew the lay of the land.

"That's cards on the table!" said Jamie, reaching over the brass topped table and patting Johnny, almost tenderly, on his forearm.

Waves of relief poured over Johnny, *I'm on a roll here*, he thought.

"You need to be rehearsing as often as you can. Two or three times a week ideally. How many times do you manage now?" Before he got the necessary answer, he added, "Get you tight as you like, couple of gigs to road test your songs again and then get you in a studio and put a couple of your best tracks down. You been in a studio before?"

Answering both questions, Danny said, "We're rehearsing once, possibly twice a week if we can afford it and we haven't been anywhere near a studio yet."

Seizing the moment, Johnny struck. "I'll pay for your room for three months, and then we'll get you into a studio to record three or four tracks – again I'll pay." Taking a gulp of his pint, he bowled on. "During that time, don't post anything online, YouTube or fucking Facebook or anywhere. I'll sort you out a couple of gigs. And I'll also speak to a couple of old contacts of mine and see what sort of favours I can pull. Get the track on local radio and the like. I've no doubt it'll sound brilliant when we," correcting himself with a quick smile, "sorry, you get in the studio. I'm 100% sure it'll be fucking ace, but let's not get carried away with ourselves…"

The four musicians looked at each other, somewhat taken aback by both Johnny's animated enthusiasm and most significantly, his offer of monies. Jamie

The Rock 'N' The Roll. 'N That

whistled between his teeth, looked Johnny straight in the eye, meeting his look with his piercing blue stare. "Give us a minute to have a quick chat and…"

Getting up from the barstool, Johnny - relieved at the opportunity to visit the gents. "Not a problem, I needed a quick piss anyhow."

"Too much detail, but we'll only be a minute or two," said Jamie with an amused smile.

Leaving the musicians to roundtable their decision, Johnny headed for the gents', with a barely contained skip in his step. Reaching the confines of the toilets, he clenched his fists and whispered, "Fucking yes," to himself. Emptying his bulging bladder at the old-fashioned porcelain 'splasher', he then took extra time and care washing his hands so that he didn't return to the table before any conclusion had been reached.

Chin-up, chest out, he thought as he walked purposefully back to the table. Sitting down without saying a word, Johnny held his breath in expectation.

Swiftly putting him out of his misery, Jamie chimed the words he had been craving to hear. "You're in! We need a helping hand for some guidance, sorting gigs and shit. And the cash. Well it's got to help and shows your commitment. We're not signing anything until we've done the practice and recording but…" Jamie paused and adding something of his own to the mix, and certainly news to his bandmates, "we're not gonna work with you just for the money. We like you and because of that, we're not signing anything now but anything we record that you pay for, then it's a five-way split between us all, I can't say fairer than that."

Quietly pleased at the offer that Jamie had made, the band were about to object but Jamie assuaged their concerns with a gentle, almost Jediesque wave of his hand. "This is all going to work out for us all. It's the start of something big, I can feel it."

Grabbing his almost empty pint glass and believing it the only appropriate thing to do, Johnny raised his glass. "I'll drink to that! Lonely Souls and something big!" One glass became five as they all lifted their glasses to meet Johnny's. As one they shouted, "Lonely Souls and having it fucking big…"

***

"Cheers Mikee," the twins said simultaneously as they tumbled from the passenger seat door of their drummer's works van. Knocking a couple of rogue fast food wrappers into the gutter from the swollen pile of cartons that was a health hazard to any passenger's footwear, Jamie picked the polystyrene boxes up and popped them in a conveniently placed wheelie bin. "Thanks man, we'll speak soon."

Cranking up the CD player, Mikee offered up a two-fingered peace sign and sped off homeward bound with the van pulsating to the bass heavy sounds of some obscure underground hip hop track.

Putting his arm around his twin brother's shoulder, Jamie hugged Dominic into him whispering - as if saying it out loud would jinx it - "It went really well tonight. Johnny will be good for us. And we are gonna crack this rock 'n' roll thing. I just know it!"

Picking up his Jamie's lead, Dominic added, "Course we will bro. It's never been in doubt…"

Taking the key from his jeans front pocket, Jamie opened the door of the cosy terraced house and saw that their mum was sat feet curled underneath her, watching a Channel Four re-run of *Donnie Darko*. Jamie looked at her, and met her loving smile, live pausing the film, leaving Donnie stood open armed with a translucent blue snake erupting from his chest. "How did my two favourite rock stars get on tonight?"

Chapter 6

"You're home later than you said," Claire said as soon as Johnny opened the front door, "I've already eaten but there's some pasta left in the fridge that you could have."

"Yeah. Ta for that," Johnny replied absentmindedly, pre-occupied by the evening's events and the commitment he had made to his new protégés. A quick mental calculation on the journey home had left him looking at a five-grand investment, plus extras if he shelled out for any equipment etc. With the forty-thousand-pound inheritance that he had banked, it wouldn't be a problem.

But.

And it was a big elephant in the room but.

It was a decision he was making on his own. He was adamant that Claire would see his nest egg as a bigger house or some such expenditure.

He knew exactly what her reaction to his covert venture capitalism would be.

Making his way into the kitchen he closed the wooden door, and turned on the digital radio, the pre-set station taking him straight to 6 Music whereby he was rewarded with Doves' wistfully perfect 'Kingdom of Rust'.

Grabbing a chilled Diet Coke, and sitting at the kitchen's breakfast bar, Johnny closed his eyes and rubbed both hands over his face, catching the rim of the can with his left elbow. He cursed loudly and jumped back before the rapidly spreading liquid could drip onto his suit trousers. The sudden movement caused the top-heavy stool to overbalance and crash loudly onto the slate tiles.

The clattering crash elicited the predictable response.

"What the fuck are you doing in there?"

And showing more concern for any potential material damage.

"I hope you've not broken any of those tiles. Or the stool!"

Clenching his jaw, but determined to quell any argument, he opened the kitchen door ajar. "Sorry, sorry. I knocked the can over. It went everywhere but everything's fine. Nothings broken," he uttered as he simultaneously scoured the Welsh quarry hewn tiles for any discernible signs of damage.

Righting the stool and breathing a sigh of relief, he grabbed a soggy blue j-cloth from the farmhouse style sink; wringing it dry, he mopped up the still fizzing liquid. Crisis averted, Johnny went into the open-plan lounge to further placate his still concerned partner.

"Hiya babe. Sorry about that. You know what a clumsy twat I can be." Johnny wasn't a huge fan of the cloyingly twee familiarity but felt under the circumstances that it was the least he could proffer as a way of keeping Claire sweet.

"I know exactly what you are like," she replied wearily, inevitably adding, "but that stuff doesn't come cheap."

Drinking back the remains of the can, and taking a moment to compose himself, Jonny offered up the palm of his right hand and said as calmly as he could muster, "I know, I know. I shouldn't have put my coat on it." He was about to offer up 'my bad' as a platitude – Claire's favourite current expression of choice – but wisely decided against this further blow to his integrity. "There's no damage done, I was lucky, won't happ—"

She cut him off mid-sentence. "Luckily! Apart from to my nerves. I was settled watching my programme before you rocked up. Where have you been till this time anyhow?"

Having been so consumed by the evenings events, he had had not formulated a plausible excuse. Stuttering slightly, "Err, I went to the gym after work 'cos I was busy at lunchtime. Then had a quick drink after with Paul. His divorce is causing him a load of mither, so I listened to him get it out of his system over a pint. Probably undoing all the good going to the gym did, but—"

As ever, she was the master of the interjection. "A text would have been nice though."

Thinking fast on his feet, he said, "Yeah, but I thought you were at your yoga class on a Tuesday night so we'd both get in at about the same time."

"Well. Bella emailed everybody to say she'd slipped a disc in her back and couldn't take the class, so I came straight home."

"Some fuckin' yoga teacher."

Turning sharply and far from happy at his attempts at the 'last word', she snapped, "Sorry?"

"Poor yoga teacher," Johnny replied, feigning innocence with an exaggerated wide-eyed stare. Adding a sincere consolatory, "I hope she's right for next week, I know how much you enjoy it." And with a final misguided stab at humour, "If you want to practise your downward facing dog, I've not had my 'birthday treat' yet…"

"If you went about asking like a grown-up, then we'll see. And stick the kettle on for me."

"No problem, proper brew or one of your hippy infusion things?" he asked, not being able to resist the barb at the panoply of weird and wonderful flavoured teabags that seemed to have multiplied every time he opened the cupboard door. Purely for his own childish enjoyment, "Conker & Dock Leaf do you okay?"

"Oh, you're so funny," she snapped back. "A normal tea please and not one of your usual stewed efforts when you forget about it because you're wasting time on the internet." Emphasising the 'normal' with cloyingly irritating rabbit's ears air quotes, Claire turned back towards the television and studiously ignored Johnny who was sticking a lazy 'V-sign' up behind her back.

"It'll be perfect, love of my life" he said, over-sincerely.

Again, sitting down at the breakfast bar, Johnny grabbed a notebook from the tray that sat atop the microwave and began to write down his proposed outlay and short-term plan for the band. Two hundred & fifty pounds per week for the rehearsal room. About a grand plus per month. Chuck them a grand or so up front for new gear, and then the studio time which he would have to price. Happy that his initial five grand estimate was pretty much spot on, he ripped the offending page from the notebook and put it into his wallet.

Turning his attention to the steaming mug, he grabbed a tea-towel and draped it over his crooked forearm, subservient waiter style.

"Madam's drink, if you would care to sample it." Bowing slightly, Johnny completed the act of contrition by carefully handing the drink over with his best winning smile. No point making an argument out of nothing.

Taking the handle in her left hand and smiling up at him, she said, "Thanks babe, you're not that bad after all…"

Chapter 7

It was the band's first rehearsal after 'that' meeting and their first paid practice session. There was a palpable difference and they opted out of their usual 'smokers meeting' whereby they would talk aspirations and ambitions.

They now had a backer, a moneyman, someone who believed in them, someone who could start to make a difference for them.

Taking off a frayed at the sleeves grey Adidas hoodie, tying it round his waist, Jamie breezily announced, "He's transferred two grand over to my bank account already, to pay for this month's practice and sort any gear out we need. I think we need to look at a new kit for Mikee," nodding over at the imposing drummer who, for a first, was already set-up and sat behind his diminutive drumkit. Idly tightening a cymbal stand, Mikee nodded his agreement.

"I can pick up a new kit for about a grand. I've had my eye on one. A metallic black Tama. It's fucking beautiful." Adding an enthusiastic, "It looks cool as fuck and won't be as small as this one. Reckon you can tap him for that?"

Looking up from his guitar fretboard and grimacing slightly, Jamie turned. "It's not about 'tapping' him up. He's investing in us. As a band. If we feel that a new kit is needed, then we buy it and tell him. It's not wasting anything, you'll have the kit to show for it and we get an even better sounding drummer…"

Always there with a wise word and conciliating statement, Jamie felt his pronouncement laid down the simple rules of their newly formed partnership.

With an ear to ear grin and trying to feign an air of casualness, Mikee reached for his phone from the backpack positioned behind his kit. "Yeah, I've got the number of a place on Oxford Road, I'll bell them tomorrow and see if they've still got the kit."

Ever the pessimist, Danny pulled his black knitted beanie further over his ears. "We're happy with this set up then, yeah?" Looking at his three bandmates individually, he said, "I mean he's the first person that we've spoken to, the first gig and we end up with the first dick that waves his wand in front of us…"

Jamie inwardly conceded that Danny was correct - he wanted all four of them to be behind the mutual decision. Deciding to discard the hoodie from around his waist, and turning to the dissenting bass player, Jamie scratched the back of his head.

"There is no situation here, we've not signed anything, Johnny has just given two fucking grand to four almost complete strangers. We've got a plan, a target to aim for. We can go in a studio and record these songs. Our songs. Our fuckin' brilliant songs that we've fuckin' written and played and played. Imagine how sick it'd be to sit and hear them back." Taking a step over to Danny, and placing a hand on his shoulder, "We've nothing to lose here, I know what you mean about him being the first guy we've spoken to, but we all like him, I trust him. Give it a few months and see where we are at." With a quick squeeze of his friend's shoulder, "We'll be right. All of us. WE KNOW WE'RE GOOD."

Nodding in reconciled agreement, he said, "Has he really sent you two grand already?"

Laughing warmly, Jamie said, "I wouldn't have said if he hadn't!"

Pulling out a roll of twenty-pound notes from the back pocket of his Levis, Jamie waved the money flamboyantly.

"I'm settling up what we owe and paying up-front for the rest of the month. We're booked in Tuesday, Thursday and a Sunday afternoon session for the next three months." He struck a C major on his guitar. "Imagine how fucking tight we'll be after a couple of months working that hard. New songs, improve on the one's we've got. Man, this is a chance that we didn't expect to get so early, let's not pick at it." Banging out another two noisy chords almost for dramatic effect, he added, "We take this chance and make things happen. Who the fuck else is out there as good as us?" Again, rising to the occasion of a rallying speech, "When was the last time we heard an album that really excited us? The Arctics, which was five years ago and before that…" Pausing for inspiration and struggling for a further example, Jamie rubbed at his chin. "…And before that it was The Libs, and that was fucking ages ago!"

Wanting to bring the talking to an end and get on with the actual rehearsal, Jamie stamped on an effects pedal with his right foot. "No-one's got anything to say these days. It's fuckin' shite out there, and we can make a difference to people, our songs can matter. Let's get them out there."Taking Dominic's lead, and sensing that the talking was done, Mikee seized the momentum, counted a loud 1-2-3 and hit the opening drum roll to 'Salvation'. Work was underway…

Chapter 8

With the new and welcome distraction of the band, Johnny had a new focus, which in turn had relaxed him, giving him a much breezier worldview. Not quite a Zen calm, but he felt happier than he had in a long while. His mind was a constant whir of thoughts, ideas, scams and flights of fantasy as to how far 'this thing' could go.

He found himself constantly reassuring himself that the songs he had heard, the live set that he had witnessed were that good. In rare moments of self-doubt and anxiety, he questioned himself, and his decision to finance the band.

Those songs.

He had only heard them a handful of times.

But that was enough.

The moments of doubt were fleeting, and he always went back to the fact that despite not having a musical bone in his body, he had a 'good pair of ears'. He knew a tune and he felt that he intrinsically knew what people wanted to hear. His opinions on what clogged up the charts and what passed for 'instant classics' were dispensed with a vociferous zeal. Much to his long-suffering friends' frustration.

It was some two months since he had met the band and their thrice weekly rehearsals were now the well-established norm. Johnny had been footing the bill for the room, and had also shelled out for a drum kit, a new bass speaker - which had gone some way to assuaging any of Danny's lingering doubts - and a distortion/effects pedal that Dominic had commandeered.

All 'expenses' were discussed beforehand and receipts were always forthcoming. He attended Thursday evenings and every other Sunday afternoons practice sessions. Progress was being made and to his ears, this was a band that had well and truly found its feet. And most importantly, a band that resolutely had its own sound.

It wouldn't be too long before they were studio ready.

And Claire.

She was the main recipient of his musical scorn. Her music buying these days extended no further than old dance compilations or what was on the

The Rock'N'The Roll. 'N That

supermarket shelves. And much to his snobbish disgust, the Mumford & Sons album seemed to be on constant rotation in her car.

He'd backpedalled somewhat here – having initially liked a track that had been heavily played on the radio – a painfully executed U-turn had been made when Johnny found out they were 'poshos' and even worse when David Cameron had endorsed their virtues.

"David fucking Cameron said he likes them. The waistcoat wearing banjo bastards!" had been the last tirade he had launched at Claire, who in fairness to her had nonchalanty re-played her favourite track, turned the car stereo up and stated to Johnny, "I'm sure you liked this when you first heard it…"

Returning home with two supermarket carrier bags – remembering to use the canvas recycling bags seemed to escape him – and resolutely sans CDs, Johnny unlocked the front door and shouted a cheery greeting, "Hello lady, I'm home."

Unusually, the TV was not on, there were no lights on and no apparent signs of life. Johnny was sure Claire was home as her car was parked outside. Putting the bags down and hanging his coat on the coat peg by the door, he again called out, "Claire. You home?"

A barely audible moan emanated from the depths of the sofa. Akin to a newly born animal that was feeling malnourished as its siblings were dominating mealtimes.

"Hiya Johnny, I'm here," was the barely audible whimper.

"You okay? What's up honey? Had a shit one at work?"

"I don't want to talk about it." Johnny had to strain to hear her.

The failsafe solution to all Northern ills was then proffered.

"You want me to stick the kettle on?"

"Yes please, and two sugars."

A Saccharine upgrade from a never to be deviated from none to two. Trouble. Definite trouble.

Had she lost her job? Someone ill? Fuck. Has someone died? Been diagnosed as terminally ill? Have Coldplay split up? Johnny thought as he weighed up the possibilities.

Johnny's mind hurtled through what had necessitated the sugar fix from the foetal figure on the sofa. Still in her work coat and shoes, Claire let out a whimper.

Just as he turned for the kitchen, his question was answered. The two words uttered by a woman in this distraught state that left no room for ambiguity.

"I've started. I've started and…" A huge wracked sob echoed throughout the house.

Johnny could only muster a sympathetic, "Shit, you okay?"

This fell way short of the desired compassion.

Way, way, short.

"Is that all you can say? I thought I was pregnant for the last three weeks…" The sentence trailed off to a whispered sob as Claire returned to staring at the blank television screen.

Needing to up the gravitas, Johnny stepped towards the prone figure - which now resembled a hibernating animal.

"Hey lovely lady, I had no idea. How could I? We hadn't even said we were trying…"

This much was true. A mutual acceptance of 'if it happens, it happens' had underpinned their view on parenthood. Claire had studied for a law degree in her late 20s and then her career then fast-tracked in her early 30s. Johnny's throwaway caveat to fatherhood was that any son/daughter and heir would inherit a fantastic record collection.

A tone of desperation entered his voice. "You should have said something. When did you come off the pill?"

Clank. The elephant in the room appeared and had blocked off all available exits. 'That question' was now resolutely out there…

Claire's reddened eyes widened owl-like, and a hint of guilt flickered across her tear-stained face. Gulping more sobs back, a hushed word came from Claire's lips. "Christmas…"

Johnny took a step back, searching with his hand for the armchair to deposit himself into so that he could process this skipped pharmaceutical bombshell.

"We really should have talked about this." Knowing that this was not the time for an inquisition, he backed off. "When you feel a little less upset, we'll sit and talk. But I'm sorry you're so…" His words trailed off limply, laced with inadequacy.

Wiping the back of her hand across her face, polka-dots of mascara formed underneath her eyes. Claire mustered a half-smile. "Thank you, I'll be fine, and we will talk but not today, yeah?"

Standing slowly and concentrating on an imaginary piece of fluff on the cuff of his shirt, Johnny said decisively, "I'll make that cup of tea for you."

Reaching the kitchen and for once deciding against the reflex action of popping music on, he filled the kettle, his mind a whirl after the homecoming events he had been party to. There was clearly no moral high ground to be sought here, but it burnt at him that the decision had been made for him rather than the conversation that should have preceded such significant life-decisions.

Stood over the sink, lost in his thoughts, Johnny inadvertently let the cold tap overfill the kettle, water rushing out over the lip, spraying up the hessian blind, he cursed softly, his mind a maelstrom of emotions.

This unforeseen development wasn't going away in a hurry…

Chapter 9

Three months passed, and the band had started to crave a break from the confines and routine of the rehearsal room. A meeting had been convened at Jamie's request.

A simple text message stating - '*Let's talk studios x*'

Johnny couldn't contain his excitement. He had left them to dictate when they felt they were studio ready. In all honesty, he had felt that they could have gone into the studio and produced more than satisfactory results after a month's rehearsals. The band were now as symbiotically tight as he could have been hoped for. A revised middle eight had also been added to 'Salvation' – it now had drop in tempo, whereby a simple acoustic and piano line underscored the chanted refrain. If this was reproduced as well as it could be when the band hit the studio, then they really would have something special on their hands.

The thought of a tangible product thrilled him. He could start to test the water and get the tracks out to his industry contacts. This would be the start of his real involvement - as much as his financial input had been hugely beneficial, this was where he would really prove himself to the band.

He also had a card up his sleeve to play tonight. A mate of his who was a graphic designer had designed several band logos, which like a schoolboy looking to impress with a vital assignment, he had printed off on to high quality paper and inserted into individual plastic wallets. The 'touch and feel' quality would work way better than displaying them on his laptop.

The workday dragged in typical fashion, but with 'b of the bang' timing Johnny was at the lift-door on the dot of 5pm. With the logo prints and notes on various studios that he had researched, all was well in the world. Just as he reached the town bound tram stop, his phone pinged the arrival of an incoming text message. Glancing down as he stepped onto the platform – it was from Claire;

'Don't forget that shopping & can we talk later. Don't be too late xx'

The Rock'N'The Roll. 'N That

Four weeks had passed since her upset and the revelation that contraception was no longer on her agenda. He welcomed the opportunity to talk, but his thoughts were solely based on the immediate future of Lonely Souls for the next couple of hours…

Firing off a quick conciliatory reply – *'Hiya all sorted, won't be too late, and we'll chat then x'*

The first part of the text bore no relation to the truth, he'd have to pick the shopping up on his way to the rehearsal rooms – turning up with supermarket bags was not the image of the savvy band manager that he was trying to portray.

Stopping off at a conveniently placed Tesco Express and relying on mental dexterity rather than the concise list that was sitting redundantly on his desk, he grabbed the essential and not so essential items and undertook a flawless self-checkout.

Arriving at the Kings at the stroke of 6pm, Johnny saw that the band had convened at their usual table and had taken the courtesy of getting him a Guinness in.

He sat down and took the top off his pint. "Who do I thank for this?" he asked, wiping the back of his hand across his mouth.

Danny saluted with a bony index finger, raised his own glass and said, "Cheers Johnny, appreciate all this. It's made a massive difference having the room paid for 'n that."

Johnny offered a handshake across the table. "Thanks man, you know I want this to work for all of us. But if you're happy, I'm happy."

Clearing his throat, and picking up the small zip-up attaché case he had bought along especially, Johnny cleared a space on the table by moving his pint & mobile to the adjacent table.

"Okay, first things first. I've had a mate of mine knock up some logos. There's about six or seven, I reckon three or four of them are non-starters, the others are decent, two of them are the business. You have a look at them and let me know what you think." Johnny passed out the plastic wallets containing the artwork. "And be as honest as you like. If you think it's shit, then tell me it's fucking shit."

Unable to resist the comedic cue, Mikee looked at the design in front of him, and audibly enough for everybody in the pub to hear, and a good few octaves too high for a man of his considerable bulk, "This one is proper fuckin' shite!"

Looking over the top of the plastic sleeve, Johnny laughed and wholeheartedly agreed. "Yeah that one's wank, probably the worst one. You passed the test big fella." Throwing up a boxer's stance, Johnny feigned a shadow-boxed punch across the table. Mikee roared with laughter and snapped a punch back, straight between Johnny's guard. The drummer's clenched paw stopped millimetres from his chin - Johnny felt that had the punch connected, he would now be horizontal on the pub's faded parquet floor.

Both grinning at the good-natured sparring, Jamie and Dominic were nodding in agreement over one design that they had held between them. Passing the wallet over to Johnny, Dominic affirmed their pleasure. "This one's fuckin' sick. It's classic looking and I can't think of anything else that it looks like."

Looking at the design, a smile washed over his face. "Exactly what I thought, this was probably my favourite one too. Danny's got the other possible runner and rider, but I love this one."

The design was done in bold black capitals against a red background, within a broken dotted white box. It looked equally striking, very cool and would lend itself to T-shirts and posters nicely, thought Johnny ambitiously.

Dan passed back his wallet, and likewise, nodded in agreement. "That one, love it. It'd look proper fuckin' smart on his bass drum."

Looking up from his phone, Mikee banged his phone down loudly. "Too fuckin' right. I know a lad who works at a signwriters, if you let me have the design, I can get that done no bother. It'll look sick."

Running with the momentum, Johnny reached for a further sheet of paper. "I've looked at some local studios, costs, quality, location and that. This is my personal choice - The Bunker. It's the other side of town, near Fallowfield, off Wilmslow Rd. A big old Victorian terrace that's had the cellars converted into a top studio space. He lets you use the kitchen and there's a lounge room that you can chill out in." Pausing for any dissention, but sensing none, he added, "He's dead sound, the fella that runs it. Called Dean. Way back when he used to do the sound in The Hacienda."

The band nodded sagely at the mention of Manchester's hallowed dance mecca - even though they would have all been at school when the club was spluttering towards its ignominious closure in the late '90s. "He'll work whatever hours that suits you, starting at midday. He doesn't do mornings. I reckon you do four tracks. You decide which ones. I'm sure we all pretty much know which four they'll be…"

The Rock 'N' The Roll. 'N That

Interjecting with a decisive shout, Dan clapped his hands together. "Salvation, Follow the Mantra, This is not Tomorrow and Speaking in Tongues!"

Looking round the table for instant approval, he said, "Well?"

Offering up a fist bump, Dominic immediately endorsed the choices. "Too fuckin' right! They'll sound fuckin' sick when we get them down!"

Assuming control and writing down the song titles, he said, "We all okay with them?"

"Fine by me," Jamie agreed, turning to Mikee, "Good for you Kong?"

Kong was the affectionate nickname that the band had bestowed on their drummer from a very early age. Having comfortably been able to get served at thirteen years old, and shaving every day by fifteen, Mikee had always been preternaturally big for his age. Mikee 'King Kong' Long. It was only ever Mikee or Kong. And no-one, repeat no-one, outside of the band called him by the latter.

Beating his chest in true gorilla fashion, and referring to himself in the third person character, which he was prone to, "Kong likes it a lot."

"I'll be picking up the tab for the studio time. It's five hundred quid a day, and I've booked ten days studio time. I know that's a lot and if you come in under, then no problem. If things are going well, then keep going and put more tracks down, never does any harm."

This expenditure added to the practice room costs and replacement gear had the outlay at close to the eight-thousand-pound mark. No small commitment, but Johnny was confident that his investment would pay dividends.

Scratching his head and frowning, he continued, "Studio time will be completely new to you, it can get tedious, and there's a lot of sitting around, but patience will pay off. You'll learn a lot which will stand you in good stead. Dean is a good 'un but he won't want you fucking about if it's wasting his time."

Dominic picked up where Johnny had tailed off. "We'll work our arses off, no fucking about, this is serious now, you'll see."

Nodding effusively, Johnny said, "And one last thing. I've booked us a gig. You've grafted in the rehearsal rooms, and with the studio time coming up, you need a chance to let off some steam and get another gig under your belt."

This was met with four very satisfied grins and much backslapping between the band. Jamie spoke first, asking excitedly, "Where and when?"

"Okay, it's a student only gig, some end of term thing at Northampton Roadmenders. There'll be a decent name indie band headlining and we'll be support. Mate of mine's son is the Ents Manager, so he did me a favour. It'll be a packed gig, with a decent soundsystem. And a room full of fit student birds which I'm sure won't go amiss with you. Only downside is they may want you to have a couple of covers under your belts, just as token crowd pleasers."

High-fives and handshakes were exchanged and 'fuckin' come on's' were uttered.

Wrapping things up, and knowing he had a pressing domestic engagement, "So we've got artwork sorted, studio time to book and a gig. Email dates that fit in with work and that and I'll get it confirmed and let you know when the gig is." Standing up and putting his coat on, and gathering up his shopping, "I'll leave you to it then, hopefully that little lot will put a spring in your step for rehearsal."

Getting up first, Jamie hugged Johnny, patting him vigorously on his back, "You're a good 'un," and kissing him on the cheek, whispered into his ear, "We won't let you down."

Leaving the pub in a state of euphoria, Johnny now had to focus on his pending conversation with Claire…

***

Arriving home only ten minutes later than promised, Johnny double checked the shopping bags and digging out his keys, opened the front door. He was greeted by the usual scene of Claire, glasses on, peering at her laptop whilst the TV chattered away unwatched.

"Hiya lovely, I've got all the shopping. You okay?"

Looking up and sliding her glasses Alice band style to the top of her blonde hair. "I'm fine, bit knackered but better after I had a bath. How was your 5-a-side?"

Johnny had been cracking on that he had been a regular on the football pitches the past few months to provide the requisite subterfuge whilst he went to see the band.

"Yeah, it was alright. I'm just going to run a quick bath if that's okay. I'll pop tea on and it'll be ready when I've finished my soak."

"Alright, use the towel that's already out and then stick it in the wash basket for me."

A 15-minute soak whilst the pasta bake ready-meal took care of itself provided the necessary sanctuary. He'd also prepared himself for the possibility of Claire broaching the 'baby chat' tonight. Tread carefully was his maxim, and don't make promises you can't fulfil…

Dressing in his 'comfies' – a pair of grey jog pants with the jog being distinctly redundant – and a deeply loved green A & F hoodie, Johnny padded barefoot down the sisal stairs carpet.

"Alright lovely lady, what do you want to drink with the pasta?"

"Better after that are we?" Claire asked facetiously.

"I'll be disappointed if I'm not called up for the next England squad," Johnny said.

Claire rolled her eyes. "I'll have a glass of that red that's already open. And it'll be water for you, being the athlete that you are."

Doing the necessary honours with both food and drinks, Johnny returned from the kitchen with a tray balancing Claire's wine glass precariously.

"Careful!" she shrieked. "It'll never come out of the rug if you drop it and they don't bloody sell that one anymore!"

Claire's encyclopaedic knowledge of the Habitat catalogue always amazed him, and sadly she was usually right. *Your specialist chosen subject…*

"Don't panic, I've got it." Deftly picking the glass up and placing it carefully on the oak table beside the sofa, Johnny placed the tray onto her lap.

Returning to collect his own tray, he reached for a lone Magners that had been chilling. Sitting on the single armchair adjacent to Claire's sofa, he let out a contented sigh as he drained a mouthful of the sweet cider.

"So how was your day then? Usual flim-flam? Another day another dollar and all that…"

"It was okay, just a lot on my mind," Claire replied.

"What like?" he replied half-hesitantly but knowing full well where this was heading.

"I've been looking on the internet."

This was never a cheap exercise, he thought.

"And I think we need to see a doctor about fertility and conception tests. Neither of us are getting any younger."

BOOM! It was right out there. Large as life and shrieking for a measured riposte. Shovelling an overloaded forkful of creamy pasta into his mouth, Johnny bought himself 10 or 15 seconds' thinking time.

Swallowing with a noisy gulp, and speaking with a calming tone, "That's quite a step." He paused. "We haven't even really discussed if we wanted a family. I've never been opposed to it, but you know, it is quite the commitment." Feeling that this was more than an adequate opening gambit, he returned to the remains of his meal.

"It is a commitment. But I really think a baby would be good for us. Make us a proper family. And I know we have never really talked about it, but I thought it was something we both wanted…"

Cute, Johnny thought, *very cute*. "No, we haven't talked about it and it has always been a relaxed sort of thing between us." Changing tack slightly, "Won't we need loads of tests and that before we looked at IVF?"

Looking up sheepishly, Claire said, "Well, babe," taking a mouthful of wine, "I've looked at it and we can speak to someone privately anytime. You know the private hospital on the Parkway?"

Exhaling softly, and reaching for his frosted glass, he said, "Sorry to be so blunt, but I've got to ask. How much are we looking at for this?"

"It's not cheap and it depends how many sessions you need if we" – with extra emphasis on the we – "decided to go ahead. But you've got that money from your dad that you've barely touched."

Oh, she has it all planned out for us, he thought.

He had to counter this, placate his partner but not commit to anything just yet. With a thinly-veiled grimace, he said, "Make us an appointment and we'll see what they have got to say, I can't say more than that for now."

A lovingly satisfied smile instantly light up Claire's face. "Ah thanks babe, I knew you'd agree with me."

Collecting up the two trays, Johnny headed for the kitchen, more than sideswiped by the speed of how things were proceeding.

Putting the bowls into the empty dishwasher, he thought, *a baby. A baby and the band…*

Chapter 10

The enthusiasm for the band's first road trip had been palpable since he had confirmed it.

June 21st. Northampton Roadmenders supporting Shed Seven. As second outings go, this was a very decent gig. A £200 fee which wouldn't touch the sides in terms of expenses. But this wasn't about the money. This was all about a 'proper gig' and seeing how they responded to a sizeable crowd. And, Johnny had cynically thought, an opportunity to see how they behaved 'on the road'.

Blue skies and sunshine were a not-oft treat for the good folk of Manchester – even in June – and this had further invigorated Johnny as he stepped into his car, picking up Jamie and Dominic on the way to Mikee's step-dad's salvage yard. Pulling away from the kerb as the car stereo parped the *'beep beep yeah'* coda to The Beatles' ode to the automobile. Johnny smiled a this-is-going-to-be-a-good-day smile.

Having volunteered to hire a splitter van, Johnny's offer had been firmly rebutted by Mikee who insisted that he'd sort them out with the 'a sick set of wheels'.

Jamie and Dominic were sat kerbside on their respective amps, guitar cases propped up in front of them, their poses perfectly mimicking each other – if rock 'n' roll did bookends. Stood by the side of them and seemingly admonishing a stiff lecture was a very attractive brunette. As Johnny pulled up alongside them, he nodded appreciatively to himself.

Good first impression, he thought to himself as he offered an overly sweaty palm. "Hiya, I'm Johnny. Johnny Harrison. I'm sure the lads have mentioned me. Glowingly." He looked over at the twins who were already heading to the rear of his car. "You must be their mum. I mean Mrs Thorne." Wiping his hand down the front of his pale blue Fred Perry polo shirt, Johnny mustered up his best smile. "You must be really proud of them. They're great lads."

"Hello Johnny. Yes, I am and yes, they are. I'm Cally. Lovely to meet you."

With the buzz of traffic noise, Johnny had to listen carefully as she was very softly spoken. Her words very precise but oh so quiet, with a pleasing, almost melodic tone to them. At 5ft 7ish, slim, almost doleful blue eyes and a soft wave of shoulder length brunette hair, it was clear where the twins had inherited their good looks from.

The twins had already opened the back of the car and were starting to load their gear. "You should see the wheels Mikee's sorted for us. Well wicked," Dominic said, as he tucked his Fender case in the boot.

There was a lull in the flow of traffic, and the delicate traces of 'Michelle' could be heard through the car's open window.

Cally smiled a perfect white toothed smile, and putting a hand up to her brow to shield her eyes from the sun. "Which one's your favourite?"

Feeling himself frown at the question, Johnny stammered, "Err, I've never thought about them like that. I err, I have had more to do with Jamie, but th—"

Punching Johnny lightly on the arm, she said, "I meant which Beatle!"

Screwing his face in embarrassment, Johnny deadpanned, "I knew that."

"I love The Beatles sooooo much!" Clasping her hands together and looking skywards, she sighed heavily, "I could listen to nothing but. Okay, I'll try again. What's your favourite album? And who is your favourite Beatle?"

"Favourite album is *The White Album*, but I do love *Rubber Soul*." Nodding towards his car, "And favourite Beatle? I can't choose. I love them all. I'm sitting on the fence on that one…"

Smiling that beatific smile again, she said, "Okay, any album would have done and favourite Beatle? Only picking out George individually is the right answer. He was beautiful. And with your surname you should have known that…"

Laughing at this Beatles based introduction, Johnny said, charmingly, "Lovely to meet you at last." Glancing down, he didn't see a wedding ring. The brothers had only ever talked about their mother, with no reference at all to a father figure.

A black cat walked haughtily along a small brick garden wall, and catching it in her peripheral vision, Cally turned around to stroke it. Looking back to Johnny, she fingered a small gold locket between her index finger and thumb. "I've heard all about you as well, Mr Harrison. You've been so good with the boys. Future of rock 'n' roll!"

"Ha, they certainly are!"

"Now you better get on your way, and I know I don't have to say this, but look after them. They're my boys and I love them dearly…"

Johnny gave his best placating nod.

The car boot slammed shut and both boys appeared beside their mum. Jamie was dressed in cut off jog pants, a faded black MC5 T-shirt and his ubiquitous white Converse, Dominic in Nike hi-top trainers, off-white jog pants and a plain navy blue long sleeved T-shirt. They shuffled embarrassingly, "Aww Mum, give us a break. We'll be fine!"

"I know you will." Putting a hand on their shoulders, she kissed them both warmly on the cheek. "I'm not worried, just enjoy yourselves and text me how the gig goes."

Waving them off with a two-handed flourish, despite the shadow casting sunshine, she gave an involuntary shiver and wrapped her arms around herself.

Turning to the brothers, Johnny said, "Your mum seems very cool."

"She's the best," Jamie replied protectively, nodding his head. "I can't wait for her to see us play live…"

***

Arriving at the salvage yard, Mikee and Danny were stood beside two large crates of Stella and a bottle of Jack Daniels - which were warming up nicely in the Mancunian sunshine.

Parking next to an antiquated Portacabin that Johnny assumed was the site office, he locked the car once the twins had unloaded their gear.

A set of keys sailed in Johnny's direction and he fumbled them to his chest.

"All yours Boss!" boomed Mikee, thumbing towards a sepia-coloured RV.

"Fuck me! Are we cooking meth or going to play a gig!" Johnny laughed as he took in the vehicular behemoth. "Is that thing roadworthy?" asked Johnny as he looked at both the dinner plate sized wing mirrors which were held in place by gaffa tape.

"Wait until you see how we've pimped it!" said Danny, with a snigger.

Sure enough, the RV had been spray painted with a pretty accurate facsimile of the band logo.

"Rock 'n' roll enough for you?" asked Mikee as he loaded on the remainder of the gear.

"If it gets us there," smiled Johnny as he pulled himself up to the driver's seat.

Chapter 11

The Roadmenders. Northampton. A curious old venue which despite an '80s makeover, had still retained the bulk of its Art Deco façade. It had a capacity of just shy of 900 and by all accounts, the evening's show would be sold out. Almost a hundred-fold increase on their debut gig. A handful of their own songs and a few covers – which remained a closely guarded secret between the band. Warm the crowd up for the main event, the perennially popular Britpop stalwarts, Shed Seven.

Finding a loading bay door to the rear of the venue, Johnny performed a neat reverse manoeuvre, despite the distractions of his boisterous cargo.

A venue operative opened the bay doors and the band enthusiastically started to unload their gear. Whistling loudly, Danny offered the blindingly obvious statement, "Fuck me, it's big. It's fucking huge."

Nudging him slightly harder than intended and almost causing him to drop his precious Marshall amp, Mikee chuckled, "This is small compared to where we are going to end up playing. Get used to it, brother…"

Johnny smiled to himself; he loved it when he heard the band offering up these little cocksure soundbites to each other. No harm in ambition, and importantly, he believed this himself. Even in the short time he had known them, their progress had been remarkable. New songs seemed to come easily to Jamie and the rest of the band always seemed to have the necessary musical creativity to fill in any composite blanks with their own flourishes. And Dominic's guitar playing just seemed to get better and better.

"Right lads. Leave your gear there and wait for your passes. You're not going anywhere without them." Pointing at Johnny with an industrially dirty finger, the building manager said, "You must be their manager or gopher or something then?"

Smirking to himself, Johnny replied, "Yes mate, I'm their manager. Where's the production office? I'll toddle off and get everything sorted. Is Ross here? I'm supposed to meet him."

"I'll take you to Ross, but just you. That lot can wait out here for you."

He turned to the band, who were visibly amused by the building manager's lack of customer service skills.

Belching loudly, Danny reached for another warm beer from the half-demolished second crate, him and Mikee seemingly having polished off a crate and a half over the past three hours. "We'll be right here and won't get up to any mischief, honest…"

The insincerity wasn't lost on the jobsworth manager, who must have been well versed at this type of boys behaving badly. "I know what you Northerners are like!"

Sighing at the needless bureaucracy, Johnny raised a 'parental' eyebrow towards the band. "Right, you lot," the latter dripping with unbridled sarcasm, "stay there and don't do anything naughty or I won't let you play with your guitars later…"

Glaring at Johnny after his unsubtle slight, the building manager reached for a sizeable bunch of keys attached to his belt by a red elastic bungee cord and opened a door to the right of the loading bay. "This way and I'll take you to Ross." Looking over his shoulder, he tutted at the band as they harmlessly play-fought amongst themselves. Johnny laughed to himself as he walked through the door, turning to see Mikee, bottle of beer between his teeth with Dominic's and Jamie's heads under each arm as they struggled in vain to free themselves.

A quick walk down the white-washed breeze block lined corridor and Johnny was shown the door to the Ents Managers production office, whereby he was introduced to Ross.

Ross McRae was small, skinny with a shaved cue-ball head. He was on his landline phone and even sat down, seemed to twitch excessively. Putting his free hand up the back of his well-worn 1989 Pixies tour shirt, he scratched frantically at an itchy shoulder blade. A quick mental calculation would place Ross at about two years old when said tour would have been in full white noise effect.

Finishing his call with an abrupt 'laters', Ross extended a friendly hand towards Johnny. "You must be Mr Harrison, my dad told me that you two go back a fair while."

"Yeah, we do, he's one of the good guys, and I owe him a drink for sorting this with you."

"Save your money Mr Harrison, he's a health nut these days. Hasn't touched a drop in years. he's more bothered about running marathons."

"Easy with the Mr Harrison lark Ross, it's Johnny. I know I'm your dad's old mate, but cut the formalities out, you make me feel ancient!"

"Alright, cheers Johnny, close the door and take a seat. This band of yours any good then?"

"Yeah, they're good, Very good. Getting them in the studio soon. This gig is a big deal for them, they've never played to such a crowd before, their last gig…" Tailing the sentence off as he realised that Ross didn't need to know that this was only the band's second ever gig.

"Cool, cool. How many passes do you need?" Reaching for a desk drawer, Ross then pulled out a small but very familiar sized parcel. "Want a cheeky livener before we crack on?"

The two not inconsiderable lines were already racked out before Johnny could politely decline. The open display of cocaine usage certainly explained the twitchy behaviour. He was clearly trying to impress on Johnny that he was far more than just his dad's little boy. *When in Rome*, Johnny thought.

"It's only a rare treat this gear man, I barely touch it," said Ross unconvincingly.

"Same as me, birthdays and special occasions only. And today is a very special occasion, eh? Full house tonight and a venue full of thirsty students."

"Cool, cool" – which seemed to be Ross's default coda – "Here are the passes, five all you need then?"

"Thanks man and cheers for the sniff."

Looking momentarily puzzled. "Oh yeah sniff, cool, cool. You Northern monkeys."

"Haha, yeah us Northern monkeys," Johnny ladled extra emphasis - elongating his already flat Northern vowels.

Scooping up the five brightly coloured fabric Access All Areas passes, Johnny stood up, vigorously rubbing his nose to ensure that no rogue traces of coke were visible. "Cheers Ross, I'll catch you later man."

Already stabbing determinedly at his desktop computer keyboard, Ross glanced up with a predictable, "Cool, cool."

Bowling back down the corridor, Johnny opened the door to see the band had found a long-deflated rugby ball that they were trying to throw quarterback-style onto the roof of the venue with limited success.

"Right, right children. I leave you for five minutes and you're already trying to wreck the place."

Putting one hand on his hip and wagging his other hand in an exaggerated school mam fashion, Johnny 'tsk tsked' at the band. "Anyhow, don't lose them. In fact, as they are the first of many passes, I'd recommend that you save it for posterity. It'll be worth a fortune in a few years."

He gulped as the bitter line of cocaine dropped in the back of his throat. Exhaling deeply and composing himself momentarily as the drug rushed into his system," I'll move the van and you lot move the gear into the venue. Just leave it on front of the stage for now. We'll wait and see how they want you to set up."

Always first with an answer, Mikee clicked his fingers, impressing himself with the loud snap. "Nice one Johnny and have you seen the toilets, I'm bursting."

"Err, yeah, just on the right I think as you get to the top of the corridor." Unable to help himself, he mirrored Ross's verbal tic, "Cool, cool." Shaking his head at himself, Johnny got into the van, reaching for a bottle of now warm water, and gulped deeply to take away the taste of the high-quality coke.

Chapter 12

Assembling their gear stage right, the band looked round the venue. As they stood in silence taking in the surroundings, the air crackled with a voice over the in-house PA system, "Alright lads. I'm Pete and your songs are in my hands tonight."

"Get yourselves set up in front of the curtain, the Sheds are already set up behind there. We'll see what you've got."

Jamie nudged Dominic and whispered to him, "Look at the lighting rig, and there's even a barrier in front of the fuckin' stage!"

"I know bro, we're gonna have to be good tonight!"

Gaining rock star confidence by the second, Danny, who was practically hopping on the spot with excitement, "We'll smash it tonight! Don't know what you're worried about."

This was either beer fuelled bravado, or he really was oozing confidence. Johnny suspected both, but felt his attitude was way better than being a mass of nerves.

"That's the spirit Danny, get the sound right and just enjoy it. Are you going to let me know what these covers are yet?"

"You'll have to wait and see!" Danny grinned across at him.

Pete's voice crackled across the PA, "Okay lads, enough of the team talk. Get set up and I'll get you sorted for tonight. Sweet?"

This request spurred the band into action and like worker ants, they swarmed the stage and had their instruments, amps and speakers set up in no time at all. Mikee had been good to his word and his bass drum now looked resplendent with the band logo adorning it.

Johnny took up a spot at the rear of the venue, giving him a view of the whole of the compact stage.

"Now then lads, give us a tune, I'm dying to hear what you've got for me..." the sound engineer requested.

The Rock 'N' The Roll. 'N That

***

Feeling the effects of four strong lagers, Johnny decided he would visit the production office to see if he could procure a further rail of coke from Ross.

"Right, I'll leave you to get ready for the gig. Stage time is 8.00pm so you've got half an hour. I'll be back just before you go on. I'm just going to square everything with the promoter."

With that, he left the band to prepare themselves in the cramped and badly ventilated dressing room.

Ross was mid-way through ordering his evening's consignment when Johnny entered his office. Double checking stage times and the length of the set, a suitably chunky line of gak was quickly procured.

With a bugle induced swagger, Johnny knocked on the dressing room. "You all decent?"

Peering round the door, what he saw made his heart race even faster. They looked like a band. A real live rock 'n' roll band eagerly awaiting their moment. Mikee was drumming percussive rhythms on the edge of a table, resplendent in a grey check fur trapper's hat complete with ear flaps which waggled in time to his drumming. Danny, still in shades was swigging on a beer, black denim jacket, skinny black jeans and battered white converse.

Jamie and Dominic both looked amazing. Jamie had a black leather peacoat worn over his jeans, with his trusty red scarf again tied round his throat. His blue eyes held a fixed determination as they darted round the room gauging his fellow bandmate's moods. Dominic was wearing a long sleeved white T-shirt with a black short sleeved shirt worn open over the top of it. Checking the tuning was just so and tightening guitar strings, the band were totally focussed, no words were being passed between them.

Few words were necessary, so Johnny kept it short and sweet. "It all starts tonight. Just enjoy this. I know you're going to be fuckin' great."

Jamie, looking impassive, leant his guitar against the rickety looking table that sat centrally in the pokey dressing room, beckoning Johnny over and indicating that the rest of the band all stood up, he instigated a 'group hug'. Speaking softly, not unlike his mum, "It starts tonight. I love you boys, and we're all in this together. Let's fucking go." Holding out a fist. "TRUST!"

Gulping back raw emotion, Johnny broke the embrace, grabbed a beer and said, "I'll see you lot out there..."

***

Entering the room, Johnny was hit by a wave of heat. It was probably two-thirds full and the chattering students were being entertained by the usual staple of indie classics. The mood felt very convivial - probably due to the 2-4-1 drinks promotion. Raising the average age by some twenty years, Johnny secured a suitable vantage point at the rear of the venue, with a perfect sight line of the stage.

Looking round at the fresh-faced students, Johnny felt a pang of regret at having missed out on this part of his education. Getting pissed/stoned/laid and a degree. Offset by the ubiquitous mass of student debt…

Snapping back to the moment, Johnny felt his stomach skip as the DJ faded out an Arcade Fire track he was struggling to remember the name of. The house lights then faded to black.

This was fucking it. He regretted that he'd not picked up another beer as his mouth was desert dry, down to a combination of adrenaline and the rising temperature within the room. And the cocaine.

Seeing the shadows of the four figures as they took take to the stage, Johnny's pulse quickened. *Thank fuck I've not crashed too much bugle off Ross*, he thought; his heartrate would have been out of control by now.

A slow thump of Mikee's newly adorned bass drum signalled their arrival, lights still down, Jamie made the introductions. "We're Lonely Souls. You're gonna love us…"

With precision timing the lighting rig kicked in and illuminated the band in searing white light, the guitars chimed in right on cue and the band piled straight into 'Speaking in Tongues'.

The venues sound system was perfect, every instrument resonated as it should; Johnny would owe the Sound Engineer a large drink if things carried on like this.

As Jamie closed his eyes and passionately sang the first chorus, three hundred pairs of female eyes and doubtlessly a good number of males, widened and took in the lead singer hungrily. He looked both gorgeous and vulnerable, yet exuded a stoic assuredness, a belief in what he was singing. *He looks like a fucking rock star*, Johnny thought excitedly. The chorus finished, and Dominic leant back slightly, his liquid guitar lines silky, yet still retaining a rawness, chiming perfectly through the speakers.

Danny stared the crowd out impassively, holding the rhythm down, his movements economical.

The Rock'N'The Roll. 'N That

Mikee, who must have already been at serious risk of overheating in his newly acquired fur trapper's hat, was a veritable blur, with his smile seeming to get bigger with every beat.

The amassed student crowd had responded to the band's frenzied energy and killer songs, and by the third number, the front third of the audience were bouncing up and down and slamming into each other. It was civilised as moshpits go, but it was exactly the reaction that Johnny had always believed the band would elicit.

Having seamlessly raced through the previous four songs without a word, Jamie now addressed the expectant crowd. "You won't have heard of us before. We're Lonely Souls. Remember the name…"

This will lift the fucking roof off, Johnny thought as Jamie introduced the last of their own set. "This is our last song before we play a few you'll already know." Looking out across the audience, "It's called 'Salvation'…"

The song had never sounded so good, the chorus was made for venues like this – bigger! By the second chorus, everyone in the room was hanging on to every single note, every single word. "*I'll be your salvation, you'll be my salvation, we'll be your salvation…*"

And then the middle eight dropped in, the lighting engineer faded the lights slightly, picking out Jamie with a red spotlight. Just as it finished the lights blazed on and Dominic launched into the fiery solo that saw the song to its chaotic conclusion.

Glancing admiringly over at his twin brother, Jamie than sang the last chorus again, his own guitar slung behind his back gunslinger-style.

The crowd went mental. Absolutely fucking mental. As songs go, it was immediate. Its anthemic qualities soaring. It was a song that people would love.

Clamouring for a beer to quench his thirst but curious to know what surprises the band had up their sleeves, Johnny made his way over to the sound booth where he had spotted a bottle of water aside the desk. Nodding at Pete and giving him a huge 'Macca' style thumbs-up, he said, "How good was that?!? Mind if I have a quick gulp of that?"

Gesturing that it was okay, Pete gratefully accepted Johnny's effusive thanks for both the drink and impeccable sound, and agreed to meet him post-show for a well-earned beer.

And now for the cover versions.

First up a note-perfect 'Helter Skelter'.

Rubbing a finger across his angular cheekbone, Jamie smiled out at the crowd. "Thought you might know that one. You've heard of The Beatles then?

"Any requests?" asked Dominic, his sweaty blonde hair now plastered to his head.

Before any response could be proffered, Danny's bassline thundered the opening to a Mancunian classic – New Order's 'Touched by the Hand of God'.

"This is our last number. We've fucking loved this," Jamie intoned politely despite the expletive. "We are Lonely Souls, you'll be seeing us again."

And with that they dropped a punked up version of a UK grime track that Johnny couldn't name - but 'the kids' loved it.

Patting Pete effusively on the back and beaming a huge smile, Johnny pushed his way through the overheated students and headed for the backstage area, flashing his pass at the security guard without even making eye contact. By the time he reached the dressing room door, the band were already in full-on celebratory mode.

Mikee was swinging Danny around in a suffocating looking bear hug, whilst Dom and Jamie hugged each other - exchanging whispered congratulations.

Bowling in to the party and shouting, Johnny was ecstatic at the mood, "HOW FUCKING GOOD WAS THAT!?! And those covers!"

All turning to the door and willing to listen to all compliments, Dan, now released from the stifling grips of Mikee, grabbed a beer and beckoned Johnny in, roaring, "You fuckin' loved us didn't you!"

"That was fuckin' blinding! They fucking loved you out there. Honestly lads, I couldn't be prouder."

The adrenaline was coursing through the room, the band talking through moments and songs excitedly, shaking heads in disbelief. The buzz was palpable.

If you could bottle this type of feelgood, the recession would be over in no time at all, thought Johnny.

"Right, sorry to be the party pooper but…"

In dreadful stage whisper fashion, Danny shouted, "Old bastard," through his rolled hand - loud hailer style.

"Yes alright, Mr I'm not even fuckin' 21 yet. Anyhow, shift the gear and load the van. Then you can get out there and find some young, student talent that will tell you that you're the future of rock 'n' roll and offer to suck your cocks for you!"

The Rock 'N' The Roll. 'N That

"Only messing boss. Tonight was sick!" said Danny. With a smile that threatened to split his cheeks.

"I'm going to have a catch up with Ross and then head to the hotel. I'll raise the average age by twenty odd years if I hang around, as young Daniel has kindly pointed out."

The band then set to with their ritual packing away of their beloved guitars, Jamie placing his sweat stained red scarf at the bottom of the guitar flight case and as always, tenderly laying his champagne Stratocaster down. The love that musicians had for their instruments was something that Johnny was always in awe of.

"Your shout first Mikee! Serves you right for stinking out the bus on the way down," said Dominic as he towelled his sweaty hair.

Rolling his eyes good naturedly at the band's playful shenanigans, Johnny reached for his wallet and chucked £100 in tens on the table. "Go and do the decent thing, watch the Sheds do their set, and get pissed. The hotel's only down the road, keys will be behind reception all bought and paid for. It's down to you to negotiate your way back there. Premier Inn. Turn right at the front of venue and it's half a mile's drunken stumble."

Having conveyed the instructions, he couldn't resist the next line, "Oh and no TVs out of the windows. We're not at that stage after one decent gig."

"Fucking spoilsport," snorted Danny, reaching up from his guitar case to shake Johnny's hand.

***

Having loaded the equipment from the vacated dressing room, Johnny sat on the rear step of the van and drank a bottle of water in one. Locking the RV's doors, he jumped back in surprise as he was met by Jamie leaning against the driver's door.

Recovering from the surprise, he said, "You okay? There must be a party to be had tonight."

"I've had one beer and I'm not feeling it. Couldn't top that gig." Jamie fixed Johnny with his piercing stare. "I'm fine man, we can grab a quiet beer at the hotel if you want?"

"Sounds fine by me J. Jump in, we're only two minutes down the road…"

Chapter 13

Standing at the anodyne hotel bar, Johnny smiled in the direction of the barmaid who had to break away from her mobile phone to take his order.

"Yeah, what can I get you?" Looking straight through Johnny, her blank stare was then hijacked by Jamie who was now leaning over the bar and craning his neck to look at the selection of bottled beers.

The affect that Jamie seemed to have on girls was Pavlovian. Like a switch had been flicked. Pushing a hand through her badly bleached blonde hair, pulling her ponytail across her right shoulder, she tried her best smoulder. "And what can I get you then?"

Jamie politely asked for a Magners with ice. Disappointed at her failed flirtatiousness, she passed the drinks across to Johnny, looking over his shoulder at Jamie, who had now taken up a seat, which conveniently, was within her line of sight.

"Eight pounds seventy please," she asked solemnly.

Handing over a ten-pound note, "Ta, and your own." Johnny took the drinks over and sat opposite Jamie. Tracy Chapman's 'Fast Car' played not unpleasantly in the background as Johnny raised his fully charged glass towards Jamie. "To a top gig and here's to many more!"

"I'll drink to that." Jamie nodded back, enjoying the bite of the sweet cider against his strained vocal chords.

"I honestly can't believe that was only your second gig!" Pausing to take a long satisfying sip, he continued, "Not many bands get to play a gig like that so soon. Not blowing my own trumpet. How come you've not played more? With songs like yours and that…"

Jamie again drank deeply, the cold alcohol relaxing him. "I wish we had played more gigs, but…"

His mood seemed to darken as he looked down at the faux-oak table top. "If I tell you something, you have to promise to never repeat it."

Slightly taken aback by Jamie's change in tone, Johnny raised both palms face up, "Of course. You know you can trust me."

The Rock'N'The Roll. 'N That

Whistling softly between his teeth, Jamie went on, "It was Dominic. At school. He had terrible acne. Really fucking bad spots man. Kids at school used to call him Dominos. Like Pizzaface but fuckin' crueller." He cringed at the recollection of his twin brother's adolescent anguish. "It never really cleared up until he was about nineteen and he then had to have some sort of laser treatment to reduce the scarring on his face. Mum took a second job to pay for him private, y'know."

"Fuck," Johnny said with a sympathetic wince.

Taking a glass draining gulp, Jamie looked Johnny straight in the eye. "Fuckers at school made his life a misery. I could have cried on his behalf. I never had girlfriends as I knew he wouldn't stand a chance with girls…" Sighing loudly. "It killed Mum. She was always proper protective of us. We had no Dad. He left her before we were born." He looked wistful for a few seconds. "She did everything she could to try and help him. Bought every soap, spot cream and treatment possible. Took him to every doctor and what d'yer call 'em, dermatologist possible. Nothing seemed to work." Knocking back a mouthful of cider, and half-laughing, he said, "And we never had pizza. Even when they'd cleared up!"

Smiling at Jamie's sacrifice, and slightly lost for words at the admission, Johnny said, "That's dreadful. Kids can be so fucking hurtful," adding positively, "But he looks great now, you can barely see the scars."

"It was tough. And the angrier he got the more anxious I became. Weird," said Jamie. His words trailing off.

"You're both out the other side now though J."

"I know. That's why he works with Mikee. He left school before his exams. Him and Mikee were tight as you like. The shit sort of stopped when he started hanging out with him. But he hated school. Fucking hated it!" Laughing at the recollection, "Some kids took it too far with Dom, so Mikee dangled one of them out a second storey classroom. Got expelled. Dom was suspended for tickling Mikee!"

"I know I shouldn't laugh," said Johnny with a snort.

"I know but imagine how he must have felt…" Jamie snapped out of the reflective mood. "Anyhow, let me grab another beer, and we can talk about our world domination!" Scooping up the empty glasses, he said, "Same again?"

"Yeah, and grab a couple of chasers. Jack Daniels would be nice," said Johnny, reaching for his wallet.

Pushing the note away firmly, he said, "Nah, my shout man. You've done enough for us today."

Returning unscathed with the drinks, Jamie sat down and took the top off his pint. "So now you know. If people ask why, we just say we didn't have the songs ready…"

"Fine by me. And you know that if," he corrected himself quickly, "When the band cracks it, Dom will be able to make up for lost time. Big style!"

Nodding slowly, "I know. But he'll always be a little insecure after taking so much shite for so long." Looking down pensively, "So you really think we stand a chance then, Johnny? Y'know. Getting a deal and making records…"

Knocking back the JD in one quick movement and clenching his teeth at the warm peaty burn, "You want me to be honest?" He met Jamie's eyes. "You will and it's going to be totally because of your songs. I've got no magic spell. I'll do everything I can for you, y'know carry on investing time and money. But this all boils down to the tunes." Leaving the sentence hanging, Johnny concluded, "This will be all about you boys. I just want to be on board for the ride."

Sipping thoughtfully at his own JD, Jamie said, "I know we can make it. I really fuckin' do. And why wouldn't you be along for the ride?"

"Jamie, you looked fuckin' great up there. When I met you at the bar that first time, and then saw you on stage, I just knew. You've got that thing, that…" Struggling to articulate himself, "Y'know, that rock 'n' roll thing. And it's your thing as well. You don't look like you're trying to be anyone else. That's the trick. And fuck me. Do the girls love you!"

Looking down modestly, Jamie smiled sheepishly. "It's not about the girls though, is it. Not to me. It's all about the songs. Other people loving our songs. That's what I want. I want that so badly."

"You'll get everything you want if this all goes to plan for you. Girls, money, fame, the lot…"

Raising the shorts glass, Jamie laughed softly, "To the lot!" adding at a whisper, "and please never say a word about what I told you about Dom."

"Not a word," said Johnny, clinking his glass against Jamie's and knocking back the spirit in one.

Closing his eyes momentarily and smiling warmly, Johnny put a hand behind Jamie's head and pulled his forehead to his. "Thanks man. That means a lot. This is gonna get fuckin' huge. I can feel it!" Releasing Jamie from the intimate grasp, he said, "One more for the road and then turn it in, I'm knackered, been a long day."

"Fine by me," replied Jamie.

"Any more and I'll be pissing all night. You youngsters and your trusty bladders, I envy you!"

"Right, I don't need to know about your toilet habits!" Jamie laughed loudly, adding with alcohol fuelled sentimentality, "You're a top bloke, Johnny. I'm glad we met you."

"Come on. You'll have me filling up here." Standing to leave the deserted bar, the two hugged and patted each other warmly on the back.

Chapter 14

The journey home had been quiet. Once the anecdotes had been spun and stretched to breaking point. Dominic had spent the entire journey surrounded by a post-coital halo of sexual satisfaction and proceeded to message said conquest for the entire journey North.

Jamie and Johnny did small talk. Principally around the forthcoming studio time and which was the best Clash album. Jamie bucking convention and pitching for the sprawling three-album *Sandinista*. Johnny played it safe with *London Calling*. Both, however, agreed that the Pistols didn't come close to The Clash.

***

A pleasant Sunday afternoon would normally have found Claire sat in their small back garden attending to the prim and proper flower beds that required very little maintenance but took on Kew Gardens-like proportions if her exaggerations were to be believed.

Upon opening the front door, he was met with the sight of her sat at the dining table feverishly reading a text heavy webpage.

Glancing up briefly, she said, "Hiya babe. How was London? Did you get me a present?"

Johnny had offered up the cover story that he was visiting a lifelong friend. An ex-pat Mancunian, now making hay in the capital. The constant subterfuge was starting to wear heavy as he'd always been very straight-bat with Claire.

"Hello lady. I've only been gone a day! Does that merit a present?"

"Of course!" Claire said with mock indignation.

"I thought you'd be out in the sunsheeinee?" The Liam Gallagher over-pronunciation of this always seemed to make Claire smile. *It's the little things* he thought.

"Well," she said, pulling her wicker chair round to face him, "I've been researching on the interweb and…"

Putting his overnight bag at the foot of the stairs and unclipping his sunglasses from the collar of his T-shirt, Johnny put his hands on his hips, and said in a jokey manner, "Go on, how much is this latest essential purchase going to cost us. Designer egg cups? Replica Ming Dynasty serviette holders? Or are we finally getting a Bose docking station? Now we're talking!"

Matter of fact, Claire retorted, "Well, it will only cost if we decide to proceed with IVF after all the tests."

Breathing up heavily through his nose, he said, "Okay. I wasn't quite expecting that today but…"

"But nothing!" Claire interjected. "We're always burying our heads in the sand about stuff, but not this. I want a baby." Hastily adding, "I think we want a baby. We talked about this a good few weeks ago but as always, nothings been said since. We're doing our ostriches and sand routine again."

Resistance was futile, and being too tired to muster any sort of an argument, Johnny agreed to go for "tests". If anything deserved finger punctuation, it was that…

"So, when…"

Before he could finish, Claire gleefully informed him, "A week on Monday at the GP's. I've booked us in at 5.30 so we won't have to finish work too early. With Doctor Davison. She's really nice."

Yup, she'll be delightful when she's talking about my spunk and asking me to crack one off into a specimen tub, he thought.

Wisely, he kept this pearl of wisdom to himself.

Resigned to what was now a fait-accompli, he said, "That sounds like that's all settled then?"

"Oh, thanks Johnny. I knew you'd be pleased!"

Glancing down, Johnny's loins stirred slightly. Claire was wearing a very tight fitting sleeveless vest bearing the logo '*Yoga Bends the Mind*'. She had clearly not been out at all that day, as she had omitted to put a bra on. Her nipples protruded exquisitely either side of the embroidered capital letters. *Now that part of making a baby I like*, he thought. Wondering if there was a complete absence of underwear, he decided an advance was very much in order.

Stepping over to her, he reached out and gently squeezed her right nipple. "You look fit in that top. Want to step upstairs with me?"

"Johnny! You always pick the worst moments! It's my time this weekend!" Rubbing his arm affectionately, she said, "And besides Michelle is coming around with some plants for the garden."

"Sorry, sorry. Fancy a drink? I'd love a Magners. Any in the fridge?" Reaching inside the fridge's cavernous insides, he grabbed a pear flavoured cider and a pint glass. "Am I alright to sit in the Hanging Gardens of Manchester? Eighth Wonder of the World and all that." Blowing a friendly kiss at Claire, he grabbed the Observer off the kitchen top and retreated to the garden.

***

"Hiya mum, how are you? You have a nice night out with Auntie Jo?" Returning home, the twins always made a fuss out of her, knowing how much she missed their company.

"Hiya boys! Tell me about the gig!" Drying her hands on a tea towel, Cally turned the kitchen stereo down, taking Fleetwood Mac's 'You Make Loving Fun' down to a background whisper.

"I had a lovely time with Jo. She'd hate it if she knew you still called her Auntie Jo though!" Sitting on the arm of the faded navy-blue sofa, she reached for Jamie's hand and gave it an affectionate squeeze. "I want to hear all about you." Looking over towards Dom, who was still engrossed in his epic textual exchange, "You look shattered Dominic. Was the hotel not that great? I hate sleeping somewhere new. That first night. I never sleep a wink!"

Oblivious to the parental concern, Dominic muttered a distracted, "Hiya Mum. Yeah. Love you too…"

Jamie laughed softly. "He's fine just a bit smitten, aren't you bro?"

Taking on a mock-scolding voice, she said, "Dominic! You haven't been with a girl, have you?" She wagged her finger. "You bad boy!"

Cally was inwardly delighted that he had been the subject of some attentive female's affections, having shared his pain during the torturous, acne ridden, adolescent years.

Finally dragging himself from his almost charge free phone, he said, "C'mon, you don't need to know these things." Shooting a half-hearted dagger look at Jamie, "Does she, Jamie?"

Heading in the direction of the stairs, Dominic said, "Anyhow, J. At least I stayed out to party. Mr Sensible here going back to the hotel with Johnny." Yawning loudly, "I'm going to have a shower then grab some kip." Yawning even more loudly, "And I'm meeting Danny for a pint later. If you fancy it. Or are you going to have another early night?"

Before Jamie had the chance to reply, his brother was already at the top of the stairs, the ping of his phone indicating yet another amorous missive had been received.

Frowning slightly and pushing a length of hair behind her ear, Cally said, "How come you didn't stay out with the boys? Was everything okay?"

"It was cool. I was absolutely fine." Sitting on the sofa and looking up to his mum, "Johnny was heading back to the hotel and the gig was so brilliant, I just wanted some peace and quiet to talk about it. And he'd been sound with us all day, I didn't want him sat on his own at the hotel. He said he didn't want to cramp our style after the gig."

"Aww, that's really sweet of you. You're a good boy." Reaching across, she placed her hand on his cheek, running a finger tenderly across his perfect cheekbone. "You seem to really like Johnny. He seems nice."

Placing his own hand on his mum's, "He is. He wants this as much as us. You should have seen him after the gig. He was absolutely buzzing."

Smiling her perfect smile, she said, "Do you want a cold drink? You must be thirsty after that long journey. I'll fetch us a juice and you can tell me about the gig."

A shout from upstairs startled them both. "GET IN!" Dom shouted excitedly. "Just had a text off Danny, we're on YouTube! Somebody recorded a couple of tracks and put them up. How fuckin' cool is that. I'm coming down. Get your laptop on!"

"Language!" Cally admonished half-heartedly. Returning with three tall glasses of fresh orange juice, she said, "Put my laptop on the table, and we'll have a look!"

Powering the laptop on, Jamie gulped back half his drink.

Typing into the browser, Jamie soon found the page. Beaming at Dom, who was stood beside them with a bath towel wrapped around his waist, he said, "How sick is this!?! And it was done by somebody we don't even know…"

The clip was far from perfect. Entirely what you would have expected from mobile phone footage. The sound was interspersed with shouts and snatches of muffled conversation. The picture focussed solely on Jamie, and 'Pollypants1992' seemed to be quite the fan judging by the "HE'S SOOOOOOOOOOO LUSH" comment that was typed underneath the gig footage.

Smiling, he was slightly embarrassed as his mum gave him a friendly nudge with her elbow. The footage was good and seeing themselves play live for the first time gave the brothers a huge rush of pride.

"Where am I then?" Dom asked peevishly.

Putting her arm round his naked shoulders, she said, "Oh don't worry luv, it's only off a camera phone, you can't see everything."

Staring raptly at the computer screen, Jamie felt as out-of-body a feeling as he had ever experienced.

It was him.

On stage. Doing what he loved. Being watched – and recorded – by other people. Loving the way his thrifty charity shop purchase looked. The red scarf setting off the whole image. The background chatter in the crowd seemed to drop just as Dom's guitar solo on 'Salvation' kicked in. It had sounded brilliant to Jamie at the time but hearing his brother's chiming guitar take over the crowd was amazing. He rubbed at the back of his neck as he felt the hairs stand up.

It was note perfect, with Dom wringing out every chord to perfection. Turning to look at his twin, he saw Dom was now stood in a fists-together boxer's stance, nodding his head to himself.

"How good does that sound? My guitar sounded wicked. Play it again bro!"

Clapping her hands with delighted abandon, and pulling both boys into her sides, she said, "Oh my boys, my beautiful boys. They're going to be famous!"

Kissing her softly on the top of her head, Jamie said, "Not just yet Mum, not just yet…"

Mirroring his brother's action, but adding with a determined assuredness, "But we will be. We definitely will be."

Looking at her boys, Cally knew at that moment that they truly would be…

***

Danny ambled up his road – ignoring the local kids who were playing kerbie with a knackered leather football – and sat down on a low, crumbling garden wall. Sparking up the last of his cigarettes, he inhaled deeply. Propping his feet up on his guitar case, he lifted his sunglasses slightly and rubbed at the still throbbing bruise on his left eyebrow. The lads appeared to buy his story of having cracked his eye when his guitar fell forward whilst he had been re-stringing it. Sucking on the cigarette deeply, Danny smiled to himself at the events of the past 24 hours. He'd never felt so alive as when he was on that stage. And chatting to girls – and well-wishing lads – had been such a buzz. Back slaps and hugs from total strangers. The most amazing of feelings to someone perennially starved of affection. The drudgery of home and unemployed life just washed away. This was what he wanted for himself. This could change everything. *This has to happen. It fuckin' has to,* he thought

Snapping from his nicotine fuelled reverie, he looked up at the little herbert who was now stood in front of him, rolling the football dextrously between his insteps. "'Ere y'ar. Have youse got a spare ciggy for us mate?"

Looking up at the diminutive would be 20 a dayer, Danny laughed, "I haven't. That was me last one. Anyhow. It'll stunt your growth, shorty."

"Well fuck off then yer tight twat. S'pose smoking give you a big nose as well?"

Skipping back a few yards before adding the finishing flourish. "'Cos you must have been on 50 a day for years!" Hearing his fellow herberts laugh at his bravado, he added his coup de grace, "and what have you got in that box? A spare nose!"

"Cheeky little cunts," Danny whispered under his breath. Nothing was going to spoil his day. Not even returning home to face his dad's scathing comments, or worse, his loose fists.

The night before the gig, Dan had been practising in his bedroom, polishing and restringing his guitar – this much of his cover story was true. He had been rehearsing his basslines listening back through a pair of oversized headphones. The resultant muffled throb could still be heard downstairs.

His mother had paid no heed to the sonorous rumble. Although when his dad had returned from his nightly visit to the Feathers – a bellyful of beer and spite – it had not been long before there had been a loud knock on his bedroom door.

"Shut that fuckin' noise up you little shite." Beating on the door. Growing angrier with each chord.

Losing patience at the lack of a subservient response, the door was then thrown open, startling Danny, who had been oblivious to his drunken father's hammering and cursing.

Ripping the headphones from Danny's head and throwing them against the bedroom wall, "SHUT THAT FUCKIN' RACKET UP!" his dad snarled.

Jumping to his feet, Danny rubbed at his ear which had been caught in the headphone cable as they were torn from him. "OW! FUCK THAT HURT! WHAT WAS THAT FOR?"

Staring at his son with rheumy eyes, flashed with booze broken blood vessels. "What was that for? To try and get you to shut the fuck up. I can't hear the tele over your constant din. Fuckin' waste of fuckin' time. Ya should put the same effort into getting a fuckin' job, ya lazy wee cunt!"

Here we go, thought Dan. The usual tirade of insults. The mental bullying. The bitterness that had engulfed his father over the past decade spewing forth. With any luck, he'd blow himself out once he agreed to put his guitar away.

"What's the special occasion? Yer mam says you've been up here all night. Aren't you usually out glue sniffing or whatever it is you young knobheads do these days…'

Even in the face of the vindictive provocation, Danny vainly tried to impress his dad. "The band have got a big gig tomorrow. I'm practising for that," he offered. Looking for the slightest shred of fatherly approval.

Leaning on the doorframe, breathing heavily, Danny's candidness was met with a disparaging guffaw. "You and yer little boyband mates playing one of them fuckin' gay bars in town? Load of shite I bet youse are!"

Staring hard at the drunk and wheezing incarnation of his father, "That's right! You fuckin' tell me how shite I am. What a disgrace I am. How I'll never amount to fuck all." His breath quickened. Surprising himself by his outburst. "Well you'll fuckin' see. I'm gonna make it with this band. And you won't see me for fuckin' dust, you sad old cunt!"

Smack. Lightning fast. His father's fist caught him on the left temple. Reeling from the punch but not wishing to show any weakness despite the tears that had started to well, Danny said softly, "Yeah that's right. That's the answer. Just fuck off and leave me alone. I'll be gone before you know it…"

His father – as ever – seemed shocked at his violent capabilities and now stood in the doorway with a look of remorse on his face. The monster in him seemed to be dispelled as soon as the violence had been meted out.

Closing the bedroom door, Danny looked in the small bedroom mirror positioned off-centre above a chest of drawers. A thin drip of blood was easing its way from an inch-long cut, right over his thick brown eyebrow. Tracing a lean finger down the bloody line, he rubbed his finger against his tongue. Staring himself down in the mirror and dabbing at the cut with a tissue. "We will fuckin' make it. Big time!" he mouthed to himself.

Chapter 15

A beer garden kind of evening. Having spent most of the day in the studio, Johnny felt that a pint was very much in order. Flirting a quick text message out to Mark and Chris, he was delighted to receive an instant response from Mark –

'Mr H, read my mind. Love a few. Printers at 6 bells?'

With Claire away on a hen party/spa day, he'd have time to himself and there was nothing better than a quiet few pints and then home clutching whatever take-out food he fancied. *Put the world to rights and all that,* he thought.

Selecting a faded denim shirt, cargo shorts and a pair of scuffed white Adidas Superstars, Johnny felt as carefree as he had been in ages. The appointment with the doctors was looming later the following week, but for now that could wait.

Shades, wallet and keys gathered up, he headed to the Printers hoping that the beer garden wasn't already heaving. Arriving on time, he saw Mark had already got two pints of lager and secured a prime slice of beer garden real estate.

"Mr Harrison. How the very devil are you?" Mark offered up cheerily.

"All good. All good man. How've you been? Let off the leash on a Saturday. You must have been a good boy!" replied Johnny before drinking deeply, sighing at the bite of the cold alcohol.

"Jenny's away at her mum's. Taken one of the kids and Barney's at his mates on a sleepover. So, I'm all yours!" beamed Mark.

A couple of hours of relaxed, good natured bonhomie together with a steady flow of strong lager lead to an easy flow of idle chatter. The seldom seen Manchester sunshine had brought a decent crowd out.

As Mark went off to catch last orders, Johnny leant back on the wooden table, stretching his legs out on front of him. Looking up, two girls in their early twenties asked if the table was fully taken. Dressed in denim shorts, strappy summery tops and towering wedged platform sandals - more suited for stumbling between bars in some Mediterranean hotspot, leaving a trail of Sambuca shot glasses and drooling young males in their wake than in a quiet South Manchester suburb.

"I'm waiting on my mate. He's at the bar. Don't mind us though."

"Nah you're alright mate. We'll wait 'til you've gone."

"Suit yourselves," he replied casually. "And mind you don't fall off them shoes. Casualty will be packed tonight the number of shoes like that I've seen."

Turning as quickly as their shoes would permit, Johnny's generosity was met by a not out of earshot cackle. "He's old enough to be your dad. And what a cheeky twat about my shoes!"

Laughing to himself, and thinking, *Bacardi Breezers, so much to answer for,* Johnny turned back to face the table just as Mark returned with the pints and two whisky chasers.

Glad that the two girls had elected not to sit at their table, Johnny lowered his voice slightly, leaning forward. "Have I told you about Claire wanting kids now?" He exhaled deeply. "She thought she was pregnant the other week and has decided that we're going to the docs to have all the tests…"

Looking at his friend for all the instant answers that a long-standing drinking partner should provide, he went on, "Didn't you go through all that bollocks when you and Jenny wanted to start a family? Looked at IVF and that…"

Mark raised his eyebrows at the unexpected change in nature of the conversation. "'Kin 'ell mate. Good luck with that. We went for the initial chat and tests, but I then fired the proverbial Death Star shot and we never looked back. Big relief as the IVF sounded bloody hard work. And expensive!" Knocking his JD back, he said, "I didn't know you were that keen?"

Sighing deeply, Johnny said, "I don't know mate. It's what Claire wants. I'm not averse to the idea. But fuck. I'm forty. As much as I'm not on the scrap heap, I never wanted to be 'old Dad'." Rubbing a hand across his face and pushing the sunglasses up to the top of his head, he let out an exasperated breath. "I've no real choice. Suppose I'll just see what the tests throw up and go from there…"

Nodding profusely, Mark said, "I wouldn't worry about that, loads of people having kids in their forties these days. Just go for the consultation and tests. That's all you can do, mate. Just tread carefully would be my advice." Lifting his glass, he continued, "Anyhow you've not mentioned this band to me in ages. What's the score?"

With the conversation having turned to his favourite subject, Johnny reached for the spirits glass and chinned the JD in one, savouring the tang of the ice as it melted on his tongue.

"It's all happening, man. Been working with them for about six months now. They're in the studio recording some tracks. Had them working hard for a few months. Rehearsing and writing and that."

"You are taking this seriously!" He sounded almost surprised. "I've not seen you in a while. What with working away and the kids. I just didn't think you'd bother after all your initial bluster."

"And why not?" Johnny said defensively.

A little too defensively.

"Fucking good opportunity like this. I'd be mad not to go for it!"

"Because—" questioned Mark, the multiple pints now negating his ability to articulate a reasoned objection. "I dunno. I suppose." Hesitating before his final salvo. "Because these things are always longshots."

"Of course they fucking are!" His voice rose. "But when they are this fuckin' good it increases chances ten-fold. No, fuck that. A hundred-fold. They are that fucking good!"

Mark was taken aback at Johnny's impassioned outburst. "What's the big plan then? If they're that great, why stick with you? Why not get somebody, like, someone professional?"

Snorting with derision, Johnny said, "Yeah thanks for that. Listen," he dropped his voice down a notch, "I've put money into them so that counts for a lot, doesn't it?"

"Fuck me mate. How much?" Mark whistled between his teeth.

"Keep this to yourself. But I'm in for about ten grand already." He paused for the inevitable judgemental comment.

"FUCK ME! That's a lot of dough mate. You sure about all this?" said Mark, shaking his head.

"Balls to the cash. I could have lost the fuckin' lot if I'd listened to some cunt of a financial adviser and stuck it in stocks and shares!" He gulped back a mouthful from his pint. "Anyhow. It's been spent now, so we'll see…"

"Okay, let's say this band make it, are you gonna jack your job an—"

Johnny interjected snappishly. "Course I fucking am! Why wouldn't I? Stick with a job I hate for another ten years or so for a big company that doesn't give a fuck about me. And then get binned off cos your face doesn't fit when you hit 50. Fuck that."

Deliberating over his words. "It's a bit mid-life crisis isn't it, y'know. It would have been a lot easier to spunk the cash on a sports car. That Ford Mustang you've always banged on about? At least you'd have something to show for it."

Johnny slammed his pint glass down, clearly irked. "A MID-LIFE CRISIS! FUCK OFF!"

The Rock 'N' The Roll. 'N That

Johnny's outburst startled the occupants of the neighbouring tables who all stopped to listen to his tirade, smothering smirks.

"You honestly think that. FOR FUCK'S SAKE MATE!"

"Sorry Johnny bu-"

Cutting Mark off curtly, and still at a free-for-all volume, Johnny continued. "WHAT'S THE WORST THAT CAN HAPPEN? I LOSE SOME CASH? OR THEY RECORD THEIR SONGS. GET A RECORD DEAL. GET FAMOUS. DRINK THEMSELVES DAFT AND BACK AGAIN. TAKE DRUGS. FUCK THAT. TAKE A SHIT LOAD OF DRUGS. FUCK SOME RIDICULOUSLY ATTRACTIVE AND OBLIGING GIRLS. START ACTING LIKE TWATS. FALL OUT WITH EACH OTHER OVER MUSICAL DIFFERENCES THAT DON'T EVEN FUCKING EXIST. START WEARING LEATHER TROUSERS. HOPE THAT NOBODY DIES. SPLIT UP. THEN DO A REUNION IN TEN FUCKIN' YEARS TIME. THAT'S IT. THE END. OH, AND HOPE THEY DON'T TRY AND TURN INTO THE NEXT COLDPLAY!" He took a deep breath. "Happy now?"

Full of beery bravado, a lad in his late teens, sporting an overly gelled spiky haircut, complete with shaved tramlines, snorted into his bottle of Smirnoff Ice. "What a twat!"

Not appreciating the eavesdropper's contribution, Johnny turned and snapped. "Oy! Parrot head. Fuck off and mind your own fucking business!"

"Alright mate! I was only messing. Keep your hair on," the gawky teen mumbled back

"Fuck sake Johnny. I didn't mean to nark you," Mark said, putting a placating hand on Johnny's arm.

"Yeah yeah, I know. But fuck, I thought you of all people would take me seriously," he said, taking deep breaths and still glaring at the parrot-headed youth who was now hurriedly drinking up.

"Listen mate, if you've invested that much cash, then you must be serious. I had no idea. Fuck me. What does Claire think?"

"What do you think? She doesn't know. It's the money I inherited, I should have told her from the off. But y'know. It'd have never happened." His words trailed off.

Wide eyed. "She doesn't know? Fuck! That's going to be some conversation."

"Yeah well, I'll cross that bridge. Don't suppose she'll complain too loudly when I start earning some proper cash." Looking at his friend and half-regretting his outburst. "They've got a gig in town next month. Come down. See how good they are. Then you'll get it."

"We good?" asked Mark.

"We're good but you're paying for the kebabs now. A mid-life crisis. Cheeky fucker! A mid-life opportunity is what this is…"

Chapter 17

"You've not forgotten about later, have you, babe? Half five at the doctor's."

"I've put loose boxers on especially. I'll see you later. I won't be late. Honest."

Trepidation was already starting to sink in.

But first a fix of studio-time…

***

"Let's get back to work," said Dean - before again hacking into his hand. Sounding like a broken tractor engine.

"Consider myself told," Mikee smiled and with four strides was back in the live room and positioning himself behind his kit.

"That's the attitude," said Dean approvingly, "says he doesn't need a click track either. I love his confidence."

The rest of them then reconvened – minus Danny who disappeared for yet another fix of carcinogens – to the rec room.

"This is going to be fuckin' brilliant," whispered Dom.

Laughing, Jamie replied, "You don't need to whisper bro, it's soundproofed in there!"

"Yeah, yeah, I knew that," Dom replied defensively, "but it is. This is gonna be amazing for us." Standing as Danny returned, "I'm going to sit in with Dean again, see what he does and that…"

Danny bounded back into the room, "How's he doing? Does it sound the business?" Snapping his bony fingers together, "Fuckin' buzzin' about this me!"

Sitting down on the battered leather sofa, facing Jamie and Johnny, the bass player was a whirlwind of unbridled excitement. Nervous tension coursing through him, "Anyhow, y'know when we crack it, make it big, what yer gonna spend yer first money on?" Wide eyed with the thought of this prospect, Danny nodded his head enthusiastically. "I had the chat with Mikee, and he said full tattoo sleeves. Proper decent ones. They'll look the

The Rock 'N' The Roll. 'N That

business on him. Not for me, I'm too skinny." Pointing at Jamie, "What about you then man?"

Tilting his head to one side, Jamie looked at Danny, "I don't know man, I've not really thought about it. Y'know, a few grand and I'd spend it on guitars and pedals, new top-class amp. Bit of nice clobber. And send our mum on holiday. She's not had one in years. Can't even remember the last time."

Smiling to himself, Johnny was as ever, intrigued by chats of this nature.

Then turning the question back to Danny, "So what about you then?"

Rubbing the bridge of his nose, just at the point where the distinct crook started. A serious look passed across his face." Don't fuckin' laugh. But I'd get this fuckin' nose sorted out." Looking beseechingly across at Johnny and Jamie, and half-expecting uncontrolled laughter, Danny narrowed his eyes. "You don't think it's funny then? Y'know an ugly little skinny twat like me bothered by how I look."

Still nothing.

"Come on, say something!"

As ever finding just the right words, Jamie leant forward, placing a hand on Danny's bouncing knee, "Don't talk about yourself like that. But if that's what you wanted, then you go for it." His hand stopped Danny's constant motion, "Just do me one favour."

Looking intrigued, Danny frowned slightly, "Go on then J. One favour."

Grinning his charismatic smile. "Yeah. Don't go taking a picture of Michael Jackson to the surgeon!"

"Haha, you wanker! Imagine how fuckin' funny that'd be! Going from this Gonzo beak to a fucked up little button nose that kept dropping off!" Falling to his side on the sofa, fits of laughter shook through his skinny frame. Sitting up after a good twenty seconds laughter, he wiped tears away from his eyes. Composing himself, "I'm serious though, just a little tweak and I'd be happy. I won't miss the odd inch or so that's for fuckin' sure…"

Enjoying the moment, Johnny leaned into Jamie conspiratorially, and in a soto voce voice from behind his cupped hand, "And before you know it, he'll be getting collagen in his lips, bit of shaping work to his chin, cheekbones…"

Nodding in agreement, "I think you're right. Slippery slope isn't it?"

Fortunately, Danny took the routine in the way it had been intended, "Yeah and some arse cheek implants, get sick of it when birds tell me I've no arse."

"That's his first royalties cheque taken care of then isn't it?" grinned Johnny.

Looking up at Johnny, Danny - clicking his Bic lighter on and off repeatedly. "And what about you Mr Manager? Bit of Botox wouldn't go amiss." Nodding at Johnny, "Them wrinkles will only get worse. And there's crow's feet starting." Pulling at his own eyes, Dan stretched his face out in a faded Hollywood-starlet facelift manner.

Far from taking offence, Johnny smiled back, enjoying the camaraderie, "Not me. Grow old disgracefully." Running a hand through his hair, "However young Daniel, if this starts to disappear, I'm getting straight on to the syrup shop and getting me a wig!"

Smacking his thighs in delight, "Haha! Imagine him with a fuckin' daft wig! Proper twat!" Snapping his fingers together frenziedly.

"All sorted then aren't we, tattoos, nose job, a wig. It's only Jamie that's going to spend his money wisely!"

Returning from the Studio room, Dom looked around the small rec room, "You all having a top time then?" as he took in the good-natured vibes.

Jamie - deadpanning and pointing over at Johnny. "You know that's a wig that he wears don't you bro?"

Looking at Jamie, and Johnny in turn, and with a look of confused perplexity, "Really? Fuck off! He doesn't?" Staring hard at Johnny, examining his hairline for any tell-tale signs of a seam. "He better fuckin' not! I don't want our manager being some daft twat with a wig!"

"Oh charming!" Johnny replied, his tone laden with sarcasm. "Give it a tug and see!"

"Isn't it called grooming when you ask young boys to give you a tug?" Jamie enquired mock seriously.

"Right you shower of piss taking twats, I'm off. Work hard and I'll catch you later."

"Laters man," said Jamie, and as Johnny reached the bottom of the stairs, he heard Dom ask, "It's not a wig is it, it doesn't look like one...."

***

A week's hard graft had seen the band nail the four tracks with a dedication that had surpassed Johnny's expectations. His daily updates from Dean meant his unwavering belief in the band was never questioned.

"Okay lads. We've got all four tracks down. We can now look at mixing them. Add some overdubs and just have a play about with them," said Dean, leaning back on the tall swivel stool as the band listened intently. "I'm gonna level with you. Even before we finish 'em off they are really fuckin' good. As good as I have heard in," blowing his cheeks out, "well, in fuckin' ages."

The pride swelled within the band. The mandatory fist bumps and nods were exchanged.

"Look. I can do my bit with songs. Get them recorded. Tinker about with them, y'know," he said, pointing behind at a dormant laptop. "Fuck me. You can polish a turd and sprinkle it with glitter but at the end of the day, it's all about the songs and you have got some proper tunes!"

Danny was lost for words, and seemed to be choking back a tear, Jamie and Dom both nodded and thanked Dean. Huge smiles in perfect symmetry.

"Your man has paid for ten days. Means we can work on these for a day or so, then look at putting down a couple of acoustic tracks. Never does any harm these days. And how about a studio jam on the last session. If you've got any half-formed ideas, we can record them live and it'll help you work on them."

Having finally composed himself, Danny fixed Dean with his doleful brown eyes. "You've been fuckin' brilliant. I knew we'd have to work hard but I've loved every second. Every fuckin' second!"

"Not bad for a miserable old cunt am I," Dean laughed heartily before coughing gruffly into his hand. Adjusting one of his many leather bracelets, he added, "I think that calls for a well-earned tea break. You can all fuck off and have a cig, yer dirty little addicts!"

"Johnny said he'd be down later, "said Jamie, leaning back against the old Victorian house. "He'll be made up with the tracks."

"How quick before he sorts us out a record deal?" asked Danny as he blew a pirouetting smoke ring.

"He'll sort it," said Mikee, readjusting the wide brimmed LA Raiders baseball cap that he had been sporting for the duration of the recording sessions. "The songs. They just sound the fuckin' business. I can't believe it's us. I knew we were good but fuck. They sound sick!"

"Let's get back to it," said Jamie, flicking a cig end into a nearby flowerbed.

***

Meeting outside the surgery at 5.25pm, Johnny kissed a clearly agitated Claire lightly on her forehead. "You alright? Ready for this?"

"I'm just glad you're here. I was worried that you wouldn't show up."

Shoving his hands into his suit trouser pockets, he said, "Thanks!"

"I didn't mean it like that. I knew really."

"Well, no time like the present. After you, lady." Stepping aside, Johnny followed Claire in and they took adjoining seats in the waiting room.

After an interminably long wait, the buzzer crackled, and the receptionist called out, "Mr Harrison. Ms Cooper. The doctor will see you now."

The two of them stood simultaneously, Johnny smiled as sympathetically as he could. "Here we go then…"

Sitting in front of the doctor, they were blinded by talk of ovarian cycles, optimum times, healthy ejaculate, sperm count, fertility, fallopian tubes, percentages, chances, absent ovulation, hormonal levels, diet, IVF, etc. etc. etc.

Johnny's head was spinning, staring at the thick pile of helpful literature that had piled up in front of them. He had confessed to having a drink, but not to excess. He sidestepped the question of narcotics with consummate ease. Claire sounded the paragon of virtue with her semi-vegetarian diet. Low alcohol intake and exercise regime. But as the doctor said repeatedly, "this wasn't about blame."

Gathering up the leaflets and thanking the doctor profusely, they were both relieved to get outside.

Anything to break the silence. "Fertility clinic and spaffing into a plastic cup. That's a date for the diary then…"

The glare delivered by Claire was enough for him to realise that this wasn't the time for banal crudities. They walked to her car in silence. Sitting in the passenger seat, Johnny reached reflexively for the car stereo.

Slap.

Claire's hand smacked him before he could. She turned to him with tear filled eyes. "I want this so much…"

"I know you do, and y'know, I'm not against the idea. I just never fancied all the tests and that." Checking himself before talking about the cost of IVF, he added, "And I don't like the idea of us finding out whose fault it is if we can't have…"

Snapping irritably, a tear rolling down her cheek, she said, "DID YOU NOT LISTEN?" Rubbing at the tear and lowering her voice, "It's not about blame! It's about finding out what we can do differently to help us."

"Okay. Okay. Sorry. I do get that, but you know what I mean. Neither of us wants to be told it's your eggs or my swimmers!"

Managing a sniffled laugh, she said, "Oh Johnny, you dick. You can call them sperm like a grown up," – with air quotes – "and not swimmers…"

The short journey home was made in silence. Johnny looking blankly at the pile of pamphlets he had on his lap.

Arriving home, Johnny popped the leaflets on the dining table. "I'll sort tea out for us, what do you fancy?"

Claire was already sat on the sofa, turning her laptop on. "I'm not that hungry. I'll sort myself out later…"

Retiring to the kitchen, he stood at the sink and stared out over the small garden, his eye fixing on a tennis ball that was nestled in one of the flower beds.

Deciding that he needed to take the initiative, he was just about to shout through to Claire, "I…"

Cutting him off before he could start, she said, "I think we should make an appointment at the fertility clinic as soon as possible. Get in quickly and you won't get in a stress about your 'plastic cup ordeal', I know what you're like!"

"I was just going to say that. No time like the present and all that," he said, trying to add as much conviction as he could muster.

Needing some respite from this, he reached for his phone and texted Jamie –

'*Alright J. How's it going? X*'

Turning the kitchen stereo on at a sensitively quiet volume, Johnny popped Nick Cave's *The Boatman's Call* on.

The beautiful minor piano chords were wistfully playing when his phone pinged –

'*Hiya man. Songs sound wicked. Get yourself down. We're making magic! x*'

Smiling at the text, and pleased that Jamie never resorted to the bastardised text speak that rendered most young people's missives nigh on indecipherable, he texted back immediately –

'*Tomorrow night. Can't wait x*'

He half smiled to himself at the last message – it sounded like he was arranging an illicit tryst with a lover. But he had to hear the fruits of their recorded labours as soon as he could.

Picking up the glass of water he had poured himself – best not have a proper drink, he had wisely decided – he went to sit on the sofa and saw that Claire, glasses firmly in situ, was looking at an IVF clinic's website…

Chapter 18

"Right lady. I'm off out for a couple. I'll pick up a pizza on the way back," Johnny said cheerily.

Sprawled full length on the sofa, her laptop balanced precariously on her stomach as she drank from a tall glass of fizzy water, Claire looked up at Johnny. "Suits you, that shirt. You should wear it more often." Fixing him with an I'm not messing glare. "And make sure it is only a couple. We've got the tests this week."

Looking down at his crisp white linen shirt, he said, "Yeah it does, ta. But how often do we get decent enough weather to start dressing like Take That." Flinging his arms out wide and tossing his head back, dramatic boy band style, Johnny laughed at his own joke. "And I'm driving so only a couple. Promise" Leaning over the back of the sofa, he kissed her on the top of her head. "And how could I forget about next week!"

Walking to the front door, he shook his head slightly as Claire had been looking at yet another 'baby making' website.

Since receiving Jamie's text, he could think of nothing other than hearing the tracks. He knew how hard the band had worked, and if there were any near as good as he hoped then this really could be the start of things…

Pulling up outside, he was met by Danny, pacing the pavement, as ever sucking his cheeks hollow on a cigarette. "Where have you been man, we've been waiting for you for the playback."

Glancing down at his watch – six-fifty precisely – "We said seven, didn't we Danny?" he said slowly.

Nodding, Danny looked at his watch less wrist, and looked up at Johnny. "Sorry Johnny. I just can't fuckin' wait. Y'know what I'm like."

Putting his arm around him, he said, "Not a problem. You fucking lunatic. I'm here now so let's go and hear these tunes."

The friendly arm round the shoulder lowered Danny's manic energy levels, and his mind momentarily flashed back to times when his father would think nothing of such a gesture.

The Rock 'N' The Roll. 'N That

Letting himself in with a quick input of the door code, Danny led the way to a room on the first floor that Johnny had not been in before. Entering the lounge at the rear of the property, Johnny saw the band, who were all sipping from cans of lager, sat on the two leather sofas that dominated the room - facing the large bay window which overlooked the unkempt garden. Either side of the window were two sizable and clearly expensive looking speakers. Housed in walnut, the speakers must have stood a good five feet high. And if they sounded as impressive as they looked…

The advent of digital files and MP3 had been a veritable musical revolution, but there was nothing better than putting on an actual tangible CD. Or if you were a real purist, vinyl. On a proper system and belting it through a quality stereo. Johnny nodded in approval. Taking a seat in the lone armchair, he gratefully accepted the can which Mikee offered him from the carrier bag at his feet.

Dean, as ever in combat fatigues, fleece and walking sandals, was, quite rightly, assuming the Master of Ceremonies role. Walking to the stereo that dominated the right-hand wall of the room, he hacked behind his hand and then with the same hand pushed his hair back. "Okay gents. I hope you remember this day fondly, as this is the first time you will have heard a playback of your songs. I think you're going to like them…"

With that he pressed play on the stereo and went to stand at the far end of the room, dead centre between the speakers.

A squeal of feedback filled the room, followed by a slow metronomic drumbeat behind it. The feedback dropped, the drums ratcheted up a beat faster, and then the raw sounding guitars kicked in. '*This Is Not Tomorrow*' roared from the speakers.

Jamie's vocals sounded brilliant. Pure emotion, with the hint of an anguished strain. With Danny and Dom's backing vocals adding perfect balance on the chorus. The bassline-driven middle eight was amazing - less frenzied and with the lead guitar perfectly placed in the mix. The guitars steaming back in for the last verse and chorus.

3.33 seconds and it was done.

Despite the clear power and anger it was the hook that grabbed you. An angry, yet hook-laden piece of protest that worked a treat. Johnny looked around the room; the band all looked incredibly serious, fixed concentration as they waited on the next track.

A skittering drum track and a spiralling guitar signalled the intro to '*Mantra*'. The guitars sounded huge. Dom had the chiming cascading solo down to perfection. The drum track had been done in one take according to one of Jamie's progress reports. Mikee might seem to be laid back to the point of horizontal but he could play. No mistake.

'*Burn the Sky*' shimmered with anger and menace – Jamie spitting the line '*so that's how the avaricious bankers thank us…*' Dom's guitar lines were economical but incandescent. No extravagant soloing but he was a guitar hero in the making.

Still nobody exchanged a word.

And finally.

The band's tour de force. '*Salvation*'.

Under Dean's tutelage, the intro was now strummed on an acoustic, before Dan's bassline laid down the groove with Mikee's hi-hats hissing like a cornered snake. The guitars glided to the forefront of the track. It sounded perfect. Anthemic. Soaring. And that chorus was crying out for mass adoration, Jamie and Dom harmonising the killer line, '*I'll be your salvation. You'll be my salvation. We'll be your salvation…*'

Stepping over to the stereo, Dean pressed pause and looked expectantly at the band for their post-playback comments.

Before he had chance to speak, Danny bowled over from the sofa and hugged Dean tightly. Pulling away, he looked round the room at the collection of beaming faces. "HOW FUCKING BRILLIANT IS THAT? HOW FUCKING BRILLIANT!"

Clapping loudly, Johnny stood and said, "It's glorious. Absolutely fucking glorious! I'm blown away. Utterly fucking blown away…"

Jamie and Dom still hadn't said a word, Mikee was excitably hugging Danny. The feeling of a job well done was rife. Dean stood on like a proud father, winking at Johnny. "You've got a fuckin' band and half on your hands here…"

Pursing his lips, and barely able to contain himself, he said, "I know! I fucking know!"

Calling for calm, Dean snapped his fingers. "And before we finish getting excited, there are a couple of acoustic tracks and a live track they jammed."

"Like it," said Johnny "Sounds like value for money to me."

And then came the 'surprise'. A track that the band had jammed around with in the rehearsal studio had now been given life. '*Only the Good Die Trying*'. A two minute forty-five second slab of furious guitars and a vocal that bought to mind Cobain at his angriest. The drums were huge in the mix and drove the track with an unbridled fury. And a call to arms lyric of '*come and watch the people take the city*'. Raw as hell, but the massive guitar hook signalled that this was more than just a work in progress.

"I've got some CDs that I burnt off for you all. Artwork courtesy of Johnny who spent ages cutting them out to size. I'd suggest you look after these. I'll pop 'em on USB sticks as well in case you crazy young kids think CD is too old fashioned for you," said Dean handing out the precious CDs.

"They look brilliant," said Jamie, smiling at Johnny. "You got a spare for our mum?"

"I think there's a couple of spare in the studio. But look after these," he added with a grin, "they'll be worth a fortune in a few years!" Looking down admiringly at the CD. "And as a little treat after all this grafting in the studio, I've booked us a gig next week. Short notice. But a band has dropped out next Friday night at Night and Day, so I said that you'd fill in. Bottom of the bill of three. But there's always get a decent crowd."

"Nice one," nodded Mikee, turning to Dean, "You should get yourself down, sure we'll all buy you a fizzy water."

Laughing, Dean replied, "I'll be there, I'll see if I can do the sound as well, I know the fella there."

"Okay, I'm off. And this," waving the CD above his head, "will be getting a proper blasting in my car!" Turning to Dean, and shaking his hand, Johnny said, "You're a top man, knew you'd do the business and, well," making an expansive gesture with his arms, "What can I say? Let's hope it all starts here…"

"My pleasure Mr Harrison. And the monies all safely in my bank account. Came across first thing today. Appreciated," said Dean, nodding his head courteously.

"I'll catch you later, and don't go plastering this little beauty over the interweb just yet, eh?"

Leaving the band listening to another playback, Johnny headed home his head reverberating with rock and roll.

Chapter 19

Two large marker penned stars on the kitchen calendar. As if either of them were likely to forget about it.

Johnny had arrived home an hour earlier than Claire and was about to embark on a bona fide medicinal wank. He had omitted to use any form of pornographic stimulation as he had deemed that this would be inappropriate. His colleague, Paul, had recently dispelled the 10CC/male ejaculate urban myth – much to his consternation as he was convinced that he'd just produced a double album's worth.

Job done, and the warm tub now safely popped in the jiffy bag, he went and showered before Claire got home. He'd been on rations that week and under strict masturbatory orders not to 'overdo it'.

Showering quickly and dressing in jeans, shirt and weekend suit jacket, he went and sat downstairs, awaiting Claire's arrival.

On the dot of 1.30pm, she opened the door looking remarkably relaxed. Barely able to stifle a grin, she put her laptop bag down by the dining table. "We all done then?" The inevitable air quotes irked as ever.

"Two cups full. Just to be safe. Waste not want not and that," he replied, keeping his face as straight as he could.

"Johnny! Do you always have to!" Claire said, grimacing.

"Yes, whatever," he mumbled back.

"We'll be off then. You going to drive, or am I?"

"I'll drive. You can carry the merch. I tried to get one of them cup carriers from Starbucks, but they don't do them for espresso cups."

A raised brow. A look of disdain. And a fold of her arms. Hat-trick.

As they left the house and headed for his car, Johnny realised that the Lonely Souls CD was still pride of place in his car stereo. Claire probably bat an eyelid at it and it would be easily enough explained away but flipping to XFM was a far better option, he thought as he reached for the seatbelt.

The Rock 'N' The Roll. 'N That

Pulling up at Wythenshawe Hospital, Johnny reached for some loose change to pay for the parking. "You ready for this?"

"Of course," Claire replied softly. A palpable tremor in her voice.

Holding her hand, they followed the signs to the fertility clinic, the jiffy bag held ceremoniously in a Tesco shopping bag.

Dr Amit was a small, chunky and friendly Asian gentleman. His relaxed tone immediately settled them, and Johnny vowed that he would refrain from any irreverent comments.

A general chat about their lifestyle was followed by a more thorough enquiry into their sex lives. Blood test and cholesterol checks were undertaken, and the doctor then politely informed them they should make a further appointment for two weeks hence. Shaking him by the hand – *I wonder how many times he thinks that he is being offered a warm wanking hand*, Johnny mused to himself – and thanking him for his time, they left and walked back to the car park.

Reaching the car, he said, "That wasn't too bad was it?"

Replying quietly, Claire said, "We'll see what happens next time then, shall we babe…"

Pulling away from the hospital car park, Johnny's mind turned to the following night's gig.

The journey home was made in silence, the 'what-if' possibilities hung large.

***

Walking down the stairs, Cal did a slow 360 turn. "Will I do then?" Wearing a pair of tight fitting dark blue jeans and an equally fitted black T-shirt bearing a logo of 'The Cult – Sonic Temple Tour' matched with a pair of just above the ankle black heeled boots, she waited for the twins' approval. Slumped together on the sofa channel surfing the music stations, Jamie turned around and laughed. "You look great, Mum. But it's only 2 o'clock! Bit early to be getting done up."

"And I've not had my dinner yet, way too nice to be getting that ready for me," added Dom.

"Get it yourself for a change," Cal laughed sweetly. Looking down at her evening's outfit of choice, she said, "Of course I'm going to get changed again. I just didn't want to let you down."

"You'll be the coolest Mum in there. No danger," chirped Dom, backtracking from his previous culinary request.

Looking at his phone, Jamie stretched and said, "Right, I'm getting a couple of hours' kip and then heading into town. What about you bro?"

"Meeting Danny and Mikee for a couple. Talk gig tactics innit," yawned Dom.

***

Night and Day. Oldham Street, Manchester. A staple of Manchester's rich musical heritage. One of the stepping stones that all the city's greats had played.

Having arranged to meet at 5pm, Danny and Mikee had arrived early and were sat at the bar sampling a cold Czech beer.

Chinking the neck of his bottle against Mikee's, Dan said, "I've not stopped playing our tracks. How about you? Your drumming sounds wicked. He did a fuckin' sick job did ol' Dean."

Taking a long draw from the bottle, Mikee said, "Same with me D-Mo. Can't believe it's us at times. Sounds sweet. He's down later as well, Dean."

Frowning slightly as he drank the dregs of his bottle, Danny was still coming to terms with the new moniker he had acquired during their time in the studio. Dan Martin. D-Mo. He'd been called worse, he thought as he signalled for two more beers.

"Top little venue this," said Mikee as he raised his bottle to his friend, "Let's fuckin' smash it tonight. Really fuckin' go for it. I've got a few mates coming down, so I wanna be good. And," glancing down at the three empties in front of them, "that means saving getting smashed till after the gig…"

"Don't look at me," Danny said indignantly, "I'd never let the band down by being off it. Never!" He made a small crossing his heart gesture and looked genuinely wounded.

"I'm only messing, D-Mo. Don't get an arse on." The nickname was thrown in again to test his reaction. Mikee knew his rhythm section amigo was still slightly prickly about it.

"I know, I know. Anyhow I need a cig. Want one?"

" Does the pope shit in the woods?"

"Only when he's been chasing after a choir boy," cackled Danny. Their addition to this malapropism never failed to make him laugh.

As they stood on Oldham Street's wide pavement soaking up the smoke and late Friday afternoon vibes, Jamie and Dom appeared. Both in sunglasses and carrying their guitar cases, looking every inch the rock stars they so craved to be.

Throwing his cigarette stub into the gutter, Dom blew out the last of the smoke. "Alright Mikee. D-Mo. We having this tonight?"

"Fuck off with this D-Mo lark. I've not decided if I like it yet. Alright Jamie," said Danny sulkily.

Laughing loudly and grinning at Dom, he said, "It's not up to you to decide! It's our nickname for you. If you don't like it then we'll just use it more!"

With a mock flounce, Danny turned to go back into the bar, mouthing 'cunts' under his breath to himself. He secretly loved the attention, but as the youngest and smallest in the band, didn't want to be the butt of the others' jokes.

As Mikee turned to follow Danny back inside the venue, Jamie noticed a magazine stuck in the back pocket of his low-slung jeans. Grabbing it, he looked at the cover and above an extravagantly tattooed couple read the title *Inked*.

Unaware of Jamie's light-fingered pilfering, Mikee span round when Jamie clipped him round the back of the head with the now rolled up magazine." OY!"

He laughed and snatched the magazine back." You weren't supposed to see that!"

"No secret dude, Danny," correcting himself with a smirk, "Sorry, D-Mo told us at the studio that you were after getting full sleeves done."

"Did he. I told him that in secret." Unable to resist the opportunity for a spot of tit for tat he said, "Did he tell you that he's gonna have a nose job when we make it?"

"Haha! He did," Jamie laughed loudly. "You'd be no good under pressure!"

Assuming positions at the bar, whilst the two other bands soundchecked, the band respectfully kept their conversation to hushed whispers. The consensus being that neither of the other bands – the headliner, The Bitter Pills, or the dreadfully named second on the bill, Jimi Jimi – were up to much. Indeed, the guitarist of the latter was under the misguided notion that he was a Caucasian reincarnation of said Jimi. Complete with a mirth-inducing silk headband and a floor-length brocade overcoat, he wrung tuneless solos out of his Fender Stratocaster which at best could be described as self-indulgent.

This had stretched the sound engineer's patience to snapping point and as the bar had to open to at 6.30, left the bottom on the bill band only 20 minutes to set-up and soundcheck.

Glaring over in the direction of the preening Hendrix wannabe, the band set about getting prepared as quickly as possible.

A cursory run through '*Mantra*' left the band far from happy. The drums were not right and a constant feedback in the vocal monitors meant that neither Jamie or Dom could hear each other's vocals.

Knowing that there was very little that could be salvaged, the band packed their equipment away until show time and retired to a nearby pub.

As they walked out, Dom couldn't resist an unsubtle mouthed 'fuckin' prick' in the direction of White Jimi - who was oblivious to the not so thinly veiled insult as he was now miming a ridiculously overblown solo to what appeared to be his doting girlfriend – she was equally absurdly dressed, with silk scarfs hanging from her wrists and a large floppy straw hat with flowers stuck into the headband, worn over a bright pink headscarf.

Hitting the pavement outside, Dom sneered, "Did you see the fuckin' state of those two? What a pair of cunts."

Putting a brotherly arm round his shoulder, Jamie said, "Don't let him bother you man. Just makes it easier for us to blow them away later…"

"I know but what a wanker. Who does he fuckin' think he is?"

Having only heard part of the conversation, Danny chirped in, "He thinks he's Jimi Hendrix, doesn't he? Thought that was obvious."

They turned and laughed affectionately towards him. "I think we got that one D-Mo…"

Heading up Oldham Street to the always inviting The Castle, the band found a table towards the back of the bar, ordered drinks and waited for the arrival of Cal, Johnny and various friends they had invited to the gig.

With their short set due to start at 9.30pm, the band had almost three hours to kill and only a limited budget, so halves were nursed and Mikee surreptitiously passed a quarter bottle of vodka back and forth under the table.

Cally and Johnny arrived in separate taxis. Both checking themselves in the reflection of the cab window as they alighted.

Given the pleasant summer weather and adding a nice symmetry to the occasion, he had decided to wear his beloved boating blazer. Matched with faded jeans, a pale blue crew neck T-shirt and brown leather desert boots. He hadn't scrubbed up bad, he'd thought as he again glanced at his reflection.

He'd barely recognised Cally as she made for the table that the band and their entourage were occupying. Dressed in the outfit she'd modelled earlier that day, Johnny took in a quick intake of breath. She looked amazing. Slim, tight fitting jeans and the heeled boots accentuated her legs and well-toned backside. The Cult T-shirt, stretched across her chest, made the pertness of her breasts even more eye-catching. With a touch of mascara and subtly applied lip gloss, together with her freshly washed brunette hair, Cally cut the picture of gorgeousness.

As Cally, clearly nervous, made her introductions, kissing both her boys fondly on their foreheads - much to their embarrassment - Danny sat wide-eyed, and it wouldn't have taken a mind-reader to establish that the expression 'MILF' was writ large between his ears.

Snapping from his thoughts, he said, "Hiya Mrs Thorne, how are you?" He pulled a wooden chair back. "Take a seat. Oh, here's Johnny."

As ever, Mikee roared the now familiar greeting, "HERE'S JOOOHHNNNNYYYY!"

Rolling his eyes and feigning embarrassment, Johnny laughed. "I'm always going to disappoint after an introduction like that. Thanks dude." Offering Mikee a down with the kid's side-shake, finished with the flourish of a fist-bump, Johnny offered to buy a round of drinks.

"Hello again Mr Harrison. A bottle of Becks. With a glass and ice please." Looking him up and down discreetly, she said, "I like your jacket. You do look the part as Mr band manager."

Johnny performed a slight bow. "Why thank you. Lads. What can I get you?" Signals for three pints of lager were acknowledged, with Johnny questioning Danny when he asked for a sparkling water.

"Couple of mates coming down. Want to be proper tight. I'm a professional, me." Looking round the table, he saw his fellow bandmates sniggering at his proclamation. "I AM!" he protested, before punching Mikee on the arm.

Returning with the drinks and sitting down next to Cal, Johnny drank down the top couple of inches from his pint and let out a satisfied sigh.

"Somebody needed that then?" Cal said softly over the top of her glass.

Hunching his shoulders slightly and blowing out, he said, "Tough week. Needed this. And tonight." He took a further sizeable gulp. "It's nice to see you down here. You'll love seeing them play live."

Leaning towards Johnny to be heard over the jukebox, and speaking in her soft melodic tone, she said, "I'll can't wait. Those tracks they recorded are brilliant."

As the band laughed and joked amongst themselves, Jamie looked across at his mum. She really didn't get out of the house as much as he would like and everything she had ever done had been for them. He smiled as he saw her chatting to Johnny, watching her trace a finger round the rim of her glass absent-mindedly.

"You've been brilliant with the boys." She glanced up towards Jamie, who was now talking over his shoulder to a couple of friends who had just arrived.

"Jamie says that every time your name's mentioned. Dom can be a little more guarded, but I can see him coming out of himself a lot more recently."

"They're both really good lads. And ridiculously talented. Dom mentioned that you do music tuition. Must be where they get their talent from."

With a slight look of remorse in her eye, she looked at Johnny, "Well there's nobody else is there…" Composing herself quickly, she said, "Right, my round. What would you like? Same again? Boys. Same for you?" Pointing at the empty glasses on the table, she picked up a small red leather clutch bag and headed for the bar.

Glancing at his watch under the sleeve of his black denim jacket, Danny, maintaining his self-endorsed professionalism, said, "Okay, let's neck these and we'll head off."

"Aye aye boss," laughed Mikee.

Stood at the bar, helping Cally with the drinks, Jamie said, "You seem to be getting on well with Johnny."

"Oh, he's just easy to chat to, isn't he," she affected an 'old codgers' voice, "and us oldies have to stick together don't we!"

Whilst they polished off the round of drinks, a setlist was hastily scrawled on a piece of paper that Jamie had procured from behind the bar.

It was only 30 minutes until they were on and just as they rolled up at the venue, Johnny's phone pinged. It was Dean –

'Sorry Johnny, can't make tonight. Minor family crisis. Next time pal'

"Balls," he muttered under his breath. After the unsatisfactory soundcheck, the lads had been holding out for Dean to save the day.

As they entered the venue, Cally took an immense amount of pleasure from having been on the guestlist. Looking admiringly at the small black stamp she had received on the back of her hand, they headed to the long wooden bar to be met by both Mark and Chris, who were both sampling a cloudy looking imported beer.

"MR H!" Putting his glass down and hugging Johnny.

Making the necessary introductions, Johnny said, "This is Cal. She's the twins' mum." He pointed in the direction of the downstairs dressing room that the band had now retired to.

Extended his hand, Mark smiled at Cally. "Lovely to meet you." And fulfilling every clichéd introduction, "And ignore anything he says about us, we could tell some tales about him!"

With mild irritation, Johnny said, "Yes, quite mate. Thanks!"

Ordering a round of drinks and leaving Cally to listen to his friend's small talk, Johnny made his way to the rear of the venue, and headed towards the dressing room.

As he got to the bottom of the stairs, he saw that the fire escape door was open, and the band were partaking in a pre-gig cigarette.

Seeing Johnny, Dom exhaled into the night air, dropping the butt into a sand-filled bucket. "Surprised that cunts not got white bedsheets on the dressing wall and vases full of flowers. The twat. Is Dean here yet?"

Johnny winced. "Can't make it I'm afraid dude, some family shit has cropped up. He sent his apologies and said next time."

"Fuck," hissed Dom. "We could have done with him after that shite before." He shook his head in frustration.

"Don't worry about Dean not being here. I'm sure the guy front of house will sort it. Have a good 'un lads, I'll see ya after!"

With a quick exchange of handshakes, they then headed up the narrow stairwell and took to the stage, plugging in as the houselights dimmed.

As the sound/light engineer picked Jamie out with a red spotlight, he adjusted his scarf, shaking out the flex of his guitar, stepping forward to the mic stand, addressing the 70 or so strong crowd. "Evening Manchester. We're Lonely Souls. We're gonna be your favourite band before you know it…"

Nodding a 1-2-3 intro, they rattled into '*Mantra*'.

***

Drawing heavily on a smoke, Dom was blazing. "THAT WAS FUCKIN' SHITE! ROOM FULL OF PEOPLE AND WE SOUND LIKE THAT!"

"It's annoying but shit happens. It could happen at bigger and better gigs than this," said Jamie, as he pulled at a loose thread on the cuff of his denim jacket.

Johnny looked round at the bands' disappointed faces, clapping his hands together. "Put it down to experience. Fuck, remember how good the last gig was. There'll be far more to remember for the right reasons," said Johnny with a placating nod.

Rolling a cigarette as he descended the stairs, the sound engineer walked straight into the band's post-mortem. Instantly bristling at the sight of him, Dom stepped forward only to be dragged back by Mikee.

Lighting his cigarette, and raising both hand up palms flat, he said, "Lads, I'm really sorry about that. Fuckin' nightmare for you. Happens now and then. It's not the newest of sound systems and we just didn't have the time. But I am sorry."

Shaking the proffered hand, Jamie said as calmly as he could, "Thanks man. One of those things. But you owe us."

Nodding enthusiastically, he said, "Fuck, yeah! I'll have a word with the promoter and make sure we get you another gig and we'll get it right next time." He drew on the ratty looking rollie. "Shame as you've got some good fuckin' songs."

Still brooding but happy to take the well-intended olive branch, Dom ground his cigarette angrily into the concrete floor, and accepted the handshake. "We'll hold you to that. It's a crackin' venue this. Fuck, I'm gutted!"

"We'll be back. Thanks," interrupted Jamie.

Not wishing to outstay his welcome, the sound engineer went to leave. "Sorry again lads, I'll sort another gig. Got to get back and do sound for Jimi Jimi or whatever the fuck they call themselves." He checked over his shoulder that said band were not within earshot. "That lead singer is a right knob…"

"He can say that again," grunted Dom. Never one in a hurry to drop a grudge.

"Let's have a drink and try and forget about this then. As Johnny said, happens to everyone at some point."

Trooping up the stairs just in time to hear the start of the second band's set, they headed to where Cal was stood, still looking solemn, her hands clasped together in front of her. Seeing the boys, she threw her arms round Jamie, looking up at him. "Oh Jamie, I am sorry. You must be gutted. But it was still great. Honestly! And you all looked brilliant up there," rubbing a hand over the top of his head, "And I'll let you have my scarf. I wondered where that had gone!"

Not wanting to spoil his mum's evening, Jamie said, " We'll have loads more gigs to come…"

Adjusting a long floral scarf, the singer said, "Thank you. We're Jimi Jimi. There's a spirit within every one of us. I know whose spirit is inside me…"

He then launched into a cod-psychedelic rock number with no discernible chorus but plenty of badly played guitar.

Unable to hide his contempt, Dom snorted into his pint, "What a fuckin' grade A cunt!"

The Rock 'N' The Roll. 'N That

"Dominic! Language," snapped Cally, momentarily forgetting where she was.

Rolling his eyes to the ceiling, he said, "Sorry but he is. I wouldn't mind but they're shite!"

Unable to contain her laughter, she agreed. "They are, Dominic, but you know I hate that word."

Just as Cal finished admonishing her son, the lead singer/guitarist then pathetically tried to segue into '*Crosstown Traffic*'. The solo was clearly beyond him, although it was met by cheers from a sizeable pocket of the crowd.

"Fuck me! I can't believe how many friends the cunt has got," said Dom, unable to contain his derision.

"DOM!" Cal scolded again, although this time with a wicked smile on her lips.

More drinks were consumed, with Johnny and Mark buying three rounds of margaritas. The mood had lifted considerably by now, and the evening's technical problems seemed to be behind them.

As The Bitter Pills – a Mod-ish looking combo – started their set, Mikee and Dom, now both in alcohol-fuelled high spirits, started whispering conspiratorially. Chinking shot glasses and knocking them back with a high-five, they headed off to back of the club, laughing to themselves as they passed the peacocking Jimi Jimi frontman, who was stood dismissively with his back to the stage.

As they reached the dressing room, Mikee and Dom could no longer contain their giggles. Peering into the dressing room, Dom looked back. "It's clear. You ready? I'll keep cover."

Stepping into the room, Dom identified the target of their ire. A guitar case painted at no small expense with psychedelic air-brushing picking out the band name – Jimi Jimi.

Popping the case open, Dom saw the Fender Stratocaster lay in its purple velvet housing. Part of him regretted what they were about to do – given his love of guitars – but this was an exceptional circumstance…

He whispered to Mikee in between snorted giggles, "Right, it's there. I'll keep cover. You do the deed." Laughing again, he put his hand over his mouth to smother the noise.

Mikee stepped into the dressing room, dropped his jeans and boxer shorts and squatted centrally over the open case. And the prone guitar.

Clenching hard, he slowly let out a long brown cable of shit right across the strings and the scratch plate of the black Fender.

Hearing Dom's whispered call of, "Hurry up!" he glanced down between his legs, looking admiringly at the parallel poo he had just deposited, hurriedly did up his jeans and placed the now closed guitar case back to where exactly it had been.

Fist-bumping before heading straight back upstairs to the bar, Dom passed the soon to be horrified singer/guitarist/cunt and patted him on the back, "Good gig, man. Good gig."

Acknowledging him with a dismissive wave, he carried on regaling his girlfriend with yet another blow by blow account of their set.

Still stifling their giggles, Dom announced that he and Mikee were going to head down the road for a change of scenery. With their own gear being safely transported home by a friend of Mikee's, the night was young.

Both Danny and Jamie agreed they would join them once the headline band had finished their set.

"You'll be okay getting a taxi, won't you?"

Putting her hand on Jamie's cheek, she said, "Of course I will. I have been into Manchester before!"

"We'll make sure she gets a cab J, don't worry," said Johnny. "I think we're going to head to Rusholme for a curry, so we'll get the one after her."

"Ah thanks Johnny, "Cally smiled, "See Jamie, good management, thinks of everything."

"Thanks Johnny, and sorry about tonight. It was all a bit shit."

"Not at all, nothing you could do. All experience isn't it." Checking his watch, "Anyhow, I'll catch you next week, so we can decide what we're going to do with these tracks."

Hugging warmly and patting each other on the back, Jamie said, "Thanks man, I'll catch ya later. And thanks for seeing that Mum's right."

Leaving the venue, the four of them headed for the nearby taxi-rank. Ensuring that Cally was safely ensconced in a black cab, Johnny smiled as she opened the window, smiling that beautiful smile of hers. "Thanks Mr Harrison, I had a good night." Hiccupping slightly as the cab pulled away, Cal turned and smiled to herself.

"She is bloody lovely mate. The arse and legs on her!" said Mark, shaking his head in admiration.

Nodding and thinking to himself, *isn't she just…*

The Rock'N'The Roll. 'N That

Chapter 20

"Johnny! The letter from the hospital has arrived. You up?" Claire shouted up the stairs.

Padding out of bed and heading to the bathroom for a pair of Nurofen and a large glass of water, he rubbed sleep from his eyes and yawned. "Give me a minute, I'll be down." Relieving himself loudly, he washed his hands and face, before heading downstairs.

Claire was sat at the dining table, still in her oversize bed shorts and skimpy vest, her glasses perched on the end of her nose. She was holding the unopened letter at arm's length, staring at it as if she could read the contents merely by concentrating hard on it.

Standing over her, he scratched the back of his head, and then pushed his hair back behind his ears as he struggled in his hungover state to find the right words. "Well, open it. It's not a Wonka Bar with a golden ticket inside. It's just an appointment date. Fancy a bacon buttie? I'm starving."

"I know, I know but…"

"But open it. It's only going to say when we go next. Rip the top. Pull. Read. Put it on the calendar. Easy!"

"Don't be so sharp, just 'cos you're tired and hungover. And you stunk of beer and curry last night. You kept breathing on me in bed," Claire harrumphed.

"That's cos I had beer and a curry. Well done CSI Manchester…"

Looking over the top of her glasses, she delivered what she perceived to be one of her stares at him. After all this time, he was impervious to them.

Heading to the kitchen, whereby he picked up a marker pen. Pulling the top off, he stood by the Parisian Scenes calendar. With the pen poised, he said, "Right, when we are going?"

"I've not opened it yet!"

"Just open it!"

"Okay, okay!" Peeling back the top of the white envelope slowly, she skimmed the two-paragraph letter. "This coming Friday. At 3.30. Can you get time off work?"

The Rock 'N' The Roll. 'N That

"Off course I can. It's on the calendar."

Setting to with the frying pan, he lost himself in thought, staring out of the kitchen window blankly.

***

Waking with a start, Jamie heard his brother cackling with laughter through the party wall that separated their two rooms. Technically speaking it was one room. Their mum had moved into the smaller second bedroom when the boys got to about ten years old. A local carpenter had erected a floor to ceiling wall in the larger front bedroom. It was a far from ideal solution, but it had proved to be an effective sticking plaster.

With the wall being so thin, communication was possible. "Fuck's sake Dom, what's so funny? It's only, "glancing at his phone, "fuck. It's only just gone half eight!"

Laughing loudly again, Dom said, "It's just a text from Mikee." Now roaring with laughter. "He said he didn't need a shit this morning!"

Unable to understand why such a missive should have amused his brother quite so much, he lifted his pillow and shoved his head under it, pulling it tightly round his ears.

Before he could return to sleep, he heard a small knock at the shared bedroom door. "Morning boys." Popping her round the door. A hint of last night's makeup smudged on her on her eyelids. "You two okay? I enjoyed it last night. It was really good of you to invite me." Yawning softly. "Either of you want a cup of tea?"

Mumbling from under the pillow, Jamie said, "Too early for me ta."

Full of the joys, Dom said loudly, "Love one. And some breakfast would be good. Thanks Mum. Glad you enjoyed it. Shame the gig was a bit shit." At this, he threw himself back on his bed in fits of laughter.

"Weirdo," Jamie grunted and willed himself back to sleep.

***

As Tuesday rolled into Wednesday into Thursday into appointment day, Johnny left Claire in bed as he set off for work. "It'll be okay. Whatever happens, it'll all be okay. I'll still love you and you might still think I'm alright."

Looking up and laughing half-heartedly, Claire already looked lost. Shrouded by a defeatist air.

"I'll see you down there., I'll get a cab from the tram stop. And I won't be late. Promise!" He blew her a kiss as he left the house, the morning drizzle not adding to his humour.

***

Meeting there at 3.25 promptly, Johnny held Claire's hand as they headed for the fertility clinic. Squeezing it for reassurance, he said, "It'll be okay," as convincingly as he could muster.

Smiling up at him meekly, she said, "Thanks Johnny. But you could have left your tie on, looks so much smarter with that suit. Cost a fortune didn't it."

"I know," he deadpanned, "my lack of neckwear will have a huge bearing on the quality control checks they've been doing on my sperms!"

"I didn't mean it like that!"

Sitting in the waiting room for no more than two minutes, they were summoned in to their appointment on the dot of 3.30pm.

Dr Atiq sat behind his desk, immaculately dressed in a charcoal grey pinstripe suit and a pink oxford cotton shirt, unbuttoned at the neck and without a tie.

"Hello again, Claire, Johnny. Nice to see you both again. How have you been?"

Both nodded silently.

Dr Atiq proceeded. "I have had a look at all the test results and you are clearly both fit and healthy people for your age."

"It's always 'for our age' these days, isn't it doctor?"

Laughing gently, he said, "Yes, it is Johnny. But neither of you have anything to worry about overall." He paused. "I have looked at the test results carefully and I can say that there is nothing wrong with your sperm count. All seems perfectly fine, slightly above average. No issue there."

There it was. An elephant had just gate-crashed the room.

NO ISSUE THERE.

There was a bombshell coming. Fuck. Fuck. Fuck, thought Johnny as he snuck a look at Claire.

Turning to Claire and looking at her, with such compassionate large brown eyes, Dr Atiq said, "Claire. There is a slight problem with your fallopian tubes. They are not letting the sperm pass as easily as they should. It isn't a major problem. But it is not going to help you conceive."

Remarkably stoically, Claire smiled as Johnny gently squeezed her thigh. "What can we do?"

"Well Claire. There is no surgical procedure to correct the problem. You could just carry on as you are and hope that you are lucky. Or you could look at a procedure to facilitate a pregnancy."

Sighing gently to himself, Johnny replayed the last phrase in his head – 'facilitate a pregnancy'. *Who said romance was dead?* he thought.

"Do you mean IVF then, doctor? I have already been looking at this online. I'd be very keen to explore this route."

"I think that is something you need to discuss. It's a very big step and a huge commitment. Both emotionally and financially. I think that you need to speak to somebody and ask them all the questions that you will no doubt both have."

Looking at them both in turn, he said, "I hope that you become a family and I'm sorry that this wasn't the news you'd hoped for. But with the procedures available, there is no reason why you cannot become parents."

Standing and shaking the doctor's outstretched hand, Johnny said, "Thank you for your time." Turning for the door, Johnny realised that Claire was still fixed to her chair.

"Are the tests definitely right then, doctor? There is no possibility that the results were wrong?"

"I'm sorry Claire but they are 100% correct. I wish there was more I could say…"

"You're sure," she said, barely audibly.

"Quite sure I'm afraid. But don't be despondent. This is the start for you. You must look at other options if you're serious about this."

Feeling Johnny's hand on her shoulder, Claire finally stood up. "Thank you, doctor. You've been very helpful," she said flatly but politely.

Leaving the hospital building and heading to the car park, Johnny said, "Come on, let's get you home. I'll drive. You got the keys?"

Reaching in her handbag and passing him the keys, Claire was catatonically silent.

With the kettle on and words not yet exchanged, Claire was slumped on the sofa, her head leant against the plump black brocade cushion.

Placing a cup tea beside her, Johnny placed the palm of his hand gently against her cheek, caressing her ear and whispered, "It'll be okay," before kissing her tenderly on the forehead.

As he returned to the kitchen to busy himself with anything that would be a distraction, he heard Claire say quietly, "It's not your fault though, is it."

Squatting down on his haunches, and ignoring the creak of his knees, he looked at her face that was wracked with distress. "Hey, hey, it's not about that. I said that right from the start. This is nature. Nobody is to blame. Don't be silly." Sighing loudly, he shook her leg gently. "Come on. Don't think like this. It could have quite easily been me with something or other that wasn't quite right."

When he didn't receive a response, he carefully took Claire's shoes off, so that she could tuck her feet under herself, and placed a nearby throw over her.

Looking up at him with tear-filled eyes, she said, "It is my fault though. The doctor said so."

Johnny returned to the squatted position. "He didn't say that. He said there was a slight issue."

Deciding that a noble retreat would be by far and away the best option, he lay on the bed staring at the ceiling rose, unable to fathom the maelstrom of his emotions. Relief that it was not down to him. Guilt that it wasn't. Pity for Claire and her burden. Confusion at what they should do next. Uncertainty at? Uncertainty at everything...

Having dozed for a good hour or so, he read a few chapters of a Dylan biography that he had been slowly ploughing through before he thought that an approach to Claire would be wise.

"Hey lady. You hungry? I'll cook."

As he walked past her to the kitchen, he glanced down at her laptop. Inevitably, there was a window displaying the procedure for the cycles of IVF treatment. A vibrant looking female face at the top of the screen exuded positivity with various contact details next to her, imploring desperate to-be-parents to contact them and have their dreams expensively concocted.

Without looking up from the screen, she said, "There's some chicken in the fridge. I got it out this morning. You could do something with that. Nothing spicy. But you know best babe."

Every drawer that he opened, or pan placed on the hob seemed to make an amplified noise, jarring against the cloying silence.

He placed the large bowls down of chicken pasta on the dining table and sat across from Claire. Grinding pepper onto the steaming food, he said, "You okay?"

"Not really," she smiled meekly, "but I just have to deal with it and decide what we do next."

Before Johnny could reply, she added, "I don't think we have any choice other than to look at IVF."

We're having a 'grown-ups' conversation, Johnny thought. Fortune favours the brave and all that.

"We do have choices though." Putting a large forkful of chicken and pasta into his mouth, he chewed slowly whilst he considered his next words.

Claire waited expectantly.

"But we do. We can carry on as we are and see what happens. We can consider treatment, or we can leave it to Mother Nature."

Staring back at him without a word, it appeared that Claire had been expecting a miraculous solution from him.

"Look, the whole IVF thing," he said, pausing slightly before taking the plunge, "It doesn't come with any guarantees. Mark and Jen looked at it. Said it was really hard work. And expensive. But then they got lucky and she got pregnant just before they decided to go ahead."

Seizing on the word, Claire snapped back, finally closing the laptop down, "LUCK! That's exactly it. It's down to luck unless you do something about it!"

More irritably than he had intended, he said, "But it's always been about LUCK!" Exhaling loudly, he took a long sip from his glass of water. "What do you think people did before the scientists in their white coats realised that they could play God?"

With what he considered to be the momentum on his side, he carried on, banging his fork on the edge of his bowl for extra emphasis. "We wouldn't all be here if it wasn't for luck and the miracle of the reproductive cycle. Difference now is you can alter your levels of luck by fucking about with nature!"

"It's not like that though is it!"

"It is! Don't get me wrong, I'm not opposed to it but it's a big step and we need to take our time to decide it's what WE want…"

"I know."

Sighing with what he hoped had been progress, Johnny ran a hand across his face.

"But I've booked an appointment for us this week. At an IVF clinic…"

Snatching up his empty bowl, he said, "Fuck's sake Claire! What did I just say?" He slammed his dish down on the kitchen work surface. "I said that we need to talk about this and you're ploughing full steam ahead and booking appointments!"

"Don't shout at me. Not now," she said pitifully.

Grimacing slightly, he said, "Sorry. I'm not shouting. I'm just exasperated that you're booking appointments before we have even had chance to chat." Shaking his head slowly, he added, "I was going to suggest we chatted to Mark and Jen, find out a bit more from them."

With an unshakeable resolve, she replied, "But we'll still go on this appointment this week though…"

Chapter 21

Band meeting. Everyone in attendance. Everyone eager for the next big steps.

Okay." He raised his glass to them all individually. "What have I got for you." Glancing down at an A4 pad on the pub table, he said, "I'm putting together a press pack so that I can send the tracks out to selected people. Radio. Press. Record companies and that. "

"How soon till we have a deal then?" asked Danny impatiently.

"Like your enthusiasm, Danny." Johnny had yet to adopt the bass player's newly acquired moniker. "To go along with the press pack, we're going to need some decent pics. I have arranged for a photographer to come down to the studio next Sunday. Take a few shots whilst you're rehearsing and then have a wander round town and he can try and do something interesting with you."

Turning to Danny," We'll look to get a gig a month and start to build momentum. I have got a mate that works over at XFM. Going to play the tracks to him and look for some airplay. All depends on what interest we get from tracks. I know, and you know how good they are, but we need other people to see that."

"Which they will," Jamie stated confidently.

Nodding towards him, he said, "As Jamie says, which they will. Lads, I'm still playing the tracks in my car all the fuckin' time and I still can't believe how good they are."

"Nice one," said Dominic. "Will be good to get some photos done."

"I'll get another round and then I'm off," said Johnny." You lot make sure you get a good night's sleep before the photo session. Want you looking your fresh-faced best!

***

Pulling up at home, he again wrestled with when it was going to be the right time to tell Claire about the band and his involvement. With so much going on with the 'baby stuff' he felt that the timing was not quite right.

Opening the front door and shouting a quick hello, he put his keys and phone down on the hall table. Claire was sat at the dining table on a chair that faced the front door. As ever there was a laptop in front of her. With a sharp intake of breath, he realised that it was his laptop.

This isn't good, he thought. *This isn't good at all.*

"You alright lady? What've you been up to?"

Wrong question. Totally the wrong fucking question.

With a tone to match the serious expression on her face. "I really should be asking you that."

Clicking the spacebar on the laptop, the browser page reappeared. The page showing Johnny's Barclays deposit account. The account where his inheritance monies had sat largely untouched for the past decade or so. The account that he had been using to bankroll the band.

Looking down at the screen with the studied focus of a forensic accountant, Claire started to list off the withdrawals, complete with dates, amounts and payees.

"WHAT THE FUCK IS GOING ON, JOHNNY? WHO THE FUCK IS SHE AND WHAT THE FUCK HAVE YOU BEEN BUYING HER?"

Taking a seat in the chair opposite her, Johnny looked at her in total silence.

"WELL? FUCKING SAY SOMETHING!"

Looking down again at the screen, she said, "That's assuming it is a woman, because some of these payments don't make any sense."

Picking his words as carefully as he could, speaking slowly and calmly, he said, "It's an investment."

With a furrowed brow like an irrigated field, she said, "An investment? An investment in what? The fucking Premier Inn? Because you paid them," glancing down, "£310.00 on the 21st June. Wasn't that when you said you were down in London seeing Rob?" – complete with obligatory air quotes.

At least spare me the fucking air quotes, Johnny thought.

Attack is the best form of defence. Onwards.

"Anyhow. Why were you looking at my bank account? On my laptop?"

"I left mine at work and needed to check my emails. You wouldn't have minded if you had nothing to hide," she replied curtly.

"I've nothing to hide." Swallowing with an audible gulp. "Nothing that can hurt us."

Taking off her glasses and looking across at him with wide owl-like eyes. "NOTHING TO HIDE. NOTHING TO FUCKING HIDE! It doesn't look like it." Placing her glasses back in place. "I've always trusted you Johnny, always."

"I've never given you a reason not to," he interrupted, "thank you for that."

Shaking her head in partial disbelief, she said, "I even knew your passwords because you're so bloody predictable and honest. *'GLASSONION99'*. On every account. You never think to change them?"

"I do when they ask. The ones that don't, I just leave them be."

Smiling and shaking her head simultaneously, she said, "So what the fuck has been going on? I checked the account to see how much was there," hesitating slightly, "to see how much was there if we decided to go ahead with the IVF…"

He grasped for any sort of moral high ground. "Oh right, so you were already spending my money on IVF. Why ever not."

"DON'T FUCKING GET CLEVER WITH ME JOHNNY!" She said, standing out of her chair with both hands flat on the table either side of the laptop. "YOU'VE NOT EVEN STARTED TO TELL ME WHAT THE FUCKING HELL YOU HAVE BEEN UP TO!"

Exhaling deeply, he put his hands behind his head, staring up at the ceiling.

"I've been making an investment. In a band."

"What the fuck do you mean? Investing in a band?" With a look of abject confusion on her face, Claire scratched her head frantically with both hands. Her blonde hair fell forward over her pained face.

"Oh, for fuck's sake. I've been wanting to tell you, but the time never felt right."

"Go on. I'm all ears as to where you have spent the best part of nine thousand pounds. NINE FUCKING THOUSAND POUNDS, JOHNNY!"

"YES, I GET IT! I have invested nine grand of my money!"

She cut him off abruptly. "IF YOU SAY FUCKING INVESTMENT ONE MORE FUCKING TIME!"

"I saw a band at the start of the year and I thought they were brilliant. Which they are," he rubbed his hand across his forehead, "and I met up with them. Decided I wanted to work with them. Invest in them if you will. And it's gone from there."

"IF YOU WILL! IT'S ME YOU'RE TALKING TO! WE'RE NOT IN FUCKING COURT!"

Happy with the absolving confession, Johnny breathed out softly. "You'd like them. They are really, good. Nice lads as well."

This casual candidness sent Claire ape-shit ballistic. Standing out of her chair, she calmly took her glasses off. Composing herself. The hum of the 'exhibit A' laptop was the only noise in the room.

She began to pace round the room. Her bare feet padding loudly against the wooden floorboards.

"I'D FUCKING LIKE THEM WOULD I? OH, THAT'S ALRIGHT THEN!" Her levels of anger rose. "AND WHAT THE FUCK HAS YOUR MONEY BEEN INVESTED ON?" Again, performing the mandatory air quotes.

"WILL YOU QUIT IT WITH THE STUPID FUCKING FINGER THING," Johnny gritted his teeth, "Gets right on my tits."

"OH, IT DOES, DOES IT!" She was now screaming at him. "I'LL TELL YOU WHAT GETS ON MY TITS," doing the air quotes thing but now with added sarcasm, "WHAT GETS ON MY TITS IS MY PARTNER SPUNKING THOUSANDS OF POUNDS ON A FUCKING NO HOPE BAND WITHOUT TELLING ME!"

Walking towards the kitchen to fetch a drink, Johnny was determined to remain as calm as possible. Drinking straight from the bottle of Becks he had just pulled from the fridge, he said, "If I had told you right from the outset, then you wouldn't have wanted me working with them. Never mind investing money in them. This could be big. This could be massive! It'd benefit the both of us if the band takes off."

Staring at Johnny as if he had been talking Mandarin, the look of disbelief on Claire's face was like nothing Johnny had ever witnessed before. "What the fuck did you just say? Benefit the both of us?" Tossing her head back, and cackling manically. "ARE YOU FUCKING MENTAL?"

Breathing heavily, unable to suppress her rage, she continued, "SO EXACTLY WHAT HAS ALL THE MONEY BEEN SPENT ON THEN?"

Johnny drank deeply from the chilled bottle. "The money has been spent on rehearsals. Recording some tracks. New equipment. And the away day gig – when I said I was at Rob's. I'm sorry about lying to you."

Gathering momentum with her rant now, Claire bowled on, "YOU'VE WASTED SOME FUCKING MONEY IN YOUR TIME," snorting through her nose as she now stood hands on hips, looking up at Johnny from only a foot away. "YOU'VE WASTED MONEY ON FANCY CLOTHES. DRINKING WITH YOUR MATES. I KNOW YOU HAVE PUT MORE THAN ENOUGH COKE AWAY OVER THE YEARS."

She jabbed a finger sharply into his chest.

"I DIDN'T MIND ANY OF THAT. I KNEW WHERE IT WAS GOING. WHAT YOU DID OR DIDN'T HAVE TO SHOW FOR IT.

IT WAS YOUR MONEY!" Again, the finger poke. "BUT THIS! YOU'VE SPENT YOUR MONEY ON SOME MAGIC FUCKING BEANS IN YOUR TIME…"

She was composing herself for a final assault.

"BUT THIS BEGGARS ALL FUCKING BELIEF! AND AT NO POINT DID YOU THINK THAT YOU SHOULD TELL ME OF THIS INVESTMENT. YOU'VE SPENT NINE GRAND ON A STUPID FUCKING BAND. MONEY THAT WE WERE GOING TO SPEND TO HAVE A BABY! A FUCKING BABY JOHNNY. NOT SOME STUPID PIPE DREAM OR SOMETHING TO HELP YOU CLING ON TO YOUR YOUTH."

Stepping into the kitchen and looking to put a little distance between him and the incandescent Claire, Johnny leant against the breakfast bar, his arms folded across his chest. "Have you finished? It was my money. I was spending, sorry investing, on this band way before any of this IVF bollocks was being talked about." He corrected himself sharply, "I say talked about, I meant you deciding that we were going to spend this money on IV-FUCKING-F!" Smacking the palm of his hand on his forehead, he said, "Anyhow. You've checked my account. There's enough money. MORE THAN ENOUGH MONEY there IF we decided to go ahead and try this bloody treatment."

With an aghast look of horror, she said, "But there might not be enough! That's the point. It costs a few thousand per cycle and with the money you've spent, if we weren't successful the first time or…"

Reeling to face her, he said, "YOU'VE GOT THIS ALL PLANNED OUT HAVENT YOU. ALL DECIDED FOR US. WE HAVEN'T EVEN TALKED ABOUT THIS!" Bringing his voice down a few levels, and with an air of exasperation, he said, "Fuck's sake Claire. We haven't even started to talk this through!"

With tears starting to form in her eyes, Claire looked at him with a lost, vacant look and then she spoke. Very slowly and calmly. "You utterly, totally selfish self-centred cunt."

The C-Bomb. She had never called him that in all their time together.

She assumed an air of resignation. Staring through Johnny as if focussing on a faraway horizon.

"Not a lot more to say then is there?" he asked.

He had never seen her look so vulnerable, but whatever words he could conjure up, however he attempted to placate her, would have fallen miles short. "Look, I'm going a walk. Let things calm down here. We'll talk again when I get back."

Heading towards the front door, collecting his keys and phone and a pair of headphones from his work overcoat pocket, Johnny turned to face Claire who had followed him to the door.

"Just go. I need to be left on my own."

Closing the front door behind him, Johnny walked down the road, his head a maelstrom of chaos. His two worlds had just collided in the untimeliest fashion...

Chapter 22

Waking at the sound of a door being banged loudly, Johnny looked round the room. He had been staying at the hotel for almost a week now and every morning he had been waking with a start, taking in the unfamiliar surroundings, before reality reminded him he was now a resident of the Premier Inn, Salford Quays.

Having smuggled a microwave into the room, stashing it during the day in his wardrobe, Johnny was now living a Partridge-like existence, eating a combination of microwave ready meals and bags of salads. Not quite on first name terms with the reception staff but it was only a matter of time…

Since the huge revelation about the band and his 'investment', Claire had asked that they have some time apart. Having been unable to face living with his mother, and both Mark and Chris not unreasonably saying that there was no room at the inn, a hotel had afforded him both the privacy and solitary that he had required.

He felt their relationship was ultimately doomed but hadn't ruled out a reconciliation - telling Claire that he would talk whenever and wherever. The band were unaware of his current domestic situation, as their 'involvement' in the breakdown of his relationship could wait.

Cabin fever was exerting a suffocating grip and he pined for his previously taken for granted home comforts – and Claire.

***

"Looking good man. Looking good. Very rock star, D-Mo," Dom said, with a little too much sarcasm in his voice for Danny's liking.

Rubbing at the sides of his newly shorn head, Danny said proudly, "Bit short at the sides, but looks good on top," smoothing the buzz cut fade at the sides and pulling tentatively at the small quiff. "I fancy the arse off the girl that cuts my hair and she said it'd look good, so I went for it. She said she'd come down to our next gig as well. Proper fit she is."

The Rock 'N' The Roll. 'N That

Nodding his approval, Dom said, "Good work. No harm with more pretty faces at our gigs. Can't wait for the next one. I'm still annoyed about the Night and Day gig." Glancing behind in Mikee's direction, who was busy setting his kit up, they exchanged a knowing wink.

Plugging in his guitar, Jamie looked round the familiar surroundings of their rehearsal room, nodding at each band member individually. "Looking good."

With the photographer due to arrive within the hour, the band continued working on the new track they had part written at The Bunker. Jamie had now finished the lyrics, which felt like a deeply noir murder ballad –

'Friend of mine, don't let me down, as you're a long time dead. A secret shouldn't be so hard to keep. Whispered promises when you're asleep. Empty vessels make most noise, don't let me down again...'

The haunting lyrics were sung with a threatening sneer, and the intent and menace of the song were beautifully underpinned by Danny's minimal bassline and Mikee's metronomic drumming. The song bringing a definite touch of light and shade to their catalogue.

On the stroke of four o'clock, an bedraggled-looking Johnny arrived, accompanied by a small but lively figure carrying a large grey canvas bag in his right hand and sporting two cameras around his neck from lurid coloured straps.

Putting a hand dramatically in front of his face, "No pictures please," grinned Dom.

Grinning at his bandmates, Danny popped his trusty shades on, instantly pulling his best 'Sid stare' at the room's whitewashed blank wall. Mikee was re-united with his trapper hat, Dom dressing like Danny in black jeans and denim jacket, but with an impressive looking pair of military boots on, worn over the jeans. Jamie had got his black leather coat on and of course his red scarf tied round his throat.

"Afternoon lads. I'm Simon. I'll be taking some pictures this afternoon. Pretend I'm not here and just get on with your playing."

Sitting down on the trusty upturned beer crate-cum-seat, Johnny rubbed a hand across his tired face.

"You okay man?" asked Jamie, clearly concerned at Johnny's tired and unkempt demeanour.

Looking up, bleary eyed, he said, "Yeah, I'll live. Thanks man."

Jamie didn't look convinced.

"Good news. My mate at XFM loved the tracks. Going to get them played on the Evening Session show," Johnny said.

"Wicked," Danny, said with the customary snap of his fingers.

"Nice work Johnny," Jamie said, still frowning at his manager.

Some thirty minutes later the photographer was done with the live shots. "Thanks fellas. Plenty for me to work with there. If we could all go outside, and I'll take a few of you outside. Just stood against the wall and that. Nothing too staged."

With the pictures all taken, Simon told them that he after he had applied a little studio trickery, he would have them across to Johnny by the end of the week.

As the band made their way back inside the building, Jamie caught Johnny by the elbow. "What's up man? Never seen you like this before. Not like you, you've barely spoken a word."

Stopping and sighing deeply, Johnny stood with his hands on his hips and closed his eyes and stared skywards. "Fuckin' hell Jamie." "Curling his arms around his head, his eyes looking bloodshot and drawn, "Problems at home. Or should I say problems not being at home. I've hit a big bump in the road with Claire." Wincing inwardly at his choice of words. "All my fault. I'm living elsewhere for now."

Jamie looked down with a thoughtful expression on his face. "I'm sorry to hear that…"

"I appreciate your concern," he said, laughing quietly, "You don't miss a trick." He checked his pockets and fished out his car keys. "Just keep this between you and me for now. I'll tell the rest of the lads when I know how the land lies," he added as cheerily as he could. "Won't stop me working with you lot though. Busy couple of weeks getting the track sent out and that."

Giving Johnny a peace sign, Jamie said, "Thanks man. Take care of yourself," patting his hand on the roof of Johnny's car.

***

"SHHH!" Dom said, looking sternly at Danny, who could barely contain his excitement. "Fuckin' shut it! EVERYBODY."

As Dominic tried to restore an air of quiet, he put a finger to his lips, looking sternly at his bandmates, who had now fallen into line with a hushed quiet.

The Rock'N'The Roll. 'N That

The voice on the radio said the words they had yearned to hear. As with everyone who has picked up an instrument and formed a band, the first measure of success was playing in front of an appreciative crowd – whatever the size. Hearing your song on the radio was very much the next big step.

"*I'm Tim and you're listening to XFM MANCHESTER. And now we have a track from a new local band that goes by the name of Lonely Souls…*"

By this stage, Danny was now literally biting down on his finger to restrain his unbridled delight.

Having bought a digital radio into the studio especially for the occasion, Johnny was perched on his usual beer crate seat, whilst the band stood around the radio, which was perched on the top of Dom's Peavey amp.

"*A four piece, made up of brothers Jamie and Dominic Thorne, on vocals and guitar. Danny Martin on bass and Mikee Long on drums. This track is called 'Salvation'. I've only listened to this the once, but it sounds like we could be hearing a lot more from these boys in the future. Let me know what you think on the usual text and Twitter and at my email. Here we go, Lonely Souls and 'Salvation'.*"

Coming across the digital airwaves, the track sounded perfect to the band. This was their moment. Undoubtedly there would be people pricking their ears as the tune played. Some of them might even remember the name of the band and the song. Some of them would nod approvingly. Some would let it pass them completely by, the radio just providing background noise for them. The song would mean more to the band than anyone else in the whole world. For now.

Predictably, it was Danny who broke the silence. "FUCKIN' COME ON! AND HE MENTIONED OUR NAMES!" Hugging Dom and Jamie under each arm, Danny's hyperactive levels of excitement were now reaching off the scale levels.

Mikee snapped his fingers, beaming his big open smile. "Nice one Johnny, fuckin' nice one!"

"I'm just as pleased as you are lads, Mike down at the station loved the tracks and said he'd get it played on one of the evening shows. I know it's not daytime, but that's not going to happen with an unsigned band."

Nodding in agreement, Jamie said, "We need to gig more and get our name out there."

Putting his hand inside the large patch pocket of the hooded orange canvas coat that he was wearing, Johnny pulled out a roll of stickers. "Which is exactly where these will come in."

Tossing the roll into Dom's outstretched hand, he said, "We can do a subtle bit of guerrilla marketing. Right up your street, eh Kong?"

Dom smiled at the awful pun. "Deffo Johnny, I'll have 'em all over the place before you know it!"

"Excellent," nodded Johnny. "Look at it as 'band awareness' if you will. Get these plastered all over town and people will start to recognise your name."

Looking down at the beermat sized stickers, Danny grinned his approval.

With the band's logo picked out in red letters against a black background, with the words '*They'll be your Salvation*' underneath, they looked the business.

"Easier than flyposting and you can carry them with you all the time. Pop 'em up, and spread the word," said Johnny. "I've had a couple of thousand printed, so I'll let you each have a roll."

"I think that calls for a pint," offered Jamie, clearly pleased by developments. "They going to play the track again, Johnny?"

"Hopefully, man. Suppose they'll see what sort of feedback they get. I'll email my mate and find out."

"Who's up for a pint then?" asked Mikee

"Sorry boys. I can't make it. Meeting a girl later," beamed Danny. "The bird that cut my hair. Loves it that I'm in a band. Meeting her in The Northern later."

"Ooh yer dark horse. Kept that quiet," Dom teased. "Think we'll have that pint in The Northern then, eh?"

Appalled at his own schoolboy error, Danny said, "Fuck off! You wouldn't?" He looked beseechingly at his friends individually. "Come on! Don't ruin this. I'm quite into her!"

Putting his arm round Danny's shoulder, Dom said, "We wouldn't do that," glancing at Mikee, "would we?"

Breathing an audible sigh of relief, Danny said, "Aw, thanks fellas. Right I'm off. Meeting her in 20 minutes. You okay taking my guitar, Mikee?"

"Cool, D-Mo. You get out there and do the business!"

Already heading for the door, having blasted some cheap smelling deodorant under his T-shirt and down the front of his jeans, he said, "See ya Sunday!"

"I'm going to have to bail on you as well," said Dom somewhat sheepishly. "I've got a hot date as well. I'm not daft enough to tell where you though. See ya laters suckers!"

Shrugging his shoulders, Johnny said searchingly, "Just us three then eh?" Anything to delay his return to the hotel, he thought.

"Good for me. Just the one though I'm up early tomorrow for work," said Mikee.

Jamie nodded his agreement whilst undergoing the ritual of stowing his guitar away.

Usual table. Usual round. Usual curmudgeonly service. The conversation was solely band based, much to Johnny's relief, as he was sure Jamie kept eyeing him in a concerned fashion.

"I'm going to look at getting a website sorted. Nothing too over-elaborate at this stage. Somewhere we can post live dates, news, videos and that," said Johnny.

"Like it," said Mikee as he once again adjusted the angle of his baseball cap. Glancing simultaneously at his watch and already drained pint glass, he said, "Want another? That one never even touched the sides."

Chapter 23

A groundswell of local support had been achieved through some regular gigging and continued airplay on XFM. A download-only single had been well received – selling almost a thousand copies. The record label interest had been a constant since the tracks were first sent out.

Hotly tipped to be the 'next big thing' out of Manchester – a somewhat dubious honour as the music press always seemed to expect the next incarnation of the 'Manc Monkey Walk'.

Having been courted by a handful of labels complete with A & R men oozing phony sincerity, a decision had been made to sign with XL Recordings – an independent label currently basking in the success and vast record sales that Adele had brought them.

A sensible advance had been negotiated, the thinking being that the smaller this sum, the less indebted the band would be. Jobs and courses had been jettisoned with much glee. Johnny had served his own notice out, and upon hearing that he had opted 'out of normality' to work full-time with the band, Claire had instructed a solicitor to draw up papers allowing her to buy him out of their house.

Having had a lawyer check over the minutiae of the contract, the band were now poised to sign their names across an actual record deal. Things would change overnight. They would now be answerable to a paymaster, dancing to someone else's tune. Working for the man…

***

The band bundled out of the classy yet understated XL offices straight into a cold drizzling January afternoon. Dusk was bleeding into the last vestiges of daylight. Eleven months from first gig to record deal. Preternaturally quick this day and age, but the adage that talent will out was writ large in Lonely Souls.

"We've fuckin' done it," whispered Dom, "We've got a fuckin' record deal!" All talking in hushed tones, as if shouting it out would negate the transaction.

A 'signing party' was planned for a select audience of two hundred that evening at Koko in Camden.

"Let's go to the venue. Get soundchecked and then head back to the hotel and have a beer," said Johnny assertively.

"We got a guestlist for later, Johnny?" Dom asked casually.

"Should do. I'll check at the venue. Let have names and I'll sort it."

Leaning into Johnny and speaking as quietly as possible as to avoid prying ears, he said, "It's Emma. The girl from the Northampton gig."

Johnny glanced down at his watch and the ubiquitous London traffic jam. "We should just hop on the tube. Venue's right next to Mornington Crescent so it'll be quicker than a cab." Looking round at the band, he said, "You fully signed up rock stars okay to slum it on public transport?"

Laughing, Jamie scratched his head pensively. "I dunno Johnny, don't want to cause a riot do we!"

With a studious nod, Johnny said, "I think we should be okay J, we'll risk it. Limo next time. Promise…"

***

Arriving at the venue, they were met by the venue's assistant manager who directed them to a hospitality room which was amply stocked with plates of expensive looking buffet food and a small bar. "Feel free to help yourselves, I'll send Zak, the sound engineer, through in fifteen minutes."

The room was adorned with dark red drapes, subdued red lighting all set against a thick black carpet.

The dramatic effect was not lost on the band. Like kids in a candy shop, they stood wide-eyed at the platters of food and the shelves of chilled beers and bottles of spirits that begged to be unburdened of their stoppers.

Coughing an attention grabbing, "Ahem," Johnny raised an eyebrow towards the band. "Look at this as a little test. Polish this lot off and play like twats and look like twats. Enjoy a couple of beers and deliver the goods later…"

Cracking a beer open whilst checking his phone, Dom looked over to Johnny. "You sort that guestlist place for me?"

"Will do. Anyone else need guestlist sorting?"

When he returned, the band were in the midst of a good-natured conversation with who he assumed to be Zak. A very good-looking black guy, sporting mini-dreads, a neatly trimmed chin beard and an aging 'A Tribe Called Quest' T-shirt was laughing and high-fiving Mikee.

"You must be Zak? Johnny. I'm their manager."

Shaking his outstretched hand, Zak said, "Excellent. Relieved you're not their Bez dancer. You Manc bands. You never know!"

Johnny smiled warmly. "No, those days are long behind me. Knees won't take it these days."

"Right then, you Lonely Souls, lets drink up. It won't go off and let's get you soundchecked," Zak said, the Southern inflections in stark contrast to the band's flat Northern vowels.

As they left the hospitality room and headed for the small auditorium where their gear was already set up, Dom's phone pinged. Pulling Johnny to one side, he said, "It's Emma. She's arrived early. Can you meet her and," scratching his head, "I dunno, let her have a drink here? I don't want her watching the soundcheck."

"Yeah, don't worry man, I'll see her in and get her a drink sorted. There's plenty of it."

"Wicked. I owe you one."

Heading towards the front of the venue, Johnny was met by an exceptionally attractive brunette, her straight bob cut hair perfectly to her jawline. In a black leather jacket, sequinned AC/DC T-shirt, skin-tight blue jeans and some fiercely spiked heeled black boots, she looked every inch the rock star's girlfriend.

Johnny just about resisted the temptation to ask her what her favourite AC/DC track was - given the younger generation's penchant for wearing band T-shirts because they 'like the logo'

Extending a hand, he said, "You must be Emma? Johnny. I'm their mana…"

Ignoring the proffered hand, Emma flung her arms round his neck and kissed him warmly on the cheek.

Choking back the overpowering smell of perfume, Johnny extricated himself from her clinging embrace, rearranging the paisley woollen scarf inside his coat.

"OH MY GOD! I CAN'T BELIEVE I'M GETTING TO SEE THEM PLAY AGAIN!" Emma squealed excitably. "Does Dom know I'm here?" She fanned herself with both hands. "THEY ARE JUST THE BEST BAND EVER! AND DOM!" Performing a dramatic little swoon, Emma was

The Rock 'N' The Roll. 'N That

positively trembling with excitement, "AND I JUST LOVE DOM. HE'S JUST SO GORGEOUS!"

"I think so too," said Johnny with a with a knowing grin, Johnny picked up the small black leather holdall that Emma had placed beside her. "I'll take you through. You can grab a drink and wait for Dom. They're just soundchecking now."

Another excited squeal." How long will they be? I SO can't wait to see him."

Leading Emma through to the darkened hospitality room, he said, "Grab a drink. The dressing room's just down that corridor. I'll tell Dom you're here," adding with a friendly smile, "Like he doesn't know already…"

Picking up a beer and heading out to watch the band soundcheck, Johnny could not have been happier.

Zak was the consummate professional and the soundcheck was conducted with the minimum of fuss. With a nod of approval, Zak motioned to Johnny that all was done.

Placing his guitar down in its stand, Jamie asked, "Nice one Zak, fancy a beer with us?"

Mimicking Jamie's turn of phrase, Zak beamed across to the stage. "NICE ONE lads, I'd love to!"

As the band listened raptly to Zak talking of bands that he had worked with, Dom slunk off to meet the expectant guest who was awaiting him in the dressing room.

Stepping back to help himself to a second plate of tiger prawns, Johnny looked at the band. His band. And smiled a contented smile.

Patting down his jacket pockets, Danny looked momentarily panicked. "Fuck. I'm out of cigs. Got a spare box in the dressing room. Gimme a minute Mikee…"

Watching him dash off in his ninety mile an hour fashion, Zak shook his head, laughing heartily. "He never stops does he!"

"Always in a hurry but happy to be here," mused Jamie.

***

Throwing the dressing room door open with a bang, Danny stopped dead in his tracks.

Dom was sat facing the door on a foldaway chair, black jeans gathered round his ankles, his hands placed on Emma's shoulders as she enthusiastically sucked on his cock. His previously closed-in-ecstasy eyes went to wide-eyed shock then straight to rolling back in grunted climax as he shot a projectile of hot sperm upwards.

Assuming a nonchalant air, she ran the back of her hand across her mouth in the definitive just-done-blow-job fashion.

"FUCK'S SAKE DANNY! WHY THE FUCK DIDN'T YOU KNOCK?" Dom snapped as he hastily pulled his jeans up. The moment well and truly sullied.

Emma, as coolly as you like, rose from her knees, stepped towards Danny, hugged him with her signature squeal and kissed him on the cheek.

Recoiling at where those pretty bee-stung lips had moments before. "Err. Hi Emma. Nice to see y'again." Making large apologetic eyes at Dom. "Sorry man, I just wanted my cigs. I'll leave you to it."

Beating a hasty retreat, Danny scooted back to the hospitality room and beckoned for Mikee to join him for a cigarette.

Exiting through a fire-door at the rear of the venue, Danny leant against the band's RV-cum-tour bus. "Fuck me, I love this business!"

Mikee accepted Dan's light. "Me too bro. Still can't believe this is all happening!"

Rocking on the spot with excitement, he said, "Nah me neither. And Dom," tossing his head back with laughter, "he's already got some bird sucking him off in the dressing room!"

Blowing smoke out with a satisfied sigh, Danny added, "Anyhow, don't crack on y'know. He wasn't best pleased as when I rocked up just as he was about to blow his load!"

***

The show started at 10pm precisely with a full complement of XL staff and invited guests making up the 200-strong crowd.

Taking to the stage in total darkness, Mikee started the set with a slow pounding of his bass drum. Zak picked the figure of Jamie out with a red spotlight. "We're Lonely Souls. But you probably knew that. We're very glad to be here and we know you're going to enjoy the ride…"

As *Follow the Mantra* blasted the crowd's senses, Johnny closed his eyes, and let out a long-contented sigh. It had only been a comparatively short journey to get this far, and it had come at a price personally. But seeing the

The Rock'N'The Roll. 'N That

band and knowing that they had a record deal in the bag, it was all worth it. One hundred percent.

Feeling a sharp pinch to bring back him from his thoughts, Johnny looked to his side and saw Emma, hands clasped to her face, making huge doe eyes at Dominic as he stood on stage, silhouetted in white light. Every inch a guitar hero. A new guitar hero for the 21st century.

Delivering a sharp-as-a-tack half hour set, the band played through their six strongest songs, finishing the set with an incendiary rendition of *Salvation*. It all looked and sounded as amazing as they could have hoped for. The delighted reaction from the gathered record company staff was quite literally music to Johnny's ears.

The only blip being a Pollock-esque spatter of dried jizz that led from the thigh of Dominic's jeans to just below the knee. It had looked particularly eye-catching under the UV strobe lighting…

***

The first 'meet and greet' went entirely without incident. The band were introduced to a stream of well-wishing faces. Shook numerous hands. Air-kissed and accepted compliments and platitudes with eager gratitude.

Dominic kept Emma by his side throughout, partially that he was such a smitten kitten but also to cover the stain on his jeans that he had only just noticed and was now discreetly trying to scratch off with a fingernail.

Performing a quick mental calculation, Johnny reckoned that this aftershow bash would be costing close to three grand - give or take five hundred quid. The assorted guests were all making merry on the free bar. All part of their non-recoupable advance.

Was he really thinking like that already? He was now part of a team. A cog in the machine behind the band. Decisions would be made for them, that he would approve or dismiss. But he would now be answerable to the label. There would be pluggers, a press officer, a marketing team, wardrobe stylists, promoters, A & R, accountants, lawyers and the label's management…

But they would always be his band.

Chapter 24

Sixteen gigs in 23 days. The band had never played consecutive gigs, never mind such an intense run of shows. Reading the email again, Johnny ran a hand through his hair and stared out of the window of the city centre apartment he was now renting. Waterside views. 24hr concierge. Underground parking. Ready-meals for one.

The label had booked them on to a UK 'toilet tour' as support act to an American college band that were currently making reasonable sized waves. This would be a real rite of passage for them. A tough slog on many levels. But they would love every fucking minute.

Once the tour was completed, it was straight into the studio to master the album.

Before that there was the small matter of a friends and family gig/party Johnny had sorted to celebrate the signing of the record deal.

Their fucking record deal!

He kept having to pinch himself that the flurry of emails that he was fielding were for him. Not some bollocks from head office regarding a new health and safety procedure that he would need to implement on behalf of the company's employees or some such shite.

The gig was to be for friends and family and a select handful of fans who had been invited via the band's website. Talking of which, Johnny thought, the old site had now been taken down and was being overhauled at the record companies expense. All happening.

He had booked The Deaf Institute – a very cool club cum gig venue in the heart of studentsville - and was currently fielding various guestlist requests from the band. Johnny was bringing his closest friends along. The texts had been sent out with a 'See I told you x' at the end. Always the last word…

***

"I think she's back, bro. Hurry up!"

The Rock'N'The Roll. 'N That

Hurtling down stairs, Dom jumped over the back of the sofa and assumed a crashed-out position to convince that he had been idling there for some time.

The front door opened and Cally smiled widely at the sight of her two sons, lazing carefree on the sofa whilst a Spaghetti Western played out to its bloody conclusion in the background.

"Hiya boys. You okay? Looking forward to tonight?" Putting her shopping bags down, she said, "I can't wait! I'm so proud of you both." She rubbed them both on the tops of their heads over the back of the sofa. "I'm beat after a day's shopping though. Got myself a lovely new top for tonight though. Got to look my best for my two favourite rock stars."

Jamie leaned back and looked over his shoulder. "Hiya Mum. We're good thanks. Just been chillin' out before tonight," he replied, feigning disinterest.

"You should go and try it on upstairs. Let's have a look at it on," said Dom kindly, but then wincing slightly as his brother kicked him with a bare foot.

"Ooh I will," shrilled Cally, "Give me a minute."

Throwing a daggers look across at his twin, Jamie whispered crossly, "I thought we were going to tell her and then let her go and see the upstairs."

Shrugging his shoulders and yawning without covering his mouth, he said, "Yeah well. I changed my mind," adding cockily, "She'll love it. You'll see."

Bang on cue, there was a surprised scream from upstairs. "What's happened to my room?" A quick dart across the landing, and another scream. "WHAT HAVE YOU TWO DONE WITH MY ROOM?"

"You best come down Mum, I'll stick the kettle on," Jamie said, slightly concerned at how she was going to take this.

"You best sit down," Dom gestured towards the empty sofa.

She perched on the edge of the sofa with a confused look on her face and her hands held to her throat.

Returning to the front room and rubbing at a rogue paint spot on the back of his hand, Jamie said, "We've moved your all stuff back into the main bedroom. Turned it back into a proper room again. For you." Taking a deep breath, he added, "Me and Dom are moving out. We've rented apartments in town. In the same block. Not far from Johnny actually."

He saw the look of resigned disappointment etched on their mum's face. Leaping up and sitting next to her, Dom put a reassuring arm around her. "We've been talking and we're going to be away so much. It'd be only fair for you to have the bigger room to yourself again."

Putting her freshly manicured hands up to Dom's face, she said, "Oh I know. I know. But I'll miss you both so much." Her eyes filled with well-meant tears. "My boys. Leaving me." Rubbing at her eyes gently, she said, "I know why. You can't have boys in a band living with their old mum." Doing an endearing little combined laugh sniffle, she said, "You best come and visit me whenever you're home!"

"Dom'll be straight round with his washing every week," teased Jamie.

"Cheeky twat! I won't." Looking at his mum imploringly, he said, "I won't and he's just as bad!"

"See! This is what I'll miss. You two making me laugh."

Adopting a serious tone, Jamie held his mum's hand. "Honestly, we'll miss you as well. But we need our own space." He pulled her by the hand. "Come and have a proper look upstairs."

Cally took in the fruits of the boys' - and some willing friends - labours. The room divide had been knocked down and the walls painted a delicate shade of linen. Her double bed and furniture were now spread out as they were intended. A new duvet cover to match the room's muted colours sat crisply on the bed, and a newly purchased rug sat at the foot of the bed in front of the pine dresser.

"Have you had one of those home makeover teams off the tele here today? It looks lovely." Letting out a stifled sob, she said, "Oh come here you two!" She hugged her boys into her sides. "I'm the luckiest mum in the world having you two. And I'm going to have to share you now you're going to be famous. I don't know how happy I am about that!"

***

The Deaf Institute was regarded as one of Manchester's coolest venues. They were playing in the room on the top floor which was tastefully decorated with black and white flock wallpaper. A huge mirrorball dominated the centre of the ceiling.

'Grown-up rock 'n' roll chic' was how Johnny had always described the place. A couple of hundred or so people would fill the room nicely, and still leave people room to get to the all-important bar. He'd stuck a couple of grand behind the bar as a gesture – an unlimited free tab would have resulted in numerous hollow-legged Mancunians leaving him facing a five-figure bar bill.

As Johnny checked his phone, he glanced out of the window of the venue and saw Danny pull up in a black cab, race round to the other side and open the door for his now girlfriend. He and Dee - short for Denise - had been going steady for a couple of months. His new oft repeated mantra was, "I can't believe how fuckin' fit she is!" Which was inevitably met with, "Neither can we…"

A good-natured gig was lapped up by the crowd. The band mingled afterwards amid much backslapping and well wishing. Cally seemed a little overwhelmed by proceedings. All the attention being lavished on her boys was a little too much for her. A combination of disbelief and trepidation of their unknown future. A reassuring word from Johnny seemed to help. "They'll be fine. They're more than ready for this. I'd stake my life on it," he offered in calming tones.

"I know," she replied in her quiet melodic tone. "It's just such a big thing. It'll never be the same again." Looking up at him with a doleful look in her eyes, she said, "You know they've already moved out?"

"I did. I did," he replied, putting a reassuring hand on her elbow. "And look what they did with your room." He glanced over at the twins who were chatting with a group of friends. "They care so much about you, honestly. And I'll always look out for them. Watch their back. Promise."

Making a cross your heart sign, Johnny hugged Cal reassuringly, her fragrant smell enchanting him. As he pulled away, he put a hand gently to her cheek. "They'll be fine. It could all just get a bit mad and that…"

"Thanks Johnny. I know I'm being daft. I'm glad you care so much. Makes me feel much better," Cal replied solemnly.

"Anyhow you enjoy tonight. Get yourself a drink and I'll catch up later." He spotted Simon, the photographer. "In fact. Gimme a minute."

Hurrying over to Simon, who had been photographing the band during their set, he said, "Hi mate. Good to see you. Would you mind taking a few pics for me?" Guiding Simon over to the brothers, he signalled for Cally to come across. "Simon. Cally. Cally. Simon. He'll take a few pictures of you all together."

Jamie saw the look of delight in his mum's eyes, and hugged Johnny, kissing him on the cheek. "Thanks man, you do know how to do the right thing at the right time."

"No worries J. And yeah. Most of the time. Most of the time man…"

In the small smoking terrace at the rear of the venue, the course of true love was starting to manifest for Danny.

As they shared a cigarette – the ultimate romantic gesture – Dee looked up at him and teased his hair into place. "You looked so good up there tonight baby. Proper little pop star I've got me."

Clearing his throat, he said, "Err, rock star please! I'm not like those fuckin' fakes you get on X-Factor!"

"SORRY! Get you. Rock star. Either way. I'm dead happy. But I'll miss you when you're away so much."

And then came the inevitable 'on the road caveat'.

"And you won't look at any other girls when you're away will you. It's just you and me now baby." She was clearly looking to test Dan's intents of fidelity.

With an anguished look, he said, "BABE! I wouldn't even look at another girl." Stumbling over his next words, he added, "Y'know how I feel, don't ya?"

"Do I?" she enquired knowingly.

He rattled his next sentence out as quickly as he could. "Y'know I love yer." Staring at her for a reaction, he repeated, "I fuckin' love you!"

"OH DANNY!" she squealed. "That's the nicest thing anyone's ever said to me. And I trust you one million percent!"

Sealing the moment with a long deep kiss, Danny then pulled out his last cigarette. "See, better than a Rolo, I'd share my last cig with you!"

Clasping her hands together and raising her right foot up slightly behind her, she said, "Oh Danny. I love you too."

As the planets aligned themselves for him, Danny inhaled deeply and blew out a long, contented plume of smoke.

A rock star. He was going to be a bona fide, real deal, genuine article motherfuckin'rock star. And he still couldn't believe how fit she was…

Chapter 25

"Oh, you dirty bastard!" said Dom, visibly appalled.

"What?" replied Danny indignantly.

"That, you dirty bastard, is your third scotch egg of the day," he added with a disgusted pull off his face.

"Well. We're in Scotland. When in Scotchland…"

"HAHA! He's got a point," laughed Mikee whilst sat on the open door of their graffitied RV/tourbus - demolishing a Big Mac in three bites.

"Dunno what you're laughing at Kong. You're sharing with him. He'll have breadcrumb coated shits at this rate, "sniggered Dom.

"Sorry Dom, forgot how you love your health food," said Mikee, pouring the rest of the fries down his neck.

He held out the sandwich box he had just opened. "Ham salad. On brown bread. And a bottle of water," Dom added smugly.

The first date of the tour was the furthest north and Johnny was beginning to wish they had done it with an overnight stop. They were four hours, two hundred and thirty miles and two service station stops down. And he was flagging. As he drained the caffeine-laced Red Bull, he stared across the car park wide eyed to revitalise himself for the remaining two hundred and odd miles.

Having sorted the accommodation himself, he had booked single rooms where cost wasn't prohibitive. For approximately half the stops, the band would be sharing rooms, but Johnny was affording himself the luxury of a single each night. There was a line to be drawn and sharing with them was most resolutely it.

"Right, chuck your shit away and let's crack on. Mikee, you can ride shotgun now. Your turn to keep me company."

In a very grown up and futile attempt to keep the RV clean and comparatively decent smelling, Johnny had insisted that all food is eaten outside of the four wheels. Only drinks and sweets/chocolate/crisps were permitted, and all rubbish was to be put in a bin bag on the back seat.

He'd felt like an overbearing school teacher when laying down the rules, but felt that some semblance of order was needed.

A further two stops and another nourishing scotch egg for Dan – he really was taking the Scottish national dish to heart. Jamie had convinced him that scotch eggs were laid by the Haggis Bird – indigenous to Scotland – which seemed a perfectly plausible explanation to Danny.

The miles rolled by. Mikee slept. Jamie busied himself writing lyrics. Dom was engrossed in his iPad and Danny provided a running commentary on everything and anything. Like a human sat nav-cum-traffic control-cum-weatherman. He'd even bought his passport along for when they crossed into Scotland. The tight bastards.

The Granite City. Unflinchingly cold and austere.

Arriving at The Lemon Tree, the band were faced with an inauspicious looking flat fronted granite-stone building.

"Fuck me it's freezing," Dom whinged as a blast of icy North Sea wind pierced his denim jacket. "Get us inside Johnny, it's fucking cold!"

"Grab the gear. I'm not leaving it all in the bus. Get a whisky down you. That'll warm your bones."

Grumbling as he grabbed his guitar case and amp, Dominic led the way, a not particularly endearing scowl on his face.

They were greeted by the promoter's rep, Alastair, a shaven headed stocky Scot, wearing a Prodigy tour T-shirt and cargo shorts. Dumping his gear down grumpily, Dom looked Alastair up and down. "MAN, you must be fuckin' mental dressing like that. It's fuckin' arctic out there!"

"Nice to meet you as well," Alastair grinned good-naturedly. "And this is warm, my soft Southern friend."

"WARM!" Dom exclaimed. "Remind me never to come 'ere on holiday."

Clearly used to temperature based outburst from bands, Alastair added, "And remind me again why we want independence from you soft shites…" His rebuttal taking the wind out of Dom's chilly sails.

They were guided through to the diminutive backstage dressing room. "Butterfly Caught have finished their soundcheck and gone back to their hotel. Stage is all yours now. Gig's not sold too bad. About 350 tickets. About three quarter full. Get the crowd going and you'll be grand."

An efficiently tight soundcheck left the band with two hours to kill before showtime. Not time enough to go back and grab some well required sleep. Nor time to get too pissed.

A cursory walk round some local shops had resulted in the purchase of the mandatory cigarettes and energy drinks but Danny had excelled himself. Having grasped the concept of 'per diem' – grown up spends, as Johnny had settled on – he had purchased a Tam O'Shanter, which he proudly announced he would wear for the Scottish dates, figuring that this would endear him to the crowd. And not at all like a patronising English twat…

***

The set was largely uneventful. Tight but the band's long northbound trek had left them tired and a little rusty. A crowd of seventy or so pseudo-disaffected Scottish youths were nonplussed by proceedings until the last three songs when there was some sporadic jumping up and down. The donning of the Scottish headwear for the last song earned Danny a hollered, "Ya look a cunt. A big nosed cunt," from an affronted Scot.

Clearly underwhelmed by their performance, the band sat around sulkily in the dressing room whilst Butterfly Caught played their set of psychedelic stoner rock. Common courtesy should have dictated that they go and catch the headliners' set, first night and all that, but they - especially Dom - were too tired and tetchy in no mood for pleasantries.

"What the fuck was that hat all about, D-Mo? You did look a right cunt," said Dominic with a surly tone.

Looking wounded, Danny said, "Thought they'd appreciate it. No sense of humour, these Jocks."

Jamie, who had been sat stoically restringing his guitar, said, "We've had a long day. We didn't play at our best. Edinburgh tomorrow. Let's get a drink and then turn it in and be bang up for tomorrow."

Regarding his brother with a frown, Dom said, "Come on J, we're on tour for fuck's sake. Least we can do is get pissed. Those are the first fuckin' rules of the rock 'n' the roll, aren't they?"

"Suit yourself Dom, I'm done. Don't wake me when you get back…"

"Whatever," Dom snapped, the exertions of the day manifesting itself with his outburst of churlish irritability.

"I'll be up for a few beers, Dom," said Mikee, lazily stretching out a yawn.

Danny, still wounded by the heckle, was busy texting Dee. Thinking that an early night on their first day on the road would appease her concerns, he said, "Nah, I'm done in as well. Johnny said there's loads to see in Edinburgh and some decent boozers so I'm gonna do that."

Snorting unattractively, Dom said, "Fuck's sake D-Mo! You're gonna go sight-seeing with Johnny? Very rock 'n' roll..."

Turning to Danny - who was now torn as to whether to submit to a night's drinking - Jamie said matter-of-factly, "You can share with me then tonight if these two are going partying."

"Yeah, cheers J, I might go for a few though. Not sure yet."

"Lightweights," grunted Dom.

***

The short hop to Edinburgh was made in relatively good spirits. Dom and Mikee had been unable to locate anywhere that resembled a party. That and a combination of a cold late-winter's night had forced a tail between their legs return to the hotel at just before midnight.

A good night's sleep had left Dom far less tetchy, but even more resolute to enjoy himself that evening. "Fuck all to do in Aberdeen last night. But I'm having it big tonight." Tapping Johnny on the shoulder from the rear passenger seat, he said, "You said Edinburgh was a decent night out didn't you?"

Glancing behind briefly, Johnny said, "Yeah, it's a superb place. Never not had a good time there. Crowd will be better tonight as well."

With the ubiquitous service station negotiated for breakfast, Johnny decided that a pub lunch would be a welcome treat as they would be seeing more than enough FriedKingMacBurgerChicken places between now and home...

***

An energised band and a far livelier crowd lead to a high-spirited dressing room. Beers were snapped open as they toasted the success of the Edinburgh gig. A confident set had been delivered – Danny wisely dispensing with his Scottish headwear. Or more accurately it was now floating in the River Forth as Jamie had sent the hat to watery grave as they were passing over the Forth Bridge.

"You seen anything of the other band yet?" asked Mikee as he drained a cold Peroni in two gulps. Putting his hand across his mouth to stifle a gassy belch, he said, "They do keep themselves to themselves."

"Fuck 'em," said Dominic as he leaned back on his chair, idly strumming his unplugged Fender. "Probably worried we'll blow 'em away. Daft Yank twats!"

"We should go and check 'em out, see what they've got," said Jamie, as he changed into a fresh white T-shirt.

"Bang up for tonight! Crowd were lovin' us. Let's go and get big. Really wasted!" said Dom.

Assembling at the crowded bar to watch Butterfly Caught deliver a reverb and feedback-soaked set, the band were soon striking up conversations with a host of amorous well-wishers.

Jamie was fielding intimate questions from a gorgeous redhead who wanted to know his favourite songwriter, food and sexual position. For what it's worth – Strummer, Chinese and the same as yours…

Also being interrogated were Danny and Mikee. However, the attentions' heading their way were from two fanboys – music students who were bombarding them with some serious muso questions. Danny's riposte of, "Can I fuck read music! I just plug the fucker in and play," was patently not the answer they were looking for.

Dominic, meanwhile, was knocking back shots with an attractive couple, the boyfriend oblivious to the outrageous flirting his girlfriend was on the receiving end of.

In between shots, Jamie leaned over his brother's shoulder, nodding towards the stage. "Not for me at all. No fuckin' tunes or melodies. They can play a bit, but we're twice the band this lot are."

"Have you seen the fat fuck on guitar? He only plays it to cover his belly!" Dom said uncharitably.

As the set came to a frenzied conclusion with ear-piercing feedback screeching through the venue's speakers, a bleary-eyed Johnny appeared, "Right. Help us get the gear loaded and I'm heading back to the hotel. I'm shagged," he yawned wearily. "Early night. Cup of Tea. Family Guy and a wank. If I can stay awake for the latter…"

"Ah, cheers boss," laughed Mikee, "Let me know if it's a good 'un." Comedic pause. "The episode of Family Guy…"

"You look done in man," said Jamie sympathetically, "I'll just drink up and we'll be with you."

"J, we've been invited to a student night at some club that Shona and," pointing at his newly-found drinking partner, "Sorry what's yer name again?" Dominic slurred ever so slightly.

"Scott," came the obliviously unoffended reply.

"Yeah. Scott the Scot and Shona have asked us to this club. Supposed to be decent."

"Nice one. Count me in. Let's just load the gear out and let Johnny get off."

With the gear safely packed away, Johnny wished the band well for the evening. "Good gig that lads, have a top night. You've earned it." Yawning loudly, "Only a short hop to Glasgow tomorrow, so we get a lie in. I won't wait up."

"Cheers boss, I'm after getting some more ink tomorrow. I'm booked in at a top tattooist down in Leith. Feel free to join me!"

"Err, yeah. Cheers Mikee. I'll leave my mid-life crisis at packing my job and splitting up with my girlfriend for life on the road with a rock 'n' roll band if that's alright."

"Suit yourself. But don't say I didn't ask. Now you get off and get your beauty sleep, "replied Mikee

"Indeed, indeed," said Johnny as he climbed into the driver's seat and headed back the short distance to the hotel.

Clapping his hands together, Dom put an arm round Mikee. "So then, Kong, shall we sniff out some chop then?" Rubbing his nose in anticipation, he said, "My new mate, whatever his name is, and his fit bird said they can sort us."

"Cool," whistled Mikee, "Still got all of my grown-up spends so far, so let's get big!"

"Excellent," replied Dom, "Proper big!"

**

A night of bad behaviour duly ensued. After being treated like proper rock stars with free entry to the club, and no queuing, the band made hay.

Jamie took the very inquisitive and equally obliging Alice back to the hotel, whereby she proceeded to ask him his life story before giving him the best blow job of his life. Ever the lady, she had indicated that 'it wasn't the right time for sex' but promised further oral favours in the morning, thus securing herself board and lodgings for the evening.

The cocaine had saved Dominic from an early bath, with the not too badly cut coke sobering him up sufficiently to have sex in a in the Ladies' with the very lovely Shona – whilst her unsuspecting boyfriend chopped a line out for Danny in the neighbouring Men's'. Upon climaxing, Dom had coarsely whispered that Shona, "Remember this when I'm famous!"

Who said romance wasn't alive and kicking...

Mikee was seeing off all comers in a winner stays on arm wrestling competition, and at a fiver a go, was £55.00 up on the deal.

Sticking to his vow of fidelity, Danny was telling all and sundry that he was going to get married when their first album went to number one. This only succeeded in alerting any listening female that he was in a band and not just your average run of the mill pisshead.

Life on the road was starting to have its perks and the band were starting to like what they saw…

***

"Satisfactory wank boss?" asked Mikee, gingerly patting down the dressing at the top of his right arm.

After only three hours' sleep, he had been up at 9am and had spent several hours at the mercies of a Leith tattooist.

"Yes. And thanks for your concern Michael. 7 out of 10. And a Family Guy I'd not seen before."

As the rest of the band assembled, Danny was busy reading the itinerary. "This is the same every day and you take us everywhere. Do we need really need this?"

"When you put it like that," he paused for dramatic effect, "Yes. It means I don't have to put a tag around your necks like Paddington. 'If lost please return to owner'. The itinerary tells you where we stay and where we play."

Packing the last of the personal luggage away, he said, "We all have a good night then?"

The half-smiles and yawns said all he needed to know. More of the same in Glasgow tonight and they'd soon be a seasoned band on the road. "All ready to do the same again tonight? Top venue and the crowd will be mad for it."

"I think we can manage that Mr Harrison. It was a good 'un last night. Were you all safely tucked up with a hot chocolate and a good book?" Dominic asked. A little too sarcastically.

"All that, ta. Remember who does all the driving and fetching and carrying when you're next getting your dick wet eh!"

"Yeah, yeah okay boss," replied Dom as he dabbed at his coke reddened nose with a used tissue.

The Rock 'N' The Roll. 'N That

***

The Glasgow, Newcastle, Preston, Leeds and Liverpool shows passed by in a flurry of booze, sexual conquests and increasingly vitamin-free diets.

Service stations were now being scored out of ten. Tebay on the M6 scoring a particularly impressive 10 out of 10, housing an authentic 'Farm Food' shop.

"Best scotch egg ever. Even though it's in England," Danny had stated with the air of a connoisseur.

Dominic was leading the way with three amorous admirers left in his wake. He'd learn about leaving his mobile number with them every time – as the morning after was spent fielding a plethora of unwanted textual promises.

Danny had 'accidentally' been the recipient of a blow job in Leeds. "But I didn't shag or her or even kiss her. So really I haven't done anything wrong!" he protested a little too loudly. And a little too desperately…

After his Edinburgh encounter, Jamie had been reticent to repeat more of the same. The female attentions were welcomed but he seemed slightly ill at ease with just how little effort he had to make.

And Mikee, aside from a broken shower cubicle door in Newcastle whilst attempting to reenact some over the top scene from his favourite porno, had been quietly enjoying himself without the hint of a grumble or moan.

An afternoon in a Preston laundrette whilst they did their much-needed laundry had elicited much dissension. Johnny's, "I'm fucked if I'm doing it for you," brought that argument to a swift conclusion.

Heading off down the M6 to Liverpool, Mikee, again riding shotgun with Johnny, piped up, "I've still not seen the main band. Fuckin' weird. They won't let us watch their soundcheck and as soon as they've done they're either back at their hotel or smoking weed in their dressing room."

"They're piss poor anyhow," sniped Dom, "Not for me at all. I've seen 'em a couple of times now and it bores me shitless."

"Anyone fancy The Beatles Museum when we get to Scouseland? I went a while back with…" His words drifted off as he turned up a Kasabian track on the radio.

A lively show in Liverpool, with the band on particularly incandescent form - although the restless natives seemed intent on reminding the band that they were 'Manc twats' between every song, only giving up when they realised they weren't another Gallagher wannabe band and could indeed play a bit.

The thought of a home stopover had been met heartily by the band and they left straight after their set. "You'd think they'd get over the fact they've not had a decent band since The Beatles," Danny had quipped whilst they were loading up at the rear of the venue. Eliciting a raised eyebrow from Johnny.

***

The domestic pitstop refreshed the band for the second and longest leg of the tour. The Manchester date saw the band at their most relaxed. A groundswell of now familiar faces gave them a partisan welcome. There was no official aftershow, but the band partied as hard as you can on a wet Wednesday in March at local favourite booze haunt, Big Hands.

Dates ticked by, notches on the bedpost were increasing daily, with Dominic revelling in the abundance of sexual offers that wafted his way. The chat Johnny and Jamie had in Northampton explained this zealous and dismissive attitude to his burgeoning love life.

Jamie began to appreciate that his voice was something that needed to be nurtured and protected, particularly with shows on consecutive days. And as his twin embraced the ready-made attention from eager well-wishers, he became more guarded.

The trusty rhythm section went about their business in a carefree eyes-wide-open fashion. Another sexual faux pas in Nottingham saw Danny admit to penetrative sex. With the extraordinary caveat of, "I never shot my load so that doesn't really count does it?" he had asked imploringly. Only to be met with a series of guffaws and howls of laughter.

Conversation turned to Jamie - with him confessing that he was not one for giving oral sex, Johnny had 'tut tutted' loudly, adding a worldly wise, "You'll learn J, you'll learn. It's an art form you have to have in your locker." A dismissive pull of his face had surprised Johnny. Especially from one so sensitive.

***

Spirits were given a further boost with the big news that Steve Lamacq had played a 'white label' track of theirs on his BBC 6 Music evening show. This was the widest exposure the band had received and the track ('Salvation') had been brilliantly well received. This felt like the start. And their Brighton gig that evening had been given a heavy plug. Momentum was building, and the tour had convinced the band that their long-harboured dream was now a rock 'n' roll reality…

Chapter 26

The penultimate date of the tour saw the band at The Haunt in Brighton. A seafront hotel with actual sea views and single rooms for all. As with most British coastal resorts, the winter season lacked the high season lustre and the rooms were a fraction of the price – not that the band needed to know this minutia.

The Haunt was an art-deco style venue a stone's throw from Brighton's stony beachfront. A full house was expected and with the band having amassed a dozen or so gigs in the past three weeks, were as tight as you like, with Jamie's on-stage confidence growing by the show.

"Big aftershow tomorrow night that the label has put on. To close the tour and that," Johnny said as he reversed their trusty but now somewhat fetid tourbus into a parking bay behind the venue.

He had maintained a healthy distance from the band once their set had finished. This was the longest time that they had spent together and having secured a record deal so quickly, he had made the conscious decision to 'behave' and show the band how professional he was. It was early days with the label and any signs of weakness with management side of things could have put him under unwanted scrutiny.

"The sound's as good as we've had all tour, and it looks full out there already," Danny added, turning off his phone having just sent the umpteenth missive of love that day to Dee. Who was apparently 'missing him like fuck'. Quite…

With the gig being on a Friday, showtime was slightly later and with the drinks promos that the venue was running, a full house would be watching Lonely Souls.

There seemed to be a tangible shift in the attitude to the band as they took to the stage. The exposure on 6 Music had given the band a 'next big thing' sheen. People wanting to say they'd seen them first. Shrouded in darkness, the band struck up, Mikee's bass drum counting them into 'Follow the Mantra'.

The Rock 'N' The Roll. 'N That

As the first song fizzed to a finish, Jamie took a moment and stared out at the sea of faces. The clapping. The pleased-to-be-here faces. The I-saw-them-before-they-were-huge smug faces.

"We're Lonely Souls. We're gonna be your favourite fuckin' band before you know it!"

Striking a minor chord from out his guitar, his presence commanding attention, "You ready for us? Cos we're fuckin' ready for you." Wiping at a bead of sweat on his eyebrow, "Brighton, LET'S FUCKIN' GO!"

Screaming into 'This Is Not Tomorrow' Jamie had never been more strident, more believing in the band's abilities. Bursting every sinew, he wrung the notes of his guitar, twisting into the mic to deliver his fiery heartfelt vocal. Mikee powered the song along, never missing a beat, and the frenzied middle eight whipped the crowd up further, Dom looking effortlessly cool as he coaxed the spiralling solo out.

The lightshow was tremendous, a separate lighting engineer able to work the stage, drowning the band in shades of red, picking out Jamie or Dominic in ultra-white spotlights when they shared a mic for vocals.

As they reached the end of the set, Jamie, now stripped of his black denim jacket, was stood, a white T-shirt plastered to him, his red scarf worn loosely round his neck, drinking deeply from a bottle of water, tossing the half empty bottle into the crowd. "BRIGHTON. YOU HAVE BEEN FUCKIN' AMAZING! This is our last song. It's called 'Salvation'. We're called Lonely Souls," pausing and flashing a quick smile at Dominic, who was adjusting an effects pedal with his foot, "AND WE ARE GONNA BE YOUR SALVATION! YOU FUCKIN' NEED US!"

BANG! The chorus as ever, sounded huge. The three-way vocal of Jamie, Dominic and Danny sounded immense. Danny picking out the groove, hopping slightly on the spot as the song soared.

Second chorus and the crowd were loving it. *"I'll be your Salvation, you'll be my Salvation. We'll be your Salvation..."*

It sounded huge.

Sky-scrapingly huge.

The drop saw Jamie lead the crowd in a mutual hand-clapping as they pushed the song to its conclusion. Standing back and watching his brother lean back, eyes closed as the shimmering solo flew skywards. It was magnificent.

They exchanged a quick glance as the song finished. There was almost a mutual knowing that they had arrived. It was all in place now. A record deal. Touring. Radio exposure. And crowds that were going to grow and grow. And quickly grow to love this band. With a knowing smile, Jamie lifted his guitar in one hand above his head, "Thanks Brighton, you rocked like fuck! We're Lonely Souls. Fuckin' follow that…"

***

Backstage, Johnny was ecstatic. He'd been stood soaking the atmosphere up, feeling the buzz that the band had generated. "Fuck me! That was outstanding lads. Fucking outstanding. Pleasure to have seen that!"

"You finally gonna join us for a party tonight then, boss?" goaded Danny, clicking his phone on to check for messages.

"I think that as it's not a school night that can be arranged," said Johnny, accepting a beer from Dominic. "That was fuckin' brilliant. Crowd loved it. Absolutely loved it. And who'd want to follow that?" he laughed, gesturing towards the neighbouring dressing room.

With the gear safely back at the hotel, which was only some two hundred yards away, showers were grabbed, and fresh clothes donned. Several of Brighton's excellent bars were visited, the band happy in their anonymity. Beers were knocked back, shots slammed, and Johnny had accepted a chunky line of coke from Mikee, a full-on bear-hug and the, "I fuckin' love you man," had been the cherry on the top.

Earlier that day, Johnny had received an email from Claire advising him that his half of the house was ready to be transferred across to her, having raised the necessary funds to buy him out. The email was curt with a pointed final line – 'You'll get your money once you've signed the papers. I suppose you'll spend it on your precious band…'

I don't need to anymore, was his immediate thought – followed by a sadness that a big part of his life was well and truly over. He'd never wanted to hurt Claire, but she had been very much collateral damage. All this beautiful rock 'n' roll was exciting him like nothing ever had before but he was still tinged with a little sadness at the finality of their relationship.

The night, that should be morning, ended at 4am for Johnny. An all-night cellar had been located and a hefty bar tab had been accrued. Upon returning to the hotel, he had been horrified to see that the bar was still open, with a few hardy stragglers demanding the night porter continue serving. With bloodshot eyes and an exhausted bladder, he said, "Right, you fuckers, I'm done. Bed. And I don't care what you say!"

***

Sleep came quickly to him, but Johnny woke with a start at 6.30am when his door was banged loudly. Upon opening it, he was met by a total stranger, clearly the worse for wear. "You seen Donna?"

"No mate, I haven't wrong room…"

Closing the door and mumbling, "Fuckin' dick," to himself, Johnny flopped onto the bed but as his hangover was now here long and loud, he couldn't sleep. Tossing restlessly did him no favours and he decided some bracing sea air and watching the sun come up would be the perfect remedy.

Throwing on a hoodie, jeans and trainers, he headed out of the hotel for the seafront. Grabbing a bottle of water from a kiosk, he wandered across the road to a flight of weather beaten stone steps that led down to the stony beach.

The beach was completely deserted, and he took a not too comfortable perch and stared out at the sea's grey blue constant motion. Seagulls the size of small dogs waltzed in and out of the tide, squawking apparent grievances at each other.

As he looked out at the half-tangerine orb that was lazily addressing the new day, Johnny felt a tap on his shoulder; turning around sharply, he was met by the band.

"What you are doing sat here like a weirdo?" Danny asked, bottle of Becks clutched in one hand. Ubiquitous cigarette blazing in the other.

"Picking up boys! What the fuck did you think I'd be doing?"

Joining him on his stony pew, the band sat in a line, Dom shielding his eyes from the semi-glare of the sun, Danny and Mikee resplendent in shades. With his legs stretched out in front of him, Jamie yawned noisily.

Looking at each member of the band in turn, Johnny smiled. "It'll never be the same again once this all kicks off. No more nights getting pissed and no-one knowing who you are." He paused as he drained the bottle of water. "It'll get like you won't be able to go anywhere. This could get fuckin' huge." Putting his arms around Mikee and Jamie who were sat nearest to him, he said, "This is gonna be some fuckin' ride. You all ready for it?"

With stoic nods, the band looked out at the horizon, individually imagining the possibilities. All was quiet until Danny broke the silence with the ultimate cliché. "I was fuckin' born for this! Course we're fuckin' ready!"

He and Kong exchanged fist-bumps. Dominic inhaled on the last of his cigarette before flicking the dimp in the direction of a inquisitive seagull, as if earwigging into a world that it would never comprehend. "I can't fuckin' wait, Johnny!"

Only Jamie seemed reflective in a deeper, more serious demeanour.

He was about to speak when Dom spotted a passing early morning dog-walker. "'Scuse me mate, would you mind taking a picture?" The five of them, wide-eyed and shivering against the bitter sea air huddled together for the snap. A perfect moment perfectly captured…

Chapter 27

"Good picture that innit?" said Dominic, choking back a yawn. "I've just sent it to Mum. She'll love it."

Jamie turned around from the passenger seat and smiled at his twin brother. "She will! Another one for her album!"

Having been the very epitome of the cocksure frontman the previous night, Johnny had noted how quiet he had been since. Glancing across at him as they left Brighton to make the short journey north to London, he made a mental note to catch him on his own and ask him if anything was troubling him.

With the soundcheck not until 5pm, the band could go to their hotel and grab some well needed sleep. Tonight's gig – aside from being the last on their very first tour – was a momentous one. The 100 Club. The legendary 100 Club. The fuckin' 100 Club where all the greats had played. From The Who to The Pistols. The club oozed rock'n'roll heritage from every pore.

Slap bang in the middle of Oxford Street, the inauspicious sign over the door doesn't exactly scream legendary rock 'n' roll venue. Thousands of shoppers pass it by daily without giving it a second glance – blissfully ignorant to the stories the venue could tell.

"Is that it?" Danny exclaimed, somewhat bemused by the fact that they were caught up in the perma-busy traffic of Central London, heading to a venue that Johnny had talked about in hallowed terms.

Exasperated at the volume of traffic that had doubled their journey time and reduced their sleep time, and at Danny's youthful impertinence and ignorance, Johnny said, "Fuck's sake, at times…" Banging the heel of his hand against the steering wheel, he said, "Don't worry D-Mo. There's a McDonalds just there. You'll be fine."

The sarcasm eluding him, Danny said, "Ah, nice one boss. I'm starving!"

Rolling his eyes upwards, Johnny shrugged his shoulders and decided to leave matters at that.

As soon as they pulled up outside, Danny, good to his word was hot-footing it to the golden beacon that was the 'M arches'.

"He's fuckin' unreal," Johnny muttered.

Just as the rest of the band had finishing unloading, Danny re-appeared clutching a sizeable brown bag full of fried delights.

"You're not taking that shite in there are you?" Johnny said incredulously.

With a look of genuine surprise on his face, he said, "Why not? I can't smoke. Fine. But eating's not banned is it?"

Shaking his head and unable to compete with Danny's logic, Johnny hoisted Jamie's amp out of the back of the vehicle.

Wanting to buy into the myth of the venue, Jamie and Dominic were looking round wide-eyed at the pictures of all the legends that had played there. "You can feel it, can't you bro?" whispered Jamie, in awe of the black and white shots that had captured such pivotal moments in musical history.

"I can't wait for this. I'm gonna head down to Carnaby Street later. Try and get some new clobber to wear," replied Dom enthusiastically.

"I'll come along, I wouldn't mind a Chinese. Nice to sit down and have a proper meal."

***

Load-in. Soundcheck. All done without a fuss. The bands growing confidence and familiarity with the whole procedure had seen them become more assertive with the various venue's sound engineers. Not brusque, just a focussed desire to get things right. Dissenting voices had on occasion been heard when being shown Lilliputian dressing rooms, but as Johnny always countered, dressing room or draughty corridor...

The 100 Club knew its place in rock's pantheon of music history, but this didn't stop the venues staff from being friendly and eager to please.

Once the soundcheck was dispensed with, the band headed off in their separate directions. The brothers went shopping in Carnaby Street's more discerning clothes shops. Danny finally conceded he needed some sleep and headed back to the hotel with Johnny. Mikee decided he wanted to go and watch some real-live 'peep-shows' in Soho.

He had a seemingly insatiable appetite for porn, and would consume it like other people would watch a favourite film. His attitude had baffled the others who regarded pornography as very much a means to an end. Not Mikee, who considered himself very much the connoisseur.

The guestlist was dominated by record label staff and the band intended to finish their first tour on a high.

After a very welcome three hours' sleep, Johnny and Danny – shades on, smoking and simultaneously texting his girlfriend – headed back to the 100 Club.

"You enjoyed this then man?" Johnny asked rhetorically.

"Enjoyed it?" He almost spluttered with surprise. "It's been the best fuckin' time of my life!" Pausing slightly, which was unusual, he said, "It's err, a bit shit at home," clamming up before he revealed too much, "but this year, with the band, meeting Dee," lifting his shades up and meeting Johnny's eye, "It's been fucking amazing. I'll always owe you. Always."

As much as this sort of comment made him immensely proud, Johnny always deflected these comments back to the band themselves. "Your songs, Danny boy. All down to your songs. Always said that's what it's all about."

"Thanks man, but it's good having you about, y'know. We could have ended up with some right dick."

Tossing his back and laughing loudly, Johnny startled a group of passing tourists. "'I'll try and take that as a compliment!"

"You knew what I meant, I'm not the best with words at times."

"I knew," he said, patting him warmly on the back.

The brothers had made some suitably rock 'n' roll purchases from a Carnaby St boutique - Dominic had picked up a classic looking vintage black leather biker style jacket, with Jamie buying a black military style shirt. Very Strummer, Johnny had noted to himself.

The show went brilliantly - the band playing with a real swagger to their set.

Lonely Souls now demanded that you listen to their music. Jamie, flanked by Dominic and Danny, was bordering on mesmeric now. Meaning every impassioned lyric. Addressing the crowd with an assuredness that was the right side of cocky but maintaining an intelligence throughout. Wearing his new shirt tucked outside his black jeans, with his red scarf worn slightly looser than usual, he had everything. The songs, the voice, the looks – those cheekbones – and masses of charisma. It was never off the shelf attitude with him. He could rock and snarl but equally show a vulnerable sensitivity.

This was more than apparent on the new song that was now getting its first live airing.

As the opening chords of the track – working title 'Long Time Dead' – sounded, Jamie's vocal rasped the lines, *'Friend of mine, don't let me down, as you're a long time dead. A secret shouldn't be so hard to keep. Whispered promises*

when you're asleep. Empty vessels make most noise, don't let me down again...'
Ears pricked up. Any semblance of conversations stopped. Heads turned to watch. Jamie, eyes tightly closed, wringing every bit of raw emotion out of the song.

As ever, 'Salvation' blazed the set to its conclusion. A slightly extended outro from Dominic had Dan and Mikee having to improvise. To the untrained ear it would have been seamless, but the rhythm section had been caught on the hop – thinking the song was over. With a barely noticeable nod, they picked up on Dom's lead, propelling the groove onwards.

Swelling with pride, Jamie slung his guitar behind his back and grabbed the mic in both hands. "WE'RE LONELY SOULS. YOUR SALVATION RIGHT HERE, RIGHT FUCKIN' NOW…" Taking a deep breath, he said, "THANK YOU! YOU'LL BE SEEING US AGAIN SOON…"

***

The aftershow passed uneventfully. The record label people seemed genuinely excited by the prospect of working with Lonely Souls. And Jamie was intrigued by the suggestion of a dub remix treatment for 'Long Time Dead'.

Full of booze, high spirits and very probably some drugs, the band left the party and headed off in various directions. Johnny went straight back to the hotel having texted Claire early in the day. The downbeat reply was weighing heavily on his mind – akin to one of those late-night alcohol fuelled texts you regretted sending the morning after…

'I only ever wanted you. And a family with you. I will miss you. Bye Johnny'

It had felt even more finite than the email and as much as his life had moved on, he still cared at the hurt he had been responsible for.

Two exceptionally attractive young females that had been floating around the party had invited Danny and Mikee back to a hotel to carry the party on. They didn't need asking twice.

A writer from the NME had been courting Jamie's attention – going under the pen-name of Sally Valley. A pretty girl from South Wales with a crop of butterscotch hair and a tree trunk thick accent.

She had chosen the self-styled name after she grew fed up of being referred to as Sally from the Valleys. They had left to go for a late coffee and to further their 'chat' in Soho. Johnny had given Jamie a quick 'just be careful' word to the wise as they had left.

And as ever, Dominic had made a beeline for the most attractive girl at the party. And having kindly unburdened her of all her coke, was now suggesting that they return to his hotel room and order some 'room service booze'.

***

The morning after the night before, Johnny awoke and clicked his phone on. Rubbing at his bloodshot eyes, he went to the bathroom to relieve himself. A satisfied sigh and a quick glance in the bathroom mirror at his Papier Mache pallor. Not too bad considering. For now…

Returning to bed, he picked his now flashing phone up. A message from Danny. The words simply read. *'Been arrested. Not that bad. Will call later'*

Sitting up with a jolt, Johnny wandered what felony half of his band had become embroiled in…

***

Lighting four cigarettes and handing three out to Mikee and their escorts, Danny was in a particularly good mood, even for him. "Did you enjoy the gig then? We were on sick form tonight. We're gonna be huge. Just you watch. I'm gonna marry my girlfriend when we get to number one!"

"You got a girlfriend then," said the dark-haired girl of the two. "Oh, that is such a shame…"

"She won't mind me talking to you," Danny replied naively.

"I'll bear that in mind then, shall I darling?" she said with a distinct purr in her voice.

"Where we headed then?" Mikee asked, draping his arm loosely round the other girl's shoulder. A striking looking Asian girl, with long straight jet-black hair.

She replied that they should go back to a hotel near the flat they shared as the bar was open around the clock.

"Sounds a plan," said Danny, wolf-whistling down a passing black cab. "What's the name of the hotel?"

"Bayswater Hotel, near Hyde Park," she said, trying to make it sound as alluring as possible.

The cab dropped them off and they sat for an hour or so. Conversation was somewhat stilted as both girls seemed disappointed that neither of the band had any cocaine about them.

The Rock'N'The Roll. 'N That

Losing interest in proceedings and resolutely determined that he would behave himself on the last night of the tour, especially as he would be seeing Dee the following day, Danny had decided that they would call it a night. "I'm just going for a piss and then we'll knock it on the head, eh Kong?"

Replying with a slight air of disappointment, Mikee said, "Fine, D-Mo. Ready when you are."

Upon his way back from the toilet, Danny passed by a sparsely light function room. As he walked by an open door, his attention was drawn by two large piles of what looked like rubber.

Closer investigation revealed that they were in fact PVC padded 'Sumo suits'.

There had been a corporate event on the previous day - held by an investment bank - and the suits had been hired as part of the 'team-building' event.

"Right. We'll be off then girls. Nice meeting you both. And watch out for us. Lonely Souls, remember!"

All the time they were saying their goodbyes, Danny had been making furtive signals to Mikee.

The girls left in a frustrated huff. "What the fuck D-Mo. I was bang in there!"

"Yeah, yeah. Plenty more where they came from. But you need to check this out!"

Hurrying back to the room, they stood giddily in front of the unattended suits.

Picking the slightly smaller of the two up, Danny said, "Help me get into this Kong. We'll have a right laugh!"

Strapping themselves into the outfits, putting the all-important headwear on, they looked patently ridiculous, but this was too good an opportunity to miss.

"There's a fire-door over there, let's go and scrap in the car park. Like Fight Club, but big fat bastards!"

Giggling uncontrollably, Danny secured his padded Sumo helmet and squeezed his now vastly increased frame sideways through the now open fire door.

After a few 'belly charges', they had both expended a considerable amount of energy trying to right themselves.

As Mikee sat firmly on his PVC padded arse, his eyes alighted on a small canopy at the rear of the hotel. Under which were parked two unguarded mobility scooters. Most large London hotels now had them available for their guests use – being especially popular with the more sizeable transatlantic tourist.

"Look over there," Mikee cackled. "There's two of them electric car things!"

Waddling over as quickly as their oversized suits would allow, they realised they had hit the motherlode. Both vehicles had keys in their ignition and were not padlocked.

They struggled to mount the vehicles, but once onboard, found the suits moulded round the cars, allowing them to start them up and drive off into the night. A rock'n'roll edition of 'Mario Kart'…

Dropping off the kerb with a bump, the two Sumo racers headed off down Bayswater Road whooping and shouting their delight.

"Look. Kong, there's a sign for Kensington Palace over there. Let's storm the gates. We can cut through the park."

Cutting up on the pavement, they headed off at a dizzying top speed of ten mph in the general direction of Kensington Palace.

Unbeknown to them a passing police car had spotted the highly unusual sight and had radioed through a call to two on-foot PCs.

As the electric cars trundled through the park, Dan challenged his friend to a race. "See that sign for the Diana Memorial Park, first one there. FAST AND FURIOUS RULES!" he shouted, "ANYTHING FUCKIN' GOES!"

They proceeded to crash into each other, padded legs kicked out to gain any semblance of an advantage.

Upon reaching the pond, Mikee stood up in his seat, claiming victory. Danny having collided with a bin, causing him to lose valuable yards.

"AND THE WINNER IS MIKEE KING KONG LONG," he roared, his fat Sumo arms waving comically above him.

Seeing his opportunity – and not wanting to be second best – Danny pulled on the largely unresponsive throttle and crashed into the back of Mikee's scooter.

Both he and the car flung forward, the car reaching an immediate stop. And Mikee, slightly off balance, flopped over the top of the handlebars into the cold murky pond.

Danny's car also plunged down the shallow bank to meet its watery grave. Jumping off and straight onto the prone figure of Mikee, who was struggling to stand under the weight of the now water filled suit. As the two figures splashed and rolled around the pond, two torchlights proceeded to pick them out.

"What the fuck!" With a look of pure confusion on his face, the PC looked at his colleague and back to the two Sumo figures. "I really have no idea…"

Slowly it dawned on the comically brawling musicians that they had company. "Mikee. Look."

They flopped off each other, sat in the middle of the pond, the two electric cars now both partially submerged and resolutely written off.

Clearing his throat, the taller of the two officers addressed the situation, picking out the two now laughing hysterically figures with his torch. "Gentlemen. At least I presume you are. I cannot wait to hear your explanation…"

***

With no idea as to which police station his errant rhythm section had found themselves as temporary guests, Johnny had no choice but to sit and wait for news.

Sitting up in bed trawling through the internet idled away an hour or so. The band now had several clips posted on YouTube – all with very favourable comments alongside them.

At 9.30am his phone rang. Grabbing it from the bedside table he saw that it was Danny. "Mr Martin. You ringing up for a solicitor?"

A somewhat sheepish and tired D-Mo replied, "No, Johnny. We're heading back from Paddington Green police station. Spent the night in the cells…"

Interrupting him sharply, he said, "So what have you done then?"

"Can you meet us at reception to pay for a cab. We're both skint. I'll tell ya later. Long story."

"You both okay though?" Johnny finally asked.

"Yeah. Just cold and tired. And starving. You stand me a Mickey D's breakfast, boss?"

Johnny realised that if he was already thinking about Bacon McMuffins, they must be pretty much unscathed.

Having showered quickly, Johnny picked up his wallet and phone and went to greet the returning jailbirds.

Sitting in the reception sipping a strong white coffee, it wasn't long before the two bedraggled figures arrived at the hotel.

Giving Mikee thirty pounds for the cab fare, Johnny couldn't help but smile with relief when he saw they were both okay.

"Let me tell you what happened then Johnny. But can you crash me a tenner to get some breakfast before it finishes, only got fifteen minutes…"

Chapter 28

"Where the fuck did you find the suits then?" asked Dominic, wiping tears of laughter from his eyes. "And the mobility scooter things. Sick touch. Just wish I'd seen the pair of you!"

"It was freezin' in the cell! We got piss wet through in the pond and they didn't have dry clothes for us," Danny moaned, hunching his shoulders at the memory. "I'm gonna get a right load of fuckin' grief off Dee. I never texted her back. Loads of missed calls as well…"

Slightly more upbeat about the whole situation, and decidedly less ashamed, Mikee clapped his large hand on Danny's shoulder. "You should have seen the police trying to push us into the back of the van in the Fat Suits. D-Mo got stuck. I think I pissed myself watching them try and get him inside."

Johnny turned around in the driver's seat to directly address the two felons. "You two can pick up the tab for this little escapade. I'm fucked if I'm paying for this one. And I don't imagine the label will be too keen to pay for it," he said sternly.

"Or too pleased to hear about it," Jamie added.

"Alright Mr. fuckin' sensible," said Dominic with a dismissive shake of his head. "Anyhow bro. Did you fuck that cutie from the NME? I had my eye on her, but got waylaid elsewhere." Leaning over the seat, he tapped Danny on the shoulder. "Fuckin' gorgeous the girl I ended up with." At that his phone pinged and he glanced down. "That's her now. No doubt to say thanks for best night of her life," he added with a cocksure grin.

Sitting up-front in the passenger seat, Jamie was reading a newspaper he had picked up from the hotel reception. Looking over at Johnny, and with a quick shake of his head, "I didn't. Had a good chat with her. She's dead cool but thought better of it y'know."

"Yeah we don't want a bad review just cos you can't satisfy her bro. Leave it to me next time!"

"Dick," Jamie muttered under his breath.

Ruffling Jamie's crop of hair, he said, "I'm only messing, J. Don't get a strop on!"

As they finally joined the M1, Johnny mentally totted up the aftermath of the tour – in excess of thirty service stations visited - Tebay the runaway favourite. Some twenty accounted for sexual liaisons. A broken shower cubicle. A new set of tattoos. An arrested rhythm section. Two written off mobility scooters. Two possibly beyond repair PVC Sumo suits. And a tourbus that needed some serious fumigating.

Offset against the fact that the band now had their first tour under their belt, national radio exposure, a record label that had big plans for them and a live set that now fizzed with pure rock 'n' roll energy, it wasn't a bad trade off.

"We gonna stop off at a service station soon, boss? I'd murder a cig and a Maccies."

Life on the road, Johnny laughed to himself. It was brilliant. Fucking brilliant…

Chapter 29

"Hello. Err, can I speak to somebody about err, an operation please," Danny asked, his voice fraught with nervous anxiety.

"Hello sir. Certainly. And what type of procedure are you looking at please?"

"Err, what kind? Err. A nose-job. A nose job innit," he said hurriedly.

"Absolutely fine. Let me take some details from you, sir, and we can arrange for a private consultation. And your name please, sir?"

"Yeah, it's Danny. Daniel Martin. But everybody calls me D-Mo…"

***

"Oh boys! You don't have to knock," Cally said, her face lighting up. "I'm so pleased to see you both! Come in and tell me all about it!"

"Maybe not all though, eh Mum," Dominic said, kissing his mum warmly on both cheeks.

Laughing knowingly, Jamie hugged his mum, giving her the bunch of flowers he had held behind his back. "Yeah, maybe not quite everything…"

"They're lovely! Thank you both," Cally said, performing the time-honoured bouquet sniff.

"Let me put these in water and I'll stick the kettle on." Passing by Dominic, who was now helping himself to some sliced ham from the fridge, she said, "Ooh that's a nice jacket love. Is it new?"

Through a mouth full of partially chewed ham, he answered, "Got it in London. Looks alright, doesn't it?"

"Get you already. With your fancy London ways!" she laughed. "And don't eat all that, I was going to do sandwiches for you."

Once the kettle was boiled and the sandwiches prepared, they sat down in the front room. The small family reunited. The world of rock 'n' roll couldn't have been further away from the good-natured scene, Cally savouring every second as it was the longest she had ever gone without seeing her boys.

***

After a couple of sound nights' sleep and two days of detoxification, Johnny was refreshed and ready to deal with the weeks offerings.

Slouched over the breakfast bar sipping a fresh cup of coffee and eating wholemeal toast whilst trying not to get too many smudges on the highly polished granite work surface, Johnny sifted through his emails.

He opened one from Claire to finalise the signing over of the house. After the London gig, he had texted her back saying that he wished she'd 'come along for the ride'. The financial deceit still weighed heavily on him and it pained him how desperate she had looked when she realised that her dreams of a family had been put on hold.

The next email completely blew Johnny's mind. It was from Simon Moran – the director of SJM Promotions. Simon had recently masterminded a Stone Roses reunion for later that summer, and the reformation had prompted huge levels of hype and excitement. Rightly so. It was a momentous occasion that few ever saw coming such was the supposed levels of animosity and antipathy between the various band members.

Staring wide-eyed at his laptop screen, he readjusted the angle of the screen as if the light were playing tricks on his jaded eyes. Letting it sink in for a moment, Johnny whooped and slapped his hand on the granite surface.

'Hi Johnny, Hope the tour went well. Just to let you know that Ian Brown heard a couple of the band's tracks and loves them. Wants to have you on the bill at one of the Manchester shows. Works for me as I can see big things happening for them this year. Regards Simon'

This was utterly without doubt the greatest email he had ever read. The Roses. Supporting the fucking Roses. In Manchester. THE ROSES! He reached for his on-charge phone and texted Jamie, trying to project an air of calm but desperate to meet up face to face to share the amazing news –

'Jamie, very huge news. Fuck that. FUCKING HUGE FUCKING NEWS! Get over here with Dom soon as x'

Staring down at his phone's screen, he willed a quick response as he re-read the email. Unbelievable. Having seen them at Spike Island, he had always loved the band, and this was just beyond superlatives.

He had to wait an hour for a reply from Jamie –

'Can't wait. I'll be over with Dom in 10 x'

The apartment intercom buzzed, Johnny leaping over in two excited bounds. "Hiya J, I'll buzz you in."

The twins were clearly not long out of bed. Dominic was in jog pants and a hoodie, Jamie in jeans, hoodie and a grey woollen beanie hat, his hair tufting out at the sides.

Rubbing sleep from his eyes, Dom gratefully accepted the coffee Johnny had prepared in advance of their arrival.

"Take a seat," Johnny motioned to the black leather sofa with a dramatic sweep of his hand. The rush of excitement had resulted in him still being dressed in his bed attire of a sloppy T-shirt and boxer shorts.

"Looking good man," Jamie said with a glance at Johnny's unkempt appearance, "Ta for the coffee." Taking a sip, "Let's hear it."

"Okay." Johnny took a deep breath, and perched on the edge of one of the tall polished chrome stools that surrounded the breakfast bar. "Firstly, the label wants to do a remix of 'Long Time Dead'. They love the track and want The XX to do a dub style remix. Really dark and stripped back. Sounds like it could be cool as fuck."

With nods of their heads, the brothers were clearly impressed. "That's brilliant news Johnny, when we going to do this?"

"Soon as. The label wants you in the studio this week." Slapping his exposed thighs with the flat of his hands, he said, "BUT!" shaking his head in disbelief, "that's not all! I still can't get my head round this" unable to stifle a high-pitched laugh, "SJM have emailed me, y'know the promoter…"

"Yeah, yeah," interrupted Dom impatiently, placing his drained cup on the breakfast bar, ignoring the drinks coasters that were haphazardly scattered.

Johnny reflexively moved the mug across, to which Dominic pulled a peevish face." You know The Roses have reformed…"

"Obviously!" interjected Dom again.

"Anyhow. Ian likes the track he's heard and wants you to play on the bill with them in Manchester."

Leaping up from the stool, Johnny performed what can only be described as a deranged person's jig. "HOW FUCKIN' GOOD IS THAT?"

Staring at each other dumfounded, the twins were speechless.

"Well, say something," Johnny beseeched.

Wide-eyed with shock, Jamie floundered for words. "Fuck me. That's," he stammered, "That's mental. Fuckin' mental."

"I don't know what to say Johnny. Man, this is just fuckin' madness. It just gets better and better." A serious look then passed over his face. "You sure about this. It's not a mistake or anything?" Dominic said. Pulling his hair off his face, he shook his head in disbelief.

"No. No, look at the email. I read it about twenty times myself. You'll be low down on the bill, but still!"

Scanning the email, his finger tracing every line slowly, Dominic turned to his brother, "Fuck me J. We're gonna be playing with the Roses!"

"Beats working," Jamie laughed.

"You were a student," Dom teased. "Never done a proper day's work in yer life…"

Yawning exaggeratedly, Jamie play-punched his brother on his thigh. "I was working my mind Dominic, we can't all be the working-class hero."

"Brilliant gig though. We need to get a gig sorted for close to the date to warm-up and a couple after 'cos people will know the name then," Johnny said adamantly.

"I can't wait… And that XX remix. How cool is that!"

Chapter 30

The recording again took place at The Bunker and was all done and dusted in under four days. Jamie's vocal was extraordinary. The dark, menacing lyrics were sung with an anguish and undercurrent of pain, with the final chorus building to an impassioned almost Cobainesque scream. It was stunning – from Mikee's metronomic drumming, the rolling bassline that Dan painstakingly nailed and Dominic's slashes of angry spiky guitar.

Upon first listen, Johnny commented that it seemed a shame to let someone 'fuck about with perfection'. It would be an album track in its original form undoubtedly – but the Jamie XX remix would raise the band's profile considerably.

***

"Daniel. Language! You know I don't approve of cursing. From you or your father."

"Sorry Mam, but if all you had to worry about was a bit of swearing…"

"I know, I know. Your fathers had a bad time of it. He was dealt a bad hand for such a good man," she said, the gentle Irish lilt in her voice still prevalent despite having lived in Manchester for forty-five years.

"I can't believe you defend the cu—" shaking his head vigorously, "I can't believe you can make excuses for him. You've done nothing to deserve what he does. And neither have I. The fucker!" Raising his hands, he said, "Sorry Mam, it just gets me like that."

"I know Daniel, but we just have to live with it. Our cross to bear." Looking up at the crucifix affixed to the front wall room, Mrs Martin crossed herself and looked towards the skies for divine guidance.

"That's what I'm trying to tell you Mam. It doesn't have to fu— It doesn't have to be like that from now on. Things can be different. And soon I hope."

"How so?" A confused look passed across her kindly face.

"Look. I've not talked about it much, but you know I told that things were happening with the band."

"I know. Your friends who you love playing music with. Such nice boys, the twins."

"Yeah, them. Anyhow. We've got a record deal. I tried to tell you, but you didn't seem to get it."

"I did Daniel, I'm not that stupid. You went away to play your songs. I know."

"But that's not just it, Mam! We're gonna get paid to make a record. And if it sells loads, then…" His words trailed off as he looked for the right words. "Right! If we sell a shitload of records, then you can leave him. I'll get you yer own place. No more getting knocked about and plates of food thrown back at you. Leave him, leave the fucker and be happy again. I miss the happy you!"

"DANIEL! I've never heard anything so ridiculous!"

"NO MAM! You used to always be happy and smiling. You can be happy again. I can make that happen. Leave him. For you. No-one else. Fuckin' leave him…"

"I told you about your cursing, but with all this stupid talk as well."

"Mam. If. No. When I get the money, then you think about it again." Looking down at his hands, his breath coming in short pants, his big eyes filled with tears. "Please Mam, think about it…"

Cupping her sons face in her hands, she said, "Oh Daniel, Daniel, my baby. You're such a good boy. I always knew that you'd do something with your life," running a hand gently through his hair, "You go and be famous. Make me proud. But I can't leave your father. It's just not the done thing. I'm sorry."

"Think about it though. And promise me you won't say a word to him." He lowered his voice to a whisper even though it was just the two of them sat in the small front room, "And don't laugh, but I'm going to get me nose fixed."

"There's nothing wrong with your nose. It was the one God gave you."

"Yeah, well the beardy all-seeing twat was a bit generous with me, wasn't he?"

Struggling not to laugh, Mrs Martin's eyes glinted with a flashing spark of merriment. Composing herself suitably and again crossing herself, she said, "Jesus and all his carpenter friends! Please don't talk about Our Lord like that. And what's wrong with your nose? Just like your grandfather's."

Rubbing at the unwanted genetic hand me down, he said, "Yeah well, it's going. I'm going to get it sorted. Have a bit shaved off it. Plenty of it, so I won't miss it."

"Danny, you're a funny one. I can't stop you doing that. It'd be your money. And I won't say a word to your father. About any of this. I promise."

"Like he'd notice anyway. Just less for him to aim at…"

***

"It is him. Definitely."

"OI! DOMINOS! OI DOUBLE PEPPERONI! "

"Don't ignore us. Ya spotty twat. Double crust and don't I get a free garlic bread with my order?"

Putting his head down, Dominic pulled his hood up, quickening his pace. Shop frontages passing him by in a melange of offers and signage. He touched the volume up a notch on his phone to block out the redundant but still spiteful insults. He knew that everything had changed, but the anguish they had caused him for the whole of his schooldays still ran deep.

"It's no good covering them up, Dominoes! I can smell the pizza from here."

Hearing the cackling from his two abusers, his knuckles tightened round the handle of his guitar case.

"Weird shaped box to be delivering pizzas, eh Dominos," came the shout, which was now getting nearer as his two abusers had now crossed the road to confront him.

"DOMINOS! You not going to stop and say hello to yer old mates from school?"

Stopping and pulling down his hood, the white ear buds dropping on to his chest. His nostrils flaring as his breath quickened. "Alright lads. Did yer say something? I didn't hear ya."

He instantly recognised his two verbal assailants, Ryan Blake and Kyle Shott – aka keep tryin' Ryan, on account of his limited academic abilities. And imaginatively enough, Kyle Shit. Schoolkids and their cunning wit…

"Alright Dominos. What yer up to? Still playing in yer shit band?"

The band had played a gig – their only other pre-Johnny live performance had been at a school battle of the bands event. A shambolically bad PA had only made their Libertines/Arctics/Beatles covers sound even worse. Jamie's voice was just breaking and the whole unedifying ordeal had put them off playing live until 'they were right'.

Putting his guitar case down and staring at them individually, Dominic said, "Ryan and Kyle, isn't it? How could I forget. Real shame we never kept in touch," bitter malevolence lacing his words.

The Rock'N'The Roll. 'N That

"Eh, don't be so fuckin' touchy. We're only having a bit of bantz!" said Ryan, his right hand shoved down the front of his acid wash Voi jeans.

"Hilarious," muttered Dominic. "Anyway. What you two up to?" His lips pursed like a twist of barbed wire.

"Not working. Y'know how it is. But we knock a bit of weed out around the estate. Pays for a night out in town."

"Remind me to join you some time," Dominic sneered.

"Fuckin' lose the attitude, Dominos!" snapped Kyle, leaning his face into Dominics.

Laughing manically, Ryan tugged at the hem of his friend's snide Ed Hardy T-shirt. "'Don't go too close, you'll catch his spots!"

"Eww! Fuck, forgot about that," he said, taking a step back, "cunt always thought he was better than the rest of us even when he had his full-on pizza face!"

"I'll be off then. Ryan. Kyle. Great to see yer both doing so well," said Dom, relieved that the busy high street had afforded him some security from more than mere verbal's. Pointing to his guitar case as he walked off, he added, "And this? Yeah. It's gonna make me my fortune, YOU FUCKIN' PAIR OF LOSERS!"

Dashing across the road at a convenient break in the traffic, Dominic headed off as quickly as he could. The insults fresh in his ears, a reminder of what was, the case clutched in his hand very much what was now.

***

"'Bout 1pm, yeah, we'll see you in there."

"Ah that's really good of you Jamie. I've not been there before," said Cal as she admired her son's new apartment. A warehouse conversion nestling proudly amidst the veneer of shiny sterile boxes that seemed to sprout up overnight like field mushrooms.

"It's got a great view over the canal as well. I still miss you both though. It's just so quiet now…"

"I know, but you knew we'd move out at some point and everything happening with the band so quickly, y'know," Jamie said as he pulled his mum into his side.

She sighed as she looked across the Manchester skyline. The infamous ship canal now reincarnated as a 'water aspect'. The canal side Victorian warehouses now occupied by the new 'digital industry' – having none of the tangibility of bygone days when cotton was the currency in the North.

Jamie stood in his bedroom selecting a coat from his wardrobe. The new apartment afforded him the privacy that he had long yearned for. A single mum before single mums were really 'a thing'. Money had always been tight. But together they had managed. If things went to plan with the band then he would be able to help her out financially, give her that breathing room that she'd never experienced.

As they made their way down the canal towpath, Cally took Jamie's hand and squeezed it. "I always knew you'd make it with the band. I just never knew how it'd feel when it did. Do you know what I'm trying to say?"

"Not really. But it doesn't matter. None of us can say where this is going to go. But we'll always be here for you. Me and Dom."

"I know. Thank you for saying it. Where is Dominic today? It would have been lovely if he could have joined us," she said, swinging Jamie's arm as carefree as the ducks that passed them by in their haphazard flotilla.

"He popped in to see me before. He was off into town to get one of his guitars repaired. It took a bit of a battering on tour and you know how precious over them he is! He said he'd meet us later."

"Quite right too!" said Cally indignantly. "Cost me a fortune to buy you both your first guitars!"

Walking in silence for a few minutes, the distant rumble of traffic not enough to break their tranquillity.

"Don't say anything to Johnny, but he split up with his partner 'cos he'd not told her about the band. And that he spent a load of money on us." He glanced at his mum for a reaction. "He told me when we were on tour, seemed like he wanted to get it off his chest. Said there was a load of other stuff, but this tipped things over the edge."

"Oh, he should have told her really. But we don't know the full story I suppose." Cally frowned slightly. "He's okay, isn't he?"

"He seems happy working with us. It's what he wanted. And especially as things are going so well. He was so made up about the Roses support slot. He loves them. Saw them back in the day. Spike Island gig and everything," he said enthusiastically.

"I don't know why they're bothering. It's all about money," Cally said flatly. "I don't know what all the fuss is about," she added dismissively.

"Don't let Johnny hear you say that! He can't wait for the gig."

"I might not even bother. All those people trying to recreate their youth. All a bit sad if you ask me."

"Come on Mum! You'll have to come along," Jamie said. Shocked that she would even consider not attending what would be their biggest gig to date by far.

Trying to sound a little more positive, she said, "People should be looking for new bands. Like you. Not looking backwards."

Arriving at El Rincon, a well-kept secret on a Manchester back street, they were greeted by Johnny, mobile phone glued to his ear. He was balancing with his heels on the edge of the kerb, every so often losing his balance and hopping back up only to perform the odd little performance again.

Ending the call and putting the phone into the inside pocket of his red Harrington style jacket. "Right. That's that sorted! Great to see you both." Kissing Cal on both cheeks, "Happy Birthday! And how are you then? You loving it being the mum of England's soon to be favourite rock stars?"

"Of course! I taught them everything they know!" she laughed, that little soft infectious laugh. The almost coquettish lowering of her head.

"Nice threads man," said Jamie, hugging Johnny.

"Only problem with living in town. Nip out to get some food shopping and come back with a two hundred quid coat! Glad you like it. Wasn't sure at first. But fuck it. Got to look the part when you're the manager of a shit hot rock band!"

Anyhow, let's go in. I've got a table booked for one o'clock. Some nice tapas and afternoon drinking. Sound good?"

"I know it's my birthday, but I've got work tomorrow. Not like you two," said Cal as they descended the dimly lit stairwell.

A perfectly enjoyable meal was accompanied by several bottles of wine. They were joined by Dominic who seemed to be bristling about something as he barely spoke for the first hour, only loosening up after he had polished off a full bottle of expensive red wine.

Cally was charm personified as she regaled innocent tales of the twins' childhood. Teaching them both to play the piano whilst they sat on her knee. Taking them carol singing dressed as Christmas elves. And buying them both acoustic guitars on their thirteenth birthdays.

The boys had a lot to thank their mum for as far as their musical development was concerned, and clearly their good looks were a genetic hand-me down. On more than one occasion, Johnny caught himself staring at her. She had the most captivating tinkling laugh, which caused her to look down, almost in embarrassment that she was enjoying herself. She had a long slender neck and a beautiful face, the cheekbones sharp before they merged with her lagoon blue eyes.

At 6.30pm, she announced that she was feeling more than a little drunk and wanted to curtail the evening before she was any the worse for wear. Johnny signalled the waiter to ring a taxi and the twins saw her safely to her carriage.

The drinking resumed in a delightfully old-fashioned pub, The Deansgate, which boasted a wonderful first floor smoking terrace.

"At the start of May you're booked into the Limehouse in London to record the album. A month or so's rehearsals. Get things tight as you like. Then recording a video straight after that, only two or three days, but means we're busy for the next couple of months. Album is pencilled in for a late September release to follow up the first single which will be out at the start of that month."

Both brothers nodded, taking in the carefully planned schedule. "All good," said Dominic, whose mood had now perked up at the mention of the recording. "Yeah, cheers Johnny. It's gonna be wicked. I just can't imagine seeing our first album in the shops. Unbelievable!"

***

"What the fuck's happened to you?" Mikee exclaimed, as Danny walked into the rehearsal room with a large white plaster over his nose and his sunglasses firmly in place.

Taking the glasses off very gingerly, he revealed two extraordinary black eyes and a thick white plaster across the bridge of his newly reconstructed nose.

"I look like a panda, don't I?" he said, laughing at his own joke. "Did you know that the male panda does a handstand when it's ready to breed. To let the female panda know he's got the horn. How funny is that? A panda doing a handstand with a massive fur boner! I heard it on that IQ show."

Johnny had to check himself not to correct Danny's malapropism.

"Fuck the nature lesson! What's happened to you, D-Mo?" Dominic asked, putting his guitar down and stepping towards Danny, for closer inspection. Not that any was required.

"You've had that nose job haven't you," said Jamie softly, realising that now was not the time for inter-band piss taking.

Sitting down on the up-turned beer crate, which was Johnny's usual perch, he said, "I had to get it done now. We're gonna be so busy for the rest of the year, and people'd suss if I had it done after we've done our video and that." Looking up at the band through bruised eyes, he said, "Don't rip the piss. You don't know what it's been like with this massive hooter all my life." Looking at Jamie and Dominic, "Especially you two pretty boys. The girls fuckin' love you…"

"Good on yer D-Mo. If it makes you happy," said Dominic, as he pinched at his own nose.

"Thanks man, and just between us eh?"

Putting a placating hand on his shoulder, Dom said, "Course man, you know that."

Chapter 31

"Room 277 J. I've got your passes and I booked a taxi for your mum. Think all the rooms are on the same floor," said Johnny as he looked out of the window of his hotel suite in The Lowry.

"Cheers Johnny. I'll grab them off you in five," said Jamie as he checked and double checked his backpack that contained his on-stage clothing.

Having handed over the passes, Johnny agreed to meet the band at 3pm, planning to get a cab across town with Cally.

Manchester was at its finest when hosting big events. And none came bigger than the first of three-hometown reunion shows by four of the City's favourite sons – The Stone Roses.

Months of speculation had born fruition when a perfectly staged press conference announced what the world had been waiting for. The Roses would be back. The original line-up would once again play live.

And although those that had bagged a ticket might be longer in the tooth, greyer at the temple, shinier of pate, and thicker round the midriff, none of this mattered. All-dayers were planned. 'Reni' hats dusted down. Monkey walks resurrected. Babysitters booked. The Roses were back, man.

And amidst all of this, four young men who weren't even born when Spike Island was a happening were now booked to play bottom of the bill to this most legendary of Manc bands. Just looking at the promotional posters featuring the band's name – albeit in small letters – had got Johnny as excited as he could remember. His band. Supporting The fucking Roses.

He'd loved being able to drop this in casually with Mark and Chris who were utterly gobsmacked – but equally desperate to secure guestlist places.

"I'll see what I can do, fellas," he'd casually said, adding a gleeful and boastful, "Told you they'd crack it bigtime!"

***

"Hi Johnny, is that you? it's Cally."

It was quite an endearing little quirk that whenever Cal called anybody from her mobile, she always asked for confirmation as to who it was, even though she had dialled the number from her mobile phone's memory.

"Hiya, yes it's me. You okay? Got your room key okay?"

The phone went silent for a moment. "Hmm. About my room. It's lovely, but it's in between Jamie and Dominic's. Now I know boys will be boys…"

"Yes. No pictures necessary! We can switch rooms. No problem. I think I've got some earplugs with me."

"Ah thanks Johnny, I'll be right across. What number did you say you were in?"

"277. Just across the corridor."

With the room switch done, they jumped into a taxi and headed off to the gig. Cally looked amazing in a brown leather jacket with a fur trimmed collar, tight black jeans and distressed leather calf-length biker boots. She was also wearing a pair of large rimmed black shades. All exceptionally rock 'n' roll and Johnny was suitably impressed.

"You look great! And the shades. Nice touch."

Cally nodded her head slightly. "Thought I'd make an effort," she replied quietly.

In his state of heightened excitement, Johnny was oblivious to Cally's subdued demeanour as he proceeded to talk ten to the dozen as they made the short trip to Prestwich.

Arriving at the park, they were hurried through the VIP gate, and headed for the hospitality area.

***

"You okay?" said Jamie as he again arranged the red scarf under his black leather jacket.

Danny had been pacing round in tight circles, drawing heavily on cigarettes. "I'm fuckin' shittin' it. Absolutely shittin' it! Have you seen how many people are out there?"

With Mikee and Dominic also strangely mute, nerves were threatening to get the better of the band.

Feeling that a dose of calm was called for, Johnny beckoned the band to huddle round him. "Okay lads. You're here 'cos Ian Brown likes your tunes. Doesn't get much better than that." Looking at each member of the band in turn, he said, "I know, and you know that every fucker out there is only here to see The Roses. There's no pressure. I promise you."

Squeezing Danny by the shoulder, given that he seemed to be in some sort of a trance, he added, "Biggest cliché in the world but just enjoy it. It's a home crowd. Drop in that you're local boys and you'll be right. I promise you!"

Back slaps, hugs and street handshakes were exchanged, deep breaths taken and at 5pm the band took to the stage.

Adjusting the mic stand slightly, with his guitar slung round his back, Jamie looked at the plethora of Madchester revivalists, and with a facade of bravado, shouted, "EVENING MANCHESTER!"

A smattering of applause heartened Jamie, as he tried to avoid looking to the horizon of the crowd. "Buses were murder getting here tonight!" A slight ripple of laughter played across the first few rows of the crowd. Smiling to himself, he said, "WE KNOW THE REASON WHY YOU'RE HERE!" And with perfect timing, Mikee hit the unmistakeable opening skittering drum groove to 'Fools Gold'. A not un-sizeable roar was emitted from the cagoule-clad crowd. "ANYWAY. WE'RE LONELY SOULS AND YOU'LL JUST HAVE TO MAKE DO WITH US FOR NOW!"

Johnny stood, stage right, approximately fifty yards back allowing him a view of them all. His innate pride swelling by the second, gulping back his emotion, he put his arms round his still disbelieving friends. "My fuckin' band that I saw that night. SUPPORTING THE ROSES! Doesn't get much better than this!"

Their set went past in a thirty-minute blur. Danny felt like he had held his breath for the entire time, and was still sat in silence some twenty minutes later.

"I felt tiny out there," whistled Dominic, as he leant back on their dressing room wall.

Having sought immediate sanctuary after their set, the band were slowly composing themselves.

"Went okay," said Jamie as he put his guitar in its case. As ever the ritual of his scarf being placed at the bottom of the case was strictly adhered to. "I'm happy with that." Thumbing in the direction of the stage, he said, "That lot are going to go fuckin' mental when The Roses finally come on. Absolutely fuckin' mental!"

The Rock 'N' The Roll. 'N That

"You seen 'em yet?" Mikee asked.

"Nah, no sign," said Dominic, "Hopefully we'll get to meet 'em later, but wouldn't be surprise if we don't. That hospitality area will be rammed later."

"Anyhow, we've done our bit. We can just look forward to seeing them now…" sighed Jamie, his relief palpable.

***

At just after 9pm, the anticipation in the crowd reached overload as the stage lights shone on the four figures that strutted on to the stage.

They were back.

And Manchester loved them for it. The crowd unifying as Mani's iconic bassline opened 'I Wanna be Adored'.

Ian Brown stood, staring out at the delirious crowd. King Monkey resplendent in a black Adidas bomber jacket, low-slung jeans and white T-shirt. Soaking it all up. Mainlining the crowd's energy into their performance. It was incredible. Every note was sung back at them. It really was what the world was waiting for. Squire stood aloof as ever, dressed to casually kill in full-on rock star red tartan suit jacket, effortlessly coaxing notes and chords from his sunburst splashed Gibson Les Paul.

***

Cally stumbled forward as the crowd surged tidally – the chorus rolling epically over them.

Regaining her balance as Johnny's hand steadied her, she turned around, an incredibly serious look on her face. "I can't do this," she whispered.

Having been unable to hear exactly what she had said, and unaware of her anguish, Johnny bent down to allow her to repeat herself. "Sorry Cally, it's amazing isn't it! What did you say?"

"I'm sorry Johnny I can't do this. I'm so sorry," she said with a barely detectable choked sob in her voice, a tear rolled down her cheek from under her dark glasses.

Carefully removing her glasses as the crowd around them jostled and celebrated the end of their returning heroes' opening track, Johnny looked down at Cally's bloodshot tear-soaked eyes.

"What's wrong?" he said, placing a consoling hand on her arm.

"I'm sorry. But he's here. I know he's here…"

With that Cally broke free from Johnny and headed off to the quiet safety of the now abandoned hospitality area.

Immediately giving pursuit, he caught up with her just as she was flashing her pass at the lone security guard.

Sitting down at a freshly cleared and cleaned table, Cally put her head in her hands and sobbed. A low, uncontrollable and wretched sob.

Bewildered by her reaction, Johnny attempted to muster up some consolatory words.

"Hey, hey. What's wrong?" He patted her gently on her shoulder, before realising that it felt like the actions of someone congratulating a Crufts winner.

After what felt like several minutes of crying and shaking, Cally looked up, her face streamed with mascara, loose strands of hair stuck to her face. "I can't tell you Johnny. I can't. I shouldn't have come. I have to go. I know he's here."

"I don't understand. Who's here?"

She sobbed loudly again. "Please Johnny, leave me alone. I can't tell you. I can't," she said, shaking her head violently from side to side. "I'm going back to the hotel. I've got to go…"

Still utterly at a loss as to what was causing her so much distress, he said, "I'm not leaving you like this. I can't." With a selfless gesture, but one tinged with a slight regret, he added, "Come on. Let's go back to the hotel. We'll get a drink and you can talk. If you want to."

Pulling Cally into his side, they headed for the exit. A lone couple, beating a retreat two hours ahead of the other 74,998.

A taxi was quickly flagged down and the fifteen-minute journey back to Manchester made in total silence, aside from the odd sniffle and blow of Cally's nose.

***

"We'll go to your room, it's bigger than mine, and we'll get drinks sent up," he said, a hushed tone to his voice as they made their way through the reception.

"I don't know. I just want to be left alone," Cally said, her sunglasses firmly in place despite the advancing hour.

"It's up to you, but it might help you—"

"If I tell you what's wrong—" she breathed out heavily, "If I tell you. Everything changes. Everything."

As much as Johnny couldn't claim to know her incredibly well, he knew enough to know that Cally wasn't prone to unnecessary dramatics.

With a strong resolve in her voice. "One drink."

They rode the lift to their floor and entered what was now Cally's hotel suite without exchanging a word.

Sitting on a small two-seater settee, still in her leather jacket and boots, Cally pulled her feet up underneath her. "I suppose I better start at the beginning."

Sipping from his glass, Johnny pursed his lips and fell silent.

Speaking in a quiet but determined whisper, she began. "Like you, I went to Spike Island. Seems a lifetime ago now." Tears again stung her eyes. "I wanted a brilliant time. For it to be the perfect day. We met some boys. Had a drink and watched the show. It was amazing."

She was breathing in short, controlled movements.

"And then it wasn't."

Meeting Johnny's increasingly concerned gaze. "We got a lift back from them. In a camper van." Anger now replaced the tears in her eyes. "And I was raped. Raped whilst my best friend in the whole world sat right in front of me. And she didn't know a thing." In slow monotone Cally repeated the fateful words, "I was raped in front of my best friend."

***

"Wake up! Come on gorgeous. There's a spliff and I've got a bottle of vodka stashed. That'll see you right." Davey shook her leg again, a bit more forcibly this time. Cal was drifting in and out of consciousness, wishing for sleep to replace the waves of nausea that consumed her.

Davey's hand reached for the waist band of her jeans and he slowly undid the top button and as carefully as possible pulled the zip down to reveal a pair of powder pink coloured knickers, embroidered with tiny yellow flowers along the waistband. Pulling the jeans down to her ankles, Davey glanced over his shoulder to ensure that he was not being observed. The garish mustard coloured curtains were pulled across the rear of the driver's compartment, giving him all the privacy he needed.

Cally lay with her head towards the rear of the camper van, face unseen by her fellow passengers. Davey loomed over her with his intent now starting to bulge under the waist band of his flared jeans. He heard her murmur as he slid her knickers down. Gazing upon the exposed wisps of pubic hair. Wetting his finger, he slowly but forcefully inserted it into Cal's exposed vagina. Pulling down his jeans and 'hilarious' Homer

Simpson boxer shorts, Davey positioned himself over the unwilling body beneath him and pushed his decidedly average sized cock into her. A squealed gasp heard only by Davey was quickly smothered as he slapped his hand across her mouth. Widening eyes and a frenzied shake of her head was all she could manage as Davey thrust forward, entering her as she tried in vain to buck against his unwanted trespass.

Please no. Not like this. I liked him, but I don't want this. Not like this. Not today. He's been so nice to me. But stop. PLEASE. PLEASE. PLEASE. PLEASE FUCKING STOP. You're really hurting me. You're hurting me so much. I'll scream and then he'll stop. FUCKING STOP.

Trying to scream. But the calloused fingers were clamped too tightly.

At least be over soon. Finish, you horrible selfish bastard. You horrible selfish raping bastard. Finish…

At 5ft 7 and a delicate size 8 – indistinguishable under her baggy garb – any resistance would have been nigh on impossible against someone almost twice her weight. The cracked vinyl on the roof forming cobwebs, mazes and spirals through her stinging tears.

With her right arm pinned against the side of the van and her sexual assailant holding her left arm down at an increasingly painful angle, she couldn't look up. Now screwing her eyes shut, but feeling they'd burst under the weight of tears. Unable to open her eyes and witness his stolen pleasure.

As the music on the tape player sped up, Davey's rough thrusting and grunting increased. His sour breath hot on her neck. A trail of spit was hanging from his gurning mouth, forming a viscous chandelier with her hair.

White noise pierced her very thinking. This was all she could hear as Davey poured himself into her. Clamping down on her mouth as he came inside her.

***

"Cally… I just don't know what to say," he said, aware of the pathetic inadequacy of his words.

"And have you not guessed the rest yet? You not worked out the dates? The years?" she said, almost goading him.

He shook his head blankly, unable to instantly work out the obvious correlation.

"Jamie and Dominic. My two boys. My beautiful babies. Who I love more than anything in the world. Can you understand now…"

After the shock of the initial revelation had started to sink in, Cally went on to tell Johnny that the pregnancy had led to her parents virtually disowning her – instigated unequivocally by her father.

That one dreadful unsolicited event could have had such long-lasting ramifications for her was stunning.

Johnny sat in silence. The disclosure had rendered him mute. The fact that these words had never been spoken to a soul before compounded their emotional impact.

Putting his empty glass down, he sat beside Cally, placing a hand gently on her cheek and tenderly wiping a tear stain away. Taking her slightly trembling hands in his, he pulled her to him, hugging her tightly into him.

Letting out a few gentle sobs, Cally returned his embrace, her head rested on his shoulder, her now unkempt hair spilling over him. After a few moments, they parted. Johnny, still struggling for words, blew his cheeks out and rubbed a hand through his hair.

Breaking the silence, her voice once again calm, she said, "Now you know. The terrible truth…"

Pulling air quote gestures caused Johnny to smile ruefully.

"I love them. But you can see the price I paid? I was all alone with them. A nineteen-year-old girl expecting twins. All alone." Reaching for her glass and taking a big gulp, she said, "I shouldn't have come tonight. Do you now realise why I was so reluctant? Why I wasn't excited for the boys? I should have loved every second of today for them…"

She drained the remaining third of her glass. "That bastard. That selfish bastard would have been there tonight. I could just feel it…"

"Cally. I don't know what to say." Having collected a further bottle of red wine from room service, he was now slowly pacing the suite with a concerned look etched on his face. "I can see why you had to leave. Totally."

The right words just weren't forthcoming. Sitting back down in the padded armchair, as he realised his pacing wasn't helping the situation, he said, "You said it changes everything. It doesn't." Narrowing his eyes slightly, he attempted to judge her reaction. "It was a terrible, terrible thing that happened to you. But you have the boys—"

"Which can feel like a constant reminder!" she snapped back. "I didn't tell my parents that I'd been raped, I thought that would make them even more ashamed of me…" Bowing her head, she let out an exasperated grimace.

"Today just bought it all flooding back for me. I tried to put a brave face on for the boys. For you. But it just made everything feel so raw all over again…"

Blurting out his next question slightly clumsier than he had hoped, he asked, "And what about your mum and dad? They've had next to nothing to do with you in all those years?"

"Pretty much," she replied bluntly. "They gave me some money to rent a house and that was it. Dad was high up in the Law Society and big at the church. Catholic. As if you couldn't guess. Said I'd bought shame on the family." Her voice resonated with a mixture of bitter anger and regret.

Swinging her feet round from underneath her, she said, "There's nothing more to say." With a slight shake of her head, "I'm surprised. I've never talked about this before. To anyone…"

At a loss for the appropriate words, Johnny said, "Cally, I'll never say a word about this. And I'm glad you felt you could talk to me." Wincing inwardly at how trite he felt his words sounded, he reached for his glass to mask their inadequacy.

Tears flooded down her face. Sobs wracked throughout her body. The deep aching hurt that was the horror she had endured all those years ago. And her boys. A constant living breathing reminder of the heinous trespass.

"I feel drained." Putting her face in her hands, Cally screamed. A muffled, "FUUCCKKK," startled Johnny.

"I'm not the best of listeners as a rule and I don't have anything to say that'd even touch the sides…" said Johnny plaintively. Tugging at his earlobe as if this would elicit him to produce some words of wisdom.

"You listened and didn't say anything stupid. That's pretty good in my book," said Cally with a rueful smile. "I'm exhausted after all that," she added whilst stifling a yawn.

Her phone pinged, and a startled look passed briefly across her face – a text from Jamie asking where they were. She whisked back her response.

'*Hi Jamie, loved the show, but felt bit unwell and didn't like all the crowds of people. Johnny brought me back to hotel. Love you both xx*'

The conversation moved on to the boys' childhood days, and her hopes and worries for their future history. Having 'held on' as long as possible whilst Cally poured out her anguish, Johnny went to the bathroom.

Returning, he said, "I'm gonna head back. If you're okay with th—" Johnny looked towards Cally, who was now curled up, her head resting on two plump cushions. Fast asleep.

Fetching an over blanket from the wardrobe, Johnny removed her clumpy footwear and wrapped the rug over her.

Picking up her unfinished glass, he sat back down in the armchair. Two sips later, he was head lolling to one side and asleep.

***

They woke with a start as the hotel room telephone rang. Johnny sat up, bleary-eyed, and tried to acclimatise himself to the unfamiliar surroundings.

Cally, now in bed, pulled the bedsheets around her as she sat up.

Picking up the receiver, she said, "Hello?" Shaking her head slightly. "Hello?"

Putting the phone down. "No-one there. I'm sure hotels do that on purpose just to wake you up."

As Johnny made his way to the bathroom. "Yeah, they're called early-morning wake up calls…"

"Very funny aren't we!"

As he entered the bathroom, Johnny tried to gauge his hangover. He was not much of a red wine drinker, and the thick end of two bottles had left him feeling decidedly rough. And the toils of a middle-aged hangover could take some shifting.

"You okay?" he asked, having finished his ablutions.

"I woke up on the sofa and got into bed. You were snoring like Godzilla, so I left you to it!"

"I meant after, y'know…" Johnny said.

"You were right. Nothing has changed. Other than someone now knows 'the truth'. I'm sorry to have dragged you away from the gig…"

Incredulously, he said, "No apologies!" And with comedic timing added, "Anyway. I can go tonight. And tomorrow.…"

"We could fall out. Quickly."

"I'm glad I could be there for you." He waved his goodbye. "I'll see you soon."

Opening his own hotel room door, he blew his cheeks out and raised his eyebrows. *That came straight out of the left field*, he thought. Flopping on to his own pristine bed, he squinted at the breakfast room service menu and then decided against as he felt the onset of his hangover – which needed shifting in order that he could resume his 'Squire worshipping' that evening.

***

"She said yes!" said Danny excitedly. "I proposed when the fireworks were going off after 'Resurrection' had finished!"

"That's a big commitment man! Y'know. I'm pleased for you and that, but you've not been together long," said Dominic, as they shared a taxi across Manchester. Neither had slept at all. A particularly lively aftershow had seen to that. Their hotel rooms had barely been touched, having been a luxury indulgence from Johnny to mark the occasion.

"You could sound a bit more pleased for me!" said Danny, seemingly hurt by Dominic's cynicism.

"Come on D-Mo, I am pleased, just a little shocked, that's all. Y'know. We're just starting out as a proper band. It's all ahead of us, man. And you're tying yourself down."

"But I love her!" Danny protested.

"Yeah, of course. And that's a good thing. But come on. You weren't exactly a good boy on tour," said Dominic, feeling that his counselling skills were suitably impressive.

"It's different now I've proposed to Dee. She trusts me," Danny replied defensively.

"Anywhere here mate," Dominic indicated to the cab driver. "You got this D-Mo?"

"Yeah, yeah. And ta for your wise words," he said slumped back into the taxi's freshly valeted seat.

"Laters D-Mo! Blinding evening. And congratulations man!" said Dominic as he leapt from the taxi.

Chapter 32

Following the Roses concert and a totally sold out local show, aside from the filming of the video to promote the first single, they would have six weeks off.

'Calm before the storm', Johnny had described it as.

However, the suspense of receiving hard copies of the album was killing them. Especially Danny.

He could not wait to see it for himself. No matter how many times he had copies of the artwork emailed to him or heard the final mix, he failed to accept that it was 'real'.

Now living with his fiancée, his world had changed immeasurably. Weekly trips to the supermarket were now the norm.

'I don't like them', 'they make me gag', and 'make sure we get more ketchup' were his stock-in-trade lines.

The concept of buying food that didn't come in a polystyrene box slathered in spicy condiments and low in nutritional value had previously been alien to him, but Dee, a resolute gym bunny and health-food fanatic was slowly but surely educating him in to a culinary world away from e-numbers and additives.

"If you steam them rather than boil them, they're lovely. Until you insist on slapping ketchup all over them!" she smiled at Danny, as he pushed the trolley begrudgingly round the fruit and veg section. "But we're getting there aren't we!"

Mustering as much enthusiasm as he could, he placed a large clump of broccoli into the trolley. A little too much domestic bliss had left him pining for his bandmates and the subsequent video shoot.

***

The video was to be recorded by a hip young filmmaker by the name of Barney Mason. A little 'too London' for Johnny – an aside to Dom that 'he'd get twatted if he went out in Manchester dressed like that' had afforded much amusement.

The Rock 'N' The Roll. 'N That

Said 'too London' garb consisted of lilac coloured skinny jeans worn rolled up three inches above his ankle, a pink T-shirt with a picture of Beethoven on the front, and glasses with thick white frames, topped off with a tartan golf-style flat cap.

Barney was never seen without a small video camera and recorded the band as they had prepared themselves for the shoot. Capturing their silent rituals, as they set their equipment up, exchanged opinions, and laughed at their constant piss-taking.

When the final edit was 'a fackin' wrap', the band were delighted with both the video and the short fifteen-minute film that Barney had edited from the captured footage. It was a brilliant introduction to the band. The short interviews providing insights into the band's individual personalities – Jamie's focussed ambition. Dominic's desire to be a part of rock 'n' roll's rich heritage. Dan's unbridled enthusiasm and lust for his new life. And Mikee. He just wanted to be the best drummer of his generation and complete his tattoo collection as soon as time/money and his pain threshold allowed.

"I love the short film. We should put that out as an extra on the album. It's really fuckin' cool. Captures what you're all about perfectly," said Johnny.

"Totally," said Jamie, "I loved working with him, hope we can do more with him."

"On the road documentary sort of thing," suggested Johnny.

"I don't know about that. The way the others carry on. It'll be full on Spinal Tap by the time of the second album!" laughed Jamie.

"They're just enjoying all that being in a band brings, J. I know you always come across as the 'serious one'. A band needs different personalities," said Johnny as he clicked his laptop from the film of the band back to his emails.

Jamie helped himself to another beer from the apartment's spacious refrigerator. "It feels like it's all in place now. Single release, video, album, tour, press. It's odd having everything mapped out for us y'know."

"You must be pleased though? People getting to hear your songs, buy them!"

"Or nick 'em. Every fucker I know seems to rip everything off the internet!" grumbled Jamie.

"You sound like an old bastard just like me!" said Johnny.

"I'm serious man! I've never ripped anything off the internet. Pisses me off when Dom and Mikee are always talking about tunes and films they've fuckin' nicked," said Jamie with a serious frown on his face.

"Record label will love you! But I agree man," said Johnny draining his bottle of Becks.

"I'm not bothered about being a multi-millionaire. I want to make money, but I don't think you should graft over something and just give it away."

Johnny looked over at Jamie, who was stood in front of the large apartment window, staring across the city's twinkling evening skyline. "You're gonna have to deal with the other side of things, J. It's not going to be just the songs and the shows. There's a ton of other shit that nobody can put into a neat schedule and plan for you. It worries me at times y'know."

"I'll be fine man, suppose it's just fear of the unknown," said Jamie as he accepted another beer from Johnny. "It's like when I talk to Dom, he just can't wait for all the fuckin' madness. It's like he feels he needs to give it the big rock star act."

He cocked his head to one side and stuck his bottom lip out slightly. "But that's what makes you so different! And people will want that. They want to see someone who is doing something they can only dream of and see that they are loving every fuckin' minute of if it!" said Johnny as he leant back on the breakfast bar.

"You're right, and I know why he's like that, but—"

"But nothing!" Johnny interjected. "Black and white. Light and shade. Yin and yang. It fuckin' works perfectly Jamie. Perfectly. Can't you see that?"

"I can," he said wistfully.

"Listen, I've got an early start tomorrow. Meeting with the label. Their bean counters. Sounds a right laugh. I'm on the early train so I'm gonna knock it on the head."

"Okay man. Enjoyed this. Nice chilled out chat," said Jamie polishing off the last of his beer.

As they hugged out their farewell, Jamie went to say something then hesitated.

"See ya soon J," said Johnny, stifling an ill-mannered yawn.

"And you. Enjoy that London. Oh, and tell 'em how made up with the video and film we are," he said, tapping his nose with a smile, "Tell 'em money well spent…"

***

"Yeah, we've got a record deal. Supported the Roses at Heaton Park as well. How wicked was that, eh Mikee?" said Dom, as they sat in a newly opened Northern Quarter bar.

The Rock 'N' The Roll. 'N That

A quiet Thursday evening had just retrieved itself as Dominic and Mikee had now acquired some serious female attention.

"I'm Jayne. And this is Davina," said the blonde as way of introductions.

"Singles' out in September. Album not long after that. We'll be all over the radio before you know it," Dominic said with a wink at Mikee.

"I'm the drummer. Dom plays lead guitar," said Mikee, as he flexed his considerable bicep to show off the latest addition to his tattoos.

"Ooh, they're lovely. Hurts doesn't it. I've just got a small one. I might show it you later!" said Davina, squeezing his bicep flirtatiously.

"Shall I get us some more drinks then, girls?" said Dominic as he stood and headed for the bar. "Shots as well? Get this party started!"

Jayne quickly reapplied her lip-gloss. Adjusting her already revealing low cut T-shirt, she made sure that her ample cleavage was set to tractor-beam effect. Her friend, who was still rubbing Mikee's biceps, stuck her tongue out slightly, having clocked her friend's sexual preening.

"Okay. Two white wines. Pints. And four Sambucas." Raising his shot glass, he said, "To rock 'n' roll. All the time!" Dominic slammed the shot back in one, banging the empty glass down on the table with an attention seeking crack.

Mikee followed suit. "To me and you bro! LONELY SOULS!"

Knocking her shot back with a grimace, Mikee's would-be conquest said coyly, "I can't see you being Lonely Souls tonight…"

Laughing at the dreadful pun, Dom signalled for more shots from the bar. As he did, Jayne placed her purse in his lap. She whispered in his ear, "Look in the zipped bit. Something you may fancy in there."

Popping the purse pistol-style down the back of his jeans, Dominic headed downstairs for the Gents'.

Securing an empty cubicle, he wiped the wooded cistern top down thoroughly and opened the purse, quickly locating the paper wrap contained within.

"Result," he whistled to himself. Chalking out a generous but not greedy line, he tightly rolled a note, cleared his nasal passages with a quick blow, and then bent over the crystalline drug and hoovered it up. The coke had been an unexpected bonus and he vowed that he would show his gratitude later that evening.

Returning to the bar and seeing the four charged shot glasses awaiting him, he smiled at Jayne. "Alright if my good friend Mikee has a little bump?"

"Go on then. But make sure that there's some left for us later…"

The magic words. As he passed the purse across to Mikee with a subtle nod, he kissed Jayne on the top of her head, his hand running down her bare arm suggestively.

***

"Just hold still. Nearly." As Dominic carefully arranged the line of coke with the tip of his bank card, he looked down with a hungry look. His handiwork carried out with the precision of a surgeon.

The coke was perfectly centred where the small of her met the curve of her arse. As she knelt perfectly still on all fours, Dominic tightened the note. "Steady! Right!"

Looking down at the arse-turned-drugs plinth, he thought that it wasn't the best he had seen over the past few months, but he loved the girl's willingness to indulge him one of his fantasies.

Grasping her thigh with his left hand, he sniffed up the coke, dabbing at a couple of stray grains with his finger and licking them off. He then slid his moistened finger into Jayne's already invitingly wet pussy.

She gasped with pleasure as Dom, rubbing at his nose with his left hand, slowly worked his finger rhythmically in and out of her.

And Mikee. Killing two birds with one stone. He had raided the fridge in Dominic's apartment and was now licking yoghurt from between Davina's legs. He was still regretting that he had not purchased a more substantial meal on the way home, but this alternative would suffice. Holding his hard cock, pulling away at it frantically whilst Davina lay back on the sofa purring as he hungrily licked away at her and the yoghurt.

Rolling on to her back, Jayne looked up at Dominic, a wicked glint in her eye. "My turn now…"

Leaning across she scooped the last of the cocaine onto her fingernail, "Lie on your back."

As compliant as a square-bashing squaddie, Dominic lay back and put his hands behind his head, all the time his greedy eyes not leaving Jayne.

Holding his hard cock in her left hand, she carefully deposited the coke onto the blood-gorged tip. Rubbing the back of her hand across her mouth, Jayne then bent over him, sucking him and the cocaine back with deep thrusting movements.

After a minute of vigorous and wholeheartedly proficient oral sex, Dominic came violently. His midriff tightened, and he groaned with sexual delight as he covered his face. "Oh fuck!" Meeting her eye as she swallowed, Dominic let out a low laugh. "You bad, bad girl…"

Chapter 33

Monday 17th September 2012. An inauspicious day in the calendar for the majority, but four young men – and one middle-aged man – were counting the days down with varying degrees of patience.

"I heard us on the radio again the other day. I'll never get tired of that," said Danny, as he leant against the wall outside their rehearsal room. Lighting up another cigarette. "Do we get paid whenever it's played then Johnny?"

"Yeah, something called PRS. You're all classed equally as the songwriters so you'll all get a small slice and the record company do as they're the publishers," Johnny replied.

"Easy really when you look at it," said Dom, struggling to light his own cigarette in the blustery wind, "Just sell a shit load of records, play loads of gigs, flog a load of T-shirts and we're laughing."

Nodding in Dominic's direction, Johnny said, "Simply but effectively put. You keep writing the tunes and nobody has a problem. Most money is in touring and festivals. Anyhow, don't you lot worry about all that, it's my responsibility."

Three weeks and counting. A relaxed programme of rehearsals was planned, Jamie and Dominic having hit a rich vein of songwriting with the nucleus of three new songs taking shape.

The record label's pluggers had done their job – the first single being lodged on the playlists of XFM Manchester and London, Radio 6, countless local stations and Radio 1 were considering it for their evening shows.

"Mikee. You're late. Been down the shops for some more yoghurt?" said Dominic as they exchanged knowing winks and a fist-bump.

Rubbing his sizeable jaw, Mikee laughed, "Get some without fruit in it next time, fudge or toffee or something."

"Whatever you say Kong!" said Dom, a wicked twinkle in his eye.

"Alright Johnny," said Jamie amicably.

"Alright J. Yeah, good ta. Busy. And busy is good," said Johnny.

The Rock 'N' The Roll. 'N That

As Johnny drank from a bottle of water, Danny grabbed his wrist. "Nice watch bossman!"

Looking down at his newly acquired timepiece, Johnny smiled to himself. "A little treat to myself. Got the money through from my house and a few quid from the label so wanted to buy something I'd remember it all by."

"Let's have a look then," said Mikee.

Johnny casually tossed the four and half grand Rolex to Mikee, knowing that his shovel like hands were a safe bet.

"Nice. Very nice," said Mikee as he inspected the watch, with its bottle green face and onyx bezel.

"I'll buy you all one when the album goes to number one," said Johnny as he put his watch back on.

"I'll hold yer to that," said Danny, with a snap of his fingers.

"My pleasure," said Johnny coolly, "You get the number one and I'll be there 9.00 Monday morning when the shop opens."

"Put it in your diary then dude," said Dominic, as cocksure as ever.

"Talking of things for your diary. NME interview lined up for start of September. Label want us to get some more photos done for promo and artwork. "Glancing in Jamie's direction, he said, "Interviews being done by your friend Sally Valley."

"Fine by me, I—"

"Good job you didn't fuck her then eh bro!" interjected Dom.

"Good job you didn't fuck her! Don't know what you've caught with all the notches on your bedpost," said Jamie.

Mumbling slightly, Dom said, "Yeah well, I'll be fine. Nothing wrong with enjoying myself."

"Absolutely bro. I'm not your keeper," smiled Jamie.

***

The day of the single release had arrived, and all concerned were behaving like expectant fathers in a maternity ward.

Flipping open his laptop, he saw that there was an email from the band's press officer –

'Johnny, hope you're well and as excited as we are about this week. Copy of the NME interview. Decent read. Speak soon. Suzzie.'

Opening the attachment, he smiled at the headline soundbite –

"IT DOESN'T MATTER WHERE WE'RE FROM, IT'S HOW BIG WE'LL GET…"

An article full of shooting from the hip soundbites and laced with cockiness culminated with a glorious payoff –

'The North Will Rise Again' and those cocky Mancs have only gone and done it again. And don't we always love them for it.

Songs, attitude, did I mention the looks and not a monobrow in sight..."

***

Wednesday would be the day that all would become clear. Mid-week chart positions would be made available. A reasonably solid indicator of where the first single would land. A band meeting had been convened in a city centre Chinese restaurant.

"That'll do for me please," said Mikee, pointing at the menu as their waitress took notes down. Sporting yet more dressings on his forearms, the tattoo sleeves were now resplendent. The 'King Kong' atop the skyscraper was now complete and was a stunning piece of art.

"Same for me," nodded Danny, "and a lager please."

"Yup, lagers all round," agreed Mikee on behalf of the band.

"We'll save the champagne until after we've heard the news, eh Johnny," winked Dominic.

They ate in comparative quiet for them. The usual ribbing was absent. They were preoccupied with a palpable nervous tension. Danny seemed convinced that anything less than a number one would be a huge disappointment. Mikee, somewhat pessimistically, was saying he'd be happy providing the placing was double digits. Jamie and Dom seemed willing for at least a top thirty slot.

The label themselves had informed Johnny that they were confident of a position in the lower echelons of the top twenty. He'd sensibly decided to keep this little nugget to himself.

A phone call was expected from Suzzie at around 2pm, and having finished their meals, they were nervously nursing pints.

With his phone ringer turned up to its maximum setting and fully charged, the shrill ringtone startled them.

"ANSWER IT!" shouted Danny.

Picking up the handset carefully, he said, "Ta for that, D-Mo. Would never have occurred to me…"

The Rock 'N' The Roll. 'N That

Crossing his arms in frustration and then reaching for his cigarettes before realising that this wasn't an option, Danny muttered to himself.

"Hiya Suzzie. Yeah, we're all here. Good thanks." The band were only able to hear one side of the conversation and Johnny had never witnessed them as church mouse quiet. "Yeah. We thought that too."

A long pause. Johnny pulled his best poker face. "Okay. I'm just going to pop you on speakerphone. One second and then the boys will all be able to hear you." Quickly adjusting the settings, he placed the phone on the middle of the not-so-pristine white table cloth.

"All yours Suzzie," said Johnny, struggling to contain the excitement from flooding into his voice.

"Good news. We've just got the midweeks in." A pause that seemed to drag interminably. "It's sitting at number 19 today!"

"FUCKIN' COME ON!!" screamed Danny.

Mikee leapt up and was now stood on his chair, his muscular tattooed arms spread wide shouting, "Nineteen, fucking nineteen," at the top of his voice.

A waitress rushed over to tell Mikee to clamber down from his elevated position only to be scooped up and spun round in an all-consuming hug, much to her amusement.

Picking up the phone, Johnny resumed the conversation. "Hi Suzzie, yeah, they're delighted. Totally made up. Yeah, we'll see where it ends up Sunday, but that's great news."

Hanging the call up, Johnny stood and accepted Jamie's hug and whispered, "Thanks man, love yer."

Summoning the still grinning waitress, the age-old cliché was fulfilled, albeit with a rock 'n' roll twist. "A bottle of champagne and five tequilas please," laughed Johnny.

The shot glasses were chinked together boisterously amid shouts of 'nineteen' and 'fuckin' get in'.

There was nothing for it but to get well and truly pissed. The band had arrived. They officially were now the proud owners of a hit record. 'Number fuckin' nineteen', as Danny was now screaming down his phone to Dee.

***

"Hello, Dominic? It's Mum."

Reflexively looking to the other side of the band, Dominic wiped his eyes.

"Hiya Mum. You okay? It's early," glancing at the bedside clock, "it's only just gone ten…"

"It's not early, lazybones."

"We were all out last night celebrating the mid-week position. Top twenty. Can you believe it?"

"I know. Jamie texted me. It's amazing news. I'm so happy for you both. But…" Cally paused as she braced herself for the pending reaction to her next statement. "I'm a bit worried though, Dominic."

"Why would you be worried? Everything's going brilliantly. I've never been happier," he said, stifling a yawn.

Steeling herself, she said, "I read the NME interview," sighing softly, "and I'm just worried that you're going in at the deep end. I'm not stupid Dominic. I know what goes on with you—" she was struggling for the right words, "boys in bands. I know what you do."

"And what's that, Mum?"

"I don't need to draw pictures and whatever I say won't make a difference. But just be careful. Please."

"Come on, Mum!" He shook his head irritably. "We've just gone top twenty and you're giving me a lecture. Jeez. You going to have same little chat with Jamie?"

A tell-tale pause gave away the answer. "Err. Of course I will."

"Really? I'll ask him later."

"Don't be like that. Please Dom."

"Like what? I'm a big boy. I can look after myself. I thought you'd be pleased for us."

"I am pleased," snapped Cally. "I said that. I cried when I heard. I was so happy. Just be careful."

"And exactly what is it that I'm supposed to be careful about?"

"I don't need to say, do I?"

Lying on his back, Dominic stared at the ceiling, an impassive look on his face. "No. You do. Tell me."

Tutting at her son's belligerence, she said, "I don't want to fall out. Sorry Dominic. But I just had to get it off my chest."

"Yeah, thanks Mum. I'll drop this chat into our next interview. How my mum says I should be careful."

"Now that's just silly talk."

"Isn't it. Lot of that going on…"

"I'll speak to you again. Bye. I love you."

"Yeah. Bye." Throwing his phone down angrily, Dominic pushed a hand through his unkempt bed-hair. "Fuck's sake," he grumbled to himself. Rubbing at his coke-raw nostrils, he rose and went for a cigarette on the apartment's small balcony.

Wiping a solitary tear from her eye, Cally clutched the phone to her chest, her mood now tinged with regret. She then cut out the NME interview and placed it in a plastic wallet. The first page in a memento book dedicated to her son's band…

Chapter 34

"She's going to be worried about both of us. Just humour her a bit. See it from her side," said Jamie as they looked through the racks of clothing.

With such a busy schedule for the foreseeable future, the twins were undergoing a spot of pre-tour retail therapy. Looking through the vintage items of varying style and quality, Dominic tutted at his brother's all-pervading sensibleness.

"What am I supposed to do then? Every time I'm gonna enjoy myself should I think of how Mum would feel. Whenever we have an interview, worry that it'll upset her." Shaking his head in frustration, he said, "This is all shit. Let's go somewhere else."

"It's all happened a little quickly for her, y'know. Just go easy on her. She just wants the best for us," said Jamie, as they headed to another clothing unit within Afflecks Palace.

"Yeah. Yeah. Sensible Jamie," Dominic grumbled.

"Just you remember that," said Jamie, winking at his brother as they entered another shop.

***

"Let's rehearse for an hour and then we'll stick the radio on at five. That sound like a deal?" said Dominic, as he tuned his guitar. "What's up with you, D-Mo? Bit quiet."

"Had a dinner with Dee and me ma and pa. The old twat was alright with me for once. Think the shock has killed me!"

"And did they like their new daughter-in-law then?" asked Mikee from behind his kit.

"Fuck off. We're not married. Not even talked about a date yet. Need to make some serious cash first," said Danny, adjusting his amp slightly.

"Lovely girl and that, Daniel. But fuck me, you won't catch me settling down anytime soon," said Dom, clearly trying to goad a reaction.

The Rock'N'The Roll. 'N That

"I didn't ask you. As long as I know that she's the right girl."

He still needled away. "I'll remind you of that next time we're out on tour and you're getting your dick sucked!" cackled Dominic.

"Yeah, well. I won't be," said Danny, muttering to himself under his breath.

"What d'yer reckon then lads? Top twenty would be wicked," said Mikee, rattling out a beat on his hi-hat.

"Can't see top ten, based on mid-week and what Johnny said. Label stats and all that," said Jamie, rubbing a plectrum idly against the side of his neck.

"Where is ol' Johnny boy?" asked Mikee, rolling a muscular shoulder.

"He texted me. Said he's got to meet with his ex. And off to London tomorrow. Got to meet the label," said Jamie, adjusting his mic stand.

"Let's work on the two new tracks' and then we'll find out where we are in the charts!" Dominic snapped his guitar lead, and tried to act nonchalant, but they all knew…

***

Glancing down as his phone pinged, Johnny discreetly snuck a glance at the message -

'Number 22. All made up. Shame it's not top twenty. Next time. And thanks man J x'

"Are you still as busy at work then?" Johnny asked, eager to maintain the small talk, although sensing that Claire's request to meet carried an agenda.

"Usual. I'm sure your working day, if you can call it that, is a little different these days," sniped Claire.

Slightly disappointed that she had dispensed with her ubiquitous air quotes, Johnny pushed back his chair and laughed to himself. "What does it matter what my job does or doesn't entail? Would have been nice if you'd asked if I was happy in my work."

"Happy in your work?" With an incredulous look on her face, it was now Claire's turn to laugh. "Why would I care if you're happy?" With a slow shake of her head. "Taking way too many drugs and hanging around with a bunch of boys' half your age!"

"Really? You actually think that?" Already beginning to regret his decision to agree to meet, Johnny sighed, and rubbed at his temple. "I care that you're happy. That you're okay."

"That'll be guilt. Pure and simple."

"Right. So that's why you wanted to see me. Thanks," grimaced Johnny.

"I still can't understand why you did it. What were you thinking? I wake up and can't believe what you were possibly thinking," said Claire, squeezing her hands together.

"Claire," said Johnny, pausing. "I said sorry at the time. I'll apologise again, but I've nothing more to say. "

"That's it? Sorry. No explanation? Nothing to add after all this time?" pleaded Claire.

"No," said Johnny. Squinting slightly, he met Claire's stare. Shaking his head slowly, he said, "You still think it was all my fault. The two situations were completely unrelated. If this is all about 'closure'." Making ridiculously exaggerated air quotes, he continued, "That I used to read about in your crappy magazines. Well…"

"It was all your fault," hissed Claire, not wishing to attract the attention of their fellow drinkers.

"There's nothing more I can say. I'm sorry Claire. Look after yourself."

"That's it? Thanks. Thanks, a fucking lot!"

Feeling his neck glands tightening, Johnny stood to leave, but slowly reached inside his jacket pocket. Pulled out his phone, opened the text from Jamie and held it up to Claire.

"Not that you're bothered. But am I happy in my work? Never fuckin' better!"

Turning on his heel, he left Claire as speechless as he had ever seen her…

Chapter 35

A top thirty single under their belts and XL's hottest new property would be playing at a record label charity event in London that week – bottom of the bill, but said line-up included Jack White, The XX, Friendly Fires and rumours of a guest slot from Adele. "It'll be great. People knowing who we are," said Dominic, as they boarded their now slightly larger tour bus. The pimped-up RV was now resigned to history.

Or more likely the scrapheap.

Not yet full on tour bus, but a distinct step in the right direction.

The guestlist read like a 'who's who' of musicians, footballers, models and I've-no-idea-but-they-must-know-somebodies. The old music hall was palpably throbbing with anticipation. A huge sign on its grand front façade announcing the evening's acts. Scalpers outside the venue were doing a roaring trade with tickets changing hands for wince inducing amounts.

At 8.25pm, minutes before showtime, a black cab pulled up, attracting the waiting scrum of photographers. A melee ensued as they jostled for position in a survival of the fittest manner.

A slim figure, with a phalanx of black-suited security protecting her from the paparazzi's prying glare, slipped through the melee of camera wielding carrion feeders, stopping for one second to allow them their picture before heading into the venue, only removing her Onassis-sized shades when she was safely inside.

"Ms Bearheart. Here are your VIP passes," said the girl at the ticket office, momentarily dazzled by the in-the-flesh beauty stood in front of her.

***

"Great set boys. It went down a storm. Jack loved it as well. He said he'll say hello after his set. And everyone at the label was delighted with how the first single dropped," said XL label head Richard Russell as he popped his in the dressing room.

The Rock 'N' The Roll. 'N That

"Thanks Richard. Top ten next time," said Dominic, as he juggled between his mobile phone and a bottle of beer from their not inconsiderable rider.

As the door closed, Mikee said, "I like him," stripping out of a sodden white T-shirt and towelling himself down. "He's cool as fuck. Must be worth a fortune as well."

"I'm just off for a cig. Anybody?" said Danny, reaching for his lighter and Access All Areas pass.

"You mean you're going to check in at home. Tell her what a good boy you're going to be," chipped in Dom.

"No. Just a cig," replied Danny defensively.

"Leave your phone here then," goaded Dom.

"Fuck off. You must think I'm stupid. Leave it with you lot! Would you? No. Well fuck the fuck off then!"

As Danny turned abruptly to leave the dressing room, Dominic pinched his overly-sensitive bandmate firmly on the arse. "OW! You weirdo!" he squealed.

"I love you really D-Mo," said Dominic, blowing a kiss in Danny's direction.

Returning the compliment as he rubbed at his stinging arse cheek, Dan pressed the speed dial on his phone. His hotline to Denise.

"We all going to the aftershow then?" said Jamie, his voice a little hoarse after the evening's gig. He had decided to pass on any cigarettes post-show when his throat felt like this.

"Bang up for it," replied Mikee, as he slipped into a fresh T-shirt, the bright white picking out the vivid colours of his tattoos.

"I think Johnny is still out front watching the bands, give us a shout if you see him," said Jamie, clearing his throat slightly and then drinking back a bottle of chilled water.

"You seen the amount of celebs that are here tonight. I'm loving this, "said Dominic, "big night tonight. Can't wait…"

***

"Nice to meet you," said Johnny as he extended his hand to the ravishingly gorgeous girl in front of him. He felt himself gulp as he made his introductions. "I'm Johnny. Johnny Harrison. I manage Lonely Souls. Best job I've ever had." Then, laughing nervously, "I say job, but it's not like it's really work looking after them. You know, I'd do it for free I love it so much…"

Realising he was waffling, Johnny laughed to himself and drank from his bottle of Peroni. Anything to prevent himself from making a twat of himself in front of this delectable and seemingly interested female.

"Amanda. And managing a band must be the best job in the world. Apart from being in the band and then that would be the best thing ever. Apart from the pressure of having to write all the songs all the time and having to go to all those parties and have to drink and take loads of drugs." Sipping from her own drink, Amanda smiled up at Johnny, her perfect white teeth illuminating it.

Johnny smiled to himself, as he felt she sounded as nervously geeky as he did. "What is it you do then? You want another drink? Or are you just talking to me so I'll introduce you to the band? I'd understand. Fewer grey hairs. Youth and talent on their side."

"Okay. I'm a vet. Yes please. A JD and Coke. And obviously. I'm as shallow as a very shallow thing, and if you've not introduced me to the band within five minutes, then I'll just go straight over to them myself and cut out the greying but somewhat charming middle man."

Taken aback by the girl's sassy sense of humour, Johnny stuttered slightly, before composing himself, "Err, JD and Coke it is. You don't look like a vet…"

"I know. This is the point where you tell me I look more like a model," she said with a coquettish smile.

A quick detour to the toilet before he went to the bar, Johnny cursed his walnut sized bladder. A gift seemingly bestowed on all men on the eve of their fortieth birthday. *May as well do a line whilst I'm here*, he thought, *I go to the Gents' that often, people will think that anyway.*

The pristine toilet top already showed the tell-tale signs of fellow recreational drug-users. Tiny grains of smeared crystalline powder, polished smears and bunched up pieces of toilet roll lay on top of the black granite shelf. A quick three step move – wrap, rack and snort and Johnny was suitably emboldened to carry on the verbal sparring with the exquisite Amanda.

"JD and Coke. I got diet, just to be safe. Wasn't sure which you wanted. You didn't say did you? Or did you?" Johnny could feel himself gabbling ten to the dozen. The coke was accelerating his thought process into an audible car-crash.

Deadpanning perfectly, she said, "Are you trying to tell me that I'm fat?"

"Er. No. I. Err, just tastes nicer. Sorry. I didn't mean that at all," said Johnny, swigging from his beer, trying to dull the effect of the cocaine.

The Rock 'N' The Roll. 'N That

Putting a slender finger to her mouth, Amanda seemed to be pondering the situation. "Well Mr Harrison, whilst we are talking about the subject of coke, are you going to share, or do I have to go and flirt with some over-paid record exec to score a line?"

Johnny's eyes widened. This girl was utterly terrific. Her attitude was such an incredible turn-on. And that was before he got to her looks – long straight dark hair, worn over one shoulder, warm almond shaped brown eyes, very little make-up and a perfectly sculpted mouth.

"Well, you don't miss a trick!" said Johnny, attempting to get the conversation on an even keel.

"Not when someone has a blob of white powder on the end of their nose…" said Amanda, the glint in her eye again causing his stomach to tighten.

Having rubbed the rogue coke from his nose as discreetly as a man with class A drugs stuck to the middle of his face could, he removed his wallet from inside his jacket pocket, passing it to her. "Never let it be said that I'm not the trusting type. Handing my wallet over to a total stranger!"

"Nice meeting you, Mr Harrison. Manager of an up and coming rock band. There should be a few quid in there, couple of credit cards. And a decent amount of reasonable quality drugs…" Giving Johnny her glass, she turned on her heel, heading off to the Ladies', casually patting Johnny's wallet against her thigh as she went.

Unable to resist, Johnny whistled softly to himself as his eyes followed her. Her long toned legs were clearly the by-product of an athletic lifestyle. The thigh length heeled black leather boots worn outside her jeans caused more than just Johnny's eye to watch her exit the room.

Returning quickly, Amanda leaned into Johnny, reaching round his back and pushing his wallet into the back pocket of his jeans. Whispering into his ear, "Thank you Johnny. There was only forty quid otherwise you wouldn't have seen me for dust."

"Well, seeing as though you came back, I'll introduce you to the band," said Johnny.

"Oh, would you! I promise I'll not get too excited and faint," said Amanda, clasping her hands together in mock girly fashion.

Strolling over to Dominic and Mikee, who were deep in meaningless conversation with two eager females, "Alright lads. Can I introduce you to somebody? This is Amanda. Very big fan apparently…"

Smiling at the neatly inserted undercutter, Amanda kissed both boys on the cheek, even throwing in a 'catching her breath in excitement' gesture. As subtle as ever where female form was concerned, Dom nudged Johnny with his elbow, an act that didn't go unnoticed by the vigilant Amanda.

"Well, thank you for that. I won't wash my hand again," she teased. "And your lead guitarist. He's such a ladies' man, isn't he? I think he liked me," she said, tossing her hair back exaggeratedly.

"I'd introduce you to Jamie, but I can't see him. Little more charming than our Dom can be on occasion," said Johnny.

It was the first time that he had bothered with any female attention since his break-up, all his energies had been focussed on the band. He didn't count his night with Cally given how gallantly he had behaved.

"We could leave if you wanted to? Or are you too busy with band business? Never off the clock. Constantly keeping a discreet but watchful eye over your young charges," said Amanda, her infectious sense of humour again amusing Johnny.

"We could leave," he said indecisively. "Where were you thinking?"

"I was hoping you could take me back to your vast hotel suite and seduce me. Leaving me with the knowledge that only an older, more experienced man can provide…"

Catching his breath, Johnny grinned at her. "You make me smile. Not like other girls, are you?"

"I bet you say that to all the girls you love and leave on the road. Girl in every town for Mr Rock 'n' Roll Manager is it?", purred Amanda.

"At least two," said Johnny, taking her hand as they left the aftershow party.

"You do know I don't usually do this sort of thing…" said Amanda as they slid into the back seat of a waiting cab.

***

"Hi Suzzie. Yeah, I'm good thanks. It was a great night. Best gig I've been to in ages," said Johnny, as he held the phone between his shoulder and ear whilst trying to simultaneously turn his laptop on. "I haven't seen the papers today or been online. There's not a problem is there?"

"Just look at the Mirror today, the 3AM gossip page. Jamie has certainly got the band in the headlines…" said Suzzie, seemingly unperturbed by developments.

"Err. I'll have a look now. Nothing bad?" said Johnny, a nervous tone to his voice.

"Not at all. Just surprised at the company he chose to keep. I didn't have him down as the celebrity-couple type. Anyhow, I'll speak soon. Oh, and you made quite an impression on my friend Amanda. I'll be changing my opinion on Northerners at this rate. Bye."

Johnny winced slightly at the last comment. The night had not gone quite the way he had planned. He wasn't sure if it was the combination of nerves, booze and bugle but he had been unable to perform when required. Once back in his hotel room the lovely Amanda had stripped down to some extremely sexy underwear, and then proceeded to undress him as they kissed on the bed.

He'd initially thought that he had been slow in getting started but had become increasingly panicked as he failed to muster even the vaguest hint of an erection.

A trip to the bathroom and a valiant attempt to cajole some semblance of life had left him sat staring at his dick which remained stoically inert – a small nub where an erect cock should have risen. Johnny had slunk back into the bedroom and had mumbled an apology to the delicious and expectant Amanda, who had been remarkably understanding towards his plight.

Avoiding the well-worn cliché that it had never happened to him before, Johnny then embarked on a sleep-free night – a heady cocktail of cocaine, frustration and dented pride seeing to that.

Clicking to the Mirror website, Johnny was met with an archetypal paparazzi picture of Jamie entering the back of a cab with Lara Bearheart.

The piece – obviously a quiet day in the world of salacious gossip – was the lead article, under the headline of *'Bear faced cheek'*. The picture showed Jamie looking at the bottom half of Ms Bearheart's very pert arse cheek as she stepped into the back of the cab. Going on to describe Jamie as *'the drop-dead gorgeous lead singer of new indie sensations, Lonely Souls, was anything but lonely as he left the hottest gig in town to go back to socialite Lara's hotel suite at the nearby trendy Sanderson Hotel...'*

Johnny knew little of Lara Bearheart, but a quick Google search revealed all he needed to know – *'Lara Bearheart is the daughter of British model Stacey Temple and Native American billionaire businessman, Awan Bearheart. His family made their fortune developing casino resort complexes on old Native American land in Connecticut. Lara herself had been a model since the age of fourteen and had recently dabbled with acting and was in the throes of trying to launch a singing career. As her parents were separated, she spends time between Manhattan and London.'*

The accompanying images showed a strikingly beautiful woman who would turn the head of any man on the planet.

It was clear that Ms Bearheart had benefitted from both her father's heritage and her mother's fine features – a perfectly heart shaped face was crowned with a jaw length bob of jet black hair. Eyes as dark as oil wells which had a certain lupine quality. A strong nose seemingly untouched by the surgeon's scalpel and a figure – unusually curvy for a modern-day model – that seemed straight off the drawing board of Disney's latest Princess.

Scanning through the images, Johnny let out a soft chuckle to himself. "Well well, Jamie. For one who's all about the music, you've certainly made a splash."

Closing his laptop, he picked up his mobile and contemplated his next conversation…

Chapter 36

"Hello. Can I help you?" said Cally as she peered round her half-open door at the stranger who was stood with his back to the door of her terraced house.

He turned and flashed his best snakeoil salesman smile. "Harvey Brown. North West reporter for the Daily Mirror. Are you Caroline Thorne?" he asked, glancing down at a well-thumbed notebook.

"I am. But what do you want?" she said, an edge of concern flooding her voice.

"Just wanted to have a chat about Jamie. Quite the star, isn't he? And people know his name after today's news story. I just wanted to ask a few questions. Then people can get to know more about him. Some direct quotes from the mum always helps," said Harvey, turning his charm tractor beam up to maximum.

"I don't know what you mean. And, err, I've nothing to say. Nothing to say at all. Goodbye." Cally went to close the door, but Harvey, a veteran at these 'doorstepping' situations was too quick and had his tired looking loafer wedged in the door frame in a flash.

"If you choose not to answer my questions… Well, you must know how it works, Ms Thorne? Anything could get printed," said Harvey, the intended menace lacing his words just as he intended.

"NO! I've no wish to talk to you ON MY DOORSTEP!" Giving the door a sharp shove, Cally slammed the door shut and leant against it as she struggled to compose herself.

She heard the reporter's voice through the door, persistent to the last. "Read today's paper, Ms Thorne. Then you'll see why you should speak to me. I'll leave my card with you should you change your mind."

Taking a deep breath, she took the card that was protruding through her letterbox and picking up her mobile phone, went into the kitchen, closing the door behind her.

"Hello Johnny? It's Cally. Can you talk?"

The Rock 'N' The Roll. 'N That

"Hey how are you," he said, detecting a slight urgency to her voice, "You okay?"

"No. I've just had a reporter on my doorstep. At my house! Asking about Jamie. What's gone on?"

"Don't worry. It's nothing bad, but Jamie has been in the paper this morning. Some model or something that he left a party with the other night. She's obviously the story and they must be looking to fill the gaps in with a bit about Jamie."

"I don't like people turning up on my doorstep Johnny," Cal said softly.

"I know, and I don't like the idea either. I'm sorry but nothing I can really do. I've not spoken to Jamie yet. Let me speak to him and I'll get back to you. Okay?"

"Thanks Johnny. I never expected this sort of thing."

***

"Hiya man. I'll buzz you up," said Jamie through the apartment's intercom.

Johnny reached the apartment and found Jamie sat with a copy of the previous day's newspaper on the breakfast bar.

"Hey Johnny."

"Hiya man. You okay?" said Johnny, putting a concerned hand on his shoulder.

He was scouring the article for the umpteenth time. "No mention of the gig. Or the single. Nothing!" said Jamie, shaking his head slowly.

Sitting on the back of the sofa, Johnny leant forward and glanced over the article again himself, "I've got to say J, she's some woman. She's beautiful."

"That's not the point!" snapped Jamie, closing the newspaper angrily.

"Sorry man. But this is the nature of the beast. Did you not know who she was or something?"

"I'd heard the name, but I don't pay attention to this sort of bullshit. Y'know, completely not my thing," laughing to himself, "But man. You're right, she is gorgeous."

"You're not kidding. You know what I'm going to ask next…"

"You're asking me to kiss and tell, aren't you?" said Jamie, smiling at last.

"Well as your management and representative," said Johnny, assuming an exaggerated serious tone.

"Blow job. Exquisite. That do you?"

"May I commend you on your discretion. And will you be remaining in touch with the young lady?"

"I dunno man. This has all been a bit of a shock. I've no regrets, but all this," said Jamie, making a dismissive gesture in the direction of the newspapers.

Looking serious, Johnny said, "You spoken to your mum today?"

"Nah, my phone's been on charge. Why?"

"I should have said earlier, but some guy from the press turned up at the house. Just being nosy. Asking questions. She didn't say anything."

"Fuck. That's bang out of order. She's okay, isn't she?"

"Fine. Just a little shocked by it all."

"Fuck me," whistled Jamie, rubbing a hand through his hair.

"As I said, this is the nature of the beast. It's what keeps these papers and magazines thriving," said Johnny as he shook the kettle.

He scratched at the back of his head. "All out of milk," said Jamie, pointing towards the fridge. "I don't want this for us. Not just yet. Un-fuckin-believable…" said Jamie, with a weary shake of his head.

"The others said anything yet?"

"You can guess, can't you? Dominic was ridiculously jealous. Said he wanted to be the first to fuck someone famous," Jamie said, laughing loudly.

"I'll leave you to it anyhow man. And give your mum a quick shout," said Johnny.

"You down at rehearsal later?"

"Yeah. I will. Few things to chat over," said Johnny.

Exchanging a quick hug, Johnny left Jamie to his thoughts.

Checking his now fully charged phone, Jamie saw two messages from his concerned mother. And one from Lara. Jamie felt his stomach tighten slightly as he opened it –

'Hello Jamie Thorne. I take it you've seen the papers. Hope it won't put you off. L x'

***

A lewd cheer echoed round the room as Jamie stepped into the rehearsal room. Putting his guitar case down, he raised his hands in front of his face. "No pictures please!"

Putting his own guitar down, Dom strode over to his twin and shook him vigorously by the hand. "Good work J. Stuffy twat. Definitely should have been me though!"

The Rock'N'The Roll. 'N That

Addressing all his bandmates, who were stood or sat with inane grins decorating their faces, Jamie said, "Right. Joke's over. I didn't know who she was. And yes, she is gorgeous. And no, I won't be telling you any more than that!"

After a couple of run throughs of the new material, the rehearsal room door opened, and Johnny stepped inside.

The track came to an end and before introductions could be exchanged, Dominic, as direct as ever, chimed up, "Well, well. Johnny Harrison. You sly old dog!" he shouted.

"Yes, go on. You've got one minute," laughed Johnny resignedly.

"Fit. Very fit," said D-Mo, nodding his head and offering up a fist bump above his bass.

Mikee made the internationally recognised divers' signal of 'okay' with a giant circled finger and thumb.

"Got to say I was impressed Mr H. She was lovely looking. Very fit. I take it you gave her a night to remember?" cajoled Dominic.

Johnny winced inwardly at the recollection of 'giving her a memorable night'.

"No kiss and tell from me. The older man definitely doesn't do that!"

"Yeah, yeah. All that bollocks. Spill," demanded Dominic.

"All I'll say Master Dominic, is that I may well see her again," said Johnny, happy with the façade.

He was still unsure as to how to play the whole Amanda situation.

On one hand, it felt very much like unfinished business – that and the fact that she was gorgeous. On the other, he felt that he would be under inordinate amounts of pressure to 'perform' this time. Having poured over the internet, he was now an expert on erectile dysfunction. Several sessions of '*me-time*' had been conducted positively but no pressure there…

"Okay. You've had your minute. Fun's over. Let's go over the schedule for the next few weeks…"

Chapter 37

Looking down at the mobile phone screen, Jamie's thumb hovered over the green call symbol. It had been a strange experience 'researching' a potential partner. He had resisted temptation for a couple of days, but curiosity had got the better of him. He didn't want to see her as some tabloid figure. He had felt that there was a connection between them, as clichéd as that sounded. They had talked for several hours about their lives so far – Jamie talking about the start of his path to potential fame, Lara talking about a road well-travelled even at the tender age of twenty-three.

And then they had kissed. After that, Lara had slowly dropped to her knees, unbuckled his belt and then blown him like he had never been blown before. Her deft tongue caused him to cum much quicker than he had hoped. After this she had stood, met his lustful stare and said, "I'll see you again, Jamie Thorne."

***

"Lara. Jamie."

"Jamie Thorne. I knew you'd call…"

Her American accent more pronounced over the telephone.

"I said I would. And why wouldn't I?"

"Why indeed."

"We're busy for the next week, some promotion work and that…"

"And that?" Lara repeated it back as a question, her transatlantic drawl making the Northernism sound decidedly peculiar.

"Y'know. Just record company stuff, but we'll be in London," said Jamie, feeling slightly nervous.

"I know. I'm just playing with you." Lara paused. "This stuff in the paper. Don't let it bother you. The assholes will make whatever shit up that they want to."

Jamie laughed softly. "I know. All a bit new to me though."

"And Jamie Thorne. You were caught on camera looking right at my ass!"

"Guilty as charged. It's a lovely arse. Who could blame me though?"

"Arse?" Lara rolled the word around her tongue. "I prefer ass."

"Can I see you again?"

"So smooth Mr Rockstar. You'll learn."

"Can I see you again please?"

"I do like you English and your manners. Thank you. And yes. Soon. I'm flying back to America next week."

"I'll let y' know as soon as I know when I'm gonna be free. And I enjoyed the other night."

"Well, Jamie Lonely Souls. I'll be waiting your call. My cell won't leave my side. Don't keep me waiting."

"I won't. Bye Lara."

"Bye Jamie Thorne."

***

There was a feel that a shift in gears had taken place. The top-thirty/top twenty-five charting single – which sounded better had been the subject of an hour-long pub debate – had seen to that. And together with the tabloid fodder attention that had followed Jamie's liaison, the band were certainly on their way to becoming public property.

Social media captured this perfectly. Public opinion was an easily measured barometer now that anybody's opinion could be registered on the digital equivalent of the toilet wall.

None of them would ever be short of offers of sex – of varying degrees of sincerity and depravity. Cutting through the cyber chaff did however reveal an all-important love for the band's songs. The expectation for the album to drop was significant – the smart kids already declaring that 'Salvation' was the best track of the year by an undisputed mile.

***

The album was three days from release. Download. Album and CD formats would soon be available for purchase – or even more widely available for illegal download Jamie had grumbled. The artwork looked tremendous – a black sleeve, with the band picked out in red shading. The all-important band name and album title picked out in bold white letters.

Ladies and Gentlemen, we give you the first long-playing set of songs by Lonely Souls – *Salvation*.

A couple of radio sessions – XFM and BBC Six Music provided more valuable exposure for them – the buzz surrounding them growing by the day. The post-album tour was now virtually sold out with venues in London and Manchester having to be up-sized due to demand.

And Jamie. He remained stoic about his romantic dalliance despite the constant cajoling and wheedling from the band to disclose the lurid details. The fact that he showed no signs of on the surface irritability was a credit to him.

'Hello Jamie Thorne. I am still in London. Aren't you lucky. I am staying at my apartment. We can meet later. If you want… x'

Johnny had also felt emboldened, having received a similar message from Amanda.

'Mr Manager. I hear you are in London. Do cal. A x'

***

Bending down to collect the post, Cally opened the familiar Amazon packaging as carefully as she could. Despite having been sent a promotional copy of the album the previous week, she wanted to ensure that she had done her bit for her boys' success, and had ordered a copy to arrive on the day of its release. Proudly looking down at the pristine CD, she rubbed a motherly finger over the cellophane film, smiling at the boys, who stared determinedly back, all Rockstar attitude and cheekbones. Placing the album centrally on the mantelpiece, and then re-positioning it slightly, she stood back and admired it, a warm smile on her face.

Unusually for her, she had a date later that evening. Having declined an invite to the album launch party, Cally had accepted an invitation for a meal and drinks from a friend of a friend. It was almost a 'blind date' – her lifelong friend Jo had encouraged her that she should get out more and had lined her up with a colleague of hers that she made met briefly. *A date. An actual date*, she thought to herself as she finally started to give thought to her wardrobe.

***

The label had organised a launch party that evening and the band were travelling first-class to London. An empty carriage and plenty of time to have a pre-party booze.

And in Dominic's case, a 'bunk-up' in the toilets.

A foray into Snapchat bought about the tawdriest of sexual liaisons. Having established with a female admirer – josie1993 – also travelling on the same down bound train. Resulting in him having a not entirely fulfilling 'jump' in the intimate surroundings of the first-class carriages' toilets.

Apparently, she did wash her hands after the sexual encounter. "She can't be all that bad, right?" Dominic had protested.

"The power of social media," Johnny said. "Could you just not have had a wank before you left your flat?" He shook his head in both bemusement and at the disposability of it all.

***

A boat on the Thames had been hired for the occasion with the band due to play a short PA. Johnny hadn't told them yet, but the idea was that there would be a flotilla set up opposite the boat, and the band would play 'London Calling'-style – he was praying for rain to complete the loving tribute in its entirety.

As well as the mounting excitement that the album launch was generating within the band, Jamie and Johnny were awaiting confirmation that their female admirers would be in attendance.

Having resisted the temptation to purchase any blue 'wood'-inducing lozenges, Johnny was a mess of nerves as he tried to focus on any expectations that might be put upon him that evening.

Jamie had asked Lara to attend the launch party, stating that he didn't care who saw them together. Lara had responded that she was already 'on the list' and promised 'not to embarrass him provided he didn't get caught staring at her ass again…'

"Tonight will be brilliant. Record company have lined it all up. You lot are in for a right treat," said Johnny, his own excitement growing as the London weather forecast was looking decidedly downcast…

***

The launch party was being orchestrated with cloak and dagger precision. Guests were to board a flotilla style launch near Putney Bridge at 8pm. This would then head back up river to Central London, stopping in front of the boat that Lonely Souls would be set up on – giving the invited guests and liggers a brilliant view of the band as they pulled off their 'London Calling'-style tribute. It was fucking genius, Johnny had mused to himself, secretly gutted that it had not been his idea.

As darkness descended, the band opened their four-song set, and as if on cue, the grey clouds that had been jostling for position started a gentle but definite downpour.

The timing of both the downpour and the flotilla arriving were perfect. The band were lined up in the classic bass/guitar/lead guitar with three mic stands – Mikee tucked just behind them on a raised platform. The penny had dropped not long before they started playing and all three 'guitarists' had clicked into full-on Clash mode – Jamie styled his red scarf into a 'Strummer bandana look'. Dan dropped his bass a notch and struck his best gunslinger poses. Dominic, borrowing Jamie's black leather trench coat, threw guitar hero poses. When the chorus for 'Salvation' kicked in for the first time, the three of them all leant into their mics, giving it the full-on rock star routine.

The brillo grey night sky and the synchronised downpour all added up to the most perfect of rock 'n' roll recreations. Aboard the floating venue, the rain sodden and booze sozzled crowd were lapping it up.

Johnny stood – a massive grin etched across his face – watching his charges announce their arrival on the flatlining UK music scene. Standing with Amanda nestled into his side, the sight of the band and the warmth from Amanda gave him a surge through his loins. *Not just yet*, he thought to himself. *Not just yet…*

Squeezing Amanda slightly harder than he had intended, he shouted to be heard above the beautifully faithful rendering, "I FUCKIN' LOVE THIS SET OF BEAUTIFUL BASTARDS!"

Wiping a tear from his eye, Johnny had just about managed to restrain himself from jumping up and down on the spot and punching the air. It had been orchestrated to absolute perfection. With the short set finished, a walkway was slung across to the flotilla and the clearly exhilarated crowd made their way across to join the band. As they stepped onto the boat, they were handed a bag containing the album, a promo T-shirt and a blood red scarf – a collector's-item not just to be put onto eBay, as Johnny insisted on telling anybody that would listen.

***

Finding a quiet, sheltered corner, Jamie chinked the neck of his bottle against Lara's. "Looked wicked didn't it?"

"Now Jamie Thorne, we wouldn't want you getting a big head, would we?" said Lara, her dark glasses still on despite the distinct lack of daylight.

"I'm glad you're here and you saw that. Brilliant idea, wasn't it? D'yer see all the people watching from the embankment?"

"I'm just glad I didn't get seasick. That boat was seriously rocking by the end!"

Jamie looked at Lara, again perfection personified. Dressed in a ridiculously towering pair of spiked heel boots, black leggings and a fitted black leather biker jacket, rock chick was like a second skin to her.

"You ready to go on to the aftershow? There are cars waiting for us," said Jamie, giving a slight shiver as the cold of the evening descended.

"We are brave, aren't we? And remember. Don't look at my ass when the paps are there. Don't make it too easy for them, huh."

"I'll tell the others, and we'll make a move," said Jamie, glad at the thought of some warmth.

"Have you calmed down yet then, Mr Manager?" said Amanda, who was now regretting wearing the thin red mac, which was offering little protection against the cold air rolling off the river.

"Ha! How good were they? I hope that there's a decent recording of it. It'll look great on the website," said Johnny, pulling his grey peacoat around him.

"Always business with you, isn't it? Suzzie told me you are very focussed."

Laughing softly to himself, Johnny said, "Oh, we've been talking, have we? Thought my ears were burning." He was quite flattered by this development.

"No harm in doing a little homework. You came out with reasonably glowing colours," said Amanda, that almost teasing quality in her voice again. "Suzzie said you work hard on the band's behalf."

Johnny cocked his head to one side and nodded in appreciation of the comment.

"I do hope that you're not all work and no play, though, Mr Harrison…"

Attempting his most sincere face, he said, "Oh I think I can make an exception. Just for tonight mind."

"Why thank you. I'm deeply honoured," said Amanda, smiling up at him.

Pulling her into him, Johnny hugged Amanda, partially against the cold, but principally to allow himself to kiss her on the forehead.

Tracing a finger down Johnny's nose, she said, "Well, thank you Johnny. That's a start…"

***

"This place is amazing," said Jamie as he drank in the luxurious surroundings of Lara's Victorian Primrose Hill apartment. A sizeable balcony with breathtaking views over London was immaculate in every detail. Her 'boho' taste was wonderfully understated, but it was perfectly apparent that nothing had happened in the apartment by accident.

"What were you expecting? Dreamcatchers and totem poles?" asked Lara - her arms folded defensively.

Jamie looked at the pictures adorning the walls – some of which depicted Native American images.

"They're my ancestors," Lara said proudly. "My father's side of the family are Navajo descendants."

Pretending that this was 'news' to him and hadn't been previously unearthed with a quick Google search, he said, "The pictures are fascinating. You're obviously proud of your heritage," hurriedly adding, "Rightly so!"

"Go ahead and fix some drinks from the kitchen. There's plenty in the fridge. Bottle of wine open on the table I think."

"I'd prefer a beer."

"Just a beer it is then," said Lara, "I'm just going to get changed."

Jamie walked into the kitchen, taking in every detail of the apartment. He had never been anywhere like this. He ran his hand across the thick wooden farmhouse style table, then trailed it over the cold to the touch granite work surfaces.

Opening the vast refrigerator, Jamie picked out two cold bottles of Michelob, popping them open before looking around for a bin to dispose of the bottle tops. Thinking better of opening all the cupboard doors, he pocketed them both.

As he turned to go back into the large living room, he heard the bedroom door close. Lara was stood in front of him, completely naked aside from a red scarf tied loosely round her neck.

"Hello Jamie Thorne."

Jamie looked at her, scanning every curve. Every single perfect detail. The dark chestnut colour of her nipples, the red scarf falling between her sumptuous breasts. The slash of jet black hair above her vagina. The muscle tone of her legs and stomach. The small surgeon's cut to the side of her right knee.

It was all he could do to remain silent and wide-eyed. Putting the bottles down, he stepped towards her and put his arms around her.

She recoiled slightly. "OW! You have cold hands," said Lara, laughing.

Pulling his T-shirt over his head, Jamie wrapped it over his hands and again pulled Lara to him, her taut body moulding into his.

"Better?" asked Jamie, before kissing her longingly.

"Much," said Lara, leading him by the hand to her bedroom…

***

As they bundled into a waiting black cab, Johnny went to speak. "Look, about last ti—"

She put a finger to his lips. "Shhhh. Don't," said Amanda as she cuddled into Johnny's side. "Hmmm, you smell nice. Let me guess?" Sniffing Johnny's neck and giving a playful nibble at the same time, she said, "I know! What do I get if I'm right?"

"Just a sec. Sorry mate. The Montcalm, on err, on Great Cumberland Place." Turning back to Amanda, he kissed her softly on her cold cheek.

As they sat wrapped into each other watching London's nightlife pass them by, Johnny felt his phone buzz. Glancing down, he saw that it was a call from Cally.

Fuck. I can't answer this now, he winced to himself. Get to the hotel, and hopefully she'll have left a voicemail. Any big deal and he would call her back.

"I thought you said you were off the clock now," said Amanda, a definite ring of curiosity in her voice.

They just fuckin' know, Johnny's inner narrative grumbled to itself. *How the fuck do they just know…*

"Err, one of the lads. I'll call them back when we're at the hotel," he replied unconvincingly.

Arriving outside London's latest must stay hotel, Johnny paid the driver and they stepped out onto the pavement. "Very nice, Mr Manager. Were you expecting company?"

"Travelodge was all booked up," he deadpanned.

Having collected his room key, they took the air-conditioned lift to his fourth-floor suite. Amanda held his hand tightly, whilst Johnny got his bedroom 'gamehead' on.

Surreptitiously glancing down, he saw that he had a message. Strolling casually over to the window, he listened carefully to Cally's whispered message. Struggling to make out exactly what she was saying, Johnny established that she had been drinking.

'Johnny? Is that you? I'm sorry to call but I just wanted to hear a friendly voice. I went out on a date tonight. A sort of blind date. Jo fixed it up for me. You've met her remember. Anyhow, it was dreadful. All he wanted to talk about was the boys and the band. He wouldn't shut up about them. I walked out of the bar and left him. Oh Johnny, it was horrible. He just wasn't interested in me at all. Anyhow. Call me if you can, but don't worry if you can't. I hope tonight was great.'

His stomach flipped slightly, knowing that there was no way he could make the call. He turned the phone off with a grimace to himself.

"Err. I was right. Danny couldn't remember the name of their hotel. I've booked them in the other side of town," he lied.

"Well if you could finally stop working, I have something for you." Amanda had taken off her red coat, which was slung across the bed, had removed her fitted T-shirt, and was in the process of unclasping her bra.

"Ah. Let me," said Johnny, striding over to her and deftly removing the bra with practised ease.

"Well Mr Manager. You've done that before…"

***

Waking the next morning, Jamie rose on to his elbows, feeling a cold draught snaking through the luxurious apartment. Craning his neck round the door, he could just make out Lara, sat on the balcony, a huge patchwork quilt wrapped around her, sunglasses on and smoking her first Marlboro (Red) of the day.

Grabbing his discarded boxer shorts and a bath towel that was neatly arranged on the top of a large antique looking wooden dresser at the foot of the bed, Jamie wrapped the towel around his bare shoulders and went to join Lara. The cold early autumn air leaving a faint dew across the neighbouring rooftops. Leaning over the balcony's wrought iron balustrade, he ran a finger down her cheek, slowly pulling the cigarette from between her lips.

The Rock 'N' The Roll. 'N That

"Perfect timing, Jamie Thorne. That's tomorrow's tabloid pictures taken care of," said Lara, as she exhaled a thin trail of smoke.

Glancing down at the pavement below, Jamie saw two long-lens cameras trained on the balcony. His presence had snapped the photographers out of their early morning inertia.

"Fuck 'em," whistled Jamie. "I don't care."

Returning inside the apartment in a swish of intricate patchwork and brown thigh, she said, "Oh you'll learn, Jamie Thorne. You'll learn."

Shaking his head slightly and with a small wave to the paps below, Jamie followed Lara inside. Having stepped out of the quilt, leaving it in a pile on the middle of the living room floor, Lara was now climbing back into bed.

That arse, Jamie thought lewdly to himself, before pulling back the covers and joining her.

***

The hotel room was shrouded in darkness as Johnny rose to pad across the room to the toilet, the cold marble floor feeling pleasant underfoot.

Catching his reflection in the mirror, he sucked his stomach in slightly, and then nodded at himself almost in self-congratulation at his performance. Relieved didn't come close. He had almost raised an arm in centre-forward like celebration as the blood had surged to his cock.

No good managing some hot young rock 'n' roll band if you can't get hard, he'd drilled into himself as way of a self-administered pep talk. Rubbing a hand across his light stubble, he scratched slightly at a white fleck of Amanda's sex that had dried on his cheek. He must have come close to breaking his personal best for oral-sex endurance. Amanda best not forget to tell Suzzie that when they conducted their next little girly chat.

Returning to bed and expecting to see Amanda's naked form, hoping to resume last night's exertions, he was dismayed to discover that the bed was empty aside from a small note scribbled on some hotel stationery.

'*Morning Mr Manager. Sorry I had to leave. Early start at work. I should have said. Thank you for a lovely and MOST satisfying evening. A x P.S don't be a stranger...*'

Sitting down on the edge of the bed, the residue of last night's sex wafting underneath his nostrils, Johnny re-read the short note and smiled. Reaching across the nightstand to turn his phone on, he then remembered Cally's message…

***

"You'll have to go. Now," said Danny, his guilt already starting to manifest itself as he itched to pick his phone up and hear Dee's reassuring tones. "Look, I had a good night, but there's twenty quid for a cab," he said, scrambling through his wallet and breathing a sigh of relief when he pulled out two rolled up ten-pound notes.

"Don't be like that," said the nameless naked form that was attempting to rub up alongside him.

He reacted by leaping out of bed and pulling on his jeans and a screwed-up T-shirt that he had tossed on to the hotel floor in the height of their passion the previous evening. Unnamed naked female then sat up in bed letting the Egyptian cotton bed sheet fall away, revealing a not-unspectacular pair of what could well have been surgically enhanced breasts.

At the sight of said breasts, Danny had a sudden flashback. He and Mikee had been wagering each other shots as to which of the attendant girls had natural breasts or were wearing underwear. All very classy stuff…

This particular female had cost Danny a slammed double tequila as she was both silicone enhanced and not wearing underwear. "But she looked like a nice girl," he had protested as Mikee had poured his forfeit.

"You weren't shy last night," said unnamed naked in a screeching high-pitched cockney accent.

Visibly wincing, Danny, never good under pressure, started to hurriedly gather up her clothing and possessions.

"'Ere, you're not throwing me out without letting me have a shower. I'm not that sort of girl." She attempted a coquettish wink, but this was lost on Danny as he busied himself trying to locate her other peep-toe suede boot.

"Yeah, yeah. You're a lovely girl, err…" then realising he couldn't remember her name, "err, gorgeous."

"Ah, you're a sweetheart ain't ya? Be good if you could remember my name…"

Freezing as his mobile phone pinged the arrival of a text message, he finally located the rogue shoe underneath the duvet which was piled on the floor at the foot of the king-size bed.

"Here's your stuff. Look, I'm late already. I've got to be somewhere half an hour ago. Err, somewhere really important!"

"Right, right. I get your hint. I'm going. But you shouldn't treat nice girls like this."

With panic threatening to engulf him, Dan tried valiantly to remain calm. "I'm sorry. Last night was great but I—" he stammered.

"I know. You've got a girlfriend and now feel all guilty. I get the hint."

As naked unnamed zipped up her dress, she said, "And by the way. It's Debs…"

Flopping down onto the bed as soon as the hotel room door had closed, he let out a huge sigh of relief. Picking up his phone, he rang Dee. "Yeah. Good, babe. Yeah, did a few too many shots with Mikee. Yeah. We'll be home about mid-afternoon. Love you too."

Hanging up, he pulled himself into a ball, willing himself to fall into a recrimination-free sleep…

Chapter 38

"Jamie! Jamie!"

Trying to enter the front door of his apartment block, Jamie put his head down and pushed through the two photographers who were blocking his path.

"C'MON JAMIE. Just a couple of pictures. You've got to be happy. Top ten album and a cracking bird to boot!" said photographer number one, wearing a black parka, and with a large camera on a thick red strap flapping round his neck.

"Is Lara any good? She looks a right dirty bitch," said photographer two, a dark grey hoodie with a thick orange gilet worn over the top.

Stopping, and tensing his jaw, Jamie turned to photographer two. "What the fuck did you just say?"

"Alright Jamie mate," said photographer one, snapping off three quick pictures. "Anything to say about your new lady friend?"

Leaning into the photographer two's face, causing photographer one to start firing pictures off with wild abandon, Jamie snarled, "I'm not your fuckin' mate! And don't speak about her like that you fuckin' scumbag!"

"Now now! No need for that. Thought you'd be pleased, record doing so well n'all," goaded photographer one.

Putting his holdall down, Jamie smoothed the front of his jacket down and opening his arms. "Go on then. Take yer picture and then fuck off. I'm not going to talk to a pair of twats like you."

"Moody little fucker isn't he," said photographer two.

"D'yer honestly expect me to have a conversation with you? Un-fuckin'-believable," said Jamie, shaking his head.

"You know how it is. Little bit of success and they get a big fuckin' ego on them. Seen it all before," said photographer one.

"And we all know that they're a little pair of bastards," said photographer two, with a nasty sneer across his face.

The Rock'N'The Roll. 'N That

"What the fuck did you say?" said Jamie, again squaring up to photographer two.

"We've got a couple of pics and you getting all shirty will make us an extra few quid. You being a silly little twat has probably done us a favour," said photographer one, putting the lens cap back into place.

"See ya around," laughed photographer two.

Picking up his holdall and entering the buildings door code, he said, "Pair of cunts."

"Jumped up little prick," came the reply.

***

"Hey Suzzie. Yes, I'm good thanks. You?" said Johnny, bracing himself for the inevitable comment about Amanda.

"I'm also good. Delighted with the album. Sold brilliantly. Better than we expected, and we think that after the tour and the second single that it'll do even better. Hopefully stick around for a good few weeks rather than drop off. There'll be a fair bit of radio play and local station interviews whilst they're on tour, couple of radio sessions. I'll let you have a full schedule in a week or so when it's finalised. You're tour managing it, aren't you?"

"Yeah. I am. Hopefully the last one. Next time will be bigger venues and we'll be able to afford a tour manager," said Johnny, as he skimmed through his email inbox.

"I'm sure you will. Don't want you being all work and no play, do we now Johnny!"

Here we go, he thought.

"The album launch party was brilliant! Loads of clips all over YouTube. Caused a real splash. And Jamie can't keep away from Ms Bearheart can he? Not doing publicity any harm at all. So far anyhow," said Suzie, clearly building up to something.

"I'm surprised to be honest. I didn't think he'd jump in at the deep end with a high-profile girlfriend." He corrected himself quickly. "Not that she is his girlfriend. I've no idea about that. It's his business."

"I'd disagree. As their manager, you need to know where we stand on these things. Stay one step ahead is my motto." Pausing slightly, she said, "And you've certainly made an impression on my friend Amanda. Not seen her like that in an age. What's your secret Mr Harrison?"

Laughing at the inevitable subject raising, he said, "Must be something in the water up North…"

"I'll have to visit some time. Once I've had my jabs," Suzzie giggled. "I'm joking! Of course. I know how you Northerners can get all touchy."

"Only when you Southerners remind us of it," Johnny shot back.

"Speak soon. And Richard sends his regards."

"Bye Suzzie."

Johnny hung up and smiled to himself. It was all going exceptionally well. Top ten album. Sold-out tour. Internet awash with nothing but positives. Life was good…

Chapter 39

"Good to be back on the road," said Mikee. "And I like the bus! On-board toilet and bunks. And a plasma screen. I've got some films in my bag for us."

"Yeah, thanks Mikee, but can you not keep those films for your own private viewing?"

"We'll put it to the vote Boss Man!" laughed Mikee as he loaded his gear into the underbelly of the bus.

It had been decided that Johnny would tour manage this tour – the venues were by and large the ones they had played as support band. This time they would be top dog with larger dressing room, longer soundcheck and a decent rider. There would be a driver, given the size of the bus and allowing Johnny to work whilst they travelled.

Simon 'Spoony' James was a well-seasoned traveller when it came to working on the road with bands. He'd pretty much seen it all.

And if he hadn't, it was because he had chosen to turn a knowing blind eye.

Rake thin, able to live on a diet of bottled water, cigarettes and Mars Bars, he had acquired more than his share of tarmac 'air miles'. And his nickname was not one to be mentioned to his face. Many a wet behind the ears novice had, however, made this mistake.

"Where's D-Mo?" asked Mikee, as he loaded the last of his kit aboard.

"No doubt saying goodbye to Dee and promising that he'll keep it in his pants," said Dominic.

"Here he is now," said Jamie, as he drank from a bottle of Lucozade, "and go easy on him, these things do just seem to happen to him."

"Alright Johnny," said Dom, as he loaded his suitcase into the hold.

"Alright lads. All looking forward to this. Bit more in the way of comfort with the transport and I don't have to drive. I'll still be in charge of the tunes though!" said Johnny.

"Well Mikee seems to think he's in charge of in-flight entertainment with his bag of award winning films," said Jamie, with a look of mock-concern on his face.

The Rock 'N' The Roll. 'N That

"D-MO!" shouted Mikee, "How are you brother? You already for a few week's fun and games?"

"Hiya fellas. Yup. Liking the bus. And a toilet!" said Danny, taking his shades off as he stowed his gear.

"Yes. And while we're on that subject. Bus rules. The toilet. No solids. Ever. At all. This isn't open to interpretation. No smoking on board. Vaping's fine. And any uninvited guests pay for their own taxi home if they wake up in the next town. All understood?" said Johnny, his arms folded across his chest.

"What's the point of a toilet if we can't use it?" asked Danny, a genuine look of confusion on his face.

"You've roomed with Mikee enough times. I'll remind you of that if he breaks the rules, "said Dom, lighting two cigarettes and passing one to Jamie.

With all the equipment loaded and everybody safely on board, their 'personal space' selected, Johnny shouted, "Next stop Glasgow!"

Leaning across the aisle, Danny said excitedly, "That means we get to go to Tebay! Those scotch eggs."

Back on the road, Johnny smiled to himself…

***

"But all he wanted to talk about was the boys and the band. It was awful!" said Cally, as she sat in Costa stirring her coffee.

"He's a nice guy. I never thought he'd be like that. I'm sorry Cal, honestly," said Jo, as she broke a bite size piece of muffin off. "Still, I'd have loved to have seen his face when you walked out."

Giggling and covering her mouth, as she had just bitten into her own muffin, she said, "Well, he deserved it. The only thing he stopped short of was asking for free tickets. The cheek of him!"

"It must all be a bit odd for you right now. I mean all that stuff in the papers about Jamie and that Lara girl," said Jo.

Sighing deeply, "I'm going to have to get used to it. It's fine with Jamie, he speaks to me regularly and I get the truth from him about stuff." Lowering her voice to a whisper, she added, "He does really like her and said he may go out to America for a couple of weeks when they've finished the tour."

"She's very beautiful," said Jo breathlessly, eating another tiny morsel of muffin.

"Isn't she! But Jamie's a very good-looking boy too," said Cally, a little more defensively than she had meant to.

"I didn't mean it like that," said Jo, laughing. "They'd have gorgeous babies!"

"Ooh, not just yet, please!" said Cally. "And did I tell you about the press guy turning up on my doorstep? It was awful. They gave Jamie a hard time as well. I hate them!"

"Suppose you'll all have to get used to that sort of thing," said Jo, screwing up her nose.

"My big worry is Dominic. He's very headstrong and seems to be enjoying the rock 'n' roll lifestyle a little too much."

"But boys will be boys," said Jo, screwing up the muffin wrapper into a neat ball.

"I know, but it just worries me. You know. All the stories you hear," replied Cally, a worried look on her face.

"What can you do though? Just ignore the papers and trust them."

"I know. And thanks. But no more blind dates!" said Cally as she hugged Jo goodbye, kissing her on both cheeks.

"I won't! And I'll be having a word with our friend after his performance! See you soon. And not so long between catch-ups next time," said Jo.

***

"Gentlemen, I'll have to ask you to go to your rooms if this level of noise carries on," said the hotel's duty manager in calming tones.

"He's the one that started shouting and kicking off though," said Danny, pointing at the irate male in stood in front of him.

"Should keep his bird happier and she wouldn't want to party with us," said Mikee, leaning back on the hotel reception's sofa.

"But they should'nae be flirtin' wi ma lassie!" shouted angry boyfriend, gesticulating wildly at Dominic and Danny.

As the duty manager tried to restore calm, the root of all the problems then proceeded to make matters worse.

Much worse.

Stood just behind her raging boyfriend and the harassed hotel employee, she again lifted her top up, flashing her bare breasts – to the wild amusement of the clearly inebriated band.

"SHE'S DONE IT AGAIN!" shouted Danny, snapping his fingers and falling onto Mikee's shoulder as he dissolved into fits of laughter.

Turning around with a look of mortified outrage on his face, angry boyfriend whirled round, only to see his flirtatious girlfriend assuming a very demure look.

The Rock'N'The Roll. 'N That

"Lovely tits," said Mikee, applauding.

"IF HE SIYS THA' ONE MORE FUCKIN TIME!" He balled his fists and breathed heavily. "I SWEAR THA' I'LL…" Looking down at Mikee, he seemed to reconsider his threat.

"Nice T-shirt by the way pal," deadpanned Mikee, pointing at angry boyfriend.

Looking down as if he had forgotten what he was wearing, angry boyfriend seemed to have a moment of clarity as he realised he was wearing a newly purchased piece of Lonely Souls merchandise.

As this comedic moment was playing out, Danny was making eyes and mouthing encouragement for flirtatious girlfriend to again lift her top. Just as she was about to perform again, the duty manager, who had clocked the prompting, whipped round and caught her just as she was about reveal all.

Ripping the T-shirt up over his head and balling it up before throwing it in Danny's laughing face, the boyfriend said, "YOUSE CAN STICK YER SHITTY T-SHIRT, YA BASTARDS! YOUSE ARE FUCKING SHITE N'ALL. I'VE HEARD MA GRANNIE PLAY BETTER SONGS. AND SHE'S FUCKING DEID. YA CUNTS!"

"Temper temper!" cackled Danny, as he pointedly smoothed out the T-shirt before handing it to Dom. "We'll stick that back on the merch stand tomorrow. Good as new."

This tipped the now bare-chested angry boyfriend over the edge. Lurching for Danny over the table of drinks, he was only stopped by Mikee, as he put an oversized paw onto the sun-starved pimply chest.

"GENTLEMEN PLEASE!" shouted the duty manger, his nerves fraying rapidly. "I'm going to politely ask if you two could leave and if you could drink up and return to your rooms."

"But we haven't done anything other than buy a drink for the lady," said Danny, a look of absolute innocence on his face.

"I'LL BREAK THOSE FUCKING SHADES ACROSS YER FACE YA CUNT!" shouted angry boyfriend, this time from a safer distance.

"I was ready to call it a night anyhow," said Dominic, finishing off his pint.

As the band stood to leave the bar area, the manager mouthed a silent thank you. The couple were now heading for the revolving door, with flirtatious girlfriend protesting her innocence. Just as they reached the door, Danny shouted after them, "Lovely meeting ya both. Keep in touch and we'll stick you on the guestlist next time we're in Glasgow."

Having been stood at the bar, taking in the whole scene, Johnny, Jamie and Spoony shook their heads, laughed and chinked glasses.

"I love this shit," said Spoony. "My round. What d'yer want fellas…"

***

"Lara. It's Jamie."

"I know who it is. Your number comes up on my phone," teased Lara.

"What time is it over there?" asked Jamie as he started to undress for bed, turning the immaculately made sheets back.

"You always ask that. It's just gone nine. I'm going out soon. Some drinks reception at a gallery opening. It's my friends so I should really make the effort even though I'm beat," said Lara as she applied the finishing touches to her make-up in the large ornate mirror that dominated the hallway to her downtown Manhattan apartment. "It's in Brooklyn. Then we're going on to a way cool bar. I'll ask them to play one of your tracks."

"Enjoy yourself. We've just played a top show in Glasgow. It was roasting!"

"Roasting?" queried Lara.

"HAHA. Sorry. Dead hot. It was packed out," said Jamie, laughing softly.

"Your accent at times!" said Lara, as she teased her into place.

"My accent! It's you Americans and your fancy expressions," taunted Jamie. "The others got a bit pissed after the show and nearly got us thrown out of the hotel."

"Pissed? See. You're at it again. You mean they were in a bad mood," Lara joked at her own expense.

"You know what I meant," said Jamie, as he slid under the sheets.

"Papers still talking about us even though I've flown back across the pond?" asked Lara.

"Not now you've flown home. They'll be back on it when you come over here." With a slight pause, he added, "or when I come out to see you…"

"Jamie Thorne. I never knew you cared," said Lara. Her accent as bewitching as ever to Jamie whenever she said his name.

"I was thinking that when we've finished this tour and what have you…"

"Oh, you had me at the 'what have you'," laughed Lara.

"Well?"

"I'll think about it. Now you sleep well, Jamie Thorne. Think of me when I'm stood around listening to boring people talking about themselves," said

Lara as she locked her front door and headed down the signature brownstone steps of her apartment building and stepped into the waiting car.

"Night, Lara Bearheart."

"Night, Jamie Thorne."

Hanging up the phone, Jamie laughed to himself. Looking round his room in the perfectly comfortable Premier Inn Glasgow, he had just had a conversation with one of the most beautiful women in the world. He was starting to enjoy this rock 'n' roll lark…

***

Settling down for bed, Johnny flipped on his laptop so that he could reply to a couple of emails, still laughing to himself about the hotel bar incident – first night of the tour and they were very nearly out on their collective ears.

Propping a pillow behind him, Johnny sat and scanned the list of emails – nothing problematic, few from Suzzie with radio airplay figures and some dates for regional radio interviews and sessions.

And then one he had previously missed from Cally.

'Hello Johnny. I feel a bit silly asking this, but look after the boys whilst they're on tour. I know that you will, but things are all happening so quickly it just takes some getting used to.

And thanks again for calling me back after I went on that awful date. I was a bit upset by it all, but I'll be more careful in future – and choosier! Take care, Love Cally xx'

Johnny had always felt a responsibility over the brothers – the whole band for that matter. And a beseeching email from their mum certainly ramped up the pressure. What could he do though? Boys in a band hanging onto the bucking bronco of rock 'n' roll and all its salacious offerings.

Girls were never not around the band and this low hanging fruit was being picked in grateful abundance.

Dominic was like a man possessed around the opposite sex, and no matter how brusque or dismissive his mood might be on any given day, it didn't seem to deter them.

Danny, as much as he continued to protest his innocence, always seemed to be under a cloud of morning-after guilt.

And Mikee, if he wasn't watching it on his iPad, was talking about his night before exploits.

Jamie, since meeting Lara, had been resolutely faithful. Quite the achievement given the numerous offers he received and the fact that there was the matter of a 3500-mile-wide pond between him and the exotic Lara.

He'd also noticed that drug usage had increased markedly – again with Dominic leading the way by a nose, ably assisted by Mikee and Danny. Jamie wasn't behind the door at having a line but seemed to use it to clear his head rather than power through to the small hours of the next day.

What could he do, he asked himself as he closed his laptop and felt a wave of sleep pass over him. With another sixteen dates of the tour to go, he vowed to be vigilant but that was really all he could do.

***

"Did you see the look on his face when he turned around and realised that his bird kept flashing her tits at us?" said Danny, his voice morning-after croaky.

Sitting over breakfast in the hotel restaurant, Dominic, also the worse for wear, choked slightly on his toast as he laughed, "And what a twat when he took his T-shirt off and threw it at you!"

"Fuckin' funny," grinned Mikee as ploughed his way through his fried breakfast with the gusto of a condemned man.

"Edinburgh tonight. Wicked time when we were there last time. Can't wait. Girls were lovely at that club we went to. Bang up for it," said Dom. "Need to get ourselves sorted before we go partying though."

***

The dates passed by with all the usual associated rock 'n' roll shenanigans – bedposts were notched with amazing alacrity. Booze was consumed like mother's milk, powders were imbibed at all hours and scotch eggs remained a staple source of sustenance.

A joyous homecoming at Manchester Academy 1 – an upgrade on the original venue, much to the band's delight – was packed to the newly replaced rafters. Friends, family and general well-wishers ensured that the gig went brilliantly. Manchester absolutely had taken Lonely Souls as their new 'favourite sons'.

A particularly ebullient Johnny had promised that they would play five consecutive nights at the city's Apollo Theatre on their next tour when he heard the news that the album had gone up to number seven in the charts.

The Rock'N'The Roll. 'N That

'I promise you! It's never been done before. But you'll see. Next tour, we'll make a bit of history,' he'd announced in front of several equally drunk witnesses in the packed dressing room.

***

"You can't just do that!" snarled Dominic as the naked girl recoiled under the bed-sheets, pulling her knees up to her chin.

Jumping out of bed and tying a bath towel round his waist, he jabbed his finger angrily in the direction of the clearly shaken girl's face.

"YOU DON'T DRINK MY BOOZE. SNIFF MY COKE. COME BACK TO MY ROOM!" Dominic started to pace the room agitatedly, the sleep-depriving cocaine preventing his adrenaline levels from dropping. "YOU TAKE YOUR CLOTHES OFF AND GET INTO MY BED AND THEN DECIDE THAT YOU DON'T WANT TO FUCK!"

Realising that he was shouting, he dropped his voice to a calmer, more measured tone.

The first of two nights at the O2 Academy in Islington had been, in keeping with the whole of the tour, a huge success. Totally sold-out, an oversubscribed guestlist and an adoring crowd who knew every word to every song. All obviously proud owners of the Lonely Souls debut album. Currently number seven and rising.

Dominic had met Grace at the aftershow and had been instantly attracted to her pre-Raphaelite head of auburn coloured hair.

As she sat in the double bed of his hotel room, the mood had soured since their initial flirtation. "I'm sorry," Grace whispered, "But I just don't want to now. It doesn't feel right. Sorry."

"Sorry!" said Dominic, his voice dripping with contempt. "Sorry doesn't cut it. I could have had any girl there tonight. Any girl that had watched the gig would have come back here." He looked at her with a dismissive shake of his head. "Any of those girls would have wanted to be here and not be fuckin' sorry," he sneered.

With a hardening of her resolve, Grace flashed a filthy look in Dominic's direction. "Maybe I'm not like those girls then." Bunching the bed sheet around her slim naked form, she said, "Don't make me scream the place down. I should go."

Standing so that she could gather her clothes and leave Dominic to brood, Grace was startled as she was pushed back on to the bed, the sheet falling away from her, revealing her coral pink nipples and perfectly tended auburn pubic hair.

"STAY!" he demanded. "We can have another drink, take things from there. No harm done eh?"

"I said I'd scream. I'm going. Now. Sorry," said Grace, once again rising from the bed.

"Go then. I hate girls like you! Fuckin' prickteasers. Prickteasers! There's nothing worse," he spat.

As Grace gathered her clothing and headed to the bathroom to dress in private, she met Dom's stare, "No. There's nothing worse is there?" Shaking her head slowly, the knots in her stomach vice-tight, she closed the bathroom and locked it shut, breathing a sigh of relief, she dressed hurriedly.

Opening the bathroom door slowly, she saw that Dominic was sat up on the bed, angrily drumming his fingers against his thigh. "I'm going now. Sorry this didn't work out as we thought it would. Bye Dominic."

Snorting with obvious derision, "You'll regret this tomorrow. What might have been…"

Picking up her small clutch bag. "Really? Maybe you should think about this too," said Grace softly. "Bye Dominic."

The door closed behind her with a metallic click. "Fuckin' pricktease," he snapped, punching the mattress repeatedly.

***

Casting his name down the guestlist, Johnny clocked an exceptionally unusual name: *'Alicia Cloudfall'*. Frowning to himself, he assumed it must be a pretentious pseudonym for a would-be shy and retiring celebrity.

Given that they had played the venue the previous day, only a cursory soundcheck was required.

Although the tour had been hectic, it had energised the band – being out on the road with a record that the public had bought. and taken to their collective hearts. Standing in the venues, Johnny had felt the connection between audience and band – the choruses were sung along with a word-perfect gusto. Jamie's sincerity, apparent in the way he delivered his lyrics. It felt like one of those 'right time and right place' moments.

At the previous evening's aftershow, Johnny had observed Jamie looking somewhat lost – clearly missing Lara, who he had hoped would have made the transatlantic hop for the gigs.

Dominic had gone off earlier than normal with a firecracker of a redhead.

The Rock 'N' The Roll. 'N That

And Mikee and Danny had done their bit to keep the share price in Jack Daniels at a quartile high.

After they had drained the last of the bottle, Danny put his arms around Johnny and Amanda, and asked the question that had been burning away at him all tour.

"Why do you call him Spoony?" As they were stood at the bar, Johnny picked up a cocktail stirring spoon and held it up to Dan's face, bottom side down. Pulling the spoon away from him, Danny watched his reflection elongate. "Oh fuck. Right! I swear I've never called it him."

"See that you don't! He's a good bloke. Just not the best looking of fellas," said Johnny quietly.

It was the last night of their first headlining tour. Their debut single, 'Salvation', was due out next week. They were, without doubt, hot property and the new darlings of the music press – something that could prove to be a poisoned chalice, Johnny had thought in his occasional glass half-empty moments. Tabloid interest was bubbling away quietly and particularly when Lara was in the country.

"Tonight. Definitely," said Jamie, as the band performed their ritual pre-gig huddle.

"You better had bro. Don't let us down," said Dominic as he hugged Jamie, kissing him warmly on the cheek.

***

Pulling his jacket around to keep the autumn chill at bay, Jamie sat at the rear of the venue on the bottom step of a metal fire escape. Sally Valley huddled next to him as they shared a roll-up.

"All happening for you boys, isn't it so," said Sally, pushing her hair behind her ears. Shivering against the cold she edged further into Jamie's side. "I said so didn't I, was right I was."

Jamie laughed, and exhaled. "You make me laugh. You sound like Yoda when you start talking with your Welsh accent. I fuckin' loves it I do," he said, putting on a dreadful Welsh accent.

"What the fuck was that supposed to be? Cos it certainly wasn't no Welsh!" Elbowing Jamie flirtatiously, Sally accepted the cigarette back from Jamie.

"But yeah. It is. I still can't believe it's all happening. The album. Man, if I never record another song I'd die a proud man. It's fuckin' brilliant." Turning to smile at Sally, he said, "But you lot still only gave it eight out of ten. It's a nine at least!"

"Get you. What is it with you Mancs and your cockiness?" she laughed.

"Nothing to do with Manchester. It's a top album. You knows it!" said Jamie, again dropping into the lamentable Welsh accent.

"FUCK OFF!" shrilled Sally, "Or it'll be seven out of ten next time. If you're bastard lucky!"

"Joking. It's fucking freezing out here," said Jamie.

"Hang on a sec. This'll warm your cockles." Sally pulled out her purse from a small canvas handbag. Opening a small paper wrap. "Hold still." And with a neat movement, she shovelled a small mound of coke onto her apartment door key. Leaning into Sally, Jamie snorted the powder up, rubbing at his nose as he ingested the cocaine.

Following suit, Sally keyed a mound up each nostril. "There we go! Ooh that's good," she said, enjoying the cold drop of the cocaine down her throat.

"What did you think of our set tonight then?" asked Jamie.

"Loved it! Obviously. And the stage dive. That was way fucking cool!" Waving her hands excitedly, she said, "OH MY GOD! I forgot. What about your scarf?"

***

Earlier that evening, as Dominic was driving the set to a close with his savage guitar solo at the end of 'Salvation'. Jamie had leant his guitar against his amp, walked to the front of the stage, stared out at the sea of expectant faces and open arms. And jumped. A relatively graceful arm extended dive. Nothing too extravagant for his first foray into the fine-art of stage-diving.

Intuitively, the crowd had caught him and started to pass him about like flotsam on a choppy tide. Rolling onto his back, Jamie had extended his right arm skyward and attempted to sing out the now familiar chorus. The exhilaration he had felt was life-affirming and like the loss of one's proverbial virginity, was an experience that would never quite re-capture that first time feeling.

As he felt the hands around him, passing him back and forth along the opposable thumb-based conveyor belt, he felt a hand pull at his scarf. In seconds, it had gone. Directing the flow of the crowd to take him back to the lip of the stage, Jamie was helped back up by a burly security guard. Sans scarf.

***

Tossing his head back and laughing loudly, he said, "I'll let you into a little secret." He whispered into Sally's ear. "Stunt scarf."

"Fuck off," she laughed, punching him on the arm.

"HAHA! I'd been planning the stage dive all tour but kept bottling it. But I knew as soon as I did it that I'd probably lose my clothes, so I bought a stunt scarf."

"Ooh, you sneaky bastard," said Sally.

"And the best of it is Johnny suggested we do an appeal to get my 'trusty' scarf back. Bit of publicity and that."

"We are learning fast, aren't we," said Sally, nodding sagely.

"Well we've got to try and stay one step ahead of you lot." He shivered against the chill. "Anyhow. Let's head back inside now. I fancy a beer."

"Don't I get a kiss before we go inside?" asked Sally coyly.

Jamie ran his thumb down her petite upturned nose and cupped her chin gently between his finger and thumb. "I wouldn't want you writing about how I kiss in your paper, now, would I?"

Making a small cross my heart gesture, Sally looked deeply into Jamie's eyes. "Brownies' honour. C'mon Jamie. You're fucking gorgeous, so you are, man?"

Pulling her towards him, Jamie put his hand on Sally's night-chilled cheek and kissed her, pulling her into him as the intensity increased.

"Hmmm. Nice," said Jamie, "but not a word in your New Musical Express Ms Valley!"

"I said Brownies' honour and I meant it, so I did," she said smiling and rubbing her hand through his hair. "Want another quick toot before we go back in?" she said, reaching for her purse.

"Why not?" said Jamie.

After the bugle had been imbibed and another short kiss exchanged, Jamie and Sally headed back to the warmth of the dressing room.

Flashing his pass at the security guard stood vigil at the characterless looking dressing room door, Jamie, holding Sally's hand, stepped into the dressing room which was now packed full of bodies wishing to rock the roll and get their own slice of the band. Drinking the scene in, he saw Johnny deep in conversation with Amanda. Mikee, as ever flexing an ink festooned bicep - an admiring female stood on her toes taking in the needlework. Dominic and Danny were stood against the back wall and Jamie flashed a peace sign and grinned at them.

Dominic froze immediately and gave a short warning shake of his head. His cocaine-heightened awareness picked up on this and Jamie's blue eyes flashed around the dressing room.

Stood in the corner, partially covered by her omnipresent security, jet-black hair matching the vintage black leather biker's jacket and tight fitted T-shirt that adorned her killer figure, was Lara.

Turning and staring at the door she slowly sipped on a bottle of cold Peroni.

Startled didn't come close as Jamie visibly gulped. His inner narrative screamed 'oh fuck' at a thousand decibels…

***

Although he had not yet thawed out from his first visit to the metal staircase, Jamie now found himself there once again.

"You should have told me that you were coming. I hadn't heard from you in weeks!" said Jamie, leaning against the wall with his arms wrapped around him. His body language both to protect him from the cold and an indication of his discomfort.

"So I see," said Lara curtly.

Offering Lara a cigarette, which she declined with a raised palm, he asked, "What's that supposed to mean?"

"I should have thought that's kinda obvious, Jamie. I'll let you have a mascara pencil if you wanna just go ahead and write guilty on your forehead."

The momentary hesitation spoke volumes. "I, err, I didn't know you were going to be here."

Rising and standing over Jamie, Lara said, "Okay," putting her hands on her hips, "So when I'm not here you're getting cosy with little blondie."

Shaking his head and stubbing out the cigarette he had been vigorously drawing on, Jamie rose to meet Lara's dogged stare. "You've got no room to talk…"

Lara stood in silence, looking impassive.

"This is pointless. I've missed you like fuck. We've been on opposite sides of the world for the past month. And as you insist on reminding me, we're not an item," he said with a shrug of his shoulders.

Mirroring Jamie's shrug of his shoulders, Lara looked more little girl lost than he ever imagined possible.

"I've missed you Jamie Thorne!"

"I've missed you," he said, putting a hand on her waist.

"I'm cold. Let's go back inside.," said Lara matter of factly. "Great set. Loved the stage-dive, Jamie Thorne. Shame about your scarf. "

Tapping his nose, Jamie held the fire door open for Lara. "I'll tell you later…"

***

Returning to the dressing room, Jamie immediately sought out Johnny. Tugging at the shoulder of his tweed overcoat, he said, "You could have told me man!"

"Told you what, "said Johnny, with a confused look on his face.

Without trying to draw any attention to them, Jamie whispered in Johnny's ear, "That Lara was here! You always check the guestlist. Every fuckin' gig. It's your little ritual. Always makes me smile. Why the fuck didn't you tell me?"

"Because I didn't know! Her name wasn't down. I promise J. I'll get the list and show you." Resisting the temptation to glance across at her, he said, "What the fuck's the problem anyhow. Thought you'd be pleased to see each other."

"If you hadn't been so wrapped up with Amanda you might have noticed she was here. I'd gone for a cig with Sally, "said Jamie, discreetly nodding his head in Sally's direction.

"Oh! You went for a cig!" He put extra emphasis on the 'cig'. "And that's my fault. 'Kin 'ell Jamie. I know you don't mean that."

"Yeah, alright, bu—"

"Meet me in the corridor in a minute," said Johnny, feeling as if everyone was staring at them.

Checking that there were no prying ears, he said, "So let me get this right. Lara has showed up and you were off getting it on with Sally. From the NME."

"Fuck's sake Johnny. I didn't know!" said Jamie.

"Proper little mess we've got here. Clearly you want to smooth things over with Lara, but you're going to have to let Sally down gently."

"I know!" snapped Jamie. "Look, I'm sorry man. It's not your fault. But you sure she wasn't on the list?"

"Sure I'm sure!" said Johnny, again checking over his shoulder that they were on their own. "Look, everyone's heading over to The Hospital Club for the aftershow. Let's see who turns up there and flip a coin, "said Johnny, before bursting out laughing.

"What the fuck's so funny," said Jamie. Struggling to stifle his own laughter

"Come here, you daft twat," said Johnny, hugging Jamie into him. "Serves you right for being so fucking gorgeous!"

Scratching his head with both hands animatedly, Jamie laughed, "For fuck's sake!"

Returning to the now-thinning out dressing room, Jamie saw that Lara had already gone.

"Problem solved," Johnny whispered, "For now…"

***

"You know I don't go kissing all the pretty boys in bands, so I don't," said Sally, sipping on a bones-warming brandy.

"I'm sure you don't. And I don't kiss all the girls that ask me," smiled Jamie, nursing his own brandy.

"And I write the stories. I don't want to be part of them," said Sally, meeting Jamie's faraway gaze.

"What's the story?" laughed Jamie

"Ha. You knows what I mean!" smiled Sally. "And make sure your second album is as good as that and you'll be right, so you will."

"It'll be even better," nodded Jamie. "You'll be the first journo to hear 'em," He kissed her on the cheek, "I promise," and then made a three-fingered gesture by his ear, "Scout's honour!"

"Oh, you were always too rock 'n' roll for Scouts Jamie. That I'm certain I am!" said Sally.

"Another drink?" asked Jamie.

"I will. But I've got to ask, so I have. You gonna chase after her tonight?" said Sally, her brow furrowing slightly.

"I dunno. I really don't. She's a world away from me." Laughing almost to himself, "Just pick up a paper and find out…"

"I will, don't worry!" said Sally.

"You any of that sniff left? Last night of the tour and all that."

"Seeing as though it be you," she said, reaching discreetly for her purse. "And go easy. I know what you lead singers are like!"

As Jamie sought a cubicle in the luxurious toilets, he checked his mobile – no messages.

A tap-tap of his credit card was echoed from one of the other cubicles, causing Jamie to chuckle to himself. A hastily rolled twenty and a sweep of his head and the hooter was hoovered. Stepping out of the cubicle and checking his reflection he caught sight of Dominic, stepping out of an adjacent cubicle.

"Alright bro. Were you talking to yourself in there?" said Dom, now also checking his reflection and dabbing at his nose.

"No. Just knew somebody else was walking the line. You okay?" said Jamie, as he started to wash his hands in the polished aluminium sink.

"Good thanks J. I was just gonna ask you the same. Got your hands full, haven't you? Said you should have left that Sally Welsh bird to me!"

"You're all heart bro," laughed Jamie. "My own fault." Turning to his twin, he said, "Number three album and a single that could go even higher. I can live with that."

"Been some year," said Dominic, feeling a cocaine-induced numbness in his front teeth.

"And it's only gonna get bigger when we start with those new songs. I love yer man. Come 'ere," said Jamie, hugging his brother into him.

"Soft twat!" laughed Dom. "Anyhow. I've got to get back out there. Nice gaff this, isn't it? Can't have you with two birds on the go and leave me all empty handed…"

***

Having resisted the urge to check his phone for over an hour, and almost ready for the hotel, Jamie looked down at his iPhone. There was the little red circle indicating he had an electronic missive.

Casually opening the icon, his pulse increased slightly. Lara. *'So where are you then?'*

No 'X' he noted to himself, and the message was almost an hour old. But it was Lara. He weighed up his thoughts quickly – Sally had gone and that had been wrapped very harmoniously. Johnny had gone off with Amanda like a love-struck puppy, having been out shopping again all afternoon.

"How much of our advance are you spending on coats?" he'd joked that afternoon as Johnny had turned up with a beautiful tan coloured trench coat. Dom had now acquired some female company. And Mikee and Danny. They had gone off to Soho on Mikee's insistence – D-Mo had a somewhat concerned look in his dilated pupils.

Fortune favours the brave, Jamie thought as he tapped out a message –

'Leaving aftershow. Can meet up. Where are you? J'

If there was no reply in five minutes, he planned to go back to the hotel. However, his phone pinged back immediately –

'Hakkasan. Get here now x'

Nodding at Dominic, he left quietly.

Arriving at the bar, a cosmopolitan and chic looking establishment just off Oxford St, he hopped out of the cab and was met by Lara.

A saucer-eyed, and for her, very bedraggled Lara. Smoking frenziedly and talking at machine-gun chatter speed. Her make-up was streaked and her hair, a voluminous tangle.

His 'spider senses' shouted trouble and he half-considered hopping back into the idling cab.

Too late.

"JAMIE THORNE!" shouted Lara, flicking her cigarette with pinpoint accuracy into the gutter. "JAMIE THORNE. SO, YOU HAVEN'T STOOD ME UP TWICE IN A NIGHT!"

"Hey Lara. Shall we go in and get a drink. Away from..." He made a sweeping gesture with his hand at the passing punters and small crowd of people that Lara had been stood with.

"OH, I'M FINE!" she said, again with some considerable volume.

But you're clearly not, Jamie thought to himself…

Turning to one of her companions, she said in a dreadful stage whisper, "I FLEW ALL THE WAY FROM AMERICA JUST TO SEE JAMIE AND HE WAS GETTING ALL SWEET WITH SOME LITTLE BITCH!"

"That's not strictly true is it? I had no idea tha—"

She cut him off sharply.

"FUCK YOU! I WAS HUMILIATED. THAT SHIT DOESN'T HAPPEN TO ME!" Making a comedic pointing gesture to herself, Lara then stepped towards Jamie, her manicured hands on her hips. "BUT MR ROCKSTAR WAS OFF ELSEWHERE. NOW HE'S SOOOO POPULAR."

"C'mon Lara. Not here, Please," he said, reaching out for her elbow.

Smack. A stinging slap rang across his right cheek.

"Fuck sake!" he yelled. He then raised both his palms up in front of him. Lara's eyes had taken on an incandescent quality. Her mocha coloured complexion had a sweat sheened pallor to it. *Somebody has done a fuck load of coke,* thought Jamie.

"JAMIE THORNE. WHO SAYS HE LIKES ME AND THEN STANDS

ME UP AND OH WAIT," she shouted, with a quick involuntary rub of her nose, "GETS ALL COSY WITH SOME BITCH BEHIND MY BACK!"

"I'm going," said Jamie, turning sharply and bumping into a stationary passer-by who had been recording the exchange in glorious megapixel technicolour…

Chapter 40

"Welcome home Jamie. You couldn't just stick the kettle on for us, could you?" said the wretchedly familiar face of photographer number one.

Their numbers had multiplied, and the two-lensed beast was now four.

"She can pack a punch, can't she?" said photographer three. A gaunt looking individual, wearing a grey canvas utility-style waistcoat.

"Looked like it hurt. Gonna take your shades off and show us the damage?" said photographer number two, leaning on a concrete bollard whilst he idly scrolled through his mobile phone.

It was thirty-six hours since the pavement incident in London and the amateur paparazzo had duly received their requisite pieces of silver for the on-the-spot mobile handiwork. Most disconcerting was the video had been hosted on the newspaper's website gossip page. It was all there in glorious sound and vision. Lara, a dishevelled and under various influences was the antagonist, with Jamie merely the unwilling recipient of the back of her vicious tongue and equally sharp backhand.

The two minutes twenty-three second clip had been given the usual tabloid spin with a completely unfounded comment that Lara's wrist had been 'badly bruised' when Jamie had attempted to lead her inside the bar and away from prying eyes.

Having seen both the offending newspaper and website on the train journey back from London, Jamie was totally expecting the camera bearing reception committee. Taking off his Aviator shades, Jamie turned and faced the scrape – this being his chosen collective noun of choice – of the press pack assembled in front of him.

"Nothing to see I'm afraid. Sorry to disappoint." Popping his shades back on, he flipped a finger in their direction. "And fuck you all very much…"

And there it was. The picture to satiate the scrape's finger hungry appetite. A volley of camera lenses clicked into action. Jamie understood this was exactly what they wanted. Returning Rockstar sporting shades giving it the big attitude.

What he wasn't expecting was photographer number four's planned provocation. "Proper tough guy aren't we Jamie. We can't wait to run the pictures of you slapping her back. That'll rain on your parade…"

Pushing his Ray-Bans up on to the top of his head, Jamie nonchalantly turned on the photographer, who had already primed his camera awaiting his reaction. "Any pictures like that are utter fuckin' bullshit. You know it and I know it. I'll get your arses sued so fuckin' quickly you'll be begging in doorways this time next month."

Looking the photographer up and down with a dismissive sneer, he said, "You fat fuckin' bullshit merchant. Go fuck yourself…"

"Nice words Jamie. Enjoy the rest of your day," laughed photographer number two.

"That'll be it for a while. Whose round is it to nip to Greggs? I'm starving," said photographer number one, rubbing his stomach absentmindedly.

***

Entering his apartment, Jamie chucked his bag onto the bedroom floor and flopped back onto the bed. Holding his hands to his temples, he screwed his eyes shut and let out an exasperated grimace. He hadn't heard from Lara since the unseemly altercation, and a text from Sally opining that he should have come back to hers for a spliff hadn't helped his darkening mood.

"Johnny. I know we've only just got back from London, but you fancy a coffee. Come around and buzz on. Cheers man."

Jamie hung up and tapped his phone pensively against his chin. He couldn't bring himself to watch the online spat again. The others had kept their own counsel when they had first seen the footage. There had almost been a realisation that they were public property now and the stark truth was there for all to see.

And Lara. She was 'off her nut'. He knew that she liked a line. They all did. But this had been something else. This wasn't the spiritual karmic girl he'd spent hours and hours getting to know.

***

"Go on then. Look at it," said Danny, as he perched on the edge of the bath.

Dee, sat in an unedifying pose on the toilet with her knickers round her ankles. "I can't. You look," she said, handing the plastic strip across to Danny.

Recoiling slightly at the piss dripping and potentially life-changing wand, Danny breathed in deeply and closed his eyes.

Opening his eyes, as Dee closed hers, he held his breath and looked down.

"Blue. It's blue," he said quietly.

Dee slowly opened her eyes, "Are you sure?"

"Course!" he said indignantly.

"Definitely blue?"

"It's blue and that means…"

"That means you're going to be a dad!" squealed Dee, jumping up from her porcelain perch, and hugging Danny, who was vainly trying not to touch her with the pregnancy divining rod.

"A dad." Rolling the words round his tongue, confusion, delight and fear were all clouding his ability to grasp the moment. "Me. A dad. I just never thought…"

"You'll be amazing! Absolutely amazing," said Dee, hitching up her skirt and pulling her leopard-print knickers back up.

Struggling to articulate, Danny stood open-mouthed. "And, err, and you'll be the best mum in the world. I just hope he doesn't get my nose," he laughed nervously.

"Oh, it's a boy is it?" said Dee, wiping tears from her eyes.

"Don't cry! You'll set me off," said Danny, his voice wavering. "And you know what I mean. I don't mind at all. Boy baby or girl baby."

"Oh Danny! I can't believe this. I do love you."

"And I love you," Danny said, still shrouded in his post-tour guilt.

Prior to the day's bombshell, he had decided that he was going to confess all to Dee and promise to never stray again if she had granted him absolution of his groupie based sins. *Forgive me Dee, for I have sinned. Many times, with many, many girls…* thought Danny

This, however, moved the goalposts. This was much more than that. It changed the sport and the shape of the goalposts. But Dan's preternatural guilt was showing no sign of abeyance…

Chapter 41

It was 6 a.m. on a typical cold and damp Sunday morning. The band had assembled to shoot the video for 'Mantra'. Barney had again been enlisted for the job, and had made the epic trek up North the previous day.

The shoot took place in the 'skeleton' framework of an apartment block adjacent to the Mancunian Way.

A cherry-picker supplied by a window cleaner mate of Johnny's and the presence of cameras had soon alerted the local constabulary.

Who, after a fumbled 'bribe' of gig tickets, had let them off with a friendly move-on…

***

After the completion of the shoot, the band, together with Barney, Ged the window-cleaner and Johnny went for a fry-up breakfast at a café on Oxford Road.

Fiddling with the salt and pepper shakers, Danny was even twitchier than normal.

"What's up D-Mo? You've hardly said a word all morning. You weren't scared of the heights were yer?" said Dominic, as he poured sugar into his tea.

"Nah. Fuck off. Not at all," snapped Danny.

"Go on then. What's up with yer?" said Mikee, hungrily glancing over in the direction of the café's kitchen area.

"Look. This is big news," said Danny, looking around almost furtively.

Interrupted by the arrival of their food, Danny hesitated before he made his revelation.

"I'm gonna be a dad. Got back off tour and Dee's pregnant," gauging his bandmates' faces for their reaction.

"Congratulations man!" shouted Mikee.

"Fuck. A Lonely Souls baby," said Dom, "Pleased for you D-Mo."

"Me too," said Jamie, "Made up for you. Really am."

"Don't look so worried. You'll be a natural," said Johnny, a quick flashback to his attempts at paternity running through his mind.

"I'll film the birth if you want," offered Barney, through a mouthful of vegan bacon.

Raising his mug of overly-sweet tea, Dominic called a toast. "To Danny and Dee! And a little D-Mo!"

Seven chipped mugs came together, and Danny mustered up his best smile.

***

"Right lads. My visa is only for twenty-four hours, so if I don't leave these Northern wastelands sharpish, I'll get scurvy or summat," said Barney, adjusting his pastel blue plus-fours. "Video will look mega. Had a quick look at some of the footage in the car over here. Love it!"

As goodbyes were exchanged, Johnny noticed Danny hanging back slightly.

"Nice one Barney. We'll await seeing the rough edit later this week."

Turning to Danny, Johnny said, "You okay man?"

"You got time for a pint? Could do with a chat. Don't tell that lot though," mumbled Danny.

"No worries. I'll make excuses and see you in Cord in five," said Johnny.

***

"Guinness do you?" asked Johnny as he caught the barmaid's attention.

"Yeah. Cheers. And thanks for this as well. Can't speak to me dad. He's a cunt. Been better lately…"

As ever, Danny was talking at speed of consciousness pace.

"Right. So, I'm a 'Dad' stand-in. Ta for that!" laughed Johnny.

"Sorry. Didn't mean it like that. But my head's in bits," said Danny, rubbing at his temples as if to illustrate this.

"Okay. I'm all ears. What's the problem?"

Taking a long draw from his pint, and nodding in approval, "I can't do this anymore."

Snapping to attention, Johnny said, "What do you mean? 'This'? You're not quitting the band?"

"FUCK! NO WAY. The band's my life. They'd have to carry me out in a box!" said Danny, with the hint of a laugh.

"That's a fuckin' relief! Don't do that to me!" said Johnny.

"We got back from tour right," he looked round and dropped his voice to a hushed whisper, "and y'know, I wasn't exactly faithful every night. I was gonna 'fess up. To Dee. Tell her I'd never do it again and set a date for the wedding and that. Next year probably," and then with a slight tug on the cuff of Johnny's shirt, "and then she tells me that she's pregnant!"

"You can't say anything Danny. Especially now. She'll go fuckin' spare. I promise!" said Johnny, in an equally whispered manner.

"Look what happened to Jamie though! What if one of the girls goes to the papers or something," said Danny with a heavy sigh, "and the guilt is killing me. Irish Catholic and all that shite." Crossing himself in front of Johnny for the first time.

"Well my son. Father Harrison says confess your sins to me and I'll absolve you of it all. Then shut the fuck up about it!" said Johnny, putting his hands palm together and offering up a prayer.

"I'm serious. I have to tell her. Look Johnny, this is my first proper girlfriend. This is all fuckin' new to me. I've got responsibilities now. I want a clean start," said Danny, gulping the last of his pint down and indicating with a tilt of his glass that it was his shout.

Returning with two fresh pints, Danny said, "What should I do then?"

"I've already told you" said Johnny, with a shake of his head. "Look. She'll never trust you again if you admit you've played about on tour. Think about it from her point of view. If it ever gets into the papers, then unless there are pictures, deny, deny and deny again!"

"I know. But now this. She wouldn't dump me now if I told her? Would she?"

"Don't fucking kid yourself! You'll be worth a few quid if the album keeps selling. You'd get proper screwed over. And you don't want that sort of a relationship with your kid, do you?"

"Course not! I'd have taken my chances before. But now! Fuck sake…"

"Danny. Just don't do it again and deal with it. That's the best advice I can give you. Honestly," said Johnny leaning back in his chair and rubbing a hand through his hair, showing a flash of grey in his temples before it fell back into place.

"Okay. I'll keep it in my pants in future. Thanks for your time Johnny. I knew I could talk to you." Grabbing his parka, Danny knocked back the rest of his pint.

"I'll see you soon. And if you need me, just call," said Johnny, zipping up his coat and pocketing his phone and wallet.

The Rock'N'The Roll. 'N That

***

Relieved to be free of the 'scrape' of photographers, Jamie entered his apartment block with ambitions no loftier than having a few hours' decent sleep. The early start for the video shoot on the back of the tour, and all the insidious pressure with the scurrilous newspaper stories had left him more than a little jaded.

Stripping down to his boxer shorts, he shut the bedroom blinds, pulled back the duvet and went to turn his phone off when he saw that there was new message.

Clicking open the envelope icon, his eyes widened slightly. Lara.

'*Hello Jamie Thorne. Think I owe you a bit of an apology. Gone back to New York. Please don't be a stranger… Lx*'

Sitting cross-legged on the bed, Jamie looked at his watch. Just gone midday, so early morning over there he thought. He fired off a text.

'*Hey Lara. Thank you. Good to hear from you. x*'

Thirty seconds later. Ping.

'*Yeah. I'm sorry for all the newspaper bullshit. I flipped out a bit. I was jetlagged and overdid it a bit. Bad combo. I just thought I'd surprise you! Lx*'

Yawning to himself, Jamie felt his head was a little too fuzzy to get involved in a set of transatlantic textual tennis, so decided he'd make his excuses and grab some sleep and pick this up later. '*I'll catch ya later. Just filming a video x*'

***

"You got anything in the fridge you could knock up into a sandwich for me?" said Dominic, reclining on the sofa in his 'usual spot'.

"I thought you said you'd just had something to eat when Danny told you his news?" said Cally, sorting through the pile of dirty tour laundry that Dominic had kindly brought round for her. Delicately pulling out a skimpy pair of white knickers between her thumb and index finger, she said, "I assume these aren't yours? Unless there is something that you're not telling me!" She laughed, in her tinkling little melodious way.

"Yeah, they are comfier when we're on stage Mum. I thought everybody knew that." Looking across at his mum as she sifted through the sports bag, he winced slightly with embarrassment. "Just chuck 'em away."

"Plenty more where they came from these days, isn't it…" Cally said, in between holding her breath as the soiled tour wear had been fermenting nicely for best part of a fortnight.

"Not me you need worry about? At least mine is all done in private. Look at Jamie plastered across the papers."

"I'm sure he's not chosen to be in the paper though," she said, having now finished separating the laundry into two piles.

"Rather him than me," said Dominic, stretching his arms out wide and yawning loudly.

"Keeping you up are we?"

"These tours take it out of you. And we were up well early this morning. Video should look sick. Although the police turned up at the end!"

"I didn't know Sting was a fan already?" said Cally, struggling to keep a straight face.

"NO! The police, no— Oh, very funny Mum. Very funny!"

Cally smiled back at Dominic, pleased with her little joke.

"No steady girlfriend for you then?"

"I wouldn't really describe Jamie as being settled. Would you?" said Dominic, a little too defensively.

"Well, she does live in America most of the time."

"You always make excuses for him."

"Not at all! I've always treated you both equally."

"I know. But you gave me a hard time last time we got back from tour. I'm just enjoying myself! Who wouldn't?"

"I realise that. I saw the evidence before. What there was of it!" Cally's eyes twinkled as she saw her son cringe slightly again. "I don't mind what you get up to, as I've said before, boys will be boys. I just hope you treat all these girls nicely."

Dominic swallowed at this comment. The hotel room incident with Grace had lingered in his mind. The worry that she might sell her story to the papers, or worse, had not escaped him.

"Course I do! Takes two to tango Mum…"

"Hmmm. Quite. Anyhow. Will a bowl of soup do you?"

"What have you got? I'd love some mushroom soup."

"Hang on. I'll just ask the chef."

"Very funny. Again."

"Well. You come around with your dirty washing and demanding to be feed. Shall I tell the papers how her Rockstar son comes around to have his errands done?"

The Rock'N'The Roll. 'N That

"Oh haha! You're on form today."

"Why thank you. I've missed you both," she said, strangely grateful for the opportunity to still be doing her boy's dirty laundry....

Chapter 42

"Are you sure it's a good idea?" said Johnny, as he washed his hands in the kitchen sink.

"I honestly don't know," said Jamie, pulling his woollen beanie hat further up his head and then scratching his forehead.

"I know you like her. But this is never going to be an easy relationship. And all the shit that keeps getting trotted out in the papers. That can't be easy…" said Johnny, flipping the kettle on.

"The only reason that bothers me is that most of it is bollocks and it detracts from the music. Look what happened to Pete Doherty. Class songwriter but he became tabloid fodder. I don't want that."

"No, I know. But there's only Dom not hit the headlines yet. After Mikee and D-Mo's little escapade." Johnny laughed to himself at the thought of them rolling round in their sodden sumo suits.

"It bothered me at first, y'know, but the album's doing so well, bit of publicity and all that…" said Jamie, as he again checked his mobile for any transatlantic missives.

"What the fuck! Life's for living. You don't go, then you'd never know. Fortune favours the brave and all them clichés," laughed Johnny. "Fish finger butty before you go? Better than any of the shit they serve in-flight."

"You do know how to spoil me! Yeah, definitely. Thanks man."

"Coming right up. Want a lift to the airport after?"

"Yeah. Cheers. But if you could stop off at my mums on the way. Want to see her before I go."

"Not a problem. How is she? Coping with all the shenanigans okay?" said Johnny, putting the fish fingers out in two neat rows before popping them in the oven.

"She's okay. All a bit weird for her now and then but…" Jamie paused for a few seconds. "Did you and h—" Cutting himself off, Jamie again looked at his phone.

"Sorry J, what were you gonna ask?"

"Nah, nothing. I'll tell her you asked after her."

"Thanks. She's a good 'un. She makes me laugh," said Johnny, slicing four rounds of brown bread.

"Yeah she is. Apparently, she was winding Dom up the other day after she found a pair of knickers in his dirty laundry bag. Cheeky twat takes it round whenever we come back off tour!"

"If you don't ask you don't get!"

"Anyhow. I've got five days in America. I've never been before, so worst case is I get to eat a McDonald's in New York," said Jamie with a smile.

"Well, that's your bucket list sorted then! A Happy Meal with a supermodel in Times Square!" laughed Johnny, pleased that Jamie could see the funny side too.

"I'll bring you back the toy," Jamie grinned.

"Oh cheers J. I can't wait," said Johnny, passing Jamie a hot mug of tea. "Just enjoy it. You'll be on her home-turf, so I guess that'll be a bit of a strange one. Are you staying with her or booked a hotel?"

"I've only booked a flight. If I need a room I suppose I'll just sort one. Play it by ear."

"At least no one will know you over there. No offence."

"None taken! That's a good thing. But anybody that's with Lara is fair game. She's never out of the papers over there," said Jamie, screwing up his nose.

"Anyhow. Eat up, you won't get food like this over there."

"Thanks man. You're a star!"

"All part of the service J."

**

'*OMG. Just seen Jamie Thorne at Manchester Airport. FIT FIT FIT #lonelysouls*'

'*Sure I've just been stood near Jamie Lonely Souls at Terminal 1. Wish my seat was next to his for next seven hours #drool*'

'*Listening to 'Salvation' on iPod and I only spotted Jamie Thorne. Cool bastard #manlove #lonelysouls*'

And with those three tweets, the feline was well and truly out of the carrying receptacle. Jamie was oblivious to all this as he dozed through the flight. Occupying himself with his iPad, he watched *Drive* for the umpteenth time, his thoughts intermittently flitting between the new songs he had been working on with Dominic on a portable eight-track studio. And Lara.

Their last meeting had been well-documented and he hoped that things were going to go a lot better than their free to view pavement bust-up. Travelling some 3,500 miles was a show of commitment, he felt. "What will be will be," Johnny had whistled to him as he dropped him off at the airport.

Having stopped off on the way to see his mum, her concern was apparent, and reading about her boys in tawdry newspaper columns was something she would never get attuned to. He'd nearly filled up when she gave him a plastic supermarket bag with a foil wrapped round of sandwiches for him. He didn't have the heart to tell her that they wouldn't allow him to take them on to the plane.

He'd been particularly attentive to how his mum and Johnny were with each other – his curiosity had been piqued. They just seemed like old friends whenever they met, although he was sure they both stole surreptitious glances at each other. He loved them both dearly, but could never quite put his finger on to why a 'relationship' between them just wouldn't sit right….

***

A yellow cab. Just like the ones you see in all the films. He was here. New York City. Manhattan. The Big fuckin' Apple….

"Times Square please man," said Jamie, gesturing to the Asian cab driver that he was fine with his hand luggage to be kept with him.

Sitting back in the cracked vinyl seat, he absorbed every detail of the cab, the driver, the neighbourhoods they passed through. And that unmistakeable Manhattan skyline.

Winding the window of the cab down, Jamie pushed his sunglasses up on to the top of his head and drank it in. The familiar vista in front of him, distorted forever after Sept '11. Featured in every New York film or music video ever made. *A bit more impressive than Manchester's Beetham Tower*, Jamie laughed to himself.

The traffic slowed as they hit the city, Jamie marvelling at sights that were already so familiar to him. The steam rising from the drains. The panoply of smells. The omnipresent NYPD. And the neon-information overload of Times Square.

The Rock 'N' The Roll. 'N That

"Here's fine thanks," said Jamie, peeling off forty dollars and pushing it through the plexiglass divide to the driver.

"Thanking you. Have a fine stay in our country," said the cab driver as he bid Jamie goodbye, already alert for his next fair.

Stepping out onto the sidewalk, he stood and like every virginal tourist, just stood open-mouthed and turned around 360 degrees. Twice.

Although he was due to meet Lara in less than an hour at her East Side apartment, Jamie wanted some time to himself.

Passing by the front of the Golden Arches of McDonald's, he ignored Danny's well-intentioned request of, "Try a Big Mac to see if it taste's the same." Tickets and fliers for a multitude of events, offers and stores were shoved in his direction at every step.

And it was the anonymity that he cherished above all else. No heads turned in his direction. No stage whispers by people asking each other if that was 'Jamie from that band'.

His home city had taken the band to their heart, but it meant that whenever he went out he was now public property. Something his twin brother was thriving upon, but left him feeling disassociated with where they were at. He loved meeting people. But this being everybody's mate before he'd even met them was a strange experience to him, and his sometimes-awkward off-stage shyness could be misconstrued as arrogance.

Having drifted in the general direction of the Hudson River, past brownstone apartments, shop fronts owned by a United Nations of proprietors, Jamie realised that he was walking in the complete opposite direction to Lara's address. Flagging down his second cab off the afternoon with a practiced nonchalance, he read the address to the driver – "Cooper Square off Second Avenue please man."

"Sure thing. You English or Australian?"

"I'm from Manchester," replied Jamie.

***

"What if it's a girl though?" said Dee, holding up a pastel shaded paint chart.

"She can still learn bass. There's a few wicked women bass players!" said Danny, trying to conceal his burning desire for Dee's bump to be a little D-Mo rather than a D-Moette.

"And what about if you're on tour or something when I'm ready to give birth?"

"I dunno. I'll be there. I promise. Whatever it takes! You know how much this all means to me. I can't wait!" said Danny, putting his arm around Dee and placing a hand lovingly on her rapidly swelling bump.

"But what if you—"

"What if nothing! I'll be there. For both of you! All I want is the album to do well, record the next one, which will be even better! You should hear some of the demos that Jamie and Dom have recorded. They are fuckin' wicked and—"

She pushed Danny's hand away from her distended tummy. "Not in front of the baby! I don't want any bad language in front of it. They can hear you already. I read it in a book!" said Dee, a hurt look on her face.

"No, they fuc—"

"DANNY!"

"No, they can't. And even if they could, they wouldn't know what I meant."

"Then do it for me please. I've stopped swearing. And smoking and drinking," said Dee, folding her arms just above her bump.

"They're in for a bigger shock than me swearing. Wait till it pops out of your fanny and gets its arse slapped!" cackled Danny with a snap of his bony fingers.

"DANNY!" shouted Dee, as she smacked him across the arse. "Don't be so disgusting! You're not on tour now," she said with a seriously cross frown.

"Sorry babe but I can't imagine how mad it'll be watching a little person pop out of you."

"Well, you can learn all about that when you come to antenatal class with me on Thursday," said Dee, with a solemn nod of her head.

"What time? 'Cos we always rehearse on Thursdays."

"DANNY! You said you'd come with me!" snapped Dee.

"Oh, it's okay. Jamie's away this week. He's gone to America to see—" Danny stopped himself as he had wanted to keep this a secret. Jamie had asked that they don't tell anybody.

"Really?" said Dee, an intrigued look on her face. As a devoted 'browser' of *Heat* magazine and their ilk, she had devoured the tabloid tittle-tattle side of the band. And this little morsel piqued her desire for fresh first-hand gossip.

"Yeah. But don't say anything. He wants to keep it quiet after all the shit that's been in the papers and that," said Danny, a serious look on his face, knowing that he had broken the promise he had made to Jamie.

"Anyhow, you shouldn't even have to ask that. And you can come to antenatal now. And every week after that…" said Dee, again folding her arms, meaning that the last sentence was a statement not a request.

"I will. But all that stuff freaks me out. An—"

"And nothing! We'll be there, Daniel Martin. For our baby."

"We'll be there," agreed Danny. He was already missing the camaraderie of the band. He loved Dee more than he thought he could ever love anybody, but he missed being with them. He missed it when he wasn't a Lonely Soul…

Chapter 43

"Mikee. Dude. It's one in the morning. This better be good. I need my sleep after the tour," yawned Johnny, as he sat up in bed, regretting not having turned his phone off.

"Sorry man. I've been out for getting big with Dom. Y'know. The usual," said Mikee, the phone tucked under his chin as he prepared a late-night Scooby-snack for himself.

"The usual. Yeah. I can imagine. Anyhow. How can I help you, Kong?" said Johnny, as he got up to get himself a glass of water.

"We were in some bar in town. I forget which one. Anyhow, we were chatting to some birds."

"Obviously," Johnny interjected, with a roll of his eyes.

"And there were some TV screens in the bar. Not the usual sort of gaff we'd go in, but these girls wanted to go in. Bit shit if you ask me," said Mikee as he pressed down on the roughly hacked slabs of bread, licking mayonnaise off his chunky thumb.

"Cut to the chase. What have you done?" said Johnny, again stifling a yawn.

"Nah, nah. We've not done anything. For a change," he laughed. "There was a clip of last week's *X Factor*. Load of fuckin' shite as ever. But some young girl. Proper cutie. Anyhow, she sang 'Salvation' on an acoustic. Slowed it right down. She can sing and that. Crowd loved it. And so did that shower of cunts on the judging panel."

"Really?" said Johnny, now more than mildly intrigued.

"Went down a storm. Bella Donna Jones, or summat like that she's called," said Mikee, biting into his overly-stacked sandwich.

"I'll have a look on the YouTube tomorrow. Don't see what harm it can do to be honest, man. As bad as that show is. If it makes people check out your album."

"BUT IT'S THE FUCKIN' *X FACTOR*!" said Mikee, almost choking on a hunk of cheese.

"I know man, but you've not played on it or anything. Don't sweat it." Plonking himself back down on the bed, "I'll say goodnight now man. And ta for the call."

"Alright Johnny. Thought you should know. Laters."

"Laters indeed," said Johnny, as he hung up the call and turned his phone off.

***

"Jamie Thorne. And nearly on time. I'll buzz you in. The concierge will show you to the elevator," said Lara. A discernible hint of excitement in her voice.

Jamie stood and marvelled at the apartment building. It was magnificent. The heavy wooden doors, with plated glass and huge brass handles, were polished to mirror like perfection. The thick red carpet cushioned his footsteps like freshly cut grass. A huge mahogany reception desk stood directly in front of him. An immaculately suited concierge stood and greeted him. His cobalt blue suit was pressed to razor cut sharpness.

"Hi. Err. I'm here to see Lara Bearheart," said Jamie quietly.

"Miss Bearheart. She is on floor nine. Apartment thirteen. The elevator is over there," said the African-American concierge, pointing in the direction of a huge polished silver door.

"Thanks man. Appreciate that." Jamie offered his hand out. "I'm Jamie Thorne. Nice to meet you," glancing down at his name badge, "Nathan."

"And you, sir," said Nathan, running a hand across his eyebrow, where the hint of a shaved tramline hinted at Nathan's off-duty personality.

"It's just Jamie," he said with a slightly bemused pull of his face. Stepping over to the elevator, he pressed the floor number and waited on the elevator to take him up to Miss Lara Bearheart's apartment…

***

"Dominic Thorne? Hello. it's Nicola from Urban Flats."

"Yeah. It's me," said Dominic sullenly. He was nursing a serious hangover following his night out with Mikee. Rubbing at his forehead he mouthed 'fuck me' to himself. This was tempered with slight relief when he realised that he had no female company to deal with.

"Hello Dominic. How are you?" asked Nicola chirpily. Far too chirpily for Dominic's liking.

"Yeah. Alright," he grunted.

"It's about the rent on your apartment. The payment was rejected by your bank, I'm afraid."

"Really?" said Dominic, a slight hint of worry in his voice.

"Yes, our records show that your bank rejected the payment on Monday. We can take a payment over the phone if that's okay with you?"

"Err. I'll have to check with my bank. Can I get back to you later?" said Dominic, rubbing his chin irritably as he willed the phone call to end.

"That's fine, Mr Thorne, but please ensure that you do as we don't want the rent to fall into arrears," said Nicola maintaining her professional veneer throughout, even though she was well aware who she was speaking to.

"I'll speak to you later, yeah?" said Dominic.

As soon as he hung the call up, he flipped his laptop open and logged onto his personal bank account site.

"Fuck," he mumbled to himself.

The monies that the band members had been paid when the signed their record deal had seemed a fortune at the time, certainly far more money than any of them had seen in their bank accounts at any one time.

A steady procession of coke-fuelled nights – and mornings, together with the irresistible pull of two new guitars and a few nice bits of clobber for his wardrobe had tanned the arse of his bank account which was shrouded in overdraft gloom.

"Oh fuck, fuck, fuck, FUCK!" he said to himself, before slamming down the lid of his laptop.

This was something that needed resolving sharpish and he had to establish when they would be getting paid again. *There must be some money due from the last tour and album sales*, he thought to himself. *Johnny. He would know. And if he didn't, then he could find out who did.*

Gulping down a pint of cold water before making the call, Dominic breathed out deeply and then rang.

"Johnny. How are yer man?"

"I'm good thanks. Nice to have a little time off after the tour. Barney has sent me over the first rough edit of the video. Looks the business. Come over and have a look at it later if you're not up to anything," said Johnny as he sat on the sofa in his apartment.

"Yeah, yeah. Definitely man. Sounds wicked. But I'll cut to the chase. I've got a bit of a cashflow problem. The fuckin' rent on my flat has bounced. I've spent a bit more than I thought I had recently…"

"Okay," said Johnny. A pensive tone to his voice.

"Right. Can you find out when we are due any more cash from the label? And how much?" said Dominic, the desperation in his voice more than apparent.

"Yeah. Course I will Dom. But I th—" Johnny said, cutting himself off as he did not want to worry Dominic unnecessarily. "I'll make a call and get back to you. That okay?"

"Yeah, thanks man. Appreciate it. I'll see ya later," said Dominic, opening the balcony door of his apartment and lighting a cigarette before drawing on it deeply.

Johnny hung the call up and pursed his lips pensively. He knew that the band were not due another tranche of their advance monies until the end of the last quarter – in December. Which would be a couple of very long months off if you were the lead guitarist of a band who had blown his wad in a very short space of time. The three and half grand Les Paul with a mother-of-pearl finish and the limited edition Gretsch in bottle green with a mahogany fretboard at a cool two thousand pounds had accounted for a big chunk of his cash. And the rest? Not difficult to identify which orifice had accounted for that…

***

Knocking softly on the imposing black oak door, Jamie tried to relax himself as much as possible. Regretting now that he hadn't bought a present or flowers, he remembered that he had a copy of their album in his bag. Hurriedly rummaging for it, he pulled the CD out just as Lara opened the door.

"Jamie Thorne." said Lara, holding a hand out towards him.

"I brought you this," said Jamie, passing the CD into her outstretched hand.

Looking down at the album, Lara frowned. "What! You've not signed it!"

"I thought I'd wait and ask what you wanted me to write."

"Where's the surprise in that? Wait there."

Lara returned a moment later with a red Sharpie marker pen, handing it to him. "Surprise me."

"I feel under pressure now," said Jamie, as he took the top off the pen, seeking inspiration as he tapped the pen against the edge of the CD case.

Leaning the plastic case against his thigh, Jamie began to write – '*To Lara Bearheart. Play me. Love me x*'

Popping the top back on the Sharpie, Jamie passed both the pen and the now-signed CD to her.

"Very cute. I won't tell you that I've already downloaded the album, so I know how good it is. I couldn't wait for you to bring me a copy."

"Downloaded! Illegally? It's types like you that are killing musicians," said Jamie, only half-joking.

"I COULDN'T WAIT!" squealed Lara.

Jamie smiled and looked down at her. Dressed in an oversized red and brown checked flannel shirt, tied at the front - revealing an attractive few centimetres of olive coloured midriff - and black leggings, Lara looked naturally gorgeous but a million miles from the public face she wore.

"Are you actually going to invite me in then?" said Jamie, picking up his bag.

"Of course. Welcome to America. And my home…" said Lara, gesturing him into the apartment with a sweep of her hand.

***

"I'll buzz you up Dom," said Johnny through the apartment intercom. He winced slightly to himself as he heard the solemn response. *This wasn't going to be an easy conversation*, he thought.

"Hiya man. Brew?" said Johnny holding up the kettle.

"Err, yeah, please, two sugars," said Dominic - a distinct absence of wind in his usual billowing sails.

"You heard from Jamie at all?" asked Johnny, trying to stall the pain of their pending conversation.

"He texted Mum to say he'd got there okay. Said New York is wicked, and we need to play there as soon as," said Dominic, his voice devoid of any excitement at that prospect.

"That's well in hand Dom. I'm getting the US deal finalised and should do some dates in the New Year. Good eh?" said Johnny, in attempt to lift the guitarists solemnity.

"Yeah. Can't wait. Sorry man, I don't mean to be a dick, but cut to the chase. When can I get paid again?"

"Okay. I spoke to the label's bean counters," Johnny lied, "and as I thought, the next chunk of the advance is due at the end of the next quarter so th—"

"In English! When does that mean?" said Dominic curtly.

"End of December. The deal was staggered dependent on certain sales

The Rock 'N' The Roll. 'N That

triggers. We had the tour money up-front. Album sales have exceeded expectations, so you'll do well come then."

"Fuck's sake! That doesn't help me now though does it!"

Johnny lifted his hands palms up. "Dom. Look, we can sort this. How much are you short and for how long?"

Looking as sheepish as he had ever seen him, Dominic sipped at his cup of tea whilst he mentally calculated his shortfall. "Couple of month's rent. Living costs and that."

"It's the 'and that' which worries me," said Johnny, "I don't want to be a broom up yer arse bu—"

"I know. I've caned it. The new guitars and kit," his voice dropping to a whisper, "and all the nights out…"

"I don't like to see you like this and I understood how and why you've got in this mess. Who wouldn't have gone a little mad…"

"Well Jamie for a starter," replied Dominic, his tone laden with sarcasm.

"C'mon. No need. You're different people. Let's just look how we can sort this."

"Yeah. Yeah. Okay man," Dom said, assuming the manner of a chastised schoolboy awaiting his punishment.

"There's not a lot we can do about the label money. Just no way of getting it paid early. The deal is tied up in all sorts of legal bollocks so wh—"

"There's nothing you can do? "snapped Dominic.

"What I plan on doing," said Johnny in calming tones, "is just between you and me. I'll front you five grand until then. I've not done much with the money I got from the deal and my proceeds from the house," he added with a slight wince, "so we can sort this. I won't say a word to the others. And you pay me back when the money comes through in a couple of months' time."

"Really?" said Dominic, a little disbelievingly.

"Really," nodded Johnny. "We're all in this together, if you'll excuse me paraphrasing our cunt of a Prime Minister. And I couldn't bear to see you like this for a couple of months."

"Could be good for the creative process, "Dom deadpanned.

"I'll sort it now. You got your bank details," pausing slightly, "or do you want it in two separate payments? So y'know…" Johnny left the sentiment hanging and Dominic took a moment to mull it over.

With a deep considered sigh, he said, "Best make it two payments. I don't suppose you'd be that impressed if I rocked up with another guitar, would you?"

"It's not my business what you do with your money, but just wind it in now and then eh," laughed Johnny.

Dominic, his mood finally lifting, said, "Johnny, man. What can I say? You're a diamond. I'd be fucked without this. I'd make a few quid busking but I'd be happier with a roof over my head!"

"I'm here to help when I can. You'll laugh about this when the monies rolling in!"

"Come 'ere man," Dom said, standing from the sofa and hugging Johnny, patting him firmly on the back. "Top man. I owe you."

"You do. Five grand!" smiled Johnny.

"Twat!" grinned Dom. "Fancy a pint later, I'm meeting Mikee and D-Mo. All the baby stuff is getting to him. Defo come out. My round," he said with a wink.

"I may well just do that. Cheers…"

***

Jamie stood and looked around the vast apartment. The views over the East River were spectacular. The panoramic vista must have added several 0s to the apartment's value alone.

"This place," Jamie whistled. "Your family must be minted," he said as he walked around the apartment slightly open-mouthed, taking in the views from all the three huge windows.

"He was a very smart businessman. People saw a dumb Red Indian. But he was one switched on motherfucker."

"It's good to see you," said Jamie, adopting a serious tone.

"It's good to see you," replied Lara. "I don't really wanna talk about last time. But I'm sorry. I guess you know why I got a little heated?"

"I do. But less said the better eh?" said Jamie. "What are we gonna do then? What are you gonna to show me? This place looks amazing," said Jamie, with a sweep of his hand in the direction of the twinkling lights of the skyline.

"Funny you should ask," said Lara as she slowly unbuttoned her shirt, letting it drop to the floor, before she then pulled the faded New York Knicks vest over her head revealing her sumptuous breasts. Standing there momentarily, before turning and heading to her bedroom…

***

"Do you have to go out? I'm tired and I thought we could have a takeaway and watch a film," said Dee, with a pout of her bottom lip.

"I've not seen the boys for a few days, and err, we need to chat to Johnny about some news about the American record deal," said Danny, pleased with himself at the justification of his proposed night out.

"But Jamie's away," countered Dee.

"Yeah, but, he err, he knows about it already. We need to speak to Johnny about it," said Danny unconvincingly.

"Well you'd clearly rather go out with your mates than stay in with us," said Dee, patting her tummy to reinforce her attempt at blackmail.

"Don't be like that," said Danny, pulling a face behind her back. "It won't be a big one. Promise," he said, putting an arm around her waist and pulling her into him before kissing her on the top of her head, his right hand gently caressing her pregnant bump.

"Go on then. You'll only sit there with a face on if I say no!"

"Ah thanks babe. I'll do the shop before then. You can put your feet up on the sofa."

***

Sat up in Lara's vast king-sized bed, wrapped around each other post-coitus, Jamie lazily rolled a tress of her jet-black hair round his finger. "As cliched as this is going to sound, that was amazing." Kissing her tenderly on the top of her head, he said, "but where are we going now? I've gotta see this place. And with you as my guide. Perfect!"

"You do realise that it's not that easy," Lara said. With extra emphasis on the 'that easy'.

"Wh— Oh. Right. Yeah, I'd not thought of that…"

"BUT!" shouted Lara, jumping out of bed, allowing Jamie to see her naked form in all its breath-taking perfection; stepping into the en-suite bathroom, she came out moments later wearing a perfectly fitting shoulder length blonde wig.

"This is my little disguise and means we can go out and get drunk and no-one will know who the fuck we are!"

"You! You sexy, clever lady are a fuckin' genius," smiled Jamie, his Northern tones in total contrast to Lara's drawled Americanisms.

After they had both showered – separate bathrooms enabled a simultaneous grooming process – and having luxuriated under the multiple jets of the power shower, Jamie felt that he had blasted any jetlag out of his system and was ready for a Manhattan night out. With a cunningly and stunningly blonde Lara Bearheart.

"We can just flag a cab down. If we turn up in a car it just gets clocked straight away," said Lara. She stood in front of Jamie – the blonde wig perfectly in situ – dressed in beat up red Converse pumps, skinny fit blue jeans a tight-fitting Queens of the Stone Age tour T-shirt and cropped black leather jacket. All thrift store vintage and the perfect outfit to blend in with any other native New York hipster barflies.

"You look amazing!" smiled Jamie.

"Don't sound so surprised!" replied Lara, as she made a last-minute check of the wig and applied a sparing amount of mascara.

"Where are we headed then?" asked Jamie.

"Brooklyn. See what's happening," sang Lara in a passable attempt at the Beastie Boys.

"Like it. I can't believe I'm here," said Jamie.

"Well Jamie Thorne. Let's party!"

An incognito night was had as they trawled from bar to bar. Jamie being turned away on one occasion for not looking old enough, much to Lara's amusement. His hilariously over the top 'Do you not know who I am' had led to them both virtually rolling round the sidewalk in fits of giggles.

Upon hitting a retro karaoke bar, they had duetted appallingly on a Meat Loaf standard before Jamie had suggested they rescued their credibility with a bar-stopping rendition of 'Gimme Shelter'. The free shots they were rewarded with after they had blasted through the Stones classic had tipped them well out of the bounds of sobriety.

"Fuck! That was brilliant, Jamie Thorne. You should join a band!" Lara laughed as she wiped a dribble of Jack Daniels off her chin.

"Here's to us and the rock 'n' the roll," Jamie shouted as they clinked shot glasses.

"It's not always this easy," said Lara, her tone far more serious. "I've normally got a camera stuck up my ass everywhere I go."

"I get that," said Jamie, whispering into her ear, "but let's just make the most tonight. I'm fuckin' lovin' this!"

"I'm fuckin' lovin' this," Lara mimicked, "Oh Jamie, you're quite the poet…" before kissing him drunkenly and passionately.

Chapter 44

"Need to borrow a tenner then, do we Dominic?" said leery and objectionably smug photographer one.

"Fuck you talking about, you fuckin' dickwad," snarled Dom, as he left his apartment on the way to meet Mikee, Danny & Johnny.

"Been a bit flash with the cash I've been hearing," said photographer two conspiratorially.

"Fuckin' pair of dicks need to sort your facts out before you start shooting your mouths off."

"Tut tut. They are easily wound up these Thorne boys, aren't they?" laughed photographer two.

Shaking his head in disbelief at the front of the photographers – and principally that they had somehow got wind of his financial plight – Dominic reached inside the pocket of his black leather jacket, took a ten pound note out of his wallet. Screwing the note up, he then flicked it in photographer one's face.

"Go and treat your boyfriend to a slap-up meal at Greggs, you fat cunt!"

"Now that's not nice, is it Dominic. What would your dad say?" said photographer two.

"Don't be daft. Remember, they haven't got one!" jeered photographer one.

Pushing the photographer back with a solid two-handed shove, Dom said, "Fuck did you say? You fuckin' cunt!"

Falling backwards like an overly dramatic continental footballer, photographer one lay on the pavement clutching his face whilst his unscrupulous colleague proceeded to snap pictures of Dominic stood angrily over the prostrate paparazzi.

"You pair of cunts! I don't know how you sleep at night." Spitting on the floor in disgust, jabbing an angry finger. "If I see either of you when I'm out tonight, you're fuckin' dead!"

"Are you picking that up or shall I," laughed photographer one as he dusted himself down.

"It'll buy us a pint and that, my friend, was gold dust…." said photographer two as he unfurled the note, kissing the Queen's solemn stare with a slobbering smack.

***

"Can we go out for breakfast? I've always wanted to go to one of them American diners and order pancakes," said Jamie as spooned into Lara.

"Hmm, Jamie. I'm tired. And I don't really do breakfast y'know. I want to sleep for another couple of hours," said Lara, pulling the bedsheets tightly around her.

"I'm wide awake though! Would you mi—"

"You go and lose yourself. Good time to wander round and see the city waking up." Lara turned to Jamie and smiled sleepily. "How can you look so good after we hit it so hard last night? I hate you!"

"You don't mind? I am starving…"

"Go. And I loved it last night. Seriously good time!" said Lara, as she turned and closed her eyes, a hint of mascara smeared under her right eye.

Getting dressed into fresh T-shirt, jeans, and a grey hoodie, Jamie popped his iPhone on and went to out to discover a bit of New York City for himself.

***

"Alright Johnny. Good to see you again and thanks again for before, y'know," said Dom as he patted Johnny on the back and exchanged handshakes and fist-bumps with Kong and D-Mo.

"Not a problem. But you don't look like a man who's had the weight of the world lifted," said Johnny with a frown.

"Don't!" whispered Dom, with a quick look to check that they were safely out of earshot. "Them two photographer cunts that hang around our apartment block were waiting for me before. Made some cheap shots about me being skint! And about not having a dad."

"Really!" Johnny exclaimed a little louder than intended.

"Shhh!" said Dom, his eyes flashing across to Mikee and D-Mo who fortunately, were stood at the bar deliberating over the first round. "How the fuck can they know about, y'know, what we sorted?"

"Fuck knows," said Johnny with a slow shake of his head.

"And that about no dad. Bang out of order. Proper scumbags."

"I hear ya Dom. But what can you do?" he said with a sympathetic shrug of his shoulders.

"Oh, and another thing," Dominic said.

"Go on," enquired Johnny.

"I sort of snapped and pushed one of them over. Cunt made a right meal of it. And the other fucker took a load of pictures." Laughing to himself, he said, "I should have proper twatted him though. He asked for it."

"So that's all over the papers sometime soon. Takes the heat off Jamie. He'll appreciate that…"

"Yeah. He'll owe me big time. What fucks me off is that somebody at the lettings company must have let the press know. That's taking the piss!"

"Too right!" said Johnny with a brisk nod of his head, "but it's all settled so it's a non-story. Forget about it and enjoy tonight. I'm sure you can just about manage that…"

"Just about," said Dom, still clearly bristling about the evening's earlier events.

***

"I brought you a cappuccino back," said Jamie, the hot liquid burning his fingertips through the cardboard cup. "And proper deli stuff, not that Starbucks tax dodging shit! How many Starbucks does one city need by the way?" Taking off his headphones, the bees in a biscuit tin chatter of Beastie Boys' *To the Five Boroughs* swarming out of the idle headphones.

"Hmm, thank you. Soy milk?" said Lara, dwarfed inside a huge white towelling dressing gown.

"Soy milk," nodded Jamie. "Three sugars."

"WHAT!" Lara squealed. Now recoiling at the touch of the cup.

"Way too easy," laughed Jamie, as he took off his hoodie, causing his T-shirt to ride up, revealing his taut stomach.

"Nice," said Lara, as she ran her hand across it.

"What we up to today?" said Jamie, plonking himself down on the huge brown leather sofa, which gave a welcoming grumble as he flung his feet over the arm.

"I've got to attend a couple of meetings. About my boutique in Greenwich and then with my management about some perfume line."

"Okay," said Jamie disappointedly. "How long will you be?"

"Should be back by mid-afternoon. Crash here and chill. Mi casa es tu casa."

Jamie laughed. One of the only lines of Spanish that he knew, and this was only due to repeat viewings of *Pulp Fiction*.

"And what about tonight?" he asked.

"Tonight. Well, tonight you go out with Lara. Restaurant opening that I got to go to. Friend of my managers. No wig tonight. You'll see the madness that goes on New York style," she said, sipping at the coffee and smiling in pleasure at the rich taste.

"And you'll want me along as your plus one?" winked Jamie.

"Of course. They've heard all about you, Jamie Thorne."

"I've got a long list of stuff I want to do, so I'll lose myself. I think I'm gonna head to Central Park. Look at Dakota Building and the Lennon stuff."

"Ooh, such a rock star cliché thing to do. And what about morning coffee at the Chelsea Hotel where Sid 'n' Nancy did their shit in?" teased Lara.

"That was next on the list," deadpanned Jamie.

"I'm going to shower and get ready. There's a key on the breakfast bar. You be careful out there and don't talk to strangers!"

"Thanks Ms Bearheart. I'll think on," said Jamie with a tap of his nose

***

"Next album will definitely get to number one. I'm sure of it," said Danny. The table of drop-dead gorgeous indie-chicks hanging on to his every word.

"He's right," nodded Dominic, doing his little trick of narrowing his eyes to accentuate his cheekbones.

"You think that it's big now, just you wait and see," said Mikee, almost choking on the ludicrousness of his own innuendo.

Johnny leant back in his chair and watched – and learnt – as three-quarters of his band went about reeling-in their impressionable entourage.

"And Johnny will tell you that we're off to America in the New Year. That is gonna be fuckin' big!" said Danny, bumping fists with Mikee.

"Off to America. In the New Year," concurred Johnny, trying to take a backseat from proceedings as he reckoned he was comfortably old enough to be these girls' father.

"Fancy coming outside for a cig?" Danny casually asked a particularly charming brunette.

Clocking Johnny raise an almost paternally disapproving eyebrow, Danny then unsubtly added, "Just for a cig like."

"So how old are you?" asked a petite perma-pout blonde.

Me?" said Johnny, feigning disinterest. "Old enough to know when it's time to call it a night."

"I didn't mean it like that!" she smiled endearingly.

"Not a problem. I've got loads to do tomorrow. I'm sure these boys will look after you and don't need me cramping their style…"

***

A glass of water and two paracetamol was Johnny's all too sensible pre-bedtime ritual if had been boozing. The additional nocturnal visits to the bathroom offset by the lack of a hangover the following morning. As he turned the light out on his nightstand, his phone pinged the arrival of a text message.

Hello Johnny
Who is this?
It's Ellie. We met in Walrus tonight. Dominic gave me your number.
Really? Why?
I like you. Do you want to know what I'm doing now…?

Chapter 45

"Oh Dom!" Cally said to herself. As she scanned down the newspapers webpage, she bit her bottom lip in between biting on an already ragged thumbnail.

Under the headline '*Lonely A***Souls*' read:

'*Manchester bad boys Lonely Souls continue to hit the top of the charts and the headlines. With twin brother Jamie in America trying to patch up his relationship with model Lara Bearheart after an unseemly fight outside a swanky London restaurant, it was left to his brother, Dominic, to play up to the band's bad boy image.*

Upon leaving his luxury city centre apartment – which had outstanding rent payments on it – Dominic violently assaulted and spat at photographers. If you look at the shocking pictures, you will see the angry guitarist stood over our prone snapper who is lying on the ground in fear of his safety.

In scenes not witnessed since Liam Gallagher was at the height of his bad boy rock 'n' roll days, Dominic Thorne seems determined to live up to every stereotype.

Not content with the brutal assault, our photographer was then threatened with further attacks should he follow Dominic as he set off on his boisterous night out.

Having grown up in a single-parent family in Manchester, the twin brothers seem to be hellbent on fighting the world at every opportunity.

We all like a bad boy but attacking a father of two going about his work is a little too much, eh Dominic…'

"Oh Dominic. What have you done now?" Cally said softly, wrought with concern.

Looking at her watch, she wondered if it was too early to call Johnny. Some consoling words from him might make her feel slightly less anxious.

"Johnny? It's Cally. How are you?"

"I'm okay thanks," said Johnny, glancing at his watch, "what's the occasion with you ringing at half nine on a wet Wednesday?"

"Have you seen the papers today?" Cally asked sombrely.

"Not yet. And I've not heard from the band's press officer. What've I missed?"

"It's Dominic. They said he attacked a photographer and they are making comments about him not paying his rent."

Taking a deep breath. "Okay. He did push a pap. But they were winding him up. He'll learn. The money thing? It's a non-story. Problem with his bank and somebody at the letting agency has been a lot out of line and must have told the press he'd not paid his rent."

"I don't like it though Johnny. They're not bad boys. I didn't bring them up like that! You know that. I hate this!" said Cally, with a slight sob in her voice.

"Nobody is saying that. It's all bullshit they are printing but it's the nature of the beast," said Johnny in a calming tone.

"I know. But it's horrible to read it."

"Don't read it."

"It's not that easy is it!" said Cally, her voice full of frustration.

"But you know the truth. That might not feel like enough. But it has to be!"

"But everybody else will always believe the papers!" cried Cally.

"Fuck em! Sorry. Look Cally. I'm not long up, I've got some stuff to take care of, but fancy meeting for lunch?"

"Really?" Her voice perked up immediately.

"Yeah, it'd be lovely to see you. Say one o'clock. Dimitris on Deansgate? My treat."

"I'd love that," said Cally, looking at her reflection in the lounge mirror.

"Okay. I'll see you then. Grab a cab as well. I'll stick it through as expenses."

"I'm looking forward to it already," said Cally, with that lovely little purr in her voice that always, always made Johnny smile.

***

"That was fuckin' nuts!" said Jamie as he again brought Lara's deli-favourite coffee in for her.

"I wondered where you had gone," said Lara, sitting up and letting the bed sheet fall seductively away from her.

"Least I can do. Free board and lodgings in New York City," said Jamie, putting on a dreadful 'Goodfellas' style New Yorkers' accent.

"I told you it would be full on, didn't I," said Lara, gratefully accepting the coffee.

"All those paps. And they do that all the time? Fuck. How do you cope?" said Jamie with a shake of his head.

"I get used to it. I've had to. I'll send you any links if you're in the pics. My mystery man," laughed Lara with a dramatic shake of her hair.

"I'd never get used to it," said Jamie, blowing at the hot coffee.

"You have to, or it drives you insane. Anyhow. Put that coffee down. Get back into bed and fuck me. I'm feeling very horny today, Jamie Thorne."

Putting down her coffee cup, Lara let the rest of the bed sheet fall away from her, sucked her index finger slowly before gently sliding it inside herself with a gentle gasp…

***

Meeting at a bar restaurant that was a little too close to Spinningfields for Johnny's liking - Manchester's new 'financial district' made up of soulless steel and smoked glass hi-rise temples of Mammon.

"Hello Johnny. This was a lovely idea!" said Cally. Dressed in a dark grey Prince of Wales check overcoat, black jeans and boots, she looked very classy indeed. Her hair was as ever worn down, but she had a pretty mother of pearl hair slide in, pulling her hair slightly away from the right side of her face.

"Hiya Cally. Great to see you. It's been a while," said Johnny, leaning across and kissing her on both cheeks.

"Nice coat," said Cally with an admiring glance. "You seem to have a different one every time I see you!"

"Oh, this old thing," shrugged Johnny. Taking said coat off he carefully hung the waxed overcoat over the back of his chair, before having a change of heart and signalling for a waiter to hang it up in the cloakroom.

"Thanks for this," smiled Cally.

That smile, thought Johnny. *Every fucking time I see it…*

"My pleasure! It can't be easy," he said, picking up the menu.

"I just worry," said Cally, raising an appreciative eyebrow as she began to peruse the menu.

"Totally understandable," said Johnny, "what would you like to drink?" as he tried to catch the eye of a passing waitress.

"It's so unfair though. They're not like that. Not like that at all! And a large red please," she said, as she balled her fists up in frustration.

"But that's the way the gutter press works. They've not had a top band to write about for a while. And they wouldn't do it if the music wasn't selling. I know that doesn't help you," he paused to order the drinks, "and you know the truth."

She lowered her voice to an absolute whisper. "That's my worry! What about the stuff they've said to Dom about not having a dad! That's awful. They couldn't know? Could they?" she said, looking aghast.

"How could they! They'll just keep lifting up rocks to see what they might find," he said in his best reassuring tones. "You're going to have to turn the other cheek, Cally. As tough as that might be."

"I'll try. But I may need these little chats with you for reassurance," said Cally, leaning her head to one side and smiling up at Johnny.

"Anytime," Johnny smiled back, placing his hand on the back of hers across the table.

Cally lifted her hand slightly and intertwined her fingers with Johnny's. "You've been so good with them. I know how much they care."

As much as Johnny knew this, it was still satisfying to have it reaffirmed and he nodded gratefully.

Realising that they had been holding hands for a good few seconds, Johnny then broke the moment. "Right. I'm starving! Shall we order?"

***

"It's been amazing," said Jamie as he started to pack his bag as he sat cross legged on Lara's bed. "I love this city!"

"It's been a blast, Jamie. And my blonde night out was my favourite in a long time," said Lara, as she stood over Jamie, a large bath sheet wrapped around her as she had just showered.

"I've got to ask. When will I see you again?" said Jamie as he checked that his iPhone was fully charged for his journey home.

"I don't know," Lara said solemnly.

"We're confirming dates in America for the start of next year, but that's ages off," he said, looking up to her and fixing her with his blue eyes.

"Jamie. Look. This is going to be a difficult relationship for a whole bunch of reasons. Let's see where the breeze takes us."

Frowning at the sentiment, he said, "I know bu—"

"But. We've had a great time. You're going to be so busy all over the world with your band. Don't put more pressure on yourself. On us," said Lara, putting her hand on the side of his face and caressing his cheekbone with the tip of her thumb.

Feeling like a child being told a blunt reality of the world, Jamie took Lara's hand in his and kissed the back of it softly.

"Don't be a stranger, Lara Bearheart," said Jamie as he zipped his bag closed.

"Not a chance, Jamie Thorne."

With a lingering hug, Jamie left her apartment and headed for the airport. His New York sojourn at an end…

Chapter 46

"Have a nice flight Jamie?" asked photographer one, as he lazily snapped off a couple of pictures of Jamie as he got out of the taxi.

"Did you kiss and make up with her then?" said photographer number two.

"Cat got your tongue?" laughed photographer one.

Lifting his sunglasses up, Jamie reached inside his jacket pocket. Tossing a small packet of in-flight peanuts towards the baying scrape of photographers, he said, "I saved these for you. Don't want you getting hungry whilst you're waiting around."

"You're all heart Jamie. All sorted with Lara? Or have you realised that she's out of your league?"

Photographer two sniggered, causing a globule of spittle to drop off his bottom lip, catching on the zip of his fleece.

"Laugh all you want. You fat cunt," said Jamie slowly. "Must drive you fuckin' mental when you're trying to sleep at night that the closest you'll get to a woman like that is crackin' one off over your pictures."

With a slow dismissive shake of his head, Jamie laughed at the photographers. "I get this now. It's all a game. And I can use you as much as you use me. And remember. You need me a damn sight fuckin' more than I need you."

"Good speech," said photographer number two sarcastically.

Photographer number one started to give Jamie a slow handclap.

"Been taking lessons off Lara, have we?"

"Truth hurts, doesn't it? Our record went gold whilst I was away. I could retire at thirty if things carry on like this. And you'll still be freezing your bollocks off desperately snapping pictures." Tossing his head back and laughing loudly, he said, "Fuck me! That's funny. I'll leave that thought with you."

"We'll be waiting for you to slip up Jamie. I'll be here. Don't you worry," said photographer one, as he opened the packet of peanuts and tossed one into the air before catching with a remarkable dexterity for a man of such girth.

The Rock 'N' The Roll. 'N That

***

"Band meeting," said Johnny, still trying to mine the *Flight of the Conchords* line for all its worth. His apartment doubling as an office-cum-meeting room.

"This better be good," yawned Dominic impatiently, "I'm knackered."

"You over your jet-lag yet, Jamie?" asked Danny, as he idly rolled a cigarette.

"It's not bad coming from East Coast, bit tired but nothing too bad, thanks man."

"Listen to the jet-setter!" said Dom. "He'll be demanding first-class or nothing before you know it!"

"Funny," said Jamie, clearly not amused.

"Only messing bro. You had a great time, so a little jet lag is a small price to pay. Or is it 'cos Lara kept you up all night?"

Danny giggled childishly and received a dirty look from Jamie.

Clearing his throat, he said, "Band meeting." Looking down at his laptop, Johnny said, "Right. If you lot can be arsed listening, I've got some big news for you."

"Sorry bossman," said Mikee, delivering a 'shut-the-fuck-up' look to his talkative bandmates.

"Cheers Kong," said Johnny appreciatively. "Okay. Where shall we start? Album went gold at the end of last month. 100, 000 UK sales. The label are delighted but not as much as we are. Next single is out at the end of November and we've got four Christmas gigs lined up – Glasgow, Manchester, Dublin and London."

"Wicked," said Danny, "there's nothing better than gigging."

"Saves you getting grief at home off Dee, doesn't it D-Mo?"

He rolled his eyes. "If you say so Dom. Can't you change the fuckin' record?"

"I could. But you get so wound up by it!"

"I'm gonna be a dad. It's not a joking matter," said Danny, again leaving himself wide open.

"As I said…" replied Dominic, as he leant over and pinched Danny's ear playfully.

"Right! Next item," said Johnny. "Festival dates are being put together and we are down to play Glasto. Possibly V and very likely T in the Park. So, get some wellies on your Christmas list as it's bound to piss down at Glasto."

Glastonbury. The place that he had met a rain-sodden and very drunk Claire, all those years ago. It would be the first time Johnny had been back to the festival since that day.

"Aren't the Stones rumoured to be headlining?" asked Jamie in an almost reverential whisper.

"Rumoured J. But who knows? They'll keep it all under wraps for a while yet."

"Imagine being on the same bill as The Rolling Stones!" said Dominic, looking as star struck as was possible.

"Okay. Next item on the agenda. Brit awards. We've been nominated for best newcomer and best single. Last one's voted for by Radio One listeners so that'll mean One Direction or some such shite will piss it. I think we stand a good chance of best newcomer though," said Johnny, as he looked at the band's reaction.

"I'm disappointed," said Dominic, pulling his bottom lip out. "We should have easily been in best album and group." With a dismissive shake of his head, he added, "If fuckin' Mumford and his bastard Sons win it, he's getting it. The posh twat in his shit clothes!"

Struggling to stifle his laughter, Johnny looked up at the guitarist's obvious displeasure. "Win the lot the year after then," said Johnny, throwing the gauntlet down.

"About the Brits," he said with a pause. "They've asked us to play live, but."

"But what," interjected Jamie.

"But. They want us to do one of those mash-up/soundclash things with," glancing down at the notes on his laptop, "Street Baby Fury. Some grime act that XL have signed. Apparently, he's up for best urban act. I haven't heard of him. But I'm not down with the kids. Word," said Johnny, making an embarrassingly bad gangster sign with his right hand.

"He's the bomb!" said Mikee, with a snap of his fingers. "Jay-Z found him rapping outside a gig at the O2. He's done some proper sick stuff. Wicked beats."

"Discovered outside the O2 by Jay-Z," said Johnny cynically, "And if you believe that one…"

"I'm not mad about that," said Jamie with a frown.

"Can't say I am," said Johnny with a nod of his head. "And they don't name rappers like they used to. What's wrong with a good old-fashioned Flavor Flav? His people are going to send across a track to our people, so we'll see," said Johnny, nodding in agreement with Jamie.

"I think it'll be fuckin' cool," said Danny, turning to his sizeable partner in rhythm.

"I hear ya D-Mo," said Mikee as they bumped fists.

"Anyhow. There's more. We've finalised the deal with XL US and the album will be released in the States in February and we'll tour it for most of March.

Supporting somebody. Not been confirmed who though yet."

"Err, Johnny. I've just worked out that Glasto is in June and that's when the baby's due!" said Danny, with a look of panic on his face.

"Bring her down. Get some druid or what have you to help with the birth. Get it done in the middle of Stonehenge or something!" said Dominic.

Trying to maintain some semblance of order and attempting to placate Danny's concerns, Johnny said, "Get me her due date and we'll take it from there…"

"Fuck's sake," Danny mumbled to himself. "I think that it's 20th June, but I'll double check." He went to text Dee and then thought better of it.

"America. That'll keep you happy then bro," said Dominic knowingly.

"Hmmm," replied Jamie, a thousand-yard stare indicating his thoughts were not quite in the room.

Seeing Danny nudge Mikee excitedly, Johnny could see there was something else on the agenda.

"Go on D-Mo. You look fit to bust," said Johnny with a playful grin.

"Let's have your laptop for a second," said Mikee, producing a USB stick from his jacket pocket.

"Err, careful. I don't want my laptop full of grot!" said Johnny.

"Like you don't look at that stuff," said Mikee with a wink. "Got to make sure you can keep your pecker up at your age, haven't you?"

"Thank you for the biology lesson, Kong."

Having accessed the Windows Media programme, Mikee turned the laptops speakers up to full volume and demanded silence. A thundering drum and bass track emitted from the speakers, with some slashes of angry guitar complimenting the beats. A sample of the Richard Ashcroft vocal then kicked in on repeat. *'God knows you're lonely souls. God knows…'*

"That's fuckin' sick," said Dominic.

Looking up proudly, Danny said, "Me and Mikee have worked on it. For when we walk out on stage. Lights down. Play that full fuckin' blast. We step out. Boom. Lights on. And we fuckin' start to tear it up!" he added, with a particularly loud snap of his fingers.

"I love it," said Johnny, replaying the link again.

"Good work," said Jamie, delighted by this little bit of studio-trickery. "Cool as fuck."

"Okay. Band meeting over. Happy with all that lot I take it?"

"Yeah. Brilliant," said Jamie, "We're going to be working on the new tracks for a few weeks now. Nice and relaxed to see how they take shape."

"Right. Get on your way. I've got work to do!" said Johnny, already checking the day's emails.

"Cheers Johnny. See you soon," said Jamie as he left the apartment, his thoughts already transatlantic.

***

Having had the London gig in December confirmed, Johnny had texted Amanda to inform her. The response of *'Hello Mr Manager. I'll see how busy I am nearer the time. I'm not just here for you when you're in town. A x'* had taken the wind out of his sails somewhat. *Modern women. Got to love 'em*, he thought. But resolutely on their terms…

***

"Lara. It's Jamie."

"Hello Jamie," said Lara sleepily.

"Are you still in bed?"

"I am. I've been working hard and just crashed out all day," she said.

"I've got some good news. We've got the American tour dates sorted. We'll be over for a month. Starts mid-February."

"Good news," said Lara. A little less enthusiastically than Jamie had hoped for.

"And we're playing London in December. It'd be great if you could make that. London's amazing in December. It'd be great," he said unabashed.

"I'll look at my schedule, Jamie. Can I get back to you? I'm tired." Lara rolled over in bed, the phone still held to her ear.

"Err. Yeah. Sure," said Jamie. "I'll speak soon to you soon then?"

"You will. Sorry Jamie. But I'm beat right now." Hanging up the call, Lara dropped her mobile phone. Right onto a piece of silver foil, scorched and burnt black in the centre…

***

"But Danny! You promised," shrilled Dee.

"It's not my fault," said Danny, as he started to strip wallpaper off the spare room that they planned to use as a nursery.

The Rock 'N' The Roll. 'N That

"It's Glastonbury the week I'm due. What if I'm late!" cried Dee, as she stood with her hands on her hips.

"I've said I'll be there, and I will!" said Danny, as he started to scrape furiously at the wallpaper.

"YOU CAN'T SAY THAT!" said Dee, throwing her own scraper at the wall. It ricocheted back, causing Danny to jump backwards.

"Fuck's sake!"

"What did I say about swearing in front of the baby?"

"Whatever."

"Not whatever. I want. No. I insist that you're with me when I give birth to our baby. Our baby, Danny." With a genuinely wounded look on her face, Dee lowered her voice. "This is the biggest thing that's ever happened to us. It might never happen again. Surely you know why I feel like this."

Wisely thinking better of telling Dee that a gold album was a pretty fucking big deal too, he hugged her into him. "It'll be okay. I promise."

***

"And then what happened?" Asked Mark, with an unhealthy level of vicarious interest.

Sat in the vault of a once oft-frequented local, Johnny and Mark were having a long overdue catch-up. Over several pints of well-poured Guinness.

Sipping from his pint, Johnny sighed and let out a low chuckle. "So, we started messaging."

"Text or Facetime?" Mark asked. A little too keenly.

"Text! For fucks sake. I'd never done anything like that before. Sexting with stabilisers I guess."

"What was she saying?"

"Y'know. I'm naked. Touching myself and that. Proper turn on."

"And what did you do?"

"Really? I'm sure even your vanilla imagination stretches that far," said Johnny.

"Did she send any pictures?" said Mark, with a somewhat pervy rub of his hands.

"No. It all went a bit pear."

"Why?"

"I was, y'know. I was cracking one off," said Johnny. Assuming a sheepish tone.

"Who said men can't multitask!" said Mark, with a conspiratorial nudge wink gesture.

"I was going to message her that I was about to err, finish."

Shaking his head at the recollection, Johnny drained his pint glass. "In all the excitement, I forgot the predictive text was on…"

"And?"

"And I said I was going to Cumbria…"

Having just taken a long gulp, Mark's eyes started to bulge as he tried to stop the drink from shooting back down his nose.

"You know what I meant to say. Obviously."

Wiping tears from his eyes, "Oh mate! What did she say after that? Ask if she needed to bring her walking boots?"

"Very fucking funny. Not a word to anyone about this. And no, she didn't message back after that…"

***

"More washing for me?" said Cally as she opened the front door for Dominic.

"Not this time, mum. But I am starving," said Dominic as he hugged her warmly.

"How've you been? It's good to have not been reading about you in the papers." She hurriedly added, "even though I know it's all a load of rubbish!"

"I'm okay. Just writing and rehearsing some new stuff. Next year is going to be amazing though," said Dom, plonking himself down on the sofa.

"Tea or coffee?" asked Cally, as she walked towards the kitchen.

"Err. Coffee. I'm knackered."

Returning with two mugs of coffee, Cally sat down on the other sofa. "So, go on. Tell me your news."

Blowing on the hot coffee, he said, "Well, we've got a few gigs on the run up to Christmas. One's in Manchester so you'll have to come to that. At the G-MEX. Massive show for us!"

"Ooh. I will. Thank you."

"And then!" with a suitably dramatic pause, "and then, we've got the Brit awards. Two nominations and we're playing and then we're off to America. A month-long tour. I can't wait!"

"That's amazing," said Cally, concealing her disappointment that she would be unable to see her boys for so long.

The Rock 'N' The Roll. 'N That

"I know! And then we've got festival dates lined up in the summer and hopefully have the second album ready to release around then."

"I still can't believe all this is happening," said Cally.

"Until you read another load of shit in the papers…"

"Until I read another load of shit in the papers," said Cally, shaking her head ruefully.

"Anyhow, I've got something for you." Pulling the large carrier bag from beside the sofa, Dominic handed it across to his mum.

"What is it?" said Cally excitedly.

"Open it."

Ripping at the brown paper that Dominic had wrapped as carefully as he could, Cally's face light up as she pulled the picture frame out of the bubble-wrap packaging revealing a gold record.

"Oh Dominic," she gasped. "Awarded to Lonely Souls for UK sales of 100,000 units." Looking up to Dominic proudly, she said, "That's so kind of you." Choking back tears, she leant across and hugged her son to him.

"Come on Mum, don't cry. It's only a little present," said Dominic, rubbing a tear away himself.

"And not many mums would ever get a little present like this. It'll be on the wall before you're home. I promise."

"Thanks Mum." He drained his cup of coffee. "Look there's something I want to talk to you about," he said, with a serious look now on his face.

"What's that then?" said Cally.

"All the shit in the papers. They've said a couple of times about having no dad and coming from a single-parent family. It winds me up."

"It upsets me too. But you know I did everything for you I could," said Cally, her voice cracking slightly.

"I know you did. That's not my point." He took a deep breath. "I want to know more about my dad. Is there anything you can tell me? Anything at all?"

Wringing her hands together, causing her knuckles to whiten, Cally stared at the wooden floorboards beneath her feet.

"What do you want to know?" she said in a whisper.

"What's his name for starters, I suppose? You've just never talked about him."

"Davey. David," she said brusquely.

"David what?"

"Err. David. David Parks," Cally said as decisively as she could. She was unsure of his actual surname, having only heard him referred to by his nickname.

"Okay. David Parks. Where was he from?"

"Manchester. He was from Manchester," replied Cally, an anguished look on her face.

Pondering his next question, Dominic frowned and rubbed at his forehead. "How long were you together?"

"Not long. Not long at all," said Cally, desperately holding back a sob.

"How long's not long then?"

"Not long at all, Dominic. He left me as soon as he found out I was pregnant." A tear rolled down her cheek as the painful lie left her lips.

"Why did he do that though? Why?" said Dom, taking his mum's hand in his.

"I don't know. I just don't know," said Cally, her voice now barely audible, the tears flowing down her face.

"Look. I'm sorry. This seems hard for you. But I need to know," said Dominic, having now joined his mum on her sofa.

"There's nothing more to know," she said, breathing deeply as she attempted to compose herself.

"But there must be!" implored Dominic.

"There isn't. He left me. And I decided that I wanted to keep the baby. Which turned out to be babies. You. And Jamie. And I've not regretted that for one second. Not one second."

Closing his eyes and kissing her on the forehead tenderly, he said, "Thank you. Honestly. Thank you for saying that. I know you won't want to hear this, but I want to try and find him. I want to find my dad."

Cally looked at him, wiping at the tears that were now streaming freely. "Please don't do that. Please, Dominic."

"I'm sorry but I have to. If he lives in Manchester, I could have walked past him in the street. He could have bought our album. I have to do this."

"You'll never find him," said Cally resolutely.

"Well I'll try. I'll try and see what happens," said Dominic, wiping his hand gently across his mum's tear-stained cheek.

"Okay. I can't stop you. But as lovely as it was to see you, can you go now. This all upsets me," said Cally, standing up and drying her eyes with a tissue.

"Look I'm sorry to have upset you, but you must understand why. I'm sorry. I'll see ya soon, yeah?" said Dominic. As he went to hug her, Cally wrapped hers arms around herself defensively.

"Of course, and thank you again for the present. It's amazing. Bye Dom."

The Rock'N'The Roll. 'N That

"Yeah. Bye Mum, and I am sorry."

As soon as the front door was closed, Cally curled up on the sofa, a cushion squeezed between her arms, and cried. And cried at the truth her son would never find…

Chapter 47

"Right then. We've done the introductions. Glasgow Barrowlands tonight. Soundcheck at 4pm. Back at t'venue for 7pm. Gentlemen. As you were. The M6 awaits," said Maggie as he read from the itinerary on his iPad. "Anybody have any questions?"

Steve Jones aka Maggie. A dyed in the wool Yorkshire man who had worked in the industry for twenty-odd years having started giving out fliers for promoters outside venues. He loved music with a passion and watched every show by every band that he had tour managed. At six feet two and a solid fourteen stone of toned muscle, he was an intimidating figure. His self-styled moniker of 'Maggie' was, to quote, "I'm a bit of a cunt from Yorkshire. A blonde haired hard-faced cunt."

Pushed in Johnny's direction by the record label, the band were still very much at the 'getting to know you' phase.

Slightly sheepishly, Danny raised his hand.

"What the fuck are you doing, D-Mo? We're not at fuckin' school!" laughed Mikee, dragging Danny's arm down.

"Danny. Yes. What's your question?"

"Err, can we stop at Tebay, near the Lake District. Wicked scotch eggs!" said Dan hopefully.

"Consider it done," said Steve/Maggie. "I'm rather partial meself. Belting little shop they have their in'tit?"

Suitably heartened by this and with the prospect of a scotch egg imminent, Danny took his seat on the tour bus with a big soppy grin.

***

Glasgow was a sweating melting pot of euphoric Scots. High on rock 'n' roll and the prospect of the festive boozeathon that lay ahead of them.

Dublin was equally triumphant. The only issue of concern being the number of cousins that Danny had to try and accommodate on the guestlist. This had caused Steve/Maggie much consternation and numerous amendments to said list. The wanker sign that Danny had made behind his back after a particularly protracted expletive-littered grumble had only just passed undetected.

And then Manchester. So much to answer for…

A homecoming gig for the band – that were now firmly lodged in the hearts of the citizens of their fair city. This was no mean feat given the roll call of bands that went before them and they were more than aware of the illustrious footprints they were treading in.

'GOD KNOWS YOU'RE LONELY SOULS! GOD KNOWS YOU'RE LONELY SOULS!'

The rhythm section-produced entrance track was going down a storm. With strobe lights whipping the audience and the sampled track roaring the announcement of the band, the crowd's adrenaline soaring even before Dominic hit the first chord of the evening.

A second-ever stage dive from Jamie resulted in him being carried almost half way to the back of the converted station hall. Upon returning to the stage, the band tore into a blinding cover version of 'Touched by the Hand of God'.

The aftershow party that followed their tumultuous set was packed to the rafters. A nearby bar had been convened for the evening and a procession of family, friends, well-wishers and blaggers ensured that the band slept until Watford the next day.

Johnny had spent most of the evening deep in conversation with Cally – to any passers-by this would have looked deeply conspiratorial, such were the hushed words they were exchanging.

And finally. London. Their own headlining show at a previous stomping ground. The Shepherds Bush Empire.

A sold-out show and a spiralling out of control guestlist had set Steve/Maggie's stress levels off the scale. He seemed to be perfectly in control of every other on the road aspect, but pleas for additional passes and places for shows just threw him into a frenzy of foul-mouthed Yorkshire turmoil.

Two names on said guestlist needed no introductions. And no ridiculous pseudonyms this time. Ms Lara Bearheart. Johnny had also made every effort to ensure that Ms Amanda Fletcher was firmly access all areas.

It had been decided that they would partake in a dressing room post-show 'Secret Santa' ritual and names had been drawn from Mikee's somewhat sweaty trapper hat as they idled through the London traffic. The rules were simple. Soundcheck and then you had until showtime to procure said present for your recipient/victim.

Names had been drawn and knowing nods exchanged.

A veritable scrape of photographers was circling the front of the venue from mid-afternoon so discreet exits under veil of headwear, hoods and shades were made just as the afternoon's light started to fade to evening.

A raucous and impeccably delivered set had seen several new tracks seamlessly introduced to their set. And after a rousing encore of 'Salvation', that was 2013 finished and boxed off for Lonely Souls.

The small matter of Secret Santa remained. The dressing room door was locked, and the band and the five presents were safely stashed in an empty bass drum box from Mikee's drum kit. Dominic had appointed himself the role of Father Christmas.

"HO HO HO. Okay boys and girls. Have we all been good as gold this year? Gold, d'yer get it?" said Dominic putting on a deep booming voice.

"Most of the time," laughed Danny, chinking bottles with Mikee.

"HO HO HO. And our first present is for Johnny. Have you been good this year, little Johnny?"

"Amanda!" coughed Mikee.

"Jealous," said Johnny, with a smile.

Accepting the badly wrapped parcel from Dominic, Johnny looked round the dressing room at the band's expectant faces.

Ripping the paper away, Johnny pulled out two small boxes – Just for Men 'touch-up kit' and 24 Viagra.

"Why thank you. Thank you very fucking much," he laughed, although the latter made him inwardly grimace at what had fortunately proved to be an isolated incident.

Glancing at the band for any reaction, he saw Danny struggling to contain his laughter. "Thanks D-Mo. You have thought of everything that an old man could possibly want!"

"IT WASN'T ME!" said Danny indignantly.

"Hmmm. Well do remind me to play high-stakes poker with you sometime soon."

"Honest! It wasn't me," he said unconvincingly.

"HO HO HO! And our next present is for Mikee."

Slowly peeling away the Sellotape off the slender parcel, Mikee then roared with laughter – fancy dress 'prison tattoo sleeves'.

The Rock'N'The Roll. 'N That

"That'll save me a fortune at the tattooist!"

Putting one on his comparatively ink free left arm, he flexed his bicep and nodded in approval.

"HO HO HO! And next present is for little Daniel Martin. Now Daniel. Have you been a good boy? My little helpers tell me that you like having your weewee sucked and kissed by naughty girls," said Dominic, with a snort of laughter.

"Very fuckin' funny!" said Danny, snatching the badly-wrapped present from Dominic.

Shaking the box slightly, he looked puzzled as he tried to guess what was inside. "New shades?" he asked hopefully.

Tearing the paper away, he looked at the box and filled up. Baby sized ear-defenders. His bottom lip trembled slightly, and he shook his head unable to speak. Rubbing at his eyes, his huge smile said everything.

Taking the box from Danny, Jamie held them up to the room. "They are wicked. The first Lonely Soul baby can come to our gigs. Love it!"

"Pass 'em back J. I'm gonna send a picture of 'em to Dee," said Danny, still struggling to maintain his composure.

"HO HO HO! And next we have a present for Jamie. Now have you been a good boy this year? I read in the newspapers that you've been doing bad things with a naked lady!" said Dominic, beaming a smile at his brother.

Opening the present, Jamie burst out laughing. "Oh, thanks Mikee. You shouldn't have!"

"WHAT!" said the drummer, convincingly feigning innocence.

Holding up the DVD, Jamie read the back of the box. "Pornahontas. Watch as the Native American beauty goes on a voyage of sexual discovery. Using her seductive power to fuck the white man out of her precious homeland. Watch Pornahontas and marvel at her sexual liberation from innocent virgin to wild cock-hungry woman."

Shaking his head, Jamie handed the box to Mikee.

"And that is not going on the player on the tour bus!" Jamie said firmly.

Looking down at the box, Mikee said, "She doesn't half look like Lara!"

"Remind me to ask her later if it was her," deadpanned Jamie.

"HO HO HO! And at last it's a present for me," said Dominic, pulling out the remaining parcel.

The opened revealed a cardboard backed plastic sealed box containing 'false glasses, nose and moustache for the prefect disguise'.

"That's wicked. I'll wear them every time I leave the flat and walk past the scrape!"

"And we have one more present," said Jamie, pulling a large flat parcel and handing it to Johnny.

Pulling back the brown paper carefully, Johnny looked proudly down at the picture on front of him. The photograph he had taken of the band on the station platform just after they had signed their record deal. Signed with individual messages of thanks and love, Johnny read them all with a lump in his throat.

Choking back his emotion, Johnny nodded a simple thank you, before he stood up and hugged and kissed each band member in turn.

A whispered 'I love you man' from Jamie had him in absolute bits and with tear-filled eyes he raised his bottle. "Lonely Souls and an even bigger and bigger AND AN EVEN BIGGER 2014!"

Five bottles all raised together and the band as one shouted, "LONELY SOULS!"

Chapter 48

As large a scrape of photographers as Jamie had witnessed greeted him and Lara as they stepped out into the cold December air, their breath clouding in front of them.

"JAMIE! LARA!" came the shouts from the scrape. Camera flashes illuminated the pavement as the photographers jostled for position.

"OVER HERE JAMIE!" "LARA! YOU LOOK LOVELY! OVER HERE!"

Jamie ushered Lara forward, guiding her by the small of her back with one hand, the other pushing away the overly-intrusive lenses. The black car was only yards away, its engine idling. The safety of the plush leather seats invitingly close.

A blinding flash in front of Jamie caused him lift his arm in front of his face. With the loss of stability he had been providing, Lara started to overbalance as a lens was thrust in her direction. Too late. As their car door opened, the heel of Lara's teeteringly high Sergio Rossi shoe snapped.

Falling forward, tumbling onto the pavement, Lara now lay full length in front of the expectant scrape.

With no thought whatsoever for her personal well-being, she was light up by a volley of flashbulbs as the photographers ravenously snapped her prone form.

Struggling to her feet, the broken heel causing her to reel again, she managed to lean against the car for support.

Wheeling on the snappers, Jamie shot them a glare that could have frozen vodka.

"FOR FUCK'S SAKE! You've got your fuckin' pictures!" he shouted, both hands flailing at the barrage of lenses in front of him.

"TOO MUCH TO DRINK ALREADY?" was one shout.

"FIGHTING ON THE PAVEMENT AGAIN?" came another.

A moment of clarity and Jamie pushed his way to Lara, who was now sliding gingerly into the car, the broken heel dangling uselessly from her right foot. Slamming the door shut, with no thought for grabbing hands and fingers, he was breathing heavily. Flashbulbs ricocheted off the car's window, hands banged on the roof and bonnet.

"FUCK!" he cried out. Turning to Lara who was wincing at both a small cut on her knee and the passing of her new favourite shoes, he said, "Fuck! Are you okay?"

"Oh, I'll live," she replied pragmatically. "My fucking shoes. Shit. My new fucking shoes! The motherfuckers!"

"Yeah, but are you okay?" said Jamie.

"I'm fine. But my fucking shoes. They were a limited edition. Motherfuckers!" Lara grimaced as she took the shoe off and mournfully shook her head.

"You must have the odd one or two other pairs?"

"Oh, Jamie Thorne. You've got a lot to learn," said Lara with a serious shake of her head.

***

Scanning his eyes predatorially around the assorted liggers and party animals, Dominic's strafing gaze stopped when he alighted on a very familiar face that was making her way towards him.

"Grace!" said Dominic, his surprise causing his stomach to flip. "I. Err. I..."

"Hello Dom. Surprised to see me?" she said with a smile.

"Err, Look I'm sorry, Can I get you a drink? "

"I will. But I didn't come for your apologies. I'm not sure why I came actually," she said, folding her arms defensively.

"Why then?" asked Dominic, his usually unbridled confidence now distinctly dialled down.

"Get me that drink. Then I'll talk to you."

Hurrying back with the glasses, Dominic discreetly ushered Grace to a quieter part of the room.

"Got you a double," said Dominic somewhat nervously.

"Not trying to get me drunk, are we?" said Grace, raising a perfectly sculpted eyebrow.

"Fuck! No. Err. I err just thought you'd li—" he stammered.

"I'm joking," Grace said sternly. Sipping at the vodka and coke, Grace smiled in approval as the alcohol bit. "Great show tonight. Nice new guitar you've got yourself."

Perking up slightly, he said, "She's a beauty. Cost me a fortune. She sounds gorgeous. Gonna use it on the next album. I won't let anybody else touch her!"

"Good to hear that you treat your guitars better than you do your women," Grace said archly.

Squeezing his eyes shut at his own faux pas, Dominic was for once speechless.

"Easy to wind up, aren't you?" said Grace, with half a smile.

"I sai—"

"I don't want you to say sorry. What's done is done." Taking a large sip from her drink, she said, "Look at me as your Ghost of Christmas Future."

Dominic looked understandably puzzled, and still resolutely speechless.

"Sorry for being so cryptic. I could easily have gone to the papers. Made a few quid for myself after our evening that went so, ahem, off the rails."

Dominic nodded, unsure where all this was going.

"Anyway. I decided against that. I'm a nice girl like that, Dominic."

His mind now racing, Dominic feared he was about to be blackmailed and looked frantically round the bar for Johnny.

"Don't panic, Dominic. All I wanted to say was. Don't do it again 'cos next time you might not be so lucky. My friend's sister is the receptionist at your record label. That's why I can come to the party."

"Thank you," said Dominic, his words dripping with relief.

"Don't thank me. I hated you for how you made me feel. But after I'd calmed down, I just didn't feel like ruining your career," said Grace softly. "Don't treat women like they are just cunt for you to use and toss aside!"

His eye's widening at her forthrightness.

"Err, thank you," Dominic said, still struggling to articulate his feelings.

"I said I don't want thanks. Just remember this and how bad things could have been."

Breathing a sigh of relief, he said, "Okay, would you like another drink?"

Tossing her head back and laughing, Grace said, "Dominic! Don't think I'm going to fuck you now!"

"I err, I wasn't."

"Good," said Grace, "and don't go forgetting your visit from the Ghost of Christmas future."

***

"I'm glad you could make it. Really good to see you," said Johnny, straightening the lapel on his purchased-that-day coat. Nip out for Secret Santa, and spend £300 quid in Covent Garden.

"Thank you," said Amanda coyly, looking sensational in a pair of wet look leggings, tourniquet tight fitted sleeveless red shirt and black peep-toe high heels. "And you too. Nice jacket by the way. You're a bit of dandy on the side aren't you," she teased.

"I like my clothes. Nothing wrong with that," he countered.

"I just want to get one thing straight whilst the night is still young," she said, sucking at her straw through bee stung lips.

He frowned slightly. "Go on," said Johnny.

"I'm not your London booty call. I've loved seeing you, but I don't work like that," said Amanda, shaking her glass indicating that a refill was required.

"Well. What can I say? That's me told. I have to say that I don't think of you like that."

"I just wanted to make it clear. No offence, Mr Manager."

"None taken."

"I'm not expecting undying commitment and swearing long-lasting fidelity, but I have principles."

"Principles are good," nodded Johnny. "I was about to say the same."

Amanda laughed warmly. "What does the manager of the music sensation of the year do with himself at Christmas?"

"Err. I've not really thought much past Christmas dinner with my mum. Then a load of cocaine, strong spirits and a smattering of self-loathing sat in my counting house looking at my riches. Something clichéd like that I suppose."

"Well, Mr Manager. My mum and dad have a small cottage in the Cotswolds that they aren't using this year. They're going somewhere sunnier."

"And?" asked Johnny.

"You could spend a few days with me after Christmas. I can get particularly lonely and horny at that time of year."

Taking no more than a few seconds to make his mind up, he said, "I like the sound of that. Err. Yes please."

"Good. That's settled. I'm not going to fuck you tonight. But you get yourself down after Christmas," said Amanda, with a look that could seduce clergy, "and well, that'll be a different matter…"

**

As the aftershow started to peter out, Dominic and Johnny found themselves at the bar, nursing tumblers of JD.

"Cheers. What a fuckin' year," said Johnny, lifting his glass to Dominic's.

"You can say that again man!" said Dominic, knocking back the rest of his oaky spirit.

"Not like you to be, err, without company," said Johnny, glancing round the room for any stray females that may have escaped Dominic's clutches.

"Night off. That Secret Santa stuff made me think I'd better be good for a few days," he said, laughing at his own little joke and the earlier encounter with Grace.

"Won't do you any harm," smiled Johnny.

"What about you? Thought you'd be off with Amanda. Proper fit!" said Dominic, nodding his approval.

Amanda was now chatting with her friend Suzzie, the band's press officer, and they were warding off the advances of two highly inebriated admirers.

"Not tonight. And yes, she is." Booze and bravado getting the better of him. "She tastes of Parma Violets. That fit."

Frowning at the obscure reference, Dominic asked "Why not?"

"Long story Dom. Anyhow. I'm done. I'm heading back to the hotel."

"For a wank?"

"Possibly," replied Johnny matter-of-factly. Leaning into Dominic, he said, "I did think I'd be guaranteed tonight, but I suppose nothing in life is," with a slight sigh.

"I'll join you," said Dominic, with a yawn.

"I'm not that type of boy! And imagine if the press found out!" laughed Johnny.

"I won't tell if you won't tell…" said Dom with a camp pout.

***

Safely ensconced in Lara's Primrose Hill apartment, Lara flopped down on the exquisitely padded sofa as Jamie paced agitatedly up and down, the floorboards creaking their resistance at each turn.

"Jamie! It's me that ended up on my ass. Chill the fuck out!" Lara implored.

Finally joining her on the sofa, he lifted Lara's bare leg up, inspecting the damage to her right knee.

"That looks sore," said Jamie. "Sure you're okay?"

"It's okay. Fetch some antiseptic from the bathroom to clean it up," said Lara with a slight wince as she tentatively touched at the cut.

Returning with a bottle of TCP and a ball of cotton wool, Jamie delicately dabbed at the cut, cleaning a few stray pieces of dirt and grit away.

The Rock'N'The Roll. 'N That

"That was horrendous. They're like fuckin' hungry animals fighting for food!" Jamie said, still shaking his head in disbelief at the scene he had just been central too.

With a shake of her head, Lara looked at the now clean and sterile cut and nodded in approval at Jamie's bedside manner.

"I'm used to it but that doesn't mean I hate it any less." She looked ruefully at her discarded shoes. "And look at them! Motherfuckers," she spat.

"Just forget about them. It's just me and you now," said Jamie as he lazily stroked her bare leg.

Running a hand through Jamie's brown hair and then letting it slide down to his cheek, she replied, "I will. I can cope though."

"I know."

"Want a smoke?" asked Lara, sitting upright.

"Yeah. Cool," he replied.

"I mean a real smoke. Too help forget about all the bad things."

Jamie looked slightly puzzled as Lara stood up and went into her bedroom, returning with a small ornately carved wooden box.

Sitting back down, she opened the box, revealing a small baggie containing rusty brown powder and a plastic tube that was scorched with a sticky residue at one end.

An alarmed look passed across Jamie's face and he looked across at Lara and frowned.

"It's okay. Honestly. It's just smoking. It just relaxes you. Makes you so chilled," said Lara, inspecting the contents of the baggie closely.

"Really?" said Jamie. Fascinated, he watched Lara slowly finger the drugs paraphernalia. "But. I heard you get addicted straight away."

"Not true. Just don't do it all the time."

Taking a small piece of aluminium foil, and placing it on the coffee table in front of her, Lara measured out a small quantity of the brown powder. Blowing through the plastic tube and wiping it on her thigh, Lara handed the silver foil carefully to Jamie.

"Hold this," she asked, and then produced a lighter from the wooden box. Holding the lighter under the foil, Lara started to heat up the tiny crystals, which responded by crackling and popping, turning into a thick viscous liquid at the flames touch. Putting the plastic tube to her mouth, Lara inhaled the thick cloying smoke, breathing deeply and closing her eyes with a contented sigh.

Opening her now glassy eyes, Lara took the foil from Jamie and handed him the tube. "Your turn…"

Chapter 49

"And the winner of the Barclaycard Brit award for the breakthrough British artist is..." The rotund presenter opened the gold envelope, wringing out as much drama as possible and announced in his cloying syrupy tones, "BEN HOWARD!"

A non-descript figure ambled on to the stage and made an anodyne speech akin to a trainee accountant accepting his graduation certificate.

The camera panned to the losing nominees' tables and the etiquette of polite applause and fixed grins was adhered to.

Mostly.

Leaning back in his chair, Dominic proceeded to make wanker signs, whilst mouthing 'who?' at the camera. Mikee and Dan had 'the finger' raised. Even Jamie was shaking his head disappointedly.

And then they headed backstage to ready themselves for their live performance. Street Baby Fury was pacing the hospitality area reciting his rhyme over and over to himself whilst studiously ignoring all and sundry.

"I said he'd never remember it all," said Dominic under his breath to Jamie.

As the band took to the stage, Fury flashed a peace sign and scooped up his mic. The premise was that he would bound on to the stage unannounced.

Striking the open chords, the band were on incandescent form as they tried to bring some life to the beige proceedings.

Slowing the tempo awaiting Fury's arrival, Dan and Mikee picked up the hip-hop beat and the rapper pinballed onto the stage. Black hoodie pulled up, shades hanging on for dear life and a red scarf round his neck.

Jamie afforded himself a small smile at the rapper's reverential nod to his band. That or he'd picked a side in the perennial LA gang wars…

"Yo Yo Yo. We be here with Lonely Souls for the Brits '13. Yeah it's me Street Baby Fury!"

Now pacing the lip of the stage, Fury continued, nodding rhythmically to the driving beats.

The Rock 'N' The Roll. 'N That

Delivering exactly what he promised, the rhythm section provided him with the requisite beats for him to drop his lyrical bombs over proceedings.

As Fury signalled the end of his rap by holding up his jewel-encrusted peace sign, the band tore into the song's snarling outro. Dom stamped on his effect pedal and a corrosive guitar line rasped through the arena.

"WE'RE LONELY SOULS. SORRY TO HAVE WOKEN YOU UP!" shouted Jamie. And with that the band left the stage with the audience screaming their appreciation at the sonic assault they had just witnessed.

"Boys! That was amazing," the high-street pretty backstage anchor presenter said faux-breathlessly. Thrusting a mic in Jamie's direction, she said, "Did you know about Street Baby Fury? You all looked surprised when he crashed the stage."

"We knew nothing about it," deadpanned Jamie, rolling his eyes as the camera panned across to him.

"It certainly raised the roof!" she carried on obliviously, giddily adding, "And he wore a red scarf just like you, Jamie!"

"Yeah. That. Or he just wanted to wind the Cripps in the audience up."

Looking slightly confused, she pointed the mic in Dominic's direction. "Hey Dom! Not too disappointed about losing out to Ben Howard were you. WE LOVE HIM!"

Big mistake. A cardinal error had just been committed. On live TV.

With a rub of his nose, Dom grabbed the mic from the hapless presenter and faced the camera.

"Who the fuck is he? My window cleaner's more rock 'n' roll then him! Bet he's back in his hotel havin' a cocoa and a bedtime story read to him."

Dominic continued unabated. "And don't start me off on 'Best British band'." His voice dripping in sarcasm. "Banjos, waistcoats and tweed trousers? Fuck off! We'll be back for that next year Marcus, you twat. If we can be arsed showing up."

Looking dumbstruck at the tirade, the presenter made an unsuccessful grab for the microphone.

"And one more thing, STREET BABY FURY! How fuckin' good was that! Anytime brother, an absolute pleasure! I'm off for a beer now and to give anyone wearing Tweed a slap. Who's with me?"

Having invited the carnage with her vacuous questions – the naïve presenter now stood looking more than a little shell-shocked.

Johnny grinned to himself. Bang. There were the tabloid titbits rights there. Picking up a complimentary glass of champagne, Johnny raised the glass flute to the band. "Loving your work lads. How about we do one to America for a few weeks and let all this hoo-ha die down?"

"Yeah, I could go that," Mikee said with a smirk

"America?" Jamie said. "D'yer think they'll be ready for us?"

The Rock'N'The Roll. 'N That

Chapter 50

Have you had your jabs, D-Mo?" asked Dominic, as they sat in the international departure lounge at Manchester Airport awaiting their flight to be called. Shades were donned, and beers being polished off with admirable gusto given their early flight time.

March 2013. A typically bleak Mancunian Tuesday morning saw the band prepare for a thirty-three date US tour support slot for Universal Gleam – 'the new Pearl Jam', a five-piece band from New York State.

First stop. Austin, Texas, to attend the prestigious SXSW music festival and conference. A headlining club gig for the band and a five-minute slot for Johnny at an industry 'round robin' style discussion about the future of the music industry and prospects for new bands.

"You don't need jabs for America. D'yer?" said Danny, looking at Johnny for guidance.

Giving him a quick shake of the head, Johnny again checked the passports and work visas that he had secured for the band. Fortunately, Danny and Mikee's little altercation with the law hadn't prevented the obtaining of said documents.

A flight to Chicago O'Hare Airport and then an internal flight on to Texas would see the band airborne for some of twelve hours. The Devil makes work for idle hands to do...

Or not. Much to Johnny's relief, the flight was event free, aside from some exuberant flirting with the flights attendants – securing them extra complimentary booze and pictures on the steps of the plane when they touched down in Chicago.

The connecting flight dragged, but at 9pm local time, they arrived at their hotel. And a round of drinks was suggested as a 'nightcap'. Which led to another. And another. And so on.

The Rock'N'The Roll. 'N That

***

Johnny looked in the mirror and blinked at his reflection. Worst. Idea. Ever. Why he had listened to Mikee and Danny of all people was beyond him.

'Drink through the jetlag'. *Jesus Christ*, he thought. The notes for the five-minute speech he was fifteen minutes away from delivering looked like a blur of random words on the page. Any coherence and structure to his thoughts were now scrambled in a haze of weak American beer and strong American spirits. And Bolivian cocaine. Which had been procured as easily as the booze.

Seeking the solace of a toilet cubicle, he sat down and put his pounding head between his shaking hands. *Okay, get a grip. It's five minutes. 300 seconds. How hard can that be?*

The premise of the speeches was along the lines of 'speed-dating'. An hour had been allocated for the ten delegates to give their talk on the future of the music industry.

With a little bit of planning and a lot less of a hangover, this would have been a straightforward exercise. "Fuck's sake," Johnny chastised himself for the umpteenth time that morning.

Having taken advantage of his porcelain perch, he felt slightly better although his stomach still growled and lurched.

A line, he thought. *That'll sort me right out.* Mikee had left a wrap with him when he had disappeared with Danny at some unearthly hour of the morning. A quick glance at his Rolex established that this was a mere four hours ago.

Popping the toilet seat down, he placed the glossy wrap on the toilet cistern. Taking out his hotel key card, Johnny carefully racked out a rail of coke. Not to too big as to render him manic – the image of Spud's chaotic job interview in *Trainspotting* sprang to mind – but enough to give him a sufficient bump to pull off the impending public speaking.

A neat two-inch white bullet sat in front of him. Breakfast in narcotic form. No milk or sugar required. Beats the Ready Brek glow hands down. Set you up for the rest of the day. Or at least until the next nutritious serving…

Leaving the air-conditioned cool of the toilet, Johnny headed to the delegates' holding area.

"Good Morning! I'm Brad," said a preternaturally young looking bespectacled conference employee. His overly enthusiastic demeanour in stark contrast to Johnny's.

Glancing down at Johnny's lanyard, he said, "Great to meet you Johnny. If you could go over and see Josh over there, he'll fit you with a radio mic."

"Thank you, err, Brad," Johnny said. He felt the cold drop of the cocaine at the back of his already raw throat.

"And don't look so worried," added Brad. "Five minutes. It'll fly by," he said with a camp flourish of his clipboard.

Heading over to Josh, Johnny rubbed at his nose and felt his stomach somersault once again.

"Hey Josh. I'm Johnny. Johnny Harrison. I believe you are the man to see about the mic things."

"Hey Johnny. Let me see. Yup. Got you. Ready for this. You're first on. Set the bar and then sit back and watch the others," Josh said, as he started to fix the radio mic to the lapel of Johnny's red Fred Perry polo shirt.

"First!" grunted Johnny. "You're fuckin' kidding me?"

"Don't sweat it. Be over before you know it!" Josh said with a reassuring pat on Johnny's shoulder.

"Hmm, yeah. No sweat," grumbled Johnny.

"Five minutes and you're on. First on and last here. Nothing like cutting it fine!" said Josh with a last-minute adjustment to the mic. "Go and wait over there, by the blue curtain and Liza will tell you when you're on."

"Thanks man," Johnny said, his inner narrative screaming at him to bolt for the sanctuary of his hotel room.

Walking determinedly over to Liza, he started to measure his breathing, the jolts of cocaine spiking his already racing adrenaline.

"Hi. Liza?"

"Yes. Hey," she looked over the top of her preppy style glasses at his dangling lanyard, "Johnny Harrison. It's nice to meet you. How are you enjoying your SXSW so far?"

"I'll start enjoying it when this is over," he grimaced.

"Oh please! Don't worry. Everything will be super! Your band are brilliant by the way! Love the album," Liza said, checking something off her clipboard.

Gulping back a cup of water from a nearby cooler, Johnny was now officially shitting himself.

"One minute and you are on," Liza said gesturing Johnny to the front of the line of other delegates who reeked of sleep, shower gel and composure.

"Good luck man. Rather you than me going first, "said Kris, a friendly looking African-American, with a neat set of mini-dreads.

The Rock'N'The Roll. 'N That

"Err, thanks," Johnny said, wiping a serviette across his sweat beaded brow.

"You okay?" asked Kris, a look of genuine concern on his voice.

"Yeah. Thanks. I'm fine. A shit and a line sorted me out before!"

As if hearing an instant echo, Johnny heard his words instantly relayed to him.

Both he and Kris froze. The radio mic. Somebody had flipped the radio mic on. The nausea in his stomach bubbled and threatened to manifest itself.

Shaking his head frantically and signalling with his eyes at Liza, Johnny pushed the palms of his hands into his pulsing temples.

Liza mouthed 'I'm sorry' and then gestured for him to take the stage.

Stepping out into the conference room and facing the three hundred equally amused and bemused delegates, Johnny took a deep breath and applying the adage that 'things could only get better' proceeded to tear up his notes…

"Well. That wasn't the start I had in mind," he said with a pause as a handful of delegates finished laughing at his misfortune.

"Before you ask. I did wash my hands. And yes, who'd have thought it. Good quality cocaine at a music convention!"

Laughter rose from the room, some of it a little shocked at Johnny's candidness.

"I had got this all prepared but after that start," he smiled with an apologetic shrug of his shoulders.

Glancing to the side of the stage, and then looking down at the mic attached to his collar. "Is thing on now?" he deadpanned.

More laughter. Right. *Fucking go for it,* he thought.

"Everybody here is here for one reason and one reason alone. We all love music. We all care about the future of the music industry. We all want to be here next year and the year after that etc."

Taking a deep breath, Johnny felt he was on a roll.

"Looking around the room, I see we are all people of a comparable generation. We grew up with our favourite bands. Our favourite albums. We invested time, money and love into these bands. They were our lives in a lot of cases. We owned vinyl, cassettes, CDs. But we owned something. We had something to show for our devotion."

Pulling out his mobile phone and waving it animatedly over his head, he said, "But today's music buying generation. They can have the whole of their music collection on this!"

Tucking his phone back into his jeans pocket, he continued.

"Download this. YouTube that. Stream this. You don't have to spend a penny to listen to music anymore. We all have bands and albums we love. I grew up loving The Stone Roses."

A few cheers erupted round the room.

"Thank you. You have excellent taste. Mine's a pint," said Johnny, raising his cup of water. "I've loved and played that album for two decades or so and it still fuckin' excites me every time. Every time I play it. After all this time, it still feels special."

A few wolf whistles were forthcoming as he continued his impassioned speech.

"And my point? My point is that it's down to us to ensure that music doesn't become ultimately disposable. We must make sure that there is music for people to love. To want to love. To want to treasure for ever. We need to find the next generations Roses. Clash. Amy Winehouse. Nirvana. Beastie Boys. Blondie. The next generations need us to find and nurture these bands. Because without us the tree will wither and die. And songs will just be another MP3 file in the latest gizmo. We must keep looking. There are bands out there. I found one that were so damn good you just had to believe in them. It proves that they are out there."

Pausing and looking around the room, Johnny took a breath and afforded himself a smile.

"The music industry needs to be investing in bands that people will invest in. Let's give them something to love. Not just download and forget about the next day. I don't want to think of people in twenty years not having a body of albums, of music, of bands that they have loved for all that time. Give them the bands. Give them the songs. And don't go for the quick fix. It's in the industries hands."

Finishing the last of his water off, Johnny breathed in deeply.

"I'm going to finish now. But. Ladies and gentlemen. Keep the faith. KEEP THE FUCKIN' FAITH! And let's find these future great artistes and give the next generations their bands to love and cherish."

As the room broke out into a generous bout of applause, Johnny clapped back and nodded his head appreciatively. With a wave, he exited the stage with a relieved, "I told you it'd get better!"

***

"I hear you had an eventful time at your conference thing," said Jamie as they boarded the metal tube that would be their home for the next six weeks.

Nursing a gargantuan hangover, Johnny blinked at the fierce early morning sunshine. "Think I just about pulled it off. Can't see them inviting me back, mind," he snorted. "Remind me never ever to listen to these two," pointing in Danny and Mikee's direction, "ever again!"

"I wish I'd seen it," laughed Danny, "a shit and a line! I'm all over YouTube later."

"Do let me know if you find it," said Johnny, finally finding his own sunglasses, "I can't wait to relive that moment over and over..."

"That's everything loaded. Next stop Houston," said Mikee as he closed the storage compartment with an unsympathetic slam.

300 kilometres. A veritable nip to the corner shops in terms of a US tour. Johnny sought sanctuary at the front of the bus, necking heavy-duty painkillers and chilled water.

The back of the bus was unnaturally quiet, he thought, having earlier heard Dominic win the shout for shotgun on the DVD player.

After 90 minutes of clear highway, feeling rehydrated and enlivened, Johnny shouted up a suggestion that they make a stop.

"Yup. Good for me," Mikee shouted.

"McDonald's please," Danny said, "I haven't had one yet."

Standing in the coach's aisle and leaning on the headrests of the seats aside him, Johnny rolled his eyes. "We've not been here 24 hours yet. I'm sure you'll survive, D-Mo. How about a genuine American diner?"

"He'll be after a scotch egg," Jamie said, looking rock star cool in a Slipknot T-shirt, faded jeans and some newly acquired Ray-Ban Aviators.

"I don't fancy getting off. Grab a burger for me," Danny said, with a concerned frown. He'd been dismayed at the excess of wide open spaces – having expected nothing but malls and neon lighting.

Dom and Mikee started cackling at Danny's newly discovered agoraphobia.

"I daren't ask! I really fucking shouldn't. But what have you told him?" said Johnny, stifling a grin.

Striking up the duelling banjos theme, and making accompanying porcus squeals, they now had tears of laughter rolling down their pasty Northern faces.

Jamie held up the box of the DVD that they had been watching – *Deliverance*.

"Oh. Good choice lads. You know that it's a documentary?" Johnny said, as he struggled to maintain a straight face.

"They told me that the middle of America is like that!" said a clearly aggrieved Danny.

"Middle America," corrected Dom.

"Middle America. Whatever," Danny snapped. "I'm not getting off in one of them quiet little towns. McDonald's means there's normal people live there. No McDonald's and you lot can bring me something. And I'll stay on here," he said with an emphatic folding of his arms.

"Less than two hours," said Johnny, somewhat bewildered. "We've been on the go for a couple of hours and you lot have convinced him that he is going to get hillbilly fucked if he isn't within 20 feet of the Golden Arches." Clapping his hands slowly, he said, "'Fucking hell. That's good even for you lot."

Looking up at Johnny, having expected a little more sympathy, he said, "But it's based on a true story!"

"Right. Danny. If we pull up anywhere that has a toothless inbred tuning a banjo, I promise that we won't stop. Deal?" Johnny said.

"I s'pose," mumbled Danny.

"And what films have we got lined up next then? *Silence of the Lambs*? *The Evil Dead*? *Independence Day*?" Johnny said, with a last disbelieving shake of his head. "There's a decent diner ahead. My shout."

***

"It's brilliant being out here," Jamie said, leaning against the thick wooden bar top and idly flicking a beer mat end over end. "Nobody knows us. We've been here a few days and even after the gigs, I'm not getting any mither."

Sipping on his Lite beer, pulling a disdainful face, Johnny leant back on his stool. "That still matters?"

"It does, yeah. There's never a minute when I'm out now. People looking and always wanting to chat. I know how bad that sounds, but it gets on top."

"Comes with the territory J. Never going to go away. Especially these days, when everybody can be a journo with their camera phones and Twitter and that."

"I don't want that. Never have."

Ordering two more beers, Johnny raised an eyebrow.

"If you mean Lara by that, then that was never part of the plan." Then sipping from his fresh beer, "Not that there was a plan!"

"You can't always get what you want after a top ten album. If you'll allow me to paraphrase," said Johnny, grinning at his own joke. "Like it or not, you are now public property. They buy your records, go to your gigs."

"And I like it here without the hassle," Jamie said emphatically.

"You're not telling me that you're going to move to LA and become a recluse?"

"Don't be soft."

"And you and Lara? I take it you're hooking up at some point now you're in the big country."

"Yeah. I'm sure we will. I haven't seen her since before Christmas, but y'know."

Pulling on his drink and looking at the label in disgust, Johnny nodded at Jamie. "You two make me laugh."

"Who? Me and Lara," said Jamie defensively.

"No!" He raised an apologetic hand. "You and Dominic. You want to be all Howard Hughes to his Great Gatsby."

"Nice touch. You're not as daft as you look!" laughed Jamie. "Remind me to tell D-Mo and Mikee that one," said Jamie with a knowing wink.

"I dunno Jamie. Next album is going to be huge. The stuff you've demoed sounds amazing. Next level. And that means more of the shit you don't like. Eye of the storm, baby!"

"Maybe I will then. Grow a massive beard and sit around writing songs and only appear to play them."

"Only one problem there."

Jamie looked across at him, slightly puzzled.

Grabbing Jamie's cheeks between his index finger and thumb and squeezing them together, Johnny said, "Look at yer little baby face! It'd take you ten years to grow a beard."

"You're just jealous of my youthful good looks," laughed Jamie as he threw a toy punch towards Johnny's unshaven jaw.

"Another drink? Or do you want to head back?"

"Why not? The gig's not for another couple of hours. And the motel is crap. Colorado is beautiful, but I'll go full diva if there's cockroaches trying to share my bed in the next motel."

Chapter 51

"I'm not saying that all American people are fat. Just that your fat people are fatter than ours," said Danny, realising the monumental hole that he was digging for himself.

"Just because you're a little skinny dude doesn't mean that you can criticise the larger gentleman," said the increasingly irate and sizeable local.

"I didn't mean... Look, I didn't mean you. Alright mate?"

"Alright mate?" repeated the antagonistic American.

"Yeah. Alright mate? Means are you okay?"

"Look he didn't mean any harm," Dominic said, playing the unlikely role of peacemaker.

"Where the fuck's Mikee?" Danny hissed.

"Gone back to the motel for a kip. We should head back."

"Hey guys," Danny said, proud of the local vernacular he felt he had seamlessly dropped into, "we've got to shoot."

"And that's supposed to be funny is it?" asked antagonistic American's cousin. His irony free T-shirt emblazoned with the slogan 'I'LL LAPDANCE FOR BEER' strained at his midriff.

"I've no idea what you mean?" Dominic said, then hurriedly finishing off his drink.

"You not get the news back in England?" he replied aggressively.

"I honestly haven't a fuckin' clue what you're on about," Dominic said, now distinctly sensing trouble.

"The school shootings. You think that shit's funny?"

"As if he fuckin' meant it like that! You dick!" Dominic said incredulously.

And that was all it took. Antagonistic American threw a powerful haymaker in Danny's direction, knocking him backwards off his stool and smashing one lens of his shades.

Leaping back off his own barstool, Dominic ducked just as a punch whipped past his jaw. The bartender who had been intently listening to

The Rock 'N' The Roll. 'N That

the conversation descend from idle bar chat to fully-fledged bar-brawl had now picked up a conveniently placed baseball bat and was pointing it in Danny's direction.

Having picked himself up off the floor, he was now wielding a beer bottle by the neck in the direction of his advancing and considerably larger adversary.

"Fuck off you fat cunt or I'll fuckin' smash this in yer face!" yelled Danny.

"Put the bottle down buddy," said the bartender, the bat hanging loosely by his side - full of kinetic danger.

The strident opening chords of Metallica's anthem 'Enter Sandman' belching out of the jukebox did nothing but increase the escalating tempo of intent that was wasping around the bar.

"I'll put it down if he backs off," shouted Danny, jabbing the bottle in front of him.

"Back the fuck off Brad," demanded the bartender in a desperate attempt to placate matters.

"C'mon Nicky! The skinny English fuck called me fat. He's getting what's coming to him!"

And with that not particularly thinly veiled threat, he again swung a meaty punch at Danny.

Who nimbly stepped aside and cracked the base of the bottle firmly across his assailant's exposed jowl.

Fortunately, the bottle didn't break. Unlike the bartender's patience.

"PUT THE BOTTLE DOWN OR YOU'LL BE SAYING HELLO TO MATILDA!" The bat was now held at shoulder height as Nicky assumed a perfect batter's stance.

Dropping the bottle with a smash, Danny raised his hands in a classic 'it's a fair cop' pose.

Peeling off a twenty dollar note, Dominic threw it in the direction of the bar, and tried to step towards the door.

"Not so fast. I think that the local sheriff needs to sort this little mess out," Nicky said. The bat now held in an 'uncocked' position.

"We have to get off. We've got a gig in about an hour," Dominic said hopefully.

Shouting through to the kitchen, Nicky said the words they least wanted to hear. "Call the cops."

The attending police officers quickly ascertained that it was only Danny who had been physically involved in the altercation and he was swiftly cuffed and carried away, leaving Dominic to make like Hermes on a bad news day and hotfoot it back to the venue and inform the band they were now one incarcerated bass player short.

***

"Fuck's sake," Johnny said, relieved that the beers he had been consuming bore little malice in terms of their alcoholic strength.

"It wasn't our fault!" said Dom, remarkably sheepishly.

"I'm not the one that needs to decide that though, am I," Johnny said, as he paced up and down outside of the venue.

"We're gonna have to cancel aren't we," Jamie said, rubbing at his temple. "What the fuck were yer thinking, bro?" he asked, half annoyed, half sympathetically.

"We were just havin' a laugh and these two fat fucks took it the wrong way," said Dominic with a rueful shake of his head.

"I suppose I best get down to the police station. I'll ring the label and get the address of a lawyer whilst I'm on my way. You lot stay here and keep out of trouble," Johnny said snappishly.

***

"Daniel Martin. He's English. He would have been brought in about an hour ago. Bit of an altercation in a bar."

Slowly perusing the roll call of cell dwellers, the female duty sergeant pursed her lips and nodded. "Martin. Daniel Martin. He is in a holding cell following his arrest, sir. Can I ask who you are?"

"Err, yes. I'm Johnny Harrison."

"And are you his lawyer?" She looked Johnny up and down.

"No. I'm err, I'm the manager of his band. They have a show in less than an hour."

"Mr Martin will be detained overnight and be in court in the morning."

Taking a deep breath and straightening out his T-shirt, Johnny said, "See, that's the problem. We have a show. Tonight. Is there no way that we can arrange for bail?" Remembering an oft-used piece of jargon from Claire's beloved US detective shows, Johnny played his best amateur lawyer card. "He doesn't present any flight risk. None whatsoever."

Quietly pleased with his turn of phrase, the wind was soon sucked from his sails.

"Really, sir? So, you're a qualified lawyer as well as the manager of a rock band, are you?"

"No. No I'm not. Obviously." Steeling himself for his next move, Johnny lowered his voice. "I'm just trying to get our boy out and back in time for the show. We might not be able to get a lawyer out until the morning."

"That isn't my problem, sir," the duty Sergeant said disinterestedly.

"Okay. Is there some local charity or police benevolent fund we can donate to? Would that make a difference?"

Putting her pen down and folding her arms, she lowered her voice to the same level as his. "I would have stuck to 'no flight risk.' You were doing okay at that point. You have just offered a law enforcement officer what could be constituted as a bribe."

"Whoah! No. I didn't mean that. I ju—"

"You just thought you'd try something like the stuff you've seen in the movies. Not smart, sir. Not smart at all." Unfolding her arms and putting her palms flat down on the desk, she said, "You're not going to be able to save the day here, sir. I'll level with you. I don't think charges will be pressed. The guy he was fighting with is well-known locally for being a hot-head."

With a resigned look on his face, Johnny nodded his head. "Any chance of seeing our jailbird?"

"Five minutes. No more than that."

"Thanks. Appreciate it."

***

Having been shown to the holding cells, Johnny saw the top of Danny's head as he sat with his shoulders slumped on the single concrete bed.

"D-Mo."

"Alright Johnny," Danny said, looking up with a tear-stained face. Rubbing hurriedly at his eyes, he said, "Don't say anything to the others! Please."

"I won't."

"What about the show? The tour! What the fuck am I going to say to Dee? I don't want to stay in prison in America. D'yer think they'll export me back to England. I could cope with that."

"Extradite," said Johnny, laughing gently at the malapropism.

"It's not funny! You're my manager. I need your help here, Johnny."

"Right, Danny. You're not making tonight's show. I've got a lawyer on the way. It's unlikely you'll be charged. But you're here overnight."

"Oh fuck. But they could send me down. You don't know that for sure."

"I don't. But I'll be back first thing. Promise you." Holding out his hand through the cell bars, Danny squeezed it gratefully.

"Not a word Johnny. And don't tell Dee," implored Danny, looking more little boy lost than cocksure rock 'n' roller.

***

"Now!"

As Danny sheepishly stepped onto the tour bus having been released without charge, Dominic pressed play on the stereo, having hooked it up to his iPhone.

The familiar slashing chords blasted out followed by Joe Strummer's strident voice ably accompanied by the band – *'Breakin' rocks in the hot sun. I fought the Law and the Law won!'*

"Here you go, D-Mo," Mikee said, throwing an artistically doctored white T-shirt at Danny.

Catching it just before it hit him in the face, he held the T-shirt up and laughed reluctantly.

"You've got to wear it for the rest of the day. And the show," demanded Dominic.

"Shirt off, D-Mo!"

Slowly taking his cell soiled grey T-shirt off, Danny put the over-sized white T-shirt over his head.

Looking down at the hastily drawn black arrows that adorned it, he again laughed. "Very fuckin' funny boys. Very funny!"

"All day D-Mo. That's the forfeit for missing a show," Jamie said.

"Yeah. Sorry about that bu—"

"IT WASN'T MY FAULT!" chorused the band.

Pointing one of his bony fingers towards Dominic. "Tell 'em Dom! You were there."

Putting a finger to his lips, Dom said, "I'm pleading the fifth!"

"What the fuck does that even mean? Danny said, screwing up his face. "Anyhow. I'm proper starving. Can we get some breakfast?"

***

"It feels like we're starting all over again. Same as our first tour support," Jamie had said.

Taking time every day to drift around the towns and cities that they were playing, having a drink or a meal in total undisturbed bliss, they had all become very relaxed within their little tour bubble.

The miles of highway had passed by remarkably event free since the bar brawl – a smattering of blow jobs, but a certain wariness had replaced their domestic take-on-all-comers' recklessness.

An intrusively rogue digit inserted inside an unexpecting orifice had caused one overly large drummer to sit down gingerly for a couple of days. But that aside, all was calm on the American front.

Dates were ticked off, with the audience apparently impressed by the latest willing entrants to join the list of the 'English Invasion'.

Conversations home were had by every form of modern communication – mobiles, texts, Skype, email. Even by public phone box…

"Lend us your phone. I need to call Dee and my phones died on me. I can't charge it until we get to the motel. And that'll be ages off," Danny said, glancing worriedly at his watch.

An unreceptive band told him in no uncertain terms that they weren't copping for his phone bill.

"Fuck ya then," Danny had harrumphed as he sifted through his pockets for change.

At the next stop, he had selected a roadside callbox and fulfilled his daily commitment to Dee.

"Hey babe… Yeah I'm okay… How 'bout you… And the bump… You won't look fat… You'll look beautiful… Even more beautiful…"

The small talk and normality of these calls kept Danny more grounded than he would care to admit to. Needless to say, his second arrest of the year had gone unmentioned.

"I love you babe. Yeah, not long now and I'll be home."

Catching movement in his peripheral vision as he leant against the foot-scuffed plexiglass, Danny started to bang his fist against the door.

Mikee and Dominic were running in opposite directions around the phone boxes perimeter wielding rolls of the roadie's best friend. Duct tape.

The rigid grey tape was now imprisoning Danny within the stuffy confines of the cubicle.

And he had just run out of change. The last noise Dee had heard being his anguished scream as he realised the prank that he had just fallen victim to.

"OY! YOU PAIR OF CUNTS!"

"See you later, D-Mo. We're just off for a beer and a bite to eat," smirked Dominic.

Lighting a cigarette, Mikee offered Danny a light through the glass.

"FUCK OFF!" shouted Danny, pushing helplessly at the door.

A group of local skate kids had gathered round the booth and were now recording Danny's anguish on their cell phones.

"Excellent punking dude," offered one spotty and lank haired youth. "How long you gonna leave him there?"

Given that he now had an audience and realising that a panicked reaction was exactly what they wanted, Danny put his shades on, light a cigarette and sat down attempting some semblance of cool.

"Laters D-Mo. We'll bring you back some McNuggets," Dom said.

Shrugging as nonchalantly as he could, Danny looked at the tip of his cigarette and blew smoke in his captor's direction.

***

"How did you manage your great escape?" asked Dom.

"For me to know and you to find out," Danny said, tapping his reconstructed nose proudly.

A ten-dollar bribe and a teenage boy's illicitly carried knife had granted him his freedom. Knocking his beer back smugly satisfied with his initiative.

"Ya should have seen your face though," laughed Mikee.

"Hilarious," snorted Danny, "Dee was really worried about me. And she's pregnant. She doesn't need stress like that," he said with a serious look on his face.

"Anyhow, no harm done eh D-Mo, and I'm sure them kids won't put it all over the internet. Next stop New York!"

Chapter 52

Although Jamie had made the journey into New York City before, he still sat in awestruck silence, absorbing the skyline and its limitless possibilities.

And Lara.

She would be at their show tonight. Two nights at the famed Bowery Ballroom. An 800-capacity venue located in uber-fashionable Lower East Side Manhattan.

"I don't care where we are playing," said Mikee, beaming his toothy smile. "It's New York fuckin' City baby!"

"You'll know the place like the back of your hand though, won't you J?" goaded Dom.

"Guided tours a speciality," Jamie retorted, ignoring his brother's jibe. "Just make sure you get some time on your own. Stick your headphones on and have a wander around."

The label had laid on a meet and greet before the show, but the two shows meant that they would have plenty of downtime.

Leaning over his seat to talk to Jamie, Johnny tapped him on his shoulder and broke his train of thought. "No guesses as to what. Or rather who you are thinking about."

"That obvious?" Jamie said, putting his headphones down on the table in front of him.

"Just a touch."

"I've not seen her for ages. It always feels a bit weird just picking up from where we left off."

"Yup. Tough gig that. Just getting back into bed with a drop-dead gorgeous model," Johnny said with a mock sympathetic nod of his head.

"Fuckin' hell Johnny! You know me better than that. It's not just about that," he said, pausing and laughing softly, "but there is that."

"Of course."

"I told you about that night we went out and she had a blonde wig on?"

"Yeah, yeah. How could I forget! You said she looked hot."

The Rock 'N' The Roll. 'N That

"You need to get laid! Is that all you can think of? Anyway. That night was amazing. We were just a normal couple."

"A very attractive very famous couple," interjected Johnny.

"NO! That's where you're wrong," Jamie said with a shake of his head.

"How so?" Johnny said, a frown appeared on his brow.

"Because that night we were just the same as everybody else. Two people having a laugh and a drink."

"And nailing a Stones classic!"

"Irrelevant. Nobody knew us. Nobody looked at us or bothered us."

"And that sounds perfect. But that can't happen all the time. Sorry to be so blunt, J."

"I know, man. I know. But it'd work if it could be like that more often," Jamie said with a rueful expression.

"Other than moving to an island and going native there's not a lot I can suggest. Lara is known worldwide. Y'know, magazines, and all the shit she advertises."

"All the shit she advertises. Remind me to tell her that later," Jamie said, then laughed loudly.

"You know what I meant," winked Johnny.

"You'll see the madness tonight for yourself. Unless we sneak past the paps," Jamie said with a self-conscious wince. "And it's for Lara, not me!"

"Girls on Film," Johnny sang. Very badly.

"Let me stick to the singing!"

"Perhaps best," nodded Johnny. "Once you've soundchecked, I'm gonna go shopping. You can't beat it over here."

"You do surprise me. You spend more on clobber than the rest of us put together!" teased Jamie.

"I have to make more of an effort at my age. You lot look good without even trying," smiled Johnny as he looked at Jamie, perfectly tousled hair, shades and a thrift store purchased Pixies T-shirt; clearly the previous owner had been quite the stoner given the proliferation of burn holes adorning it.

Interrupting the moment, Danny then shouted up in a distinctly un-Palinesque manner, "Fuck me! It's massive. You'll never find your fuckin' way round!"

***

"Hello? Lara. It's Jamie. I, err, I thought that you'd be at the show tonight. You okay?"

Hanging up the call, Jamie paced up and down the alleyway to the rear of the venue muttering to himself. He considered making another call and then put his phone away.

Dominic and Mikee leant out of the large steel loading bay door, sharing a cigarette and a beer.

Jamie, away with his thoughts, was momentarily startled as he turned around. "Alright, I didn't see you there."

"You okay bro? You looked miles away," asked Dominic.

"Yeah. I'm good. Top set tonight. Decent crowd and that."

"This place is brilliant. I'm definitely getting me some sex in the city tonight!" Dominic said, laughing at his own joke, and as ever thinking ahead with his loins.

"AND," corrected Jamie.

"What?" asked Dominic blowing smoke and looking confused simultaneously.

"Sex AND the City," corrected Jamie.

"Okay smartarse. Don't ruin my joke. You know what I meant," said Dominic spikily.

"You expecting company J?" asked Mikee. His Empire State Building tattoo complete with King Kong swatting planes was resplendent on his upper arm.

"Not in this back alley…" said Jamie, vainly attempting to inject some humour to overcome his frustrations.

"Haha. No, I meant—"

"I know who you meant, dude. Cheers. But she hasn't shown. Bit of an odd one," said Jamie, as he accepted a cigarette off Dominic. "Cheers bro." He inhaled and almost chewed on the smoke. "Fuck. What is that?"

"I've been trying different cigs whilst we've been here. These are called," he looked at the packet, "American Spirit Full Flavor or summit."

"Jeez. They'd stop a tiger in its tracks!" coughed Jamie.

"Lightweight," laughed Dominic as he took an exaggerated pull on his own cigarette and nearly a coughed a lung up for his bravado.

"I'm gonna give her one more call and if nothing, I'll join yer for a beer," said Jamie, as he popped his collar up to ward off the chill of the night air.

"Good to know we've got our uses," said Dominic, having just about recovered the use of his larynx.

"You know what I mean bro," said Jamie as he pressed call on his phone.

Straight to voicemail again. Her familiar voice *'Hey. This is Lara. Leave me a message or don't. Your call. Bye.'*

Having already left two messages, Jamie decided that a third would look decidedly desperate.

"Fuck's sake," he muttered under his breath.

***

Bzzz.

Bzzz.

Jamie stood on the pavement outside Lara's apartment building, pulling his woolly hat further down over his ears, partially to ward off the cold of the New York morning, and in frustration at being stood on the outside looking in.

He peered hopefully through the plate glass door, but did not recognise the on-duty concierge.

With a dejected grunt, he headed back to the hotel, hoping to catch the rest of the band before they surfaced for 'Johnny's New York City Tour' – his passable accent had impressed Jamie far more than his singing.

If he got back quickly enough, he could pretend that he had played this far cooler than he had. Flagging down a yellow cab – *I'll never tire of that*, he thought to himself – he was soon back at their art-deco Hotel on 91 and Broadway.

Grabbing a New York Times and a coffee from an adjacent deli, he popped his headphones on and strolled into the hotel's compact reception area. Mikee was already up and about and was sat, engrossed with his mobile phone.

"Alright Kong?"

"Hiya J. You up and about already as well?"

"Yeah. Fancied some fresh air and a coffee. Rooms are a bit stuffy if you keep the window shut."

"And you have to keep the window shut to keep the noise out," nodded Mikee, "I hear yer man."

"Want some?" said Jamie, offering across his freshly ground coffee.

"I'd love a cwoffee!" laughed Mikee, pulling off the New York accent almost as passably as Johnny. "You should see the itinerary the bossman has lined up for us today. Empire State. Harlem. Everything!"

"Obviously," smiled Jamie.

"And then Ground Zero and Statue of Liberty. He's booked us a driver and a people carrier, so we can stop where we want as well," Mikee said excitedly.

"Sounds wicked. The others are coming along as well?"

"Should be. Dominic managed to get his sex in the city sorted. As always!" Mikee said, nodding approvingly.

"And," said Jamie, with a slight shake of his head. It was one of his mum's favourite programmes – until the tragic second film – and it was one of her bugbears that so many people got the show's title wrong.

"What?" asked Mikee, with a confused look.

"Never mind," said Jamie with a smile, "Here's Johnny and D-Mo."

***

"NEW YORK. THANK YOU SO MUCH! I can't tell you how good it feels saying that," said Jamie, adjusting his scarf slightly and wiping a hand across his sweat soaked face. "We're gonna leave you with this one. It's called 'Salvation'. We're Lonely Souls. AND WE'LL BE BACK!"

Dominic's solo was hitting incandescent heights as his technical ability was growing in proportion to his confidence. The girls loved his good looks and the boys wanted to talk guitars and chord changes with him. *He'd never been happier*, Jamie thought to himself as he glanced stage right and saw his twin totally lost in the spitting spiralling solo that he was unleashing. *Cool as fuck. And he's my brother.*

Raising his guitar and taking a slight bow to the crowd. "NEW YORK FUCKIN' CITY! SEE YA SOON."

And with that, they were done. Their first US tour in the bag. There was just the small matter of establishing if Ms L. Bearheart had been in attendance.

Beers were downed in their poky graffiti riddled dressing room – which Mikee was painstakingly adding to. His height allowing him to easily access the comparatively blank canvas of the ceiling. Balancing precariously on a chair, that threatened to splinter into matchwood at any second.

"You been able to check the guestlist for me, man?" asked Jamie as discreetly as he could.

"Not yet. I was watching your set. Give me a minute to down this and I'll check for you," Johnny said. "You were good tonight. Dom was on fire."

Overhearing the compliment, Dom raised his bottle in acknowledgement, before returning to the rail of cocaine that Danny had just racked out for him.

"Thanks man." With a slow shake of his head, he said, "I'll be gutted if she doesn't show."

"I'm sure she'll show. You know what women are like. Bit of drama just to keep you on your toes," Johnny said, with one eye on the diminishing pile of coke.

The Rock 'N' The Roll. 'N That

***

As the band stood and watched the headline band finish their set, Jamie's phone vibrated in his pocket. Snatching it out, he finally saw what he had been waiting for. A text from Lara.

'Hey Jamie. Sorry I've not been in touch. Had a virus and my doctor ordered me to stay in bed. I hear you killed it in NYC. Love lots L x'

Reading and re-reading the message for any hint of ambiguity or sub-text, Jamie cursed to himself.

Aside from him not getting to see her, he felt it also made him look 'a right twat' in front of the rest of the band.

He stepped back into the sanctuary of the dressing room, and sat down to ponder his response. The first time they play in America, and she is five minutes away. In bed. He'd been hoping that she might have surprised him and showed up at one of the other dates, but appreciated her work commitments, 'advertising shit', were always exceptionally pressing.

With much deliberation, he replied – *'Hey Lara. Sorry that you're not feeling well. Shame you missed our shows. We fly home tomorrow afternoon. I can come and see you…. J x'*

Composing himself and with a final bout of profanities, he went to join his bandmates to celebrate the last night of their first US tour.

***

"Twins?" said the achingly cool hipster chick. Skinny as a green tea and cigarettes diet, the black-haired Cleopatra-alike admirer was making no secret of her desired cardinal sins. "I've never fucked twins," she said matter-of-factly.

"I have to tell you Tyra, that is going to stay that way. Certainly, as far as these twins are concerned," said Dominic, with a dismissive shake of his head.

"Shame. You're both so hot," Tyra purred.

"Mikee is your man to talk about threesomes, but you'd need to bring along a pretty friend," Dom said, pointing in Mikee's general direction.

"I have lots of pretty friends. Marcus is beautiful. Shall I introduce him to your friend?" Tyra said, arching an eyebrow.

"That's not the sort of threesome he has in mind. But ask him. Definitely," laughed Jamie.

Just then, his phone buzzed again. Glancing at Dom, he excused himself.

'Hey Jamie Thorne. Bring me chicken soup. The deli on the corner opposite my building opens late. Love L x'

Screwing his nose up in frustration, Jamie weighed up his options. He had promised the boys that he'd party with them on the last night of their tour. But he wanted to see Lara. And most of all, he wanted Lara to answer his questions.

"My shout, bro. Another beer? And a shot," Jamie said, returning to the fray of the aftershow.

Their blistering set of rock 'n' roll, coupled with them being English – and in the twins' case, exceptionally good looking – meant that they were never short of attention. The New York scenesters had some sort of sixth sense when it came to identifying the next hot talent.

Beers and shots were dispensed with. Covert invitations for convivial trips to the washroom to share a line were readily accepted. Heads were nodded appreciatively at compliments and at tunes played over the bar's ageing sound-system. Or 'real vintage shit' as the bar owner had described it to Jamie as he ordered another round.

As he returned with half a dozen bottles of Michelob, Jamie glanced over at where Johnny was stood. By himself, idly flicking through the old-fashioned vinyl-only jukebox.

Excusing himself, Jamie went over to him and gently shoulder-charged him in the back.

Reeling round, Johnny was holding his mouth as he had just cracked the bottle he was drinking from against his front teeth and was trying not to drip beer on his newly purchased coat.

"Oh shit! Sorry man. I didn't realise you were drinking," Jamie said, raising an apologetic hand.

"It's okay seeing as though it's you," Johnny said, gingerly pressing a thumb against his teeth.

"Why are you stood on your own?"

Gesturing round the bar, he said, "C'mon J. Look at them. All these hip young kids. I'm old enough to be their fuckin' dad!"

"Last night of the tour man! You have to have a drink with us," Jamie said.

"That's good of you J. But I've seen your set. That's enough for me. I don't want to be making a twat of myself in front of this lot."

"C'mon. They're alright, the crowd we're with," Jamie said, nodding his head in the direction of the fashionistas.

"J. The last thing I want is a sympathy shag off one of them just because I'm your manager. I don't want to give them an excuse to see even more of their $150 dollar an hour therapist."

"Don't be soft, you—"

Cutting Jamie off, Johnny said, "If I can borrow your favourite expression, it's all about the music."

Smiling, Jamie placed his hand on Johnny's shoulder. "You do like a bit tired."

"Oh cheers!" Johnny said, mock-indignantly. "Six weeks on the road with you lot. Is it any wonder?"

"As long as you're okay," Jamie said.

"I'm fine J. I'm gonna get back to the hotel. There's bound to be some adverts on the TV that I've not seen yet."

He hugged Jamie to him. "I love yer man."

"You too," Jamie said, kissing him on the cheek, the smell of heavy spirits hot on his breath.

"I'll see you tomo—"

He was interrupted as the door to the bar crashed open.

The whole room turned towards the gate crasher.

Jamie's face dropped.

Lara.

A clearly not really that ill and wide-eyed Lara.

"Fuck," he mumbled under his breath.

Marching over to him, Lara stood in front of him with that familiar ballsy hands-on-hips pose.

"Jamie Thorne."

"Lara. You said you were ill in bed," Jamie said, looking more than a little taken aback. He breathed a gentle sigh of relief that he had been chatting to Johnny.

"WHERE DA FUCK IS MY CHICKEN SOUP?" asked Lara. Her accent became notably more native-Manhattan when she was either angry or off it.

"What?" Jamie said, thinking fast on his battered Converse. "Is chicken soup some secret code I don't know about?"

The rest of the bar had now dropped to hear a pin drop quiet as they eavesdropped the irate exchange. Camera phones were rapidly deployed as the partygoers turned into on the spot reporters. Fortunately, a swift intervention from Mikee quickly curtailed this.

"You know exactly what I mean!" Lara said, her dilated pupils blazing.

"I actually don't," Jamie said, "Look, let's step outside and talk."

Trying to hold Lara by the elbow and steer her out of the bar, she slapped his hand away angrily.

"When you didn't show at my apartment, I got mad."

"I did! Last night," Jamie snapped.

"Fuck you Jamie Thorne," Lara snapped back.

"And tonight, I'm having a drink. On the last night of our tour. With my friends," Jamie batted back.

Lara slowly shook her head. "Not good enough."

Pursing her exquisite lips together, Lara stared at Jamie. Her eyes a dead giveaway of her narcotic intake.

"I don't play games, Lara. You know that."

"Neith—"

Jamie cut her off before she could get out of second gear.

"I was gutted when you didn't show last night. And you'd only texted me a couple of times." Hesitating slightly, he added, "And you don't seem that ill."

"I was ill. But I'm better now," Lara said, her hands placed on her hips.

"I can see that. So why didn't you text me?" He shook his head in frustration at the Jekyll and Hyde nature of her personality. "You're here now. Do you want a drink?"

"Get me a beer," snapped Lara, "And a shot of JD!"

"You have been ill though?" asked Jamie.

"I have. My doctor said that I've been working too hard. Burning the candle at both ends," Lara said, fortunately now an awful lot calmer, after her earlier dramatic whirlwind entrance.

"I know this isn't easy. Us," Jamie said, as he peeled distractedly at the label of his bottle.

"I told you that," Lara said, rubbing at a tiny tell-tale crystalline white speck on the inside of her nose.

"You did."

"So, we carry on and see where this shit takes us then?" Lara said, before kissing Jamie on the mouth.

"I'm glad you showed up. But fuck me…" Jamie said.

"I blame you, Jamie Thorne. I'm not used to chasing after someone."

"Well now that you are here, I can ask you."

"Ask me what?" Lara said eagerly.

"Come to Glastonbury. You owe me after missing the last two nights."
"How did you know I wasn't already going?" Lara said coyly.
"'Cos I hadn't asked you."
"I can't wait," she said, "now let's finish these and head back to mine."
"Need me to pick up any chicken soup on the way?"

***

Having decided that it had been a good time to leave, Johnny stepped out on to the sidewalk and let out a deep breath. Feeling his phone vibrate, he looked at the message. Cally.

'Hiya Johnny. Thank you for the picture. It's great. I've put it as my screensaver. I've missed them so much. It'll be great to see them. And you xx'

Smiling to himself, Johnny sat down on a metallic bus stop bench - festooned with elaborate street graffiti. Earlier that day he had taken a picture of the twins at the top of the Empire State Building, arms around each other, smiling down the camera. The Manhattan skyline in the background not quite stealing the show.

'Hi Cally. Not long now. They've loved it here, but they've missed you. And it'd be good to see you when we get home x'

Rubbing his hands across his tired face, Johnny thought of Cally. The way he caught her smiling at him. Or at least that's what he thought…

Chapter 53

"I've just bought some wellies. And I treated myself to a couple of nice summery dresses in case it doesn't rain," Cally said, as sat with her feet curled underneath her on the sofa.

"It'll be brilliant but it's mad that you're going," Dominic said.

Cally frowned her displeasure. "I hope you don't mind?"

"No! Not at all," Dominic replied unconvincingly.

"When I found out The Stones are playing," Cally said, clapping her hands together softly.

"Same stage but different day. We're playing Saturday. Those Mumford twats are headlining that night."

"Dom!"

"They are. I can't stand them. And they dress like utter wankers."

Unable to resist laughing at her son's outburst, she said, "I'm going to get the train down on Saturday morning."

"I'm glad it's not just Mick and Keef that you're coming to see," Dominic said as he sat and admired the framed gold disc that sat pride of place in his mum's front room.

"And I may get to meet Lara. Jamie told me that she's going to be there."

"You'll know about it if she's there," Dominic said, idly checking his phone as it shuddered at the arrival of a text message.

"What do you mean by that?" Cally asked, edging forward on the sofa.

Dominic hesitated, not wanting to breach his brother's trust." She's just a bit high maintenance at times. D'y'know what I mean?"

Cally nodded and waited for her son to carry on.

He ran a hand across his blonde hair, which he had taken to wearing in a top knot - the days of hiding his face behind curtains of lank hair long behind him. "It's just these public kick offs that she seems to get off on. It'd do my head right in."

"Jamie says she's lovely. Most of the time," Cally said.

"Most of the time," Dom said and then screwed his face up. "Just a bit too split-personality, yeah?"

"I'll hopefully get to meet her and make my own mind up," Cally said.

"I'm sure she'll be on her best behaviour if you do. She's good at that fake PR shit."

"Another drink? Anything to eat?" Cally asked as Dominic finished off his cup of tea.

"No. I'm good thanks." Taking a deep breath, Dominic sat up and leant forward. "Look Mum. I know I've not mentioned it in a while, but I've got nowhere trying to track down my dad."

Cally's mood changed instantaneously.

"I just wanted to know if there was anything more you could tell me. Anything?"

"Such as?" Cally replied softly.

"A middle name? Date of birth would be really helpful," Dominic said.

"I don't have any of those things. I told you that."

Sighing, Dominic said, "I know. I know. Nothing at all? It's just a bit, just a bit odd y'know."

"I told you. He left me as soon as he found out I was pregnant. I'm sorry Dominic, but I'm not hiding anything from you." Her stomach knotted as soon as the lie once again left her lips.

"You can't have been with him long to know so little about him," Dominic said slowly.

"What are you trying to say?"

"I, err, I don't know what to think."

"If there was anything else I could tell you, I would," Cally said emphatically, knowing full well that her son was attempting to trace the impossible.

"Not a lot more I can say."

"I'm sorry Dom. Just nothing more I can say," Cally said, her resolve growing.

With a shrug of his shoulders, Dominic reached out for his mum's hand. "I know. Thanks. And next time I'll see you is in the mud at Glastonbury!"

"Don't say that! It'll be glorious sunshine. Think positive," Cally said, with a squeeze of her son's hand.

Getting up to leave, Dominic smiled and then said, "Just don't forget those wellies…"

***

"Three days. I'm due three days after you play Glastonbury!" Dee said. Her patience had worn thin over the course of what had been a difficult first pregnancy. "I'm in my last two weeks. My waters could break at any time."

"I know. And I can't wait," Danny said as they sat in the beer garden of their local waiting on their food.

"Can't wait for what! The festival or our first baby?" Dee said, placing both hands on her hugely distended stomach.

"THE FUCKING BABY!" Danny said exasperatedly. "Obviously the baby."

"What have I said about swearing in front of baby?"

Rolling his eyes, he said, "Look how many times do I have to tell you that I'll be there for you."

"I don't not want you to go to Glasto, but it worries me, it worries me tha—"

"I WILL BE THERE!" Danny shouted, banging his first down onto the edge of the woodworm pockmarked table.

"You better be, Daniel Martin. You better be."

***

"I'm already packed," Lara said as he sat on the sofa in her apartment blowing softly on her freshly painted nails. Her own brand. Naturally.

"I can only imagine," Jamie said, as he paced up and down his new apartment, the mobile phone clamped between his cheek and shoulder as he pulled the protective wrap of a newly-purchased sofa.

He had recently moved to a building that had its own reception and concierge. There was parking accessed by a security gate and these two features provided Jamie with a reasonable shield of privacy from the permanently in-situ scrape of photographers.

"Don't be like that," Lara said, "I have to pack for every eventuality."

And every photo opportunity, thought Jamie.

"I've sorted somewhere really cool for us to stay. Well, Johnny's sorted it. But it'll be great."

"I can't wait," Lara said, wincing at a slight smudge on her index finger.

"Me to! And we get to see The Stones," Jamie said excitedly.

"They got nothing on us, Jamie Thorne," Lara said, smiling as she recalled their incognito karaoke turn.

"Glastonbury it is."

"I'll see you there. And don't bring that Manchester rain with you…"

Chapter 54

Stepping back onto the tour bus having collected the precious Access All Areas accreditation, Johnny handed them out. "And don't fuckin' lose them."

Looking out across the sprawling site, the band – all Glastonbury virgins – were all taken aback by the size of the farm-cum-decent sized town as their bus rolled through the Artistes' entrance.

Johnny sat and tapped his pass rhythmically against his nose. His last visit to the festival had resulted in him meeting Claire. On the back of his father's death and a subsequent broken relationship, he had literally bumped into Claire whilst she danced on her own outside a beer tent.

He still harboured deep regrets about their ending and the band were a constant reminder of the subterfuge he had immersed himself into. But what a gold disc rock 'n' roll reminder they were.

The band were planning on finishing their set with a new track that they had just finished recording at the legendary Monmouth Studios.

They had been particularly keen on the idea of working there after Johnny had informed that the Roses had recorded *The Second Coming* there.

Dominic had acted suitably reverentially and the guitar parts that he had laid down were by far and away his best work to date.

Unfortunately, the tour bus equilibrium was not quite right. The twins and Mikee couldn't have been more relaxed as the bus parked up. Danny, however, was a tightly-coiled mass of panic and running the risk of a repetitive strain injury such was the frequency of his phone checking.

He'd convinced himself that Dee was going to go into labour the second they took to the stage and such was his anxiety, the band had even absconded from their usual winding up duties.

Placing a calming hand on Danny's shoulder, Johnny looked at the pre-occupied bass player in the eye. "You'll be right D-Mo, I promise you. You'll be there. You've got my word."

Nodding solemnly, Danny lowered his sunglasses. He clearly hadn't slept in days.

"Fuck," whistled Johnny under his breath.

"I know," Danny said, "I'm shagged. And that's before the baby is born."

"Look, I know your mind is elsewhere, but enjoy this and then we've got a couple of weeks off before we go to Japan."

"Thanks man," Danny said unconvincingly, as he pushed his shades back into place and reflexively checked his mobile again. "But you'll get me there?"

He placed his hand on Danny's shoulder. "Promise."

Bundling off the tour bus, the band donned shades and rock 'n' roll attitudes.

"Where we heading first?" Mikee asked, both arms now fully resplendent in painstakingly applied ink.

Dragging on his cigarette like his life depended on it, Danny had gone into a state of telecommunications-induced panic. "FUCK! I've lost my mobile signal. I knew that'd happen once we rocked up onto a fuckin' farm in the middle of nowhere." Staring dejectedly at his phone, shoulders slumped, he muttered and cursed to himself.

"Here you go D-Mo. I've got full bars. You can use mine," Dominic said, holding his own phone out.

"Thanks man, but it seems to be sorted now," Danny said, genuinely touched by his bandmate's offer.

"I'm off to find some druids," Mikee said, his energy levels rising in the fresh summer air.

"Think on Kong. We're on at five tomorrow," Johnny deadpanned.

He had considered offering a 'do's and don'ts' list but knew that it would have fallen on deaf ears. "I'm going to hospitality. I'm starving. Anyone?" Johnny asked hopefully.

"Sounds good," Jamie said. He was expecting Lara's arrival later that afternoon and clearly did not want to be AWOL for that.

Dominic and Mikee did their farewells and headed out to imbibe their inaugural Glastonbury experience.

***

The first night's headline act was Arctic Monkeys, and all had agreed that they would meet up to watch them. Hopefully with one Lara Bearheart in tow, and a bass player still awaiting the call of fatherhood.

"My round," Johnny said as he pulled his wallet out of the pocket of his trusty cargo shorts.

"Lara is getting here about four," Jamie said. Excited and apprehensive in equal measures – the not knowing which Lara would show being the root cause of the latter.

Carrying the three pints back to a table that Danny had commandeered, Johnny set them down and then returned with three unappetising looking plates of Chinese spicy beef noodles.

Jamie instantly pulled his nose at the culinary offering in front of him.

"I hear you, J. But nobody comes here for the Michelin starred food," Johnny said, as he wound the greasy and already congealing noodles round a wooden fork.

The afternoon passed convivially. Beers were sunk. Celebs were spotted. Further MSG soaked noodles were wisely avoided. And phones were checked. Regularly.

"You're both going to run out of juice if you check them that often," Johnny said. Principally to Danny – who fortunately seemed a little more chilled now he was a few beers to the good.

"I can charge it on the bus, can't I?" Danny asked

"You can charge it on the bus. Yes," Johnny replied.

"She's here!" Jamie said excitedly. "I've texted her where we are."

Wearing a short-sleeved black fitted shirt with epaulettes, worn open over a 'wife beater' style white vest, jeans, worker style boots and his beloved Aviators, Jamie couldn't have looked cooler if he tried.

And he didn't have to. His consummate style seemed like a second skin. The band had so far dispensed with the record label's offer of a stylist – "Fuck that. I can do my own shopping," had been Dominic's curt response.

One round of beers later and Lara made her entrance.

And what an entrance it was.

Dressed in a Native American Indian style waistcoat, revealing an incredibly sexy flash of 'side tit', vintage denim shorts, with a huge belt, and topped with a culture clash of footwear – a pair of brown cowboy boots. Her hair had been gathered in two small bunches. Topped off with a matching pair of Aviators, she looked nothing less than sensational.

The crowd literally parted as she casually sauntered through the hospitality area. Heads were turned, sunglasses lowered, and nods of appreciation were made by both lustful males and jealous women.

The Rock'N'The Roll. 'N That

"Jamie Thorne. Hope you've got me a beer waiting," Lara said, blissfully aware of the stir she had just caused.

Standing up and hugging her warmly, he said, "Nice shades." Stepping back a pace, Jamie looked her up and down. "You look amazing."

"Glad you approve," Lara replied, genuinely pleased at the compliment, which made Johnny smile given how many times a day she must be told how good she looked.

"Dunno where Dom and Mikee are. They disappeared as soon as we got here."

"I'll get the beer in," Danny said, having almost fallen off the bench as he tried to discreetly look at Lara's perfect breasts.

"Thanks D-Mo, a white wine please."

Looking slightly perplexed as it was only ever the band or Johnny that called him that, Danny went to collect the round of drinks.

Lost in their own little bubble as they caught up, Johnny was left to coax non-baby conversation out of the expectant father.

***

Having enjoyed a triumphant set from Friday night's headliners, the band had then gone their separate ways.

And Jamie had escorted Lara back to their luxury board and lodgings.

An exclusive band-only camp site adjacent to the hospitality area was home for luxury camper vans and tents of every description.

Including Jamie's piece de resistance – a Tipi-style tent.

Pulling back the canvas flap, Jamie ushered Lara inside.

With a small trail of fairy lights running over the headboard of the futon style bed, Lara was impressed - which was quite the feat for a millionaire socialite model.

Kneeling in front of each other, they slowly undressed.

Jamie unbuttoned her leather tasselled waistcoat as they kissed deeply.

Pulling his own shirt and vest off, they fell on to the mattress passionately wrapped around each other, Lara's nipples hardening at Jamie's touch.

"Jamie Thorne. This is perfect. Just perfect."

Taking her boots off and sliding her denim shorts over her toned legs, Jamie's eyes widened when he saw that she had dispensed with any notion of underwear.

Propping herself up on her elbows, Lara slowly opened her legs, rubbing an index finger against her already moistened lips. "Go down on me. Now!"

Licking at a horse-chestnut dark nipple, Jamie rolled on top of Lara. "Not now," he said as he groaned softly and slid his hard cock inside her inviting wetness.

***

"Cheers Tex. Sounds great," Dominic said.

Johnny had dispensed with the services of Maggie as tour manager. A combination of finances, missing doing the job himself and principally that he had scared the living shit out of the band with his draconian attitude.

However, a guitar tech was now in the band's employ.

Tony 'Tex' Hardy.

Given his predilection for watching Westerns on whichever tourbus he was on and a punning nod to his occupation, Tex was a more than apt nickname.

"That Les Paul plays like a dream. And she looks beautiful. I gave her a clean and polish before," Tex said in his rich Devon accent, before handing the guitar back to Dominic.

Inspecting it lovingly, Dominic nodded his approval. "Nice one. Pop it on the stand for me. I'll pick it up on stage then rather than walk on with it."

"You're on in two," Johnny said, staring out across the sizeable crowd. He estimated that there must have been a good forty thousand people in attendance.

Pushing Cally - who had arrived bang on time that morning - forward slightly, she gasped. "I've never seen so many people like that."

The band formed a huddle whilst Jamie said a few words. As they broke, Dominic and Jamie then hugged each other. "Let's fuckin' have this bro. Give 'em a proper show!"

And with that, the band took the stage.

Jamie dressed as he was yesterday – but with his red scarf knotted round his throat. Naturally. Dominic. Head to toe in black, ignoring the rising temperatures and sticking with his leather jacket. Danny, all shades, sneers and denim was bouncing on the balls of his feet and Mikee, a white vest and shorts showing off his tattoos to maximum effect. And his now somewhat musty smelling trapper hat.

Fists raised, cocksure nods and waves were dispensed to the crowd. Jamie adjusted his mic stand slightly. "GLASTONBURY. YOU FUCKIN' READY FOR THIS, RIGHT?"

The Rock 'N' The Roll. 'N That

Straight into 'Salvation'. The song choice caught the crowd unawares given that it had always been a traditional set-closer.

It worked perfectly. The band had deliberated over the set-list, flipping it on its head after much debate.

Looking out and seeing the first hundred metres of the crowd bouncing up and down, singing every word back to them, vindicated the decision immediately.

Dominic peeled off the blistering solo without even breaking sweat. Every single pair of eyes in the crowd were drawn to the band as the song concluded.

"GOOD AREN'T WE," Jamie shouted, before drinking from a bottle of water and spraying the remains over the sweat soaked front-row.

Johnny and Cally stood stage-right - mesmerised. "Fuck. They are on fire today," Johnny said.

Lara stood in total silence, her manicured hands held to her face, which was a look of wonderment and adoration.

The rest of the set continued ablaze. Mikee's drumming was nothing short of miraculous, driving each song on with unerring precision.

Halfway through the set, Danny had unfurled a small DIY flag over his bass amp. Beamed out across the crowd and TV land, 'LOVE YOU DEE. WE'LL SOON BE 3!' A little corrective nudge from Johnny with the punctuation had saved him any widespread embarrassment.

'Long Time Dead' dropped the tempo slightly, the withering lyrics delivered by Jamie in smouldering fashion.

And then Dominic addressed the mic. "THIS ONES FOR MICK 'N' KEEF!" They then roared into the Stones' underplayed classic 'Heartbreaker', Mikee having programmed his sequencer to replicate the songs famed brass section.

Cally clapped her hands together in delight as her boys hammed it up by leaning back to back throwing ridiculously over the top rock 'n' roll poses.

As Jamie took over the lead guitar line, Dominic swapped his Les Paul with Tex for his trusty Fender.

"THIS IS OUR LAST SONG. IT'S A NEW ONE," Jamie shouted.

"YOU'LL FUCKIN' LOVE IT!" Dominic added, as he adjusted his guitar strap.

"IT'S CALLED 'YEAR OF THE STRANGE."

Closing a Glastonbury set with a new song. That's the measure of the balls on this band, thought Johnny.

And the kerosene dripping, psychedelic flecked song was a perfect set-finishing show stopper.

The anthemic chorus took the crowd up a further gear and had classic written all the way through it.

Dominic stamped on his pedals, coating the song in a caustic yet beautiful guitar line.

Leaving Dominic to do the heavy-lifting, Jamie had dispensed with his guitar and was stood on the lip of the stage working the crowd into a final frenzy.

The song crunched to its conclusion, the band waved triumphantly to the crowd and then performed an exuberant group hug.

And in a little moment of Glasto magic, Jamie took his signature scarf off and tied it round the neck of his guitar. Then holding it aloft in two hands, jumped down off the stage and stood in front of the security barrier as admiring hands pawed at him.

***

"You okay, Danny? Gig's out of the way now. You're all clear," Johnny said, still on a total adrenaline high after the set.

"That was fuckin' superb. We smashed it. Totally smashed it. D'yer think Dee will have seen the flag?"

"I'm sure she will, D-Mo. Nice touch that."

"And she's only got to hold on for two days and we're home."

"You'll be right. And what a set."

Putting his trunk-like ornately decorated arms around Danny and Johnny, Mikee said, " How good was that? Best we've ever played!" Squeezing them both into a Python like embrace he added, "And me and you never missed a beat, did we bro. Kong and D-Mo pinning it the fuck down."

"Fancy a beer Mikee? Think you've earned it," Johnny said, as he attempted to wriggle free from the drummer's sweaty grips.

"Yup. We can now get big. You up for that D-Mo?"

With his nose glued to his phone, Danny looked up. "Err, yeah. Deffo." Glancing down at his phone again, he said, "Dee saw the flag. She said the baby kicked at the same time!"

He looked up at them with tears in his big brown Irish eyes before popping his shades firmly back into place.

And with that, Lonely Souls and their select entourage hit Glastonbury with the sole intention of getting suitably dazed and confused.

***

Realising the insistent grumble was not just in his head, Johnny rolled over on the double mattress and picked up his mobile phone.

Danny. Seven missed calls from Danny.

It was 4 am. He had barely slept, and his head was pounding.

As he attempted to compose himself, the phone rang again.

"Hello.," Johnny croaked. The noises emanating from his vocal cords sounding like sandpaper rubbing against a crumbling dry-stone wall.

"Johnny. It's me. It's fuckin' happened. I fuckin' knew it would!" Danny said in a heightened state of panic. His words merging into a one shrill, jumbled blur of shrieked vowels, and dropped consonants.

"Calm down. What's happened," he said as he looked around his yurt style tent for a bottle of water he was sure he'd left by the side of the bed only hours before.

"Dee. She's been taken to hospital with constrictions!"

"Contractions. But never mind." Rubbing a hand through his unruly bed hair, he said, "Right. We need to get you home."

"I know. But it'll take for fuckin' ever!" Danny said, his voice close to breaking.

"Gimme a minute to get dressed. Where are you?"

"Err. Hospitality. Me and Mikee have been here for a while. I've not been to bed."

"I'm about five minutes from you. We'll sort this. I promised, and I won't let you down," Johnny said, his tones as calming as he could muster.

Whipping on his jeans, a hoodie and a woollen beanie hat he had brought along in case the night time temperatures dropped, Johnny quickly met up with the expectant rhythm section.

It wasn't difficult to spot them.

Danny was smoking and pacing up and down in the classic 'father-to-be' manner, the tip of his cigarette performing frantic circles like a hyperactive firefly.

"Thank fuck. You're here. Now get me home. PLEASE!"

"Okay. We need to get you to an airport. Bristol is the nearest. I reckon we can get you to the hospital in a couple of hours or so"

"TWO HOURS Fuck's sake. She could have given birth by then!"

Frantically trying to perform a mental calculation, Johnny reckoned they would be a good hour clearing the site. A taxi to Bristol. And then hope that they could get their boy on a direct flight. Or worst-case scenario via London.

"Have you got the keys to the bus then?" Danny asked, as he light another cigarette.

"No. Have I fuck! Why would I have them," Johnny said, still thinking over the permutations. "And I couldn't drive it anyhow."

"FUCK!" Danny yelled, as he started to punch his forehead in frustration.

"I can boost a car," Mikee said, as calmly as a man offering to go and fetch the morning paper.

"You can what?" Johnny asked incredulously.

"I can hotwire a car for us. No problem."

"Really?" You sure?"

"Piece of piss. My step-dad owns a breakers' yard. He owns a few businesses. That was the one me and Dom used to work at," Mikee said, cool as you like.

His mind racing at the possible pitfalls, Johnny decided that if fortune didn't favour the brave then they'd end up in prison, but this was a mission of mercy.

They could 'boost' a car – *The Fast and the Furious has a lot to answer for*, he thought – and be there and back in four hours. No-one need even know…

"Right. Fuck it. Let's do it."

***

They left the hospitality area and headed for the artistes' car park. It was predominantly made up of buses and vans of every size. But there were enough cars to choose from.

"Okay. Nothing too flash. But pick one that'll get us there," Johnny said, pulling his hood over his head.

This elicited a bout of nervous laughter from the soon-to-be-a-dad bass player. "Fuckin' hell Johnny. Could you look any more suspicious?"

Realising his mistake, Johnny lowered his hood. "Yeah. Point taken. It's just 'cos I was cold."

"Bullshit," Mikee coughed. "Perfect. That Astra there. I can do that no problem."

"Go for it," Johnny whispered as Danny light up yet another cigarette, wishing at times like this that he smoked.

Smashing the quarter light window, Mikee reached inside the car and opened the passenger door. Squeezing his huge frame under the dashboard, his thick fingers worked with dextrous accuracy and some twenty seconds later, the car sparked into life.

He wiped his hands together. "Done," Mikee said proudly.

Bundling into the car, Johnny checked the mirrors, adjusted his seat and strapped himself in. *A mere drunk driving and stolen vehicle charge away from a world of trouble*, he thought as he took a deep breath and reversed out of the parking bay.

"Bristol here we come," Johnny said, his voice an octave or two higher than normal.

Reaching casually over, Mikee turned the car stereo on. "TUNE!" he said as The Prodigy's 'Firestarter' belted forth.

"Fuck's sake Mikee," Johnny said, snapping the stereo off. "You'll draw attention to us."

Flicking the stereo back on, he said, "You'll draw attention to us without the music on."

"You've done this before! But knock it down a couple. My head's pounding."

Leaving the site through the designated exit some ten minutes later, their mission of paternity well underway.

"Check your phone and see what the flight times are," Johnny said as they pulled onto a quiet B- road. Helping himself to an already opened packet of Haribo and relishing the sugar fix, he breathed a sigh of relief as the first part of their crime had gone undetected.

A couple of minutes later, Mikee said, "It's almost half four now. There's a flight at just gone six. You could be at the hospital for about eight, D-Mo."

Danny did not respond. He just sat staring out of the window shaking his head and muttering to himself.

Ninety minutes later and they were at Bristol airport. It was virtually deserted aside from the early morning cleaners and one manned check-in desk.

A few keyboard strokes later and Danny had the necessary tickets in his shaking hand.

"Thanks man. You're both fuckin' lifesavers. I owe you. Big time," Danny said before he hugged Johnny, struggling to stop his scrambled emotions get the better of him.

"Get yourself on that plane. And keep us posted, yeah?" Ruffling Danny's dark hair, Johnny smiled, and said, "Right. Get gone!"

***

The return journey was made in pretty much total silence as Mikee proceeded to polish off a sizeable McDonald's breakfast he had insisted that they purchase as soon as they left Bristol.

As the site appeared into view, Johnny breathed out and rubbed a hand over his face.

"Just flash yer pass and stay calm," Mikee said.

And it was that easy. Showing the AAA passes to the bored security guard, they were through.

Navigating back to the exact same spot, Johnny parked up and started to wipe the cuff of his hoodie round the steering wheel and door handle.

Snapping his fingers and laughing loudly, Mikee said, "Man, you watch way too much tele!"

Pulling out his wallet, and taking out a hundred pounds, Johnny opened the glove compartment and placed the folded notes into a clear CD case.

"You'll still go to Hell," Mikee said, with a nod of approval.

Grinning sheepishly, Johnny breathed a huge sigh of relief. "I know. But hopefully I'll get day-release. And if I can use Danny's favourite expression, let's get something to eat. I'm starving."

"Me too," Mikee said as he rubbed his stomach, "that Maccies barely touched the sides!"

***

"She's lovely," Lara said as she spooned into Jamie.

"Who is?" he mumbled, rubbing sleep away from his eyes.

"Your mom."

"What bought that on?" Jamie asked, propping himself up on his elbows.

"Oh nothing. I was chatting to her last night whilst you were indulging your star-struck admirers."

"I hardly left your side," Jamie said, sensing a hint of jealousy.

"And Johnny. He makes me laugh. He's good at the grumpy old man routine!"

"Don't call him old!" Jamie said. "Johnny's cool."

"Kinda good looking as well," Lara teased.

"Haha. I'll have to watch out then!" Jamie said, then laughing gently, "What did you talk about with my mum?"

Oh, just stuff," Lara replied breezily.
"What sort of stuff?"
"Girls' stuff."
"Be more specific."
"It's private," Lara said, also sitting up, but holding a woollen blanket over her bare shoulders.
"Be like that then," Jamie harrumphed.
"If you must know, she talked about how proud she is of you both."
Jamie smiled. And then slowly pushed the blanket away and placed a hand over one of Lara's already hardening nipples.

***

"IT'S A GIRL!" Mikee shouted, as he read the rest of the text message. "And there's a picture of them all," as he held up the phone for all to see.

Looking at his own phone, Jamie read out the full message that they had all just received. '*Made it back in time for the birth of Dominique Angie Martin. Can't remember her weight as me heads all done in. Would have named her after you lot if she had been a boy – but she can be little D-Mo! Love you all x PS Can't believe I'm missing the fucking Stones!!*'

As they all looked at the message on their own phones and duly sent texts of congratulations back, Johnny disappeared off to the bar and returned with a bottle of champagne and seven glasses and handed them out to the band, Cally, Lara and Dominic's latest lady friend.

Eleanor – a stunningly beautiful 'young' Stevie Nicks lookalike, who wafted around innocently in a diaphanous flowing dress and bare feet.

Her apparent innocence, however, hadn't prevented her from sucking Dominic off on one the ancient ley lines that bisects the Glastonbury Tor.

"I don't normally buy into the champagne lark. But this is a special occasion," Johnny said, looking decidedly bleary-eyed. "Raise your glasses," he glanced down, "well, plastic glasses, but you know what I mean. Dan, Dee and Dominique Angie Martin!"

The plastic flutes clinked together with a dull 'thwok' and the smiles and bonhomie was notched up yet further.

"She's lovely," Johnny said to Dominic as they stood together for a picture as Lara was now brandishing a camera and freely taking snaps.

"I actually like her. A lot," Dominic replied.

"That's novel for you," Johnny said, playfully elbowing Dominic in his ribs.

"HEY! I like em all, but," he replied indignantly.

"I know what you meant," Johnny said looking across at Eleanor who appeared to be swapping fashion tips with Lara.

As daylight began to gracefully ebb away to dusk, a charge of expectation coursed across the festival site.

The Rolling Stones were half an hour from playing.

"He'll be doing a line of Sanatogen to get himself sorted," Dominic said disingenuously.

"Dominic!" scolded Cally, "that's the Rolling Stones you're talking about."

Dom looked to Johnny for validation.

"Don't get me involved," Johnny replied, as he reached for his beer.

"Ready to go and watch them then?" Jamie asked.

"There's a small cordoned off area we can watch from," Johnny said. "We all got our passes?"

Eleanor smiled demurely across to Johnny. *She really is a vision of loveliness*, he thought, mentally blocking the image of her on her knees in the morning dew smoking Dom off.

"I've got Danny's pass if that's okay," she said sweetly.

"I'm sure he won't mind," Johnny replied, checking himself not to be too captivated by her alluring charms.

"Hang on a sec," Cally said, "I want to put my wellies on. It looks like rain."

Leaning on Johnny for support, she slipped out of her cowboy boots and changed into her wellies.

"There. All done! Thank you."

Johnny discreetly looked her up and down. Wearing a pale blue gardenia print dress, with a cropped faded denim jacket tied round her waist - *even with the practical rubber footwear, she looked utterly, delightfully gorgeous*, he thought.

Clapping her hands together, Cally said, "I so can't wait for this. I love them!"

The select entourage headed for the show. Hands held, arms around each other, drinks necked and spirits high.

A barnstorming set from the greatest rock 'n' roll band in the world.

Simple as that.

The perennial classics were delivered with Devil-may-care abandon before the inevitable rain shower came, drenching the ecstatic masses.

As the greatest of greatest hits set was drawing to a close, Johnny and Cally found that the crowd's momentum had separated them from the rest of the party.

Closing with the triumphant lilting beauty of *You Can't Always Get What You Want* - a myriad of mobile phones captured the moment.

Fireworks blazed and cascaded as the last chord finished and they were swept along with the ebb and flow of the crowd as they headed back to the hospitality area.

Johnny felt a sudden tingle jolt him as Cally grabbed his hand, squeezing it tightly, but slowly rubbing the back of it her with her thumb.

As they reached the exit to the AAA pen, they were ushered swiftly through, still holding hands.

The fireworks continued to blaze overhead, the collective oohs and aahs thick in the air.

Johnny stepped aside from the hospitality-seeking throng and pulled Cally to one side.

Putting a hand to her face, he pushed away a tress of her hair, which was now in rain sodden ringlets. Tiny white droplets of styling product were dripping onto her bare shoulders from the ends of her hair. Placing her own hand onto Johnny's face, they looked at each other unblinkingly.

And then they kissed.

A deep and urgent pent-up kiss. A perfect in the moment kiss.

Separating, Johnny could feel his heartbeat hammering inside his chest as Cally put a hand to her throat and smiled up at him, shivering slightly.

"Thank you," she said.

Totally lost for words, Johnny leaned forward and kissed her again…

***

"Not a problem as far as I'm concerned," Johnny said as Dominic stood hand in hand with the bewitching Eleanor. "There's plenty of room on the coach."

Jamie had bid Lara and her multiple outfit changes goodbye and seemed particularly deep in thought.

Having successfully aided and abetted his partner in rhythm to attend the birth of his daughter, an unusually jaded Mikee was powering his way through a bacon baguette. Resolutely of the non-vegan variety.

Cally hung back, seemingly now reluctant to be part of the rock'n'roll ensemble.

The coach trundled slowly through the soggy car park, and headed off on the long road home…

Chapter 55

"Oh Dom. It's lovely. I can't believe you've only lived here a month. It looks exactly like I imagined it would," Eleanor said as she twirled around in the large front room of Dominic's newly rented property.

He had taken the house as it had a tanked-out basement that he intended to convert into a home studio, together with a large decked patio that he had designs on kitting out with a hot tub. Electronic gates and the thick dense shrubbery affording him some much-coveted privacy had sealed the £1800-per-month deal. The days of rental payments bouncing were long gone following the album achieving platinum status.

"I love the place," Dominic said, "And I want you to move in."

"Seriously?" Eleanor said with a squeal, momentarily losing her dreamy cool.

"Deadly," Dominic replied.

"I would love to. Totally," Eleanor said as she flung her arms around Dominic's neck.

"Let me show you round and tell you all about my plans for the place," Dominic said as he scooped her up off her feet.

***

"I'll pick you and Dom up... No problem... Yeah, about midday," Johnny said.

A visit to the see the first addition to the Lonely Souls family was a top priority, before a couple of weeks' downtime to prepare for a seven day/five gig whistle-stop tour of Japan.

Hanging up the call, Johnny sat down and looked at his phone and read the same text message repeatedly as he deliberated over his reply – '*Hi Johnny. So tired after Glastonbury but worth it. Think we need to talk. C xx*'

They had shared a tent that evening, although things hadn't yet moved to the next level – a combination of factors, namely the damp canvas surroundings, but Johnny's booze intake had again left him somewhat lacking.

The Rock'N'The Roll. 'N That

When reaching for his cock, Johnny had been met with a shrivelled nub the size of a jeweller's loupe. He'd switched lanes quickly and hushed whispers of 'let's not rush things' prevented any further humiliations.

A relationship with the boy's mother was out of the question, he felt, and he had been wrestling with the dilemma since they boarded the coach to depart Glastonbury. It felt like a breach of their trust.

The conversation could not be put off – '*Hiya Cally, Me too, takes it out of you! I'm going to see Danny & co with the boys. I can see you anytime this week x*'

An instantaneous reply – '*Thanks. Tomorrow. Dukes at 6pm? Xx*'

***

"Ah Danny, she's beautiful so she is," said Mr Martin Sr, as he held his granddaughter for the first time.

"Oh Dee. I can't tell you how proud we are," cooed Mrs Martin. "And she looks just like Danny's Grandma."

"Does she?" Dan asked with a quizzical look on his face. "Don't remember her very much."

"She's got her eyes, that's for sure," Mrs Martin said, with a beatific smile.

"I'll just go and fetch us a cup of tea, shall I?" said Mr Martin.

Grabbing his cigarettes, Danny followed his father out of the ward. "Fancy a cig? I'm gasping."

"I will. Thanks son."

A mixture of pride and frustration bristled through Danny. The birth of his daughter. His parents' first granddaughter had brought the family closer together than they had been in years.

Offering up both a cigarette and a light to his father, he inhaled deeply.

"This is good. Things are better."

Mr Martin blew the smoke out of his lungs and let a small satisfied sigh leave his lips. "It is, Danny. Me and your ma are so proud."

Danny pursed his lips slightly whilst he let his father continue.

"Not just your little 'un. The band. Everything."

"I spoke to me mam," Danny said, as he looked fixatedly at the tip of his cig. "She says things have been better."

Mr Martin closed his eyes and nodded ever so slightly.

Meeting his dad's rheumy gaze. "You were a cunt. A right fucking cunt. To me. To Mam. I've fuckin' hated you for so long…"

"And I'm sorry. Truly sorry"

"I told her to leave you. Move out. But she wouldn't."

"Wha—"

"I wanted her to be happy. And she is now," Danny said, speaking slowly, enunciating every word. "If you ever lay a finger on her again. Ever throw anything at her again. Harm a hair on her head. I'll fuckin' kill you. And you'll never see your granddaughter again."

"I won't Danny, I promise. She's a good woman. Always was. It was ju—"

"I know why. Doesn't make it right. But you've got a fresh start. A second chance. Don't fuck it up."

Bowing his head slightly, Mr Martin put both hands on his son's shoulders. "Thank you, Danny. I won't."

***

"Jamie. It's me," Johnny said through the gate intercom.

Like Dominic, Jamie had also sought the sanctuary of a new house away from the intrusions of Manchester. A small rural cottage north of the city centre. The rustic security gates led to a long pebble driveway, meaning the house was totally obscured from the road and most importantly prying lenses.

His need for privacy becoming of paramount importance - having completely stopped going out into Manchester over the past few months.

"I'll buzz them open. Any company out there today?" Jamie asked.

"All clear," Johnny said as he nosed his Audi through the slowly opening gates.

Jumping into the passenger seat, shades and woollen hat in place as ever, Jamie said, "Right, next stop Dominic's new place."

"I haven't seen it yet. It's supposed to be quite something."

"It is. Costing him a fair few quid. But the views from the back are amazing," Jamie said.

"Never does anything by halves though," Johnny said. "Pop the postcode in the sat nav for us."

Half an hour later, they pulled up at Dominic's 'House on the Hill'.

"Alright. I'll be out in a second," Dominic's voice crackled through the intercom.

Leaving the front door, Dom kissed Eleanor goodbye and sauntered over to the car without a care in the world.

"You still got company then?" Jamie asked his brother as he adjusted his seatbelt in the rear of the car.

The Rock 'N' The Roll. 'N That

"She's moved in with me," Dominic replied matter-of-factly.

"What?" both Jamie and Johnny replied in perfect unison.

"Yeah," Dom said calmly. "We just clicked at Glasto. Never felt like that before. Just felt right. For the both of us."

The front of the car remained speechless.

"I've had enough of fucking around. And I didn't do any sniff all weekend either. I feel great."

"Ahem," Johnny coughed.

"Well, y'know what I mean. I didn't do any after I met Eleanor," Dominic said.

Jamie shook his head slowly. "I hope you know what you're doing, bro."

"Don't worry about me. And we won't be all over the papers like you and Lara."

"Fair point," Jamie replied as he stared out of the window, somewhat taken aback by his brother's personality makeover.

***

"Look at you! A natural already," Jamie said as Danny sat by Dee's hospital bed, his newly born daughter cradled gently in his arms.

"Alright fellas. Brilliant to see ya," Danny said with a number-one-record-proud look on his face.

"She's beautiful, really beautiful," Jamie said, as he gently ran a finger down her three-day old cheek.

"Good job she's not got your nose, eh D-Mo," Dominic said as he leant over and then kissed his bandmate on the forehead.

"Is that the best you've got? Time you changed the record." Dan replied with a newly acquired Zen calm.

"And how are you doing? We know you did all the hard work despite what D-Mo says," Dominic said, before he kissed Dee on warmly on both cheeks.

Johnny then pulled out a parcel and handed it to Dee. "We've got a few little bits for you and the baby. Just glad we got your boy here back on time."

"Hmm, thank you. And I heard ALL about that," Dee replied. The look on her face indicated she was not unduly concerned at the dubious methods that had been employed. Opening the badly wrapped parcel, she pulled out an assortment of tiny bibs and T-shirts, holding up one which read *'Daddy's little Rock Star'*.

"They're wicked," Danny said with a trademark snap of his fingers. "Thanks. For everything. Mikee was in before as well, so now you've all seen her."

"She's perfect. You're gonna be great parents," Johnny said, seeing something before him that he felt had most certainly passed him by.

"And don't you be taking him off on tour all the time then," Dee said, scolding Johnny with a pointing finger.

Raising his hands mock-defensively, Johnny said, "Don't blame me! It's the record label."

"Nicely sidestepped, man," Jamie said with a smile.

"Let me get a picture," Dominic said, pulling out his phone - which already had a picture of Eleanor as the screensaver.

Danny and Dee put their arms around each other and held up their 5lb 8oz tiny bundle for posterity.

"Lovely that, D-Mo," Dominic said.

"You like her name then? Sort of like Dominic, and D-Mo. Wicked innit," Danny said, beaming like only a proud parent can.

"Still can't believe you missed The Stones. And to spend an hour in their dressing room was wicked!" Dominic said, with a sly wink at Johnny and Jamie.

"Fuck off! You never?" Danny said, looking aghast, even with Dominique, nestled in his arms.

"DANNY!" Dee barked. "What have I told you about swearing in front of her?"

"Sorry babe. But fu— I mean The Stones! I can't believe it."

"I think that our Dominic is winding you up," Dee said, as she caught the stifled sniggers that Dom was struggling to contain.

"Wanker," Danny muttered, before raising an apologetic hand in the direction of his daughter's long-suffering mother.

***

"Red please. Large," Cally said as she took a seat on the busy canal side terrace. Fiddling with her sunglasses, tell-tale signs that she was more than a little agitated.

"No problem," Johnny replied, with a slight gulp, realising that this little chat would not be plain sailing.

Returning with the drinks after a protracted wait at the bar, Johnny said, "How are you? Believe you've been to see Danny and Dee. Baby's beautiful, isn't she?"

"She is. And I heard all about your little escapade in getting him home on time."

"Good to know people can keep a secret. No harm done. Car was left where we found it," Johnny replied with a nervous slurp on his pint.

The Rock 'N' The Roll. 'N That

"All very *rock 'n' roll* as you boys are so fond of saying."

"It was needs must. We didn't just nick a car for the sake of it," Johnny replied - a little too brusquely. *Talk about stating the obvious* he thought.

"It was a great couple of days," Cally said, leaving the comment hanging, waiting for Johnny to give the hungry elephant in the room an iced bun.

"It was," nodded Johnny. "All of it." *Okay, that was a solid opener,* he thought.

Cally raised an eyebrow and smiled across the table at him. "All of it. That's good to hear."

"Course it was. I'd be lying if I said that it wasn't. And, y'know. Us. That was great too."

"Y'know," Cally mocked. "For someone with the gift of the gab. At times..."

"You know what I mean," Johnny said, still floundering for the right thing to say.

"I don't actually," Cally replied pointedly.

"Okay," Johnny said, steeling himself. "Okay. It was amazing, and I really like you. Why wouldn't I?" Taking a deep breath, "But—"

"*But*," interjected Cally.

"But, it puts me in a tricky situation."

"*It*," Cally said, before downing half her glass in one gulp.

"Sorry. I meant us. Us. It puts me in a difficult one with the boys."

"How so?" asked Cally.

"Our professional relationship," replied Johnny matter-of-factly.

"Oh. I see. What do you think they'd say?"

"I have no idea. Honestly. But, y'know."

"No Johnny. I don't know," Cally said tersely.

"I work with them. On a daily basis. To be having a relationship with their..." Johnny paused as if the next word sounded awkward to his ears.

Cally filled in the gap. "With their mother."

"Yeah. With their mother," Johnny said sheepishly.

"But the boys really like you, Johnny. You and Jamie are so close. It's like..." It was now Cally's turn to cut off herself short.

"I know. And that's what makes it so difficult. This was never part of the plan. Not there was ever any great Masterplan..." Reaching across the table, Johnny put his hand onto Cally's.

"Go on," Cally prompted, glancing at her now empty glass.

"Look. I do like you. I really do. But this. Us. It'd complicate things so much," Johnny said with a genuine look of frustration in his eyes.

Cally closed her eyes and sighed. "It doesn't have to be like that. We could take things steady. See how they go."

"I'd have to speak to the boys. Right from the start. And I don't know if I can. Y'know, things are going to get huge with the next album an—"

"If you say *y'know* one more fucking time!" It was unusual for Cally to proffer an expletive, but this was heartfelt. "What you're saying is that the band and their album is more important than anything we might have." Finishing off her drink and hurriedly gathering her bag and glasses. "Thanks a bunch Johnny. At least I know where I stand now."

"Cally! C'mon," Johnny said, pushing his own chair back and reaching out for her bare arm.

Pushing his hand away, Cally turned on her heel and with a shake of her head, said, "Thanks Johnny." And with that she was gone, pushing her way through the crowd of post-work drinkers.

Sitting, staring at his pint and reeling at just how bad that the exchange had gone, Johnny cursed to himself. The band and his unswerving loyalty to them looked they had just cost him a relationship for the second time.

***

"Sounds amazing. Just try it with a D minor before the chorus," Jamie said as he and Dominic sat in the darkened rehearsal room. Their chairs were close to each other, a shared mic stand positioned between them. The short shadow cast between them gave the impression that they were conjoined.

"Yeah, hang on. Right. On three. With the vocal," Dom replied as he lovingly caressed the scratch plate of his champagne coloured Epiphone guitar.

Clearing his throat, Jamie sat, hunched over the mic which. The scrawled lyrics on a piece of paper lay between his feet.

'The silence between us is so profound. I double dare you to make a sound. So don't you talk to me, don't you talk to me…'

The impassioned vocal was underpinned by a snaking, ghostly guitar line that rasped and whipped around the room.

"I'm gonna double track that. It'll sound brilliant. Opening track of the album. Love the way it builds," Dominic said as made a minor adjustment to the neck of his guitar.

"I love the guitar sound. Worth the money wasn't it. Fuckin' gorgeous and sounds amazing," Jamie said.

"That's eight, maybe nine tracks we've got sorted. I've got three more I'm just working on. Not quite ready but you'll fuckin' love 'em bro."

Jamie leaned forward and kissed his twin brother on the forehead. "Difficult second album? Never in any doubt."

"We're back in the studio when we get back from Japan. I want this done and out by the end of the year," Dominic said determinedly.

"Christmas Number One then eh?" Jamie said with a chuckle.

"Number One album. No fuckin' about this time," Dominic replied.

Chapter 56

'Kong padded around his freshly laundered lair. Prodding disinterestedly at a piece of fruit, he scratched a lazy paw across his forehead. Walking naked around the room, he tensed his chest as he caught sight of his reflection. Flopping backwards on to his bed, he lay staring at the ceiling, his all-consuming need to mate preoccupying his every primal thought. The black bamboo bars of his bed were cold to the touch as he wrapped his fingers around them, squeezing them in his mighty grip until he heard them creak their resistance.

Rising to his full height, Kong again paced up and down, looking expectantly at the silent door.

Drinking deeply, he wiped a muscular forearm across his mouth, the dark hair on his chin bristling - abrasive to the touch. Making a deep guttural noise, he rubbed his stomach and drank deeply again.

A sharp, precise knock on the door of his lair alerted his senses. His eyes narrowed, and he felt his pent-up seed surge. Opening the door, he was met by two identical raven-haired females. Beautiful to behold in every detail.

Beckoning them in with a sweep of his unfurled hand, Kong closed the door behind them and smiled to himself.

Each girl placed a brown leather holdall to the floor and bowed slightly...'

***

"Fuck," Danny exclaimed. "This place is unreal."

As blunt as his summary was, it remained an oft muttered sentence by first-time visitors to Tokyo.

"And this is only the airport," Dominic said with a low whistle.

A prestigious slot at the Mount Fuji Festival with club dates either side saw the band arrive in Japan as wide-eyed tourists in a whole new land.

Narita International Airport was a visceral bombardment. All sleek metal walkways and glass fronted express elevators. Products were smacked right in front of you. An unavoidable sensory overload of adverts all screaming for attention.

It's like something straight out of Blade Runner, thought Johnny

Cars had been politely declined as the band, and particularly Johnny, wanted to experience the 'bullet train'. A quick transfer and they were aboard the Tokaido Shinkansen travelling into the heart of Tokyo. Speeds of up to 200mph rendered most passengers mute as townscapes blurred past them in an almost indecipherable blur.

Taking their pre-booked seats, Johnny looked at *his band*. As much as they were 'strangers in a strange land' and no-one would recognise them outside of their forthcoming gigs, they looked like a band. Unmistakably.

That 'gang mentality' exuded from them whenever they were together. This was their inner sanctum. You could get a party pass for the night, but no-one was allowed permanent residency.

Slouching back in his seat and propping a black desert boot-clad foot on the arm of the empty seat in front of him, Dominic had an insouciant second nature swagger whenever he was in public, exuding confidence with his every fluid movement or glance. The torturous days of 'Dominos' were long, long gone.

Jamie seemed to ooze Rockstar cool even if he was dressed in TV viewing scruffs. Totally comfortable with his exquisite good looks, his piercing blue eyes burning with intensity – when they weren't covered by his favoured Aviators.

Now resplendent with his tattoo sleeves, Mikee was a living breathing tribute to rock 'n' roll. A close-cropped haircut and beard, always dressed simply yet stylishly, the 'don't fuck' attitude poured from him. Which always amused Johnny as he was soft as shite and would do anything for you – provided he was suitably topped up with food, drink and pornography.

And Danny 'D-Mo' Martin. He'd made the gear change from fatherhood back to fully signed up rock 'n' roller with practiced ease. His leather jacket zipped right up to his reconstructed nose, shades fixed on, dark hair now slightly longer again and worn in thick Sid-esque spikes, sneering and glowering at everything that he wasn't quite familiar with.

Heads turned, people stared and whispered to each other as the four-headed shaded up rock 'n' roll creature talked amongst themselves.

Johnny sat in silence, wrapped in his own thoughts. He'd not spoken to Cally since he had been so brusquely put in his place. Having contemplated speaking to the twins about the *'situation'*, he had erred on the side of caution.

If there was a relationship to disclose then he felt that he would have done, but to tell them about something that didn't exist seemed a little futile.

"Shame you're all loved up Dom. These Japanese women are beautiful," Mikee said with a sage nod.

Dominic looked over the top of his shades and smiled. "I'm a one-woman man now I've met my Queen."

"Sh'yeah right," Mikee said with a dismissive snort.

"You'll see," Dom said with a curt nod, "You'll see."

"You've only known her a few weeks. I know you Dom. Remember that," Mikee said with a tap of his nose.

"Plenty of that still. Still love my nose to the straw. But I'm bang into Eleanor."

Looking away from the window, Jamie laughed at his brother's comment. "Bang into her! So, you moved her in. Whatever happened to good old-fashioned romance?"

"What? Like you and Lara?" Dominic needled back.

"Never said I loved her, and I'm not living with her," Jamie sparred.

"Only 'cos she lives so far away. Otherwise you'd be following her round like a lost puppy. I've seen you."

Sensing that the jet-lag might be causing the inter-band banter to go a little further than normal, Johnny intervened. "Right. We're nearly there. They'll be a car waiting outside the station to take us to the hotel."

***

"Did you see how many people had a red scarf on?" Jamie asked breathlessly, having thrown everything his jet-lagged body could muster into their closing track. They had reverted to 'Salvation' as a set-closer for the 'new market'.

And the audience had loved it. Japanese crowds were notoriously respectful but also exceptionally willing to show their appreciation. They were quick to fall for bands and Jamie and Dominic were soon installed as the objects of their desire and worship. With precise subservient bows and innocent giggles, the youth of Japan formed an orderly queue so that could shake hands with the boys and have pictures taken. Selfies. Inevitably.

Jamie and Dominic had best part of an hour's 'meet and greet' to fulfil, and if the previous day's gig had been an indicator, they would come back with an armful of miscellaneous fan gifts – which had included numerous sketched pictures, items of clothing and plenty of red scarfs.

The Rock'N'The Roll. 'N That

"Just me and you then, Mikee," Johnny said as he and the muscular drummer chilled in the dressing room. "All the others are spoken for now."

"I can't wait for what I've got lined up," Mikee replied with a slow nod of his head.

Frowning slightly, Johnny asked, "Go on?"

"Threesome."

"Okay," Johnny said. "You make it sound so easy."

"It is. I've ordered two girls for tomorrow night. Not cheap. But top drawer. All done and dusted. Online," Mikee said calmly. "I love Japanese women," he added.

"Two birds with one stone. If you'll excuse the pun," Johnny said.

Mikee laughed and crushed his can, tossing it with impressive accuracy into the bin situated on the other side of their spacious dressing room.

Opening another can, Mikee raised it to Johnny, "Here's to birds and stones then."

"Birds and stones," Johnny echoed.

Looking across at Mikee, Johnny thought how little he had changed since they had first met.

He remained totally nonplussed by the under-the-microscope levels of attention the band received, happy in the knowledge that the band were getting the plaudits they deserved. And that he was being recognised as a drummer of considerable talent. Success having enabled him to indulge his vices of expensive drum kits, his deep thirst for pornography and his need to adorn much of his upper body in intricate inkwork.

Don't fuck with Mikee and he won't fuck with you.

***

"Massive spike in sales after Glastonbury. The record company have just emailed figures across," Johnny said as they travelled from Tokyo to Osaka on a luxurious tour bus.

Danny, as ever, was having a Skype conversation with Dee and cooing down the crystalline 6000-mile digital link at his daughter's beautifully carefree face.

"A spike? Get you with your jargon," Dominic said, looking up from his iPad. "You're getting good at this, aren't you?"

"If you count reading out record company emails as *getting good*, then yes. Wait till I get on to territories and units. You'll get hard," Johnny replied.

"I will if you tell me how much we're going to earn this year," Dominic said, suddenly very interested in Johnny's missive.

"There'll be turkey on the table this Christmas. And let's just say you'll be able to do better than last year's Secret Santa."

Handing over his own iPad to Dominic, Johnny said, "Look at the figures. Bottom right. That's a projected gross."

Screwing up his face and handing back the iPad and using a line from *The Usual Suspects,* complete with Hispanic accent – one of the bands favourite tour bus films – "In English please."

"You'll all pull out over a hundred grand. Comfortably. With all the sales, touring and festival monies," Johnny said.

"Imagine going to the cashie and seeing that," Mikee said, with a satisfied rub of his hands.

"A hundred grand," Dominic said with a low whistle. "You know we want to get the second album out by the end of the year, don't you? Those figures won't include that?"

"Jamie said that you'd demoed most of the songs. Don't know if the label will want it out this year though. Not whilst the first album is still selling so well," Johnny replied. *Get the second album right, and the world really will be their oyster,* he thought.

"If it's written and recorded, it's out," Dominic said, a little too boorishly.

"Let's get it recorded before we start with the ultimatums, eh Dom," Johnny said.

Hanging up his Skype call, Danny asked, "What have I missed? How long until we get there? I'm gonna stick *Fight Club* on again."

"We're gonna be rich. About three hours. And it's still the same person but with a split personality," Mikee replied, answering all three of Danny's questions in one go.

***

Bowing slightly, the two women slipped out of their floor length robes. The exquisite ivory dropped to the floor forming silken puddles. The alabaster skinned women again bowed in total silence. Their jet-black hair had a 'just-washed advert' sheen to it, both wearing it in the same shoulder length style.

Aside from one physical difference – one girl was notably fuller of breast – they looked identical. Kong patted the bed either side of him and beckoned his soon-to-be conquests over to his King-sized bed.

With an almost indiscernible shake of their heads, the women put a finger to their lips. This was a perfectly synchronised performance and Kong was happy to be sat in the select audience.

Turning to face each other, they proceeded to run their hands seductively over each other's bodies. Hands flickering over the slight rise of their partners' perfectly tended and shaven mounds.

Kong sat up on the bed, catching his breath slightly as he felt himself harden at the act that was being performed for his pleasure.

Again, patting the bed, signalling for his exquisite mates to join him, his ardour was pushed yet further as the fuller breasted girl slowly dropped to her knees whilst her partner with balletic poise put her right leg over her kneeling partner's shoulder. She then gave out a low guttural moan as she felt a tongue seek out and dart at her clitoris.

Kong grasped his now fully erect cock, unable to contain his skyrocketing urges. A sharp shake of the standing girl's head caused him to reluctantly desist. He breathed out heavily through his nose, struggling to maintain his composure.

The oral sex routine was performed in exact reversal and then they stepped slowly over to the bed.

Unable to contain himself, Kong roughly kissed each woman in turn, pulling a hand from each of them down on to his throbbing erection. Flipping the smaller girl on to her back, Kong hunched down and licked her hungrily, from her slender neck down to her wet cunt.

As he performed oral sex, Kong's exposed backside was soon playing house to an unwanted guest.

The other girl had collected a not inconsiderable vibrator from her bag and having applied a perfumed lubricant, slid it into Kong's unprotected arsehole.

Yelping with the shock, he spun around and flailed a large paw, catching the girl flush on her cheek. Making the slightest of squeals, the girl removed the vibrator and bowed apologetically before stooping and then sucking Kong's considerable cock with deep long swallows…

***

"Where's Mikee?" Jamie asked as he lounged across the black leather chaise lounge in the hotel's sparsely furnished reception. "Not like him to be late."

"I've texted him and not had a reply," Danny added. He was still in awe that he had been able to procure a full McDonald's breakfast that tasted exactly like the one he could purchase at home. In buttfuck America. In France. Etc, etc.

"I'll give him another five minutes then get reception to ring his room," Johnny said.

After the five minutes had elapsed, Johnny strolled over to the brightly light reception desk and enquired after one Mr M. Long.

"No reply from his room. I'm going up to check," Johnny said with a slight frown as he recalled the earlier conversation with the sexually ambitious drummer.

Taking the express elevator to the fifth floor, Johnny knocked firmly on room 505's black panelled door.

Nothing.

Knocking again firmly, Johnny thought he heard a vague grunt from the other side of the door.

Putting his head to the door.

Another knock. Another stifled grunt.

"Mikee. You in there?"

"Grrrmmm," came the muffled reply.

"You okay man? Can you open the door?" Johnny asked urgently.

"Neerrrmmm."

"Right. Give me a minute. I'll get a spare room key."

Returning to the reception and after a minutes cajoling, Johnny obtained the necessary swipe card and standing in front of room 505, took a deep breath.

Swinging the heavy door open, Johnny stood stock still at the vision that met him.

Kong was facedown and completely naked. Hogtied to the bamboo bed frame by plastic snap handcuffs, his mouth was covered by a strip of thick black insulation tape.

To top off the humiliation, a pair of his thick Zildjian drumsticks had been roughly inserted into his arse.

Wincing with sympathy, Johnny strode over to the bed and slowly pulled the tape from Mikee's mouth.

As delicately as he could, he extracted the drumsticks. Regretting he'd removed the tape before said sticks, Mikee let out an anguished moan. The ancient Greek fable of Androcles and the Lion flashed through Johnny's mind, but this was swiftly extinguished as he looked at the sticks' tips - a fusion of blood and shit.

He couldn't see Mikee's recently acquired drum sponsors looking to use this image as part of their up-coming marketing campaign…

Having been sucked dry to climax, Kong had eventually fallen asleep and the wounded girl had then exacted her sadistic revenge. The swollen welt on her cheek would cost her at least a week's work although this act of vengeance would go some way to assuage her irate employer who would take great amusement from the mobile phone pictures that had been gleefully taken.

Taking in Mikee's discomfort, Johnny said calmly, "I won't tell them. Honestly."

Pulling against his plastic binds, Mikee said, "There's some nail scissors in my toiletries bag," nodding in the direction of the bathroom.

After a couple of minutes frantic hacking, Kong was freed from his shackles. Throwing a bath towel in his direction, Johnny slumped into a padded leather armchair. "What the fuck happened? I know you said you were expecting company, but I guess this wasn't on the menu."

"I dunno man. I woke up like this after the girls had left." Holding a hand gingerly to his tender-to-the-touch arse, Mikee grimaced. "I think I hit one of them by accident 'cos she shoved something up my arse and…"

"Fucking hell," Johnny said, his tone sympathetic as he had never seen the affable drummer in anything closely resembling pain or distress. "Look, get yourself showered and sorted. Bang some painkillers down and sleep on the bus."

"It's bleeding," Mikee whimpered as he inspected his thick index finger.

"I've got some Savlon in my bag that you can have. I don't think a plaster will do any good," Johnny said, laughing nervously.

"It's not funny," moaned Kong.

"I'm not laughing man. Honestly. I'll grab it for you and bring it back up. Gimme a minute."

"Please Johnny. Don't say anything," Mikee said beseechingly.

With a silent shake of his head, Johnny returned to the reception to collect the soothing antiseptic cream for the anally distressed drummer.

***

"Are you feeling any better, man?" Danny asked the prone drummer - a look of concern on his face. "I'm just glad you didn't have that Pufferfish I've heard about. It can kill you stone dead!"

"Thanks dude. I'll live. I'm just not eating for a while," Mikee said through gritted teeth.

Johnny had told the inquiring band that their sexually-adventurous drummer had been struck down by food poisoning and that if anybody dared attempt a 'Japanese Flag' joke, the forfeit would be considerable.

"If you don't cook it properly, the tetrodotoxin can kill you. Absolutely true! You've got to be licensed to cook it. How fuckin' mad is that!" Danny said.

Looking up and blinking in surprise at Danny's *QI*-depth knowledge of Japanese cuisine, Johnny then smiled at the neat subterfuge.

The coach rumbled north-east in the direction of Mount Fuji and its namesake Festival.

The blue skies outside were not, however, a reflection of the turbulent storm clouds that were gathering at the rear of the bus.

Slamming the lid of his laptop down, Jamie slapped his Aviators into placed and began to inwardly seethe.

He had become a digital scab-picker where one Ms Lara Bearheart was concerned. As much as he tried to resist the web-browser based temptation, he could not help himself from scouring the more scurrilous, largely US-based sites for news and pictures of the object of his desire.

This particular search had done him no favours.

A very drunk and very high Lara had been *papped* quite literally falling out of a limousine. Her no-doubt ridiculously expensive high heel had caught on the seat belt as she exited the car resulting in a graceless fall to the sidewalk.

This little scenario would normally have elicited nothing but sympathy from Jamie and a well-intended text message.

However.

Lara had been helped to her feet by the other passenger in the car. An up-and-coming Hispanic NBA player. A ridiculously good looking and athletic specimen, by the name of Jesus Cavaz.

Jesus had miraculously risen from the confines of the limousine and proceeded to floor two of the photographers with lightning-fast jabs. The remaining paps had fled the scene when he proceeded to throw the fallen snappers' camera at them with both unerring accuracy and velocity.

Then in a very public show of chivalry, he scooped Lara into his arms and placed her back into the security of the car.

"Fuck. Fuck. Fuck," Jamie cursed under his breath.

The Rock'N'The Roll. 'N That

***

The festival site was nothing short of awe-inspiring - set at the foot of the 4000-metre splendour that is Mount Fuji.

The only person who failed to be impressed was Jamie, who, unlike him, was mono-syllabically brooding.

Johnny frowned at this attitude but erred from probing any further other than a well-intended, "You alright J?"

This was met by a mumbled 'fine' and Johnny backed off – his own paranoia kicking in that Cally had told the boys of his unwillingness to get serious. *Nonsense*, he thought, but it still niggled at him.

Whatever Jamie's state of mind was, it was reflected in a fiery, verging on venomous performance which had the crowd rocking from the first chord. Resisting the urge to stage dive, Jamie had however tossed a 'stunt' scarf into the crowd, causing momentary pandemonium.

Mikee had discreetly smuggled a small cushion onto the stage and secreted it on his drum stool. Given the pain that he was clearly in, his performance was as fluid and dextrous as ever.

As the band finished their set with an incendiary version of 'Salvation', Jamie bowed politely and said thank you in perfect Japanese.

"Nice touch J. I never knew," Jamie said as he patted them individually on the back as they filed off stage.

"Hotel receptionist taught me this morning whilst we were waiting for Mikee and the Blowfish," Jamie replied, catching his post-gig breath.

"Fuck off J! You can take the piss all you like but that crosses the line!" Mikee said with a laugh as he flipped Jamie.

***

Lonely Souls' first tour of this captivating new territory had gone brilliantly, the label's management wanted them to tour there again early in the New Year with bigger venues and more dates.

The tour itself had resulted in two upheld vows of fidelity. A quietly seething lead singer. A blinding new song getting its first live airing. And a drummer who would resolutely never forget his first threesome.

Chapter 57

Having returned home, a twisting jealousy gripping his stomach, Jamie nearly tripped over the pile of post on his doorstep – tracking his new address proving to be no issue to those determined enough.

He had yet to formulate his plan of attack but wanted resolution as to where they stood. Having had such an amazing time at Glastonbury not four weeks earlier, it troubled him to see her falling out of cars – new suitor in tow.

Eight hours.

Eight hours before he could contact her. Yawning slightly, Jamie decided that the only way to make that time pass was to reacquaint himself with his bed.

Having *borrowed* a couple of sleepers off Johnny, a deep dream-free slumber came easily to him.

***

"It's beautiful. I love it. Thank you," Eleanor said as she held up the multi-coloured silk kimono.

"I knew you'd love it," Dominic said. "Try it on."

"Just one second," Eleanor replied as she pulled her vest over her head and wriggled out of her black leggings. Sliding the kimono over her naked body, she twirled round with a giggle. Catching sight of her reflection, she then pouted seductively at her homecoming Rockstar, and then let the shimmering garment drop down from her shoulder.

"I've missed you…"

Dominic wanted to tell her this that this was the first time that he'd been on tour and not slept with a plethora of women. As much as his fidelity sounded like a declaration of love in his head, the words didn't quite convey the intended sentiment.

"Come here," he said, pushing the exquisitely tailored gown aside, and kissing her deeply. "I've missed my Queen."

Scooping her in his arms, Dominic carried the naked Eleanor to the bedroom. He had some well-deserved catching up to do.

***

"She's grown so much. I can't believe it!" Danny said, as held his six-week-old daughter to him, choking back a tear.

"We've missed you, haven't we," Dee said, in the high-pitched tones of a mother talking on behalf of a baby.

"You look great too babe. You and Mummy have been busy!"

"I miss you both. But I am gonna be away a lot, y'know."

"We know that, but we can buy nice things with all the money daddy earns, can't we baby."

"Johnny said we're due a decent payday later this year and that's before we even think about the second album. Which we're gonna start recording as soon as."

"Where?" Dee asked, her tone reverting to that of an adult.

"Err, not sure yet. But probably back to Monmouth. We loved it there. And it's not too far."

"It's far enough! And you'll be away for weeks on end," Dee snapped.

"I won't. Anyhow. I can't drop everything, can I?"

"I'm not asking you to leave the band. Obviously. But just don't be away all the time, babe."

"I won't," Danny mumbled.

"Now pass me that bottle, she's ready for her feed…"

***

"Can you tell exactly what was inserted, Mr Long?"

Mikee rolled his eyes and looked down at the nondescript carpet tiles. *He's revelling in this,* he thought. *Fuck it, I'll just tell him.*

"A pair of drumsticks. I had a pair of drumsticks stuck in my arse."

"I'm sorry Mr Long. Did you say drumsticks?" the doctor asked, peering over the top of his half-rimmed spectacles. "And why did you do that?"

"I didn't!" Mikee shook his head exasperatedly.

The doctor grimaced but nodded at Mikee to proceed.

"I'm a drummer. In a band. I was on tour. Having a threesome," he said somewhat proudly. "Anyhow, I fell asleep and woke up tied up with me drumsticks stuck up my arse." Hoping his candidness would shock the Doctor sufficiently to enough for him to drop the supercilious tone he had assumed.

"I. I, err. I—" the doctor stammered.

"Never heard anything like it?" Mikee said with a chuckle.

Struggling to compose himself, the doctor said, "I've dealt with numerous patients who have a variety of items in their respective orifices, but this is quite exceptional…"

Mikee nodded. Verging on proud.

"Well Mr Long, you may well have damage to your anal muscles. Nothing more than bruising I'd expect. The bleeding should subside. Hopefully the bowel won't be damaged, but I think you need to be referred to a hospital for further checks."

"I'll have to tell somebody else this story all over again? Great," Mikee harrumphed.

"Well, err, no. My notes will be comprehensive, and I'll make sure they know exactly what occurred."

"Y'know what. I can go private. I don't trust the hospital not too blab it. Too many people there. Let me have a specialist's number."

"Certainly, Mr Long. I'll find the necessary details for you. Please. One moment." The doctor tapped at his desktop computer and scribbled a name and number down. "There you go, Mr Long. I hope the appointment goes well. I'm sure that there won't be any lasting damage. But you can never be too careful…"

***

"I never said anything about us being exclusive," Lara said.

"And I didn't ask. But, y'know, I thought we had an understanding," Jamie said as he paced up and down, craving a cigarette but not wanting to smoke inside his new house.

"You've been away on tour. Again. I don't know what you're doing. And I don't want to stop you enjoying yourself. Fuck, Jamie. You're in one of the best bands in the world. I know how these things work."

"I'm not like that. You know that."

"Not like every other Rockstar that's ever fucked his way around every town and city around the globe?"

"No," Jamie replied bluntly.

"We live on the other side of the world from each other. We're great when we're together b—"

"But nothing," Jamie interrupted. "I really care, Lara. I get you. I get all the bullshit you have to deal with."

"Jamie Thorne. You are different. I know that. I do. But it'd be impossible."

"Impossible?" Jamie rolled the word around his tongue. "Not if we didn't want it to be."

"Look, Jamie. I'm not serious with this guy. He's a big deal over here and we just hooked up for a night." Lara paused. "C'mon Jamie. You know how it works by now. We were good for each other's column inches."

Jamie closed his eyes and gritted his teeth.

"Look, I think I may be over in London in a few weeks. Let's meet up then."

Grasping the futility of the situation, Jamie said, "Okay. Fine. Let me know. But don't be a stranger…"

Hanging the phone up, Jamie felt his chest tighten and his breathing quicken. Sitting down, he put his head between his knees and tried to slow the short, sharp panting breaths down.

"Fuck," he hissed between hyperventilating breaths.

After a minute or so, his breathing returned to normal, and more than a little shaken, Jamie flopped down on the sofa and thought of how calm he'd felt when Lara had offered him *that smoke…*

***

"It's all booked, Jamie. Just had confirmation from the label. Tom Duffy all confirmed to produce as well. Ten weeks' studio time and then it can be mastered after that," Johnny said, as he sat in his apartment scrolling through numerous emails. Studiously avoiding the pile of invoices and receipts that were more pressing.

"Brilliant. Dom will be made up. He's totally loved up, but I know can't wait to get into the studio to get this album done," Jamie replied.

"Cool. I know Danny is just the same. He's loving it with his little 'un but think he wants some band time soon."

"Me too. Get this right and we're—" Jamie struggled slightly for his words. "Well, proves the first one wasn't a fluke."

"I know you'll get it right and fuck, no-one has said the first album was anything less than brilliant."

"Y'know. Difficult second album and that."

"Yeah, yeah. We need to catch up soon for a drink. Not the same now you have moved out of town."

"We should. Just been enjoying my own space and no mither," Jamie said. "Come over and pick up a curry and some beers. There's a couple of spare rooms to crash in."

"Cheers J, we'll sort that."

"Nice one Johnny. Speak soon. Chuck all the dates and stuff on an email for us all."

Johnny hung up the call. He hadn't seen anywhere near as much of Jamie since he had sought privacy in his little house in the country. There was no correlation but the situation with Cally had knawed away at him and it worried him that the brothers knew something was afoot.

***

Week one of recording album number two and the band were shacked up at Monmouth Studios.

"FUCK OFF!" Mikee threw his empty can at the 52-inch plasma screen that sat pride of place in the studio rest room. Fortunately, the can sailed past and hit the wall, leaving a wet splat. "That's the second fuckin' idiot that's covered one of our songs. I fuckin' hate this shite."

"Don't watch it then," Johnny said as he popped the offending can in the bin and wiped the stain down with his shirt cuff.

"Don't hate the player, hate the game," Danny said, with a sage-like nod.

"Very profound D-Mo. That one of your own?" Johnny said.

"No, I heard so— Oh, fuck off. Very funny," Danny replied, with a wounded look on his face. "True though innit."

"Compliment in one way I suppose. Great for sales," Johnny said before he was sharply cut off by Mikee.

"Woah woah woah! We don't want some *X Factor* knobhead getting anywhere near one of our songs. You can fuck the money. I'd rather be skint," Mikee said, with a suitably appalled look on his face.

"I agree," Danny said, "And I don't want my daughter thinking that's what paid for her education."

Both Mikee and Johnny looked at him with bemused looks..

"She's two months old. Getting a little ahead of ourselves, aren't we?" Johnny said.

"It's the principle," Danny replied, leaning back and putting his shades on. "You know I'm right."

Chapter 58

"I'm glad you called," Jamie said, just about keeping a lid on his delight.

"Be at my London apartment at midday tomorrow," Lara replied. "And be discreet, let's try and have a camera free day. Or what is it you call them. '*A scrape*?'"

"I'll be there. Until Friday," Jamie said as he clenched his fist.

"Until Friday, Jamie Thorne."

"YES!" he shouted to himself as he punched the air.

Returning to the confines of the studio, Jamie felt a wave of relief wash over him.

"Last track and we're all done," Dominic said as he saw his brother. "You already to pin that vocal down. Need some fire in your belly, bro."

Good job he didn't hear that phone call then, Jamie thought to himself.

"I'm spitting fire. Let's do this," Jamie said, pulling a serious face that was in stark contrast to his newly re-discovered inner glow.

***

The band had four days of down time so were going their separate ways – Dom was whisking Eleanor off to Paris, Danny was heading home for family time and Mikee was off to Prague on his cousin's stag do.

Jamie only had one thing on his mind.

Lara.

Pulling his collar up and his woolly hat down, Jamie sat on the platform virtually unrecognisable behind his sunglasses.

Two uninterrupted hours of First Class train travel followed by a cab saw him direct to Lara's North London apartment.

And no scrape of photographers when he arrived. All good so far.

Buzzing her on the intercom, he took a deep breath and muttered self-encouragement under his breath.

"Jamie Thorne. And right on time."

"Fashionably on time. It's the new late. Can't believe you've not heard," Jamie said.

As Jamie entered the apartment – the door being on the latch – he saw Lara busying herself packing a small wicker hamper.

"Never had you down as a domestic goddess," Jamie said, as he put his small overnight bag down on the huge leather sofa.

"Full of surprises," Lara replied coyly.

"Aren't you just," Jamie said, with just enough intent to make his point.

Lara looked over her shoulder, frowned and stuck her bottom lip out slightly, in what Jamie perceived to be an apology.

He felt his stomach flip slightly. She looked beautiful. With a minimal amount of makeup on, her hair tied up in a pleated ponytail which was resting like a whip on her left shoulder.

"Aren't you going to ask what I'm doing?"

Stepping up behind her, and putting his arms round her waist, Jamie looked down at the hamper which was brim-full of food and bottles of beer.

"We going somewhere?" Jamie asked.

"A picnic." She shut the hamper with a self-satisfied flourish. "At the top of Primrose Hill."

Raising an eyebrow quizzically, he said, "Really? Very rock 'n' roll."

"Problem?" Lara said as she spun round and kissed Jamie on the cheek.

"No. But won't there be uninvited company?"

"Nope. They don't know I'm here."

"I'm sure won't that last long when you spread half of Waitrose's finest out at the top of some hill," Jamie huffed.

"We'll be fine, Jamie Thorne. You worry too much."

"Hmm. Anyhow, am I okay to grab a quick shower?"

"Sure. But I can't join you. I've only just dried my hair," Lara said with a twirl of her ponytail.

"Gimme five minutes. And I am starving!"

"Wait till you see all the stuff I've got us," Lara said, like a proud teenager at a yard sale.

Freshly showered and changed, Jamie, as ever, looked like the consummate Rock Star – Vintage Jeans, Black Denim Jacket and Aviators.

Lara gave his just waxed hair a quick corrective tweak. "Perfect. You always look so gorgeous, Jamie Thorne, and never have to make any effort. So unfair!"

He shrugged and picked up the hamper – letting out a slight grunt at the weight of it.

"There'll be a car at the back of the building waiting for us. We can use the back entrance. Just to be safe."

"Wish you'd told me about that before," Jamie replied. "Might have made life a little easier."

"I've only just been given a key for it. If I'd known about it…" Lara said.

Loading the hamper and themselves into the car, they headed off for some early autumn alfresco dining.

***

Idly ticking off a handful of emails – principally concerned ones from the label as to when the album would be finished. A pre-Christmas release and marketing campaign was planned and despite Johnny's constant reassuring, they seemed somewhat jittery.

Firing off yet another conciliatory email, he was about to close his laptop down when an email popped up from their press officer.

'Hey Johnny, Hope all good. Album all on track for the October release I believe. Just a quick heads up. A friend of mine has just told me that Lara is in the country and has 'tipped off' the press about her whereabouts. Seems she's doing some self-promotion for a new clothing line and wants to maximise publicity for the launch. Your call if you want to speak to Jamie. Suzzie.'

Pulling a perplexed face, Johnny scratched behind his ear and let out a frustrated grumble.

Tricky one. Jamie was big enough and old enough and could be very prickly where Lara's shortcomings were concerned. What's the worst that could happen –a few papped shots in the paper. Lining tomorrow's recycling bag, he decided. It wasn't an unheard-of practice, but it certainly left a nasty taste. It was Lara all over…

***

"It's been so hard whilst you were away," Dee said, looking jaded with traces of dark circles starting to form under her eyes. Her hair scraped back and a baby sick-flecked A & F hoodie completed the struggling first-time mum image.

"Shouldn't that be my line," Danny said, with a misplaced smirk and a grab of his crotch. "C'mon give her to me."

"Not fuckin' funny!" Dee said, as she turned her shoulder away, shielding their on-the-verge-of-tears-yet-again daughter from him.

"Ahem. Language."

"Fuck off Danny. I'm exhausted," Dee snapped back.

"I'm home now, c'mon babe," Danny said as he put his bag down and reached into the fridge, hunting out a beer.

"And if you're after a beer, then you're out of luck. I've had enough on my plate," Dee said before rocking her daughter gently and shushing her softly.

"Okay. I get it, you've been on your own with our little princess," Danny said as he rubbed a bony finger under his daughter's chin. "But I'm here now. I can do my bit."

"But you're only home for a few days," Dee groaned. "Are you sure they need you? Can't they do your parts without you?"

With a wounded look on his face, Danny wrested the bundle of gurgling baby from Dee, her eyes widening at the sight of her returning father. "I hope you don't mean that…"

"I've heard Dom say he can play bass in his sleep," Dee said, taking the conversation into uncharted and distinctly hostile waters.

"Fuckin' hell! Dom says he can do pretty much anything but don't believe everything he says," Danny snapped back, his raised tones startling his daughter.

"I need you here. You know what I meant."

"Not really. It sounded like you're saying the band could manage without me. MY FUCKIN' BAND!"

Dominique screamed loudly, and tiny pearl like tears flowed down her screwed up puce-coloured face.

"Sorry darling. Mummy doesn't mean to talk such shit," Danny said as he attempted to placate his daughter's histrionics.

"Mummy does mean it. I can't cope on my own," Dee said, holding the palms of her hands to her temples and letting out an anguished grimace.

"We'll get help sorted for you. I can afford it," Danny said as he surveyed the carnage that was their kitchen. Pots of baby food littered the work surface and the sink was overflowing with bowls and feeding bottles.

"I'd rather you were here, but I suppose…" Dee said, leaving the sentence trailing as a wave of relieve seemed to pour off her.

"You tell me what you need, and I'll sort it. I need both of you to be happy. But I need the band."

The perfect triangle of his life wouldn't be complete without each component.

***

"I love it that no-one can see us," Eleanor said, following it up with a contented giggle as she raised her arms over her head and let her exquisitely pert breasts rise above the bubbling waters of the newly installed hot-tub.

Dominic looked over and placed his beer down on the thick pine border and pulled her over to him. As he kissed her softly, he felt Eleanor's hand snake beneath the surface and pull at his already stirring cock. Leaning back and closing his eyes, he thought, *it doesn't get much better than this. Second album nearly in the bag and sounding sensational – especially the guitar parts – beautiful and doting girlfriend. And a hot-tub with sensational views overlooking his hometown…*

"Don't finish me off in the water," Dominic said in between contented grunts. "The guy that installed it said not to block the filters."

"Spoilsport," Eleanor purred. "Sit up on the edge then," she said as she positioned herself in front of him.

With a satisfied smile, Dominic hoisted himself out of the water and let her suck him off to a satisfying climax. Turned out things could get even better…

***

"*I'll be your Salad-vation*" read the typically-tabloid punning headline. "*Lara Bearheart, over in the UK to promote her newly launched clothing line, but still found time for her bad boy but oh so pretty on/off Rockstar boyfriend as they frolicked raunchily during a picnic on Primrose Hill yesterday. Jamie Thorne never seems to be far away when Lara hits town and our exclusive pictures show that their alfresco dining brought out the wicked side of them. They kissed in between mouthfuls of the expensively packed hamper and downed two bottles of white wine – Lara also seemed quite intent on seeing what the lead singer was packing under his jeans as she constantly ran her hands over him. Dressed in her own clothing line 'Bearheart', Lara looked amazing as she lay back and let Jamie kiss her. Busy with the launch of her personally designed fashion label and with*

Jamie just putting the finishing touches to his band's second album, the picnic clearly showed they still have time for each other no matter how busy they are. We hope Jamie didn't get dressing on his jeans!

"Fuck's sake," Johnny said to himself as he scanned down the article. Their press officer had been right. The public picnic had been a pre-prepared stunt to boost Lara's profile whilst she plugged her new brand.

Frowning and running a thumb over his eyebrow, Johnny felt perplexed as to whether Jamie needed to hear about this. The article read like an advert for her launch and was so obviously a plant. *Hopefully Jamie will work that out for himself*, Johnny mused with an irritated scowl.

***

The morning after the papped picnic, Lara and Jamie were lay on the king-size bed in Lara's apartment.

"When will you be back? We're in America again before Christmas but I want to see you before then," Jamie said.

Putting her hand on his taut torso, Lara replied, "I don't know. I'm busy with the launch Stateside. Got to see how it goes."

Taking a deep breath, he said, "I don't like this just seeing each other when our paths cross, y'know."

"And as I have said before, that big pond makes it difficult. And I don't see you moving to the States. You rock stars always head to L.A anyhow," Lara said before she kissed Jamie, almost patronisingly, on the forehead.

"I know bu—"

"There's no buts. How can we commit when we live so far apart?" Lara said with a neatly rehearsed line in evasion.

"I suppose," Jamie said with a grumble.

Rolling over to pick up his mobile that had just pinged, Jamie flicked open the message and let out an exasperated sigh. "It's from my Johnny. We're all over the papers again after our picnic. I said it was a bad idea!"

"You're fucking shitting me," Lara said convincingly. "How the holy fuck could they have known?"

"Not a clue," Jamie said with a shake of his head. "They get everywhere."

"They surely do," Lara said, before she slowly slipped under the thin summer weight duvet and set about satisfying Jamie's morning glory…

***

"Oh Dominic! Absolutely. And Eleanor Thorne has such a lovely ring to it."

"Talking of which," Dominic said, and with a flourish, he produced a small black velvet box which had been concealed under a bath sheet by the side of the hot-tub.

Eleanor's eye's widened as she flipped open the clasp and saw the exquisite vintage diamond ring contained within. "It's so beautiful," she cooed as the ring slid over her finger.

"Careful with it in here! I don't want you losing it if the fit's not right."

"It fits perfectly. I love you, Dominic."

"And I love you, my Queen."

"When are you thinking?" Her voice full of nervous excitement.

"Soon. We're off to America sometime in October. Vegas? Find a cool little chapel and then book a sick hotel for the aftershow."

"But what about my parents? And your mum?" Eleanor said with a slight frown.

"Fly them out. I wouldn't want them missing their beautiful girl getting married."

"That's lovely. But they always saw me getting married in our village church. It's so pretty, Dom. You should see it," Eleanor said, in her most beseeching tone.

"I don't really see me in some church," Dom replied with a slow shake of his head. "And this way it'll be more private. We can always have a massive party here when we get back."

"I suppose," Eleanor said.

"And it'll be proper rock 'n' roll and that in Vegas," Dom said. "I'll sort it then?"

"Of course," Eleanor said softly, already dreading the conversation with her somewhat staid parents.

Chapter 59

"I really can't be fucked with these things. Load of fakes just here to be seen," Johnny said as he finished off his umpteenth beer of the evening.

"You British do like to moan and bitch. And so sarcastic," Lara said as she rubbed at her nose. Again.

"It's a Mancunian trait. Unique to us rather than the English in general. I like to see it as grounded pragmatism," Johnny replied, as he beckoned the bartender for another bottle.

"These meet and greets are all part and parcel of the music business though. You can't bite the hand that feeds," Lara said.

Dressed in a short black multi-tiered ballet skirt and a black gravity defying silk strapless bodice, Lara was in full siren mode – with both men and women unable to stop themselves from staring to take in her beauty. Her thick kohl eye make-up gave her a seductive smoulder that she utilised to maximum effect.

"Bit fucking pointless if the band aren't even here though," Johnny grumbled as he sank yet another beer. Frowning at the bottle, he said, "What is it with you Americans and piss weak beer?"

"Charming," Lara said. "You have got one on you tonight."

"Yeah. I'm just gutted that the lads are the other side of the country because of this storm. Sorry, hurricane. You always have to do things bigger and better over here, don't you," replied Johnny as he tugged irritably at the collar of his Fred Perry polo shirt.

"Can you please chill the fuck out! They'll be fine. The airlines aren't flying in to New York, so they'll be in Vegas still. Quiet night in and that."

Johnny chuckled to himself. "And that. We'll make a Manc of you yet."

A five-day stag-do for Dominic taking in the musical hotspots of New Orleans, Tennessee and Vegas had now been extended by at least forty-eight hours whilst the hurricane over the Eastern seaboard subsided. Johnny had cut the occasion short by a day to attend a record label management meeting in New York. Quartile projections, territories and units saved him from a fourth day of relentless drinking.

Followed by the small matter of the 'happy day' itself. Eleanor flying out to join the party – under some duress as her parents were blissfully unaware of their daughter's pending Sin City-based nuptials.

One blushing bride.

One wasted groom.

And three very trashed best men…

The record company had laid on a celebration party for the band as a reward for 250,00 sales in the last quarter. Not a massive number in terms of the US market but solid enough to garner the label's thanks and for them to exercise their 'option' on the band.

As the band had separate US management, Johnny's job was quite easy Stateside, operating in more of a tour manager capacity, merely relaying information to the band that their American paymasters had decided upon.

Lara reached into her clutch bag and, grabbing Johnny's hand, palmed him a small glass phial.

"This is my decent stuff. I don't hand it out to just anyone. But given that I'm stuck with you, I may as well have you in a good mood. We might do *piss weak* beer, but great coke is something we can get."

"Ta for that. I'll go and give it the Pepsi challenge then," Johnny said as he headed off in the direction of the restroom.

A full-blown hurricane – sweetly named Trudy – had decimated the Eastern seaboard and had rendered pretty much all modes of transport impossible. The band were grounded in Vegas and all that she had to offer for at least another 48 hours. The hotel bill would be astronomical without Johnny's intervention and he'd asked them to busk on the main strip to fund their inevitable excesses.

Returning from his nose-powdering, Johnny – heartrate now a few BPMs faster – felt narcotically invigorated.

Handing the glass phial back, he said, "You weren't fuckin' kidding."

"I don't bullshit about my coke," Lara said as she popped the phial back into her clutch bag.

"How long until your apartment's sorted?" Johnny asked, before gulping down a beer in a vain attempt to smooth out the coke's bitter aftertaste.

"The architect says three weeks. But it'll be longer. For sure."

"Not just a coat of paint and a new front door then," Johnny deadpanned.

"No. I was bored of the old place and this was a cheaper option than moving. Prices in the city are still not value for money," Lara said.

"Never had you down as the property tycoon."

"No. You probably thought I was just some dumb model with all my talents down here," Lara said jutting her chin down in the direction of her sumptuous and irrefutably impressive breasts.

"I'd say brains and beauty. But that'd be such a fuckin' cliché," Johnny said, before catching a drop in the back of his throat. "Fuck me! That coke is extraordinary."

"Don't be going all lightweight on me, Johnny Harrison," Lara said, her smile revealing the finest dentistry that the dollar could buy.

"Don't you worry about me. I'll be right," Johnny said, as he stifled yet another gag reflex at the frozen lump that was lodged in the back of his throat. "You're racking up some bill at your hotel then?"

"What is it you guys say? Slum it?" Assuming a passable Northern accent, she said, "You don't expect me to slum it d'yer?"

"Haha! Very good. You're learning," Johnny said.

"Look. This party is dying. And I have a gift for Jamie. Why don't we go back to my suite and you can ring him from there? Check on your boys. Kick the ass out of the room service and that," Lara said.

"I dunno. My hotel is right across town. But I won't be sleeping in a while after that hooter. Fuck it. Yeah, and we can call Jamie and see if Vegas is still standing."

"I'll call my driver to collect us. I'm sure you can knock back another couple of beers in the time it'll take him to get here."

"Knock back. Like it. You really are picking up the lingo. I'm not arsed about a car. We can get a cab. I still buzz off a proper yellow New York taxi."

"Hmm. And get papped with you? I have standards!" Lara said.

"Yeah. Fair comment. Supermodel seen with saucer eyed middle aged greying man doesn't quite cut it."

"You're not wearing too bad. But no," Lara said with a schoolgirl-like giggle he had not previously witnessed.

Lara's driver arrived ten minutes later, and they slipped through a side entrance and made the short six-block ride across town to her hotel.

As they pulled up, Johnny let out a low whistle. "Fuck. This place is amazing. It'll be costing you a mint!" he said in a whisper.

"Did I forget to tell you? My father owns the place. I'm comped whenever I want to stay."

Taking the elevator up to the top floor suite, Johnny felt like Charlie in *The Great Glass Elevator* with his Willy Wonka possessing some seriously strong cocaine rather than outlandish confectionery.

The Rock 'N' The Roll. 'N That

Swiping the door open, Lara threw her clutch bag on to a plush looking leather couch and gestured around the vast suite. "Welcome to my humble hotel room."

Johnny stood literally open-mouthed as he took in the surroundings. The room was glass on three sides, offering the most spectacular views of Manhattan.

"Fuck me! This place is amazing. You could see the whites of King Kong's eyes the Empire State is that close."

"I took an injunction out against him. To stop him peering in!" Lara said. Again, with the little giggle in her voice. "Help yourself to a piss weak beer. I'll rack out a couple of lines."

As Johnny opened the jet-black fridge and helped himself to a Michelob, he pressed call and rang Jamie.

Voicemail.

"Jamie. It's Johnny. I'm in New York. Sorry you lot are all stuck over there. Party was pretty crap without you all. Just having a drink with Lara. She wanted a chat so bell me back, yeah. Cheers J. Love yer man."

"Oh, that's so sweet!" Lara said as she looked up from the glass table. A thick rail of coke and a hundred-dollar bill sat there invitingly. Calling out to Johnny like a drug-addled Bisto Kid.

"Jeez. That one'll finish me off!"

"Pussy," Lara goaded.

"Yeah right," Johnny said as he took in a deep breath and polished off the girder like line in one satisfying snort. "You could knock a buffalo out with that!"

The next hour passed by quickly, with Johnny repeatedly checking his phone for Jamie's return call.

Conversation centred mainly around the band and inevitably, Jamie.

With the pure cocaine emboldening Johnny by the minute, he leant back in his armchair and fixed Lara's stare.

"I know what you did in London."

"Do tell. What did I do in *that London*?" Lara replied, clearly intrigued.

"I know," Johnny said as he idly tapped the rolled-up note on the heel of his desert boot.

"Go on then, Mr Smartass. What did I do?"

"You tipped the press off. You told 'em where you and Jamie would be. When you went for that picnic."

"That? Well, aren't I the Wicked Witch of the East then."

"Not really. But it's a shitty trick. Especially when you were with someone you care about."

"Johnny. Johnny. I knew you knew. Don't play the innocent with me. You know, and I know it's all a game. All a fucking game that we play. The music business. Show-fucking-business. It's all one big motherfucking game and don't pretend for one second that you don't know that," Lara said. Her voice mixed with frustration and sadness.

"Course it is. And obviously I fuckin' know it's a game. But come on. It was Jamie you were using to flog your brand!"

"Right," Lara said, annoyance creeping into her tone. "So poor defenceless Jamie didn't use me to raise the profile of his little band. Fuck you!"

Lara's demeanour had changed as quick as the flip of a switch.

"Bollocks he did!" Johnny snapped back.

Pausing, Lara glared at Johnny and then burst out laughing. "Bollocks. What does that even mean?"

Leaning over the table, Lara chopped out two more sturdy looking lines.

"Look I know you love Jamie. And you want to protect him and the rest of the band, but they are big boys. They know the rules. You'd be surprised."

"I know, but you can see my point?" mumbled Johnny.

"I do know that Jamie would walk through Hell for you. Barefoot. That's some control. Especially as he's the talent. No offence."

"None taken." Johnny met Lara's stare. "It's not control. Nothing like it."

"Level with me. Yes or no answer. Don't fucking bullshit me," said Lara, leaning forward in her plush armchair. "Did you tell Jamie that you knew it was a set-up for the press?"

Johnny pursed his lips, letting out a low whistle. Meeting Lara's stare, he replied. "Yes. Yes, I did."

"Son of a bitch! I fucking knew it. Control. All about control. Motherfucker!"

"It's got nothing to do with control. I have Jamie's back. Nothing more than that," replied Johnny coldly.

"BULLSHIT! It's control. You telling Jamie so he thinks you're the good guy. CONTROL!" Lara said, slapping the flat of her hand on her thigh for emphasis.

"If that's what you want to think," Johnny countered.

"Because I'm right! Do I want to be in control of my life? Fuck yes! And if that means playing the game then I want it on my terms. MY RULES," said Lara, her voice rising as she became more animated.

The Rock'N'The Roll. 'N That

"If that's your mantra, who am I to argue."

"Admit that it's a control thing," Lara challenged.

"It's not! I love him. Fuck, I love them all!" said Johnny, wiping a rouge dribble from his nose.

"Been your meal ticket, haven't they? You could say your salvation from the rat race…"

"Very good," replied Johnny, adding a sarcastic slow-clap. "

"I'm now seen as a businesswoman. Not just some model blessed with great genes. You know how hard it is to achieve that? As a woman. As a Native-American woman?" said Lara as she paced the room, silhouetted elegantly against the Manhattan skyline. "I truly care for Jamie, but I have never promised him anything. Ever!" Lara was rattling out her impassioned cocaine fuelled speech, jabbing a French polished nail in Johnny's direction.

"Point taken," said Johnny with a slug of his beer, feeling his pulse racing with the coke that was pinballing around his bloodstream.

"Finally! Thank you. Do I get an apology?"

Don't push it thought Johnny but decided it prudent to take the sting out of the situation.

"Okay. Sorry. Apology accepted?" said Johnny.

"Apology accepted. You over-protective dick!"

"Thank you," Johnny said as he accepted the proffered 100-dollar bill from Lara and swooped over the line which disappeared in one brisk flourish.

"Okay. After you upset me with your rude smartass routine, I've another question for you."

"Shoot," Johnny replied. "The least I can do given your fine hospitality."

"What is it with you English guys and the whole not eating pussy thing?"

"Excuse me?" Johnny said as he almost choked on both his words and the ice cube of coke in his throat.

"I've dated two English guys and neither of them would go down on me."

"What can I say? It's always been something I've had in my locker. As you Americans are fond of saying. Give and take. That's always been my motto."

"Pity Jamie never felt like that. Obviously not his thing."

"I remember telling him once that it was rude not to. He clearly doesn't listen to everything I tell him."

"Shame," Lara replied. "He'll learn. Hopefully."

"And after that little bombshell. I'm off to the toilet and then I'll call a cab."

"I'll call my driver for you."

"Don't worry. I'll walk for a bit and then grab a cab. Don't think I'll sleep for a week after that bugle. Walk will do me good," Johnny said as he dragged himself out of the armchair and headed for the bathroom.

Relieving himself with a muted sigh, Johnny looked at his reflection and saw how wide his eyes were. His pupils were penny-sized ink blots, and his nostrils an angry red - speckled white with the heavy duty ching.

Okay. Coke in a luxury hotel suite with the supermodel on/off girlfriend of the lead singer of your band. *Time to go, Harrison*, he said to himself.

When he returned to the suites living room area, Lara was nowhere to be seen. *Good time to make my excuses,* Johnny thought to himself.

"Lara. I'm off now. Shame we couldn't get hold of Jamie."

No reply.

"Lara?" Johnny said enquiringly.

"In here," came the reply from behind the black ash bedroom door.

Johnny stepped tentatively towards the door and popped his head round.

And stopped dead in his tracks.

Lara was sat astride the bed, naked from the waist down. Having discarded the black lace tutu, she was now sliding two fingers slowly in and out of her perfectly clean-shaven pussy.

"Hey Johnny. Coke always makes me feel so God damn horny."

Speechless didn't touch the sides.

Johnny stood transfixed.

Away from the liberal anything goes world of online porn, he had never seen a woman like this in the flesh. And certainly not one sat masturbating a matter of feet from him. Everything about her seemed high-class glossy magazine perfect. *Fuck. She is*, he remembered.

"Cat got your tongue?" Lara said coyly, before gasping at her rhythmic exertions.

"Err. Yeah," Johnny stammered. His mind screaming at him to get the fuck out of the hotel suite.

Immediately.

"You going to prove my little theory wrong then?"

"What?" His vocabulary was now limited to grunts and one-word exclamations.

"You going to show me that English men can eat pussy?"

Johnny closed his eyes and felt his stomach and scrotum tighten simultaneously.

The Rock'N'The Roll. 'N That

"Well. Least you can do for me after all my hospitality. Ooh, that's so good," Lara said as she again emitted a satisfied moan.

Shaking his head slightly, Johnny was rooted to the spot. He glanced down at her cunt. If Disney went adult and did vaginas this was it. A perfectly symmetrical designer vagina.

"Get on your knees, Johnny. Taste me." Her hand moved quicker as she slid another finger into herself.

Stepping towards the bed, his head spinning with conflicting messages, Johnny sank slowly to his knees and ran a hand up her right leg, pushing it to the side.

"Good boy. I knew you wouldn't be able to resist."

Johnny went to slip his polo T-shirt over his head.

"NO!" Lara snapped. "Fully dressed. You eat my pussy and that's it."

The surreal nature of the whole scenario slammed home to him.

"And don't even think of touching your cock. That can wait until you're back in your little hotel room."

Leaning his head into her and feeling the warmth of her slick pussy, Johnny was processing the sexual orders that were being barked at him.

Removing her wet fingers to allow Johnny to lick at her, Lara lay back on the king-sized bed and let out a low sigh.

The coke had shattered Johnny's thought process. His tounge darted at Lara's pussy, her slickness forming on his chin.

Feeling Lara's stomach muscles tense as she sat up, Johnny leant back.

"Don't stop I'm nearly there."

Bending forward, Johnny carried on subserviently.

As Johnny, head bent, Lara flipped on the video camera on her iPhone and recorded some 'jumpy' footage in the mirror that faced the bed.

Then, pushing his head back with a red-soled Louboutin heel, Lara rubbed languidly at her clitoris and brought herself to a panting climax.

Crossing her olive legs, Lara looked down at Johnny, whose hand was now hovering over the buckle of his belt like an expectant Wild West gunslinger.

A barely perceptible shake of her head caused him to slowly lower his trigger finger.

"Well, well, well. Mr. Integrity. Just the same as every other fucking guy. Thinks with his dick."

Johnny looked upwards, a look of abject mortification splashed across his face. And her warm pussy juice on his chin.

The dominant look on Lara's face told him all needed to know.

"I've got Jamie jumping whenever I snap my fingers. The band make it big over here, then I might just marry him. Who knows."

Closing his eyes, Johnny felt like he might be sick there and then.

"And as for you. Mister stumbles across a band and gets lucky. Dumps his girlfriend for the big bad world of showbiz. I've got you exactly where I want you. Don't ever try and fuck me over and think you've got the measure of me."

Johnny went to speak, but Lara cut him abruptly off.

"I knew you would have told Jamie. It's all quite sweet, this little paternal routine you pull."

"But I do ca—" Johnny stammered.

"I can see how much you care. Now fuck off back to your hotel room and jerk yourself off to your heart's content, "said Lara caustically.

Standing to leave, Johnny reeled towards the bedroom door. As he reached for his coat, he heard Lara in a sing-song voice.

"Oh Johnny! Next time you see your beloved Jamie. Look him in the eye and tell him I miss him. Mwah."

Stabbing at the elevator button, Johnny felt tears forming in his eyes and a bilious rush in the pit of his stomach.

The express drop of the lift did him no favours and as he exited the hotel's revolving door, Johnny bent double with his hands on his knees and dry-retched, spitting Colombian laced bile onto the sidewalk.

Holding his hands to his face, he rubbed the ball of his thumbs into his eyeballs in a vain attempt to extinguish the scene that he had just been central to. Despite the driving rain, a myriad of sunspots exploded in front of his eyes.

"What the fuck have I done," he said to himself.

Almost oblivious to the lashing down rain which seemed to come from the sidewalk itself such was the velocity. Already soaked to his T-shirt, the rain washed the dried sex off his face. Stumbling away in the vague direction of his hotel, his drug-induced indiscretion screaming at him at every step…

Chapter 60

"What the fuck do you lot look like?" Johnny said as he met the band in the hotel reception. The achingly hip Philippe Starck interior design seemed to wince at the band's boisterousness.

"VEGAS BABY!" Danny shouted, clearly still under the influence and oblivious to his surroundings. Heads turned from across the other side of the reception. Three of the band had shades firmly locked in place despite the gloomy weather, the exception being Mikee who had acquired a new trapper hat – the loosely hanging flaps forming large mutton chop sideburns.

The band were all sporting street vendor printed T-shirts bearing images of each other.

Mikee's had a picture of an elegantly wasted Jamie stood by the side of a swimming pool, soaking wet, with his T-shirt slung over his shoulder, the top button of his jeans undone, shades on and a cigarette hanging from his lips. He looked beautiful. And Johnny was already picturing the image on various band merchandise.

"Nice T-shirts, lads. Little souvenir from Vegas?" Johnny asked.

"Top time," Danny said, with a snap of his fingers, followed by a tap of his nose.

Looking up from his coffee, Jamie slid his sunglasses onto the top of his head. "What's up man? You look terrible."

"Think I've picked up some bug. Not feeling at my best," Johnny said, meeting Jamie's concerned expression but feeling a wave of guilt smother him.

"We've got to soundcheck later. But apart from that we're clear all day. You get your head down. Sleep it off and be right for the show," Jamie said, patting Johnny's arm reassuringly.

A final show of the year would see the band play bottom of the bill at Madison Square Garden supporting Black Keys. Even the lowest slot on the undercard couldn't diminish the band's excitement at playing at such a prestigious venue.

"Thanks man. I will. But you'll be alright without me."

"You look fuckin' terrible," Dominic chimed up. "Couldn't hack the pace with us, eh boss?"

"Yeah, cheers Dom. Appreciate your concern," Johnny deadpanned.

"After soundcheck, I'm off guitar shopping and to pick something up for Eleanor. Check out one of the big department stores," Dominic said chirpily.

"Well, seeing as you are all safely here. In body but possibly not mind, I'll turn it in again," Johnny said, stifling a yawn.

"You been worried about us, dude?" Mikee asked, a beer cradled in his shovel sized hand.

"Always, Mikee. Always," Johnny said before he headed back to the sanctuary of his room. Just him and his painkillers. And his gnawing guilty conscience…

***

"Great show Jamie!" cooed Lara, having ensured that she was the first well-wisher through the dressing room door. Full backstage accreditation was never ever beyond her capabilities. "You looked amazing up there. You rocked like a motherfuckers!"

Jamie smiled and nodded his head slowly but appreciatively. "Thanks Lara. You on your own?" he asked pointedly.

Having been sat on the adjacent armchair to Jamie, Johnny – nursing a sparkling water – had nowhere to turn and had to acknowledge Lara's presence.

"Hiya Lara. Glad you enjoyed it. They were on top form tonight," Johnny said between tentative sips.

"Oh Johnny. Hey. You look a bit peaky. Our little night out wasn't too much for you was it?" Lara asked with the flicker of a wink.

"Johnny's not feeling too great. Been a full-on year, hasn't it man!" Jamie said, before leaning over and kissing Johnny on the cheek.

"Oh Johnny. You've perhaps eaten something you shouldn't. It mustn't have agreed with you," Lara said. Shooting Johnny a knowing glance.

"Something like that," Johnny grumbled into his bottle.

"JAMIE! DOM! Someone wants to meet you," Tex – the perennially chipper guitar tech – shouted around the door.

Jamie made eyes that he was already occupied.

"Free guitars on offer. It's the dude from Gretsch I told you about."

Dom was already across the room, signaling frantically for his brother to join him.

"Gimme a minute," Jamie said. "And be gentle with Johnny. Don't know what you did to him the other night but he's very fragile."

Johnny grimaced as Jamie stepped past him.

"I'll look after him, Jamie Thorne. Don't you worry. But don't be too long," Lara said with an added purr to her voice.

As soon as the dressing room door had closed behind the twins, Johnny turned to Lara, and hissed under his breath.

"Very clever. Very fuckin' clever aren't we. Just because you acted the perfect cunt and showed me your perfect cunt, don't think I'm going to be dancing to whatever your fucking tune is."

"Tell him then," Lara said matter-of-factly. "Man the fuck up and tell him. Imagine how hurt poor Jamie would be."

Johnny fell silent.

"Exactly. I wonder if they've held your shitty old job open for you, Mr. Manager?"

"I'd love to know what you're trying to prove," Johnny said. "And anyway. There's no proof. None whatsoever. Jamie's hardly going to believe that his greying middle-aged manager is suddenly fighting off sexual advances from models!"

"You don't think?" Lara said with an archly raised eyebrow.

Pulling her mobile phone from the pocket of her leather jacket, she proceeded to scroll through the applications before holding the screen in front of Johnny's face.

The home-made movie crippled Johnny's stomach again and he gulped down the last of his water. The screen showed some dimly light footage of Lara reflected in a mirror with a male head buried deep between her legs. It was hard to make out much detail.

Aside from the green face of the Rolex Submariner that was clearly visible as the 'giver' pushed his hair back. That and the trade mark two stripes on the collar of a Fred Perry T-shirt.

"That proof enough? Like I said. I'm in control," Lara said emphatically.

"Yes. Yes, it is," Johnny said flatly. "But don't," Johnny implored. "Please don't. What does it achieve?"

"What it achieves is that you'll keep your nose out of my business. Think on. Don't try and be so fucking smart in the future. We understand each other?"

The Rock'N'The Roll. 'N That

"We understand each other," Johnny said with a meek nod.

"Good. And by the way. Great action. It's true about the older man being more experienced," Lara said as she leaned across and kissed Johnny on the cheek.

"Look at you two all cosy," Jamie said as he returned, carrying a brand new Gretsch guitar case. "Free guitars for me and Dom. How fuckin' sick is that!"

"Nice," Johnny said, struggling to get his words out of his bottom of the bird-cage dry throat.

"What were you showing Johnny?" Jamie asked.

"Just my latest sex-tape," Lara said sarcastically. "Looks nothing like me. She's coyote-ugly."

Scrolling through her phone again, she handed it to Jamie.

Johnny thought he'd be sick there and then as he felt his eyes widen and his stomach constrict simultaneously.

"Wicked!" Jamie said. "You must have been really close. I didn't spot you."

"I love it in the pit," Lara laughed. "You know me. Can't get enough of the rock and the roll. Especially you guys."

Trying to contain his relief, Johnny excused himself to go to the bathroom.

"Is he okay?" Lara asked, feigning concern with consummate ease.

"Just a bit burnt out I think," Jamie replied. "He'll be fine. We've got a couple of weeks off over Christmas."

"Christmas. That reminds me," Lara said. "I've got you a Christmas present. I hope you haven't forgotten mine…"

***

"I can't wait to get home," Danny said as they queued at JFK Airport. "I've missed my girls."

"Yeah. We could tell that in Vegas," Dominic said smugly.

"Err. What happens in Ve—" Danny started to say.

"Don't give me that bollocks of a cliché," Dom snorted. "You couldn't wait for that stripper to drag you back for a private dance."

"If you hadn't wanted to go in there, it would never have happened," Danny replied.

"My fault then, isn't it? Obviously," Dom sneered.

Shaking his head and returning to his iPad, Danny proceeded to grumble to himself for the next couple of minutes.

As they finally passed through US Customs, the band stripped off their coats, shoes, belts and passed them through for inspection.

"Pain in the arse, this. Every time we take a fuckin' flight," Danny moaned as he collected his belongings from the grey plastic tray.

"Excuse me sir. Is this yours?" asked the burly Customs official as Jamie's personal effects passed in front of him.

Jamie froze on the spot as the officer opened his bag and took out his iPad and opened the black plastic sleeve.

Sensing Jamie's panic, Johnny put his hand up. "No, that's mine. I must have left it at the hotel. Wondered where it was."

Radioing through to his colleagues, he said, "Would you mind collecting the remainder of your belongings and stepping this way please, sir."

"But Johnny," Jamie whispered.

With a quick shake of his head, Johnny silenced Jamie and followed the Customs officers, struggling to walk and hold his jeans up as he hadn't had time to replace his belt.

**

"Sir. Is this your iPad? Even though you weren't carrying it?" asked the Customs officer.

The iPad sat dead centre of the cold-metal table in the interview room. And alongside it sat a small incriminating plastic baggie with the dregs of some so far unidentified white powder.

"I left it on our tour bus and Jamie must have picked it up for me," Johnny said as confidently as he could.

"And the powder? Can you tell me what it is?"

"Bit of coke. I bought it from a guy at the aftershow last night. Not really my thing, as a rule."

"Really?" said the officer disbelievingly. "We'll be checking what it is. But in the meantime, we will be holding you here and suggest you call your lawyer…"

**

"Fuckin' Hell J!" hissed Dominic. "I can't believe you'd carry anything through customs! How fuckin' stupid."

"I forgot," Jamie said slowly. "I honestly forgot about it."

"What do we always get told! Dump anything before you get to the fuckin' airport," Dominic said as he stared at his brother.

"Fuck's sake," Jamie said as he put his head between his hands.

"Look bro. If you say it was only a tiny amount, he'll get off with a fine. They're not going to bang him up."

"I know. A bit of coke. They won't send him down for that. Surely." The lie paining Jamie as soon as it left his lips.

"And all that fuckin' waiting around whilst they searched our gear. We could've missed our flight!" Dom said.

"I said I'm sorry. I just forgot," Jamie whispered.

"Well. It'll be Johnny that you need to say sorry to. He fell on the fuckin' grenade for you."

"I know. I can't believe he'd do that for me…"

Chapter 61

"Fuck! Is it good to see you," Jamie said as he hugged Johnny.

Having established when his return flight was due to land, Jamie and Dominic had taken a taxi to Manchester Airport.

"How was *Con Air* for you then man? Did they manacle you to the seat?" Dominic asked, as he then mirrored Jamie's hug.

"Very fuckin' funny," a weary looking Johnny replied. "Thanks for meeting me. Good to see a friendly face. That was a fuckin' nightmare."

"So just the fine then?" Jamie asked.

"Two grand fine and I won't be going to the Land of the Free again in a hurry. No chance of getting back in now. But rather me than you, eh. At least you lot can still conquer America!" Johnny said, putting on the bravest of faces.

"Yeah. Thanks man, I owe you," Jamie replied sheepishly.

"I owe you! There's an understatement," Dominic added unnecessarily.

"Fuck's sake, Dom," Jamie said.

"Yeah okay. Right. Think this calls for a pint," Dominic said as he flagged a taxi down.

"Just the one," Johnny mumbled, still clearly a little shell-shocked by the past thirty-six hours. "You're buying."

Arriving at a quiet pub not far from Dominic's 'House on the Hill', Jamie and Johnny took a seat whilst Dominic called the drinks in.

"We need to talk," Johnny said as soon as Dom was occupied with the round.

"What?" Jamie asked, feeling the guilt flush his cheeks.

"You know. The fuckin' drugs. Wasn't just a bit of sniff!"

"I don't know what you mean," Jamie said, the gulp in his throat giving him away all too easily.

"It'll wait, J. But fuck. Don't do this to us. You're way, way better than that shit," Johnny said as he put his hand on the back of Jamie's.

"If I knew what you were banging on about, I could agree with you," Jamie relied tersely.

"It'll wait, J. But it's good to be home with my arse intact. I'm still way too pretty for prison," Johnny said as he accepted the pint off Dominic.

He raised his pint to meet the brothers' glasses. "Thank fuck!" Johnny said succinctly.

"You really fell on a grenade there man," Dominic said, "I've already told this dick he should have dumped it. Schoolboy error."

"Yeah Dom. You have told me. Many times. And I fucked up. I know that," Jamie said quietly.

"Look. It's done now. Better me than you. Band's never gonna crack America without a lead singer. Simple as that," Johnny said. "They'll let me back in one day. Maybe."

Jamie exhaled wistfully. His brother then put an arm around his shoulders, realising quite how manifest Jamie's guilt was.

"Few weeks off now. It'll do us all good. Next tour starts in February. Noses clean until then, eh," Johnny said as he drained the last of his pint. "My round. That one didn't even touch the sides."

"What you doing for Christmas, Johnny?" Dominic asked. "You should come around to ours. You're coming, aren't you J? And Mum will be coming along."

"Didn't know you could cook? Getting proper domesticated, aren't you?" Jamie said.

"Fuck that. Eleanor has got some caterers sorted. You both gonna come? Christmas at the new Mr. & Mrs. Dominic Thornes'. Still can't get my head round that," Dominic said.

"I'll see my mum during the day but if it's after that then count me in," Johnny said. "Why not?" *Aside from the prickly situations with Cally*, he thought.

"Good for me," Jamie said.

"Wicked," Dominic said. "Mikee said he'll come along after he's finished at his. I'm still working on D-Mo."

"Here's to Christmas dinner at your House on the Hill," Johnny said. "Looking forward to it."

***

Dumping his bag down in his apartment, and bladder fit to burst after the three rapid pints followed by what felt like an interminably long taxi ride,

Johnny slumped onto the toilet and sighing, head in hands, and luxuriated in what he termed a 'lady wee'.

A much-needed body and soul cleansing shower left him feeling human again, although his emotions were still a maelstrom of relief and guilt after the bands relatively brief American sojourn.

A stag-do. A marriage. A major sexual indiscretion. And a *Midnight Express*-esque 'drug bust' had taken its toll. And as Johnny finished shaving, he saw his drawn features reminding him of it all too vividly.

Flipping on his laptop, he browsed through the emails that had been unanswered for the past forty-eight hours.

One sprung out immediately causing his stomach to constrict on itself.

Lara Bearheart.

"I don't fuckin' need this," Johnny said to himself, rubbing a hand across his freshly-moisturised forehead.

"*Hello Johnny Harrison. Well aren't we the hero of the hour! Somebody got a guilty conscience? I'm sure Jamie was suitably grateful. But why wouldn't he be? And the lengths someone will go to not be allowed back into America. But don't worry, Johnny, I'll be over in England a lot next year. Lots of new lines to promote. Anyway, you bask in your moment of self-sacrifice. You deserve it. No hard-feelings. And by the way. It was my pleasure.... Happy holidays. Lara*"

"Cunt," Johnny hissed as his mind flashed back to that last ten minutes in her hotel suite.

And as much as he tried, it was nigh on impossible to delete from his wank-bank…

Chapter 62

"Hello stranger. Long time no see! Few more grey hairs since last time. I would have bought you some 'Just for Men' for your secret Santa if I'd known," Cally said, sitting herself next to Johnny.

Having positioned himself under the ozone eroding patio heater, Johnny had steadily polished off several large JDs in an alcohol-fueled attempt to assuage his omnipresent guilt whenever he was around Jamie.

This guilt was magnified as Jamie was constantly acting like he now had a life-debt to Johnny after the airport incident.

"Hiya Cally. Yeah, proper silver fox these days. All that rock and the roll catching up with me," he said as he ran his hand through his silver flashed hair. "How are you? It's good to see you." He then leaned across and kissed her warmly on both cheeks.

"Looks good longer as well. Nothing like a mid-life crisis, eh? Grow your hair and tour the world with a band," Cally replied. The dig wasn't lost on Johnny.

"Ooh. Very cruel. I'm hoping that the open-top sports car and trophy blonde are waiting for me under the Christmas tree."

Cally huddled closer to Johnny. "Budge across, you're hogging all the heat."

Laughing softly, Johnny hunched along and allowed Cally some of the artificial heat that was permitting them to sit outside on this seasonally satisfyingly frosty Christmas Day. "Great view isn't it?"

"He's got good taste. He surprises me at times. Jamie was always the sensitive one. But look at this place. And he's married! One of my baby boys a married man!" Cally said. Her tinkling laugh at the end of the sentence caused Johnny to briefly close his eyes and bask in the moment.

"She's beautiful. And he seems really happy. It'll be good for him," Johnny said.

"I'm worried because he's so young. But he seems to have really grown up the past few months. And rather this than the, ahem, constant womanising," Cally said, edging closer into Johnny's side.

The Rock'N'The Roll. 'N That

Draining his glass, Johnny laughed, "C'mon, he was j—"

"Stop! If you're going to give me that cliché about him just being a young lad in a band. He didn't even know the names of half the girls he was sleeping with."

"I was going to say good looking, and really talented young lad in a band. But I won't," Johnny deadpanned.

"Funny as ever, I see," Cally replied, more than a little flirtatiously.

"Same old Johnny." Slapping his hand to his forehead, he said, "Fuck. I've just referred to myself in the third person! It's official. I've been lost to the beast of rock 'n' roll!"

"I always knew it," Cally said. "Look. I know it's not really the time, but I do understand why you said what you did."

"What?" Johnny replied, gulping hard.

"Putting the band before…" Cally's words trailed off as she stared out across the Lancashire hills.

Placing an arm around her shoulder, Johnny pulled her into his side. With a slow shake of his head, he said, "You don't know just how difficult that was. But thank you."

"It hurt, Johnny. But I understood after a while. By the way. Terrible Christmas Jumper. You win!"

"This? It's not that bad? Wait till you see Mikee's!" Taking her chin between his finger and thumb and looking into her eyes, he said, "And thank you. I've never stopped caring though. Never."

"Me neither. Now go and get me a top-up," Cally said, holding out her empty red wine glass.

***

The Christmas dinner was a perfect occasion. Both Mikee – with a new and equally spectacularly tattooed girlfriend in tow – and D-Mo with Dee and baby Dominique all turned up to make it a full-on Lonely Souls affair.

And Mikee's cap sleeve Christmas jumper did indeed trump Johnny's for crass festive tackiness.

Standing at the foot of the table, Dominic stood and clapped his hands together. "Right. Shut it. You noisy rabble! Thank you."

Raising a glass of expensive Champagne, he said, "I just wanted to say on behalf of me and my beautiful new wife that I love each and every one of you. This has been the best year of my life by a fuckin' mile!"

"Language, Dominic!" scolded Cally, then giggled behind her hand.

"Yeah. Thanks Mum. Anyhow. Here's to next year and more of the same."

"Another wife? You're shameless, Dom," Danny shouted, before snapping his fingers in delight at his own joke.

He was quickly put in his place when Dee aimed a discreet elbow jab into his ribs.

"Your turn next D-Mo. Make an honest woman of her before she realises that she's too good for you! Anyhow. Next year. Our biggest tour ever. Album number three and worldwide domination baby!"

Hands were smacked on the table and shouts and whoops of encouragement filled the room.

Leaning over and kissing Eleanor, Dominic lifted his glass over his head. "BEST BAND IN THE WORLD!"

Which was echoed back by the exclusive guestlist.

***

Waking up, Johnny rubbed at his eyes, and then glanced to his right.

Cally.

They had shared a taxi back in the direction of Manchester and a nightcap at Johnny's had been mutually agreed upon.

And this had led to the inevitable.

Having made eyes at each other throughout the lavish Christmas dinner, the nightcap had been sidestepped and a long embrace on the sofa had swiftly led to the bedroom.

Rising as slowly as he could and searching for anything to cover his nudity, Johnny winced as the bed creaked slightly. Grabbing at a pair of boxer shorts, he tiptoed to the bathroom.

"You weren't so modest last night," he heard Cally say hoarsely.

"You want a coffee?"

"And a fruit juice please. But don't think that this counts as breakfast in bed for one minute," she replied after a clearing of her throat.

"Gimme a minute," Johnny said. Turning on the bathroom tap so she couldn't hear him relieve himself through the paper-thin apartment walls, he returned a few minutes later with the coffees and juice on a tray.

"Hmm, thank you," Cally said as she gulped back the juice.

Sitting down on the bed next to her, Johnny felt his stomach tighten as the quilt dropped away as she leant her head back to empty the glass.

She let the sheets sit in her lap and smiled up at Johnny.

"Don't say anything." Looking her straight in the eye, he said, "You know. But I'll say it anyhow."

Cally went to speak but Johnny held up a finger to shush her.

"You know what I'm going to say. I love you. I've loved you for ages."

"I knew," Cally replied softly. "But where does this leave us? What's changed?"

Johnny sighed before draining his juice in one. Wiping the back of his hand across his mouth, he said, "I don't know." Hesitating as he sought the right words. "I want to be with you…"

Frowning slightly, "So you admit to being in love with me and are going to tell Jamie and Dominic about us then?"

"I will. I'll quit the band. But n—"

"When, though," Cally snapped. "And don't you dare say when the time's right! But in the meantime, come here and kiss me like you mean it…"

Chapter 63

Reeling to the back door of his house, Jamie fumbled with the lock, his breath catching in short sharp gasps. Air. He needed fresh air. Desperately.

Dropping to his knees, he sucked up the cold winter air in grateful but difficult gulps.

Falling onto his backside, Jamie put his head between his knees and started to take in measured breaths. Wiping the hyper-ventilation induced tears from his eyes, he leant back on the cold stone wall, the dampness cooling his prickly sweats.

"What the fuck," he mumbled repeatedly.

Returning to his abandoned laptop, he refreshed the screen that had been the catalyst to his anguish.

An 'open-heart confessional' interview with Lara in an American glossy magazine.

The headline had sent Jamie's world spinning off its axis.

"No, I'm not drinking. I'm having a baby!"

The article had gone on to detail how Lara had collapsed at a fashion event and then been carried out and an ambulance called.

This hadn't been alcohol-induced, but down to severe morning sickness leaving her dehydrated.

The killer sentence had been Lara's sign off to the interviewer – "I'm happy. So happy. I'm going to have a little rock star baby…"

This isn't happening, he'd said to himself.

Picking up his mobile, he called Johnny. Controlling his breathing again, he collapsed back in the sofa with relief when Johnny answered upon the first ring.

"J. How are ya man?"

"Hey Johnny. You about? I need to see you. Now."

"Fuck. You okay, Jamie? Sure. Yeah. Want me to come across to you? I'll be with you in half an hour."

"Thanks Johnny. Soon as you can. Please…"

***

Jumping in his car. Johnny punched the stereo off as he tried to clear his head.

He knew that Jamie was not one to make a drama of things, so this had to be a matter of urgency.

Lara?

Cally?

Both?

Johnny shook his head to clear his self-absorbed thoughts.

Jamie had clearly got a problem and had called him. *Don't make it all about you*, he pondered to himself.

Door-to-door in twenty-two minutes, he buzzed the intercom and Jamie buzzed the gates open without speaking.

Knocking twice on the door, Johnny pulled his large-check overcoat around him as he waited for Jamie to open the door.

The door opened, and Jamie stood before him in his boxer shorts and his 'unique' Vegas T-shirt – Mikee's jutting jaw staring up at Johnny and looking a lot more at ease than Jamie currently did.

"Fuckin' hell. Johnny, I can't go on tour. I need to get a flight to America. Now."

"Whoa! Slow down, J. What's wrong?" Putting a reassuring hand on Jamie's shoulder, he said, "Tell me. Sit down. Tell me what the fuck's happened."

"It's Lara."

Johnny tried to disguise his panic, but only needed to do so for a matter of seconds.

"Lara. She's pregnant. And says it's mine."

Slumping back into the sofa, Jamie's breaths again began to quicken sharply.

"How the fuck did this happen. Stupid question," Johnny said, correcting himself.

"Look at my laptop. Read the interview. I found out in a fuckin' magazine interview. What the fuck?"

Skimming through the article, Johnny kept glancing up at Jamie, who was now sat with his head between his legs again, sucking up oxygen and wiping tears away.

Letting out a low whistle, Johnny blinked in disbelief. "Fuck. I can't believe she hasn't spoken to you about this. Bang out of order."

"I know," Jamie mumbled. "I can't cope with this. I have to go and see her. Today."

"But the tour starts in two days, Jamie."

Realising the crass insensitivity of his comment, Johnny held up an apologetic hand.

Jamie looked little-boy lost and the last thing he needed to hear was his pending tour commitments.

"Call her. You need to speak to her. As soon as possible."

"I will," Jamie said. "Will you stay whilst I speak to her?"

"Of course, I will man. I'm here for you. Always."

***

"You said that last night in Edinburgh," Dominic said, a look of brotherly concern on his face.

"I'll be fine," Jamie replied.

The inner sanctum of the band and crew – and Johnny – were the only people Jamie was communicating with. He'd refused all press/radio/fan meet and greets, citing a sore throat.

Which probably was not far off the truth. He had been delivering his vocals in a fit to breaking point style, his vocal chords straining like an errant bull terrier yanking at its leash.

Sitting nursing a beer in the sterile breeze block dressing room, Johnny pulled absentmindedly at a loose thread on the sleeve of his check shirt – the ubiquitous uniform of the middle-aged man – and looked across at Jamie.

Dealing with the triple whammy of his own personal sexual interaction with Lara, a burgeoning romance with the twins' mother and Jamie's obvious demons following the 'media baby' bombshell.

Jamie had confided in him that they hadn't even had sex the last time they had met – after their MSG show – but Lara was adamant he was the 'baby daddy'. He'd been dissuaded from taking the trans-Atlantic trek at Johnny's behest, but was desperate for resolution of the latest twist in his 'relationship' with Lara.

Having to tread carefully with his advice, Johnny had tried to convince him that Lara was consumed by the 'fame game' and that she didn't realise the hurt she caused by her actions. Jamie - still teetering on the brink of inconsolable - nodded solemnly, agreeing to confront her as soon as possible.

Chapter 64

"OY!"

The band were about to navigate a scrum of largely well-intentioned fans as they headed from the sanctuary of their tour bus to the artistes' entrance of the Newcastle O2 Academy.

A metal security fence was teetering precariously as the north-eastern crowd jockeyed for prime position, pushing forward as the band disembarked – who were to a man wearing sunglasses despite the cigarette ash skies.

Last to step off the bus was Johnny, and the second he put his box fresh Adidas clad foot onto the tarmac, he saw the fence topple.

A kettling effect ensued resulting in the band being separated into individual pockets.

Band security was vital at times like this and this was overseen by one man. Major.

A veritable beast of a man, whose collection of jewellery made Mr T look like an agoraphobic supply teacher. He had earned his moniker given the rank he had held within a now defunct Hells Angels chapter.

"OY! YA BIG DAFT CUNT," came the initially faceless shout from the jostling mass.

Mikee, at the rear of the party, pushed on. His considerable bulk easing his passage. Until.

"AYE! YOU. YOU UGLY TWAT!" the abusive Geordie shout persisted.

Wisely he kept his head down. He was forced to stop as the bottleneck would not ease up given the numbers in front of Jamie.

"FUCK. YOU'RE EVEN UGLIER CLOSE UP! YOU JACAMO WEARING CUNT!" The sartorial insult was bellowed down Mikee's ear.

Glancing to his left, he saw the deliverer of such hostile tidings – a humpty-dumpty faced bloke in his late twenties. Sporting a beer stained Newcastle United polo shirt with a chunky gold rope chain worn resplendently outside it. Flouting his wealth for all the world to see.

Offended more by the fact that this badly dressed miscreant should question his own wardrobe, Mikee leant forward and delivered the shortest and sharpest of headbutts.

The reaction to his action was devastating.

The discourteous Geordie's nose exploded like a bottle of ketchup that had been run over by a ten-tonne truck.

Blood formed in a sash down the front of the t-shirt. Screams went up as he collected himself and windmilled a sovereign-clad fist towards Mikee.

Catching the frame of Mikee's Vegas-bought Ray-Bans resulted in a second act of violence. Swinging an elbow into the already splattered nose, the abuser collapsed to the floor in a mess of humiliation and cartilage.

He rose to his knees and held the bridge of his nose. His little finger raised at a right angle much to Mikee's amusement.

"*YOOFRUCKINCRUNTI'MGONNASUEYERFRUCKINBIGTIMEYER BASTARD!*"

A swift yank on the collar of his denim jacket and Major was dragging the indignant drummer into the confines of the venue.

An hour later and one cancelled show.

"Fuck 'em," D-Mo said emphatically. "If they fuck with the band then they don't deserve a show."

"Not quite that simple. As much as I admire your sentiment, it's me that'll have to sort this fucking mess out with the promoter. It'll cost us a few quid if the shows not re-arranged," Johnny said.

A soundcheck had been dispensed with, given that they were sans drummer and unlikely to play that evening. Cups of coffee were being sipped at whilst they waited for news on Mikee's arrest.

"Didn't see it. Unfortunately," Dominic added helpfully. "But he must have given him a proper crack."

"Not helping dude," Johnny said as he checked his iPhone for the umpteenth time.

Jamie sat silently in the corner of the stark dressing room, meticulously peeling an AAA sticker from the flight case of his guitar.

An all-consuming silence hung over them like the onset of January 2nd.

Then Johnny's phone rang like a digital harbinger of doom.

"Charged with GBH and they are going to hold him overnight," Johnny reported dolefully.

"Back to the hotel then," Dominic said.

"And batten down the drawbridge to protect us from the angry locals," Johnny added. "I'll get Major and see if the coasts clear at the back."

"Bound to be a fuckin' scrape of press out there by now," Jamie muttered, before returning to the last corner of the sticker that was resolutely refusing to give up without a fight.

"Only you two left without a conviction," D-Mo piped up cheerily, nodding in the twins' direction.

"Really not helping Danny. Not fucking helping at all," Johnny said.

***

"Not great," Johnny said, as he sat on his hotel bed swathed in a freshly laundered towelling robe. He laughed to himself when he realised he was pulling his stomach in even though he was only chatting to Cally over the phone. Breathing out slightly, he pulled the robe across the 'tour paunch' he felt he had amassed.

"Oh no! It's just dreadful what she has done. My poor Jamie. I just never thought she'd be like that. She was lovely to me when I met her at Glastonbury," Cally said. The pain crystal clear in her voice.

"The lovely Lara has many facets unfortunately. I think Jamie reckoned he knew her. Or she was more like her real self when they were together. Which I think she was most of the time," Johnny said in between sips of room service brandy.

"He'll be okay. I'm sure he will. He'll just retreat into himself for a bit. He'd do it as a little boy if he was upset. Dominic was always a lot more brash. Even when they were little, he'd come out fighting whilst Jamie would brood on stuff."

"You know I'll be looking out for him more than ever," Johnny said, closing his eyes as the last of the brandy soothed him.

"I know. Thank you."

"I miss you. Big time," Johnny said.

"I know that too," Cally said. "I'll see you at the Manchester shows though."

"Night lovely lady."

"Night Johnny."

Hanging up, Johnny thought about another brandy, just to see him on his way too sleep. The conversation with Cally felt like a snatch of normality. Although since having told he loved her, they'd hardly seen each other given his workload.

***

"Do the '*I Fought the Law*' thing you did for me in America," Danny implored as the tour-bus pulled up outside Newcastle Central Police Station.

"It won't be a funny a second time," Dominic said as he offered out a handshake to the hulking drummer.

Mikee had been released without charge, as the recipient of his expertly aimed head butt had decided against furthering the case. Guestlist places and some signed merch had seen to that. Much against Mikee's better judgement.

"I'd rather have taken the rap than have that fucker think he's got the better of me," Mikee said as he took up his place on the bus. Having flipped the finger to the waiting photographers, as he mock lunged at them, he'd also guaranteed his place in tomorrow's tabloids.

"Anyhow. Get me out of this shithole and find me something to eat. Room service was fuckin' shite in there."

Jamie looked on stoically – a brooding presence at the back of the bus. "Calm down. He's not done twenty years on Robben Island."

Johnny raised an eyebrow at Jamie, who reverted to staring out of the window, barely blinking such was his trance-like state.

Which would not to be helped by the latest press release from Lara which Johnny had just been sent by the label's press officer.

The edited lowlights surrounding her fictitious miscarriage made for cringeworthy reading.

"*I'm heartbroken. I've lost a real living thing. A soul has died inside me and with him – I'm sure it was a boy – a part of me has died. I'm fine physically but mentally I'm in pieces. My sympathy goes out to all the other women who have suffered this loss. I'm going to take some time out to come to terms with this and grieve. I hope people respect my loss and privacy during this time…*"

"Fucking horrible cunt," Johnny said to himself.

He'd been bracing themselves for Lara's 'closure' of this fabricated stunt, but this interview would do Jamie no good at all, Johnny thought.

A 'fake pregnancy' story had been concocted by Lara's people in an attempt to save face after Lara had dropped a stop-a-runaway-truck-in-its-tracks strength speedball. The resultant publicity needed extinguishing and the phantom pregnancy/miscarriage yarn did the job.

The only collateral damage being Jamie's mental wellbeing.

Re-reading the piece to take in the bare-faced horror of her crassness, Johnny shook his head in disgust and pondered about when to break it to Jamie.

***

The kettle steamed almost at boiling point and Jamie stood transfixed by the droplets that formed on the mirror in his hotel room.

Passing a hand quickly through the hot vapour, Jamie then closed his eyes and held his right hand directly over the kettle.

1.2.3.4.

I'll stop when it gets unbearable.

Now.

Fuck.

The pain seared through his hand and up his arm as angry blisters bubbled on the palm of his hand. And Jamie looked at them. Focussing on it. Channelling it. Feeding on it. Wanting it to consume him. To take away his inner pain.

***

"Glad that you're back fit Jamie. Must have been annoying to have to cancel four dates after your accident," Sally said as she sat alongside Jamie at the back of the bus.

It had been agreed that Sally Valley would spend 24 hours on the road with the band – taking in two gigs and interviewing them for an NME cover story.

"Yeah. I should be getting an underling to make hot drinks for me," Jamie deadpanned.

"I'm sure you can afford it these days," Sally said with a laugh.

"I'm not like that though!" Jamie snapped.

Johnny was earwigging and felt Jamie was still way too prickly for any sort of an interview. Even to a 'friend of the band' like Sally.

"I didn't mean it like that," Sally replied defensively.

"It's not about the money. Never has been."

"But it's a by-product of any band when they are successful. It's not a criticism, Jamie. Honest it's not."

Accessing an application on his iPhone, Jamie held the screen in front of Sally's face.

The Rock 'N' The Roll. 'N That

"How much?"

"Sorry?" she replied.

"How much? What does the balance say?" Jamie asked. A serious look on his face. His blue eyes flashing with frustration.

"Thirty-two grand. And a few quid. Nice," Sally said.

Returning to his phone for a minute, Jamie again held up the phone.

"How much now?"

"Fuck! Twelve grand. What the fuck have you just done?"

"Given twenty grand to charity. Their need is greater than mine." Letting out a heavy sigh, he said, "That's what I think of money. Not fuckin' bothered."

"Right Jamie. I get your point. Do you want me to print that?" Sally asked, shaken by this previously unseen side of Jamie.

"It hardly makes me Richie Manic but it's your call," Jamie said as he put the phone down on the table in front of him and proceeded to stare out of the blacked-out bus-window.

***

"Doesn't make pretty reading, J. I'm sorry man. It's not what you needed but we knew it was coming," Johnny said as they sat in Jamie's hotel room, sipping on an early morning coffee.

"I know man, but reading it in black and white. Fuck. It's just so calculated," Jamie replied with an exasperated shake of his head, pushing a hand through his ruffled 'bed hair'.

Leaning back in the armchair, positioned to the foot of the bed, Johnny looked at Jamie. The most popular 'new' rock star in the country. A prodigiously talented songwriter. Ridiculously good looking. And one of the most genuine people you could hope to meet. Yet, sat in front of him now, Johnny saw a helpless young man. Unable to comprehend what he had unwittingly been party to.

"It's hard to see you like this. What the fuck was that all about with Sally on the bus yesterday?" Johnny said as he drained his cup.

Bristling at the mention of his impromptu charitable donation, he said, "Fuck it. Shows what's important and what isn't. What does it matter? It'll be back in my bank before I know it looking at the way second album is selling. I'd do it again," Jamie said, his eyes not leaving Johnny's once. "You know I didn't start this band to make money, don't you?"

Jamie said this more as a statement than a question.

"Course I do, man!" Johnny replied without missing a beat.

"I'm in this so I can play my tunes with our band and stand there at the end of the night with my guitar held over my head. That fucking simple," Jamie said in a steady tone with his jaw set tight. It sounded like the ultimate rock 'n' roll mission statement coming from him.

"I get it," Johnny said, breaking away from Jamie's stare. "The people that love you are just worried you know. You have the accident with your hand. You're keeping yourself to yourself so much. It's only because we care."

"I know you spoke to my mum," Jamie said. An almost challenging tone to his voice.

"Yeah. That's no secret. She was worried when she heard about your hand. I told what happened. You had an accident."

Sighing deeply, Jamie rubbed the palms of his hands across his face, pulling the skin taut across his cheekbones.

"She's worried. If she doesn't hear the truth from us. From me. All she's got is the bullshit in the papers and that."

"I know," Jamie replied. "But that's the problem. Whatever I do. I can read what I did on any day by just reading Twitter or some such shite!" Letting out a frustrated grimace, he said, "I mean for fuck's sake, there was a video on YouTube of me walking down the street a couple of weeks ago. What the fuck is all that about?"

"We've done this before, J. You do what you do, and the public see you as their property," Johnny said.

"Once the tour's done, I'm off for a few months. I need a break from all this. Go somewhere where I can walk down the street without any hassle," Jamie said.

"You've got another three months," Johnny replied. He knew the exact date was closer to four but felt that pedantry was perhaps not what was needed right now. "You want some advice?"

"Go on," Jamie said leaning forward on his elbows.

"Don't just go out and have meaningless cheap and dirty sex. You'll know when you're ready. And it's not as if it'll be hard to find when you are. But, take it from someone who cares. It'll do you more harm than good," Johnny said, his gaze not dropping once as he looked at the vulnerable figure in front of him.

Laughing softly, Jamie smiled at Johnny. "That's the absolute opposite of what anybody else would say." He cracked a grin. "And that's why I love you man."

"Just get your head down. Talk to me. Talk to the rest of 'em. As fucking daft as they might appear at times. They all love you, J. No-one likes to see you struggling."

The Rock 'N' The Roll. 'N That

"I can do it. I love playing and being with the others. I just don't need all the bullshit."

"I've got your back, J. You know that," Johnny said as he lifted himself out of the armchair, trying to ignore the faint creak from his knees as he did so.

"Thanks man," Jamie said as he started to get out of bed.

"Woah! Keep it decent," Johnny said as he put a hand to his eyes.

"Don't worry I'm dressed," Jamie said as he stood up, revealing a pair of white Calvin Klein trunks. "If you ever let me down, then it's time to jack it all in. Come here."

Hugging with a back slap, Jamie kissed Johnny on the cheek. "Right. I'll be down in half an hour. Show to do tonight. I'll be right."

"I know man," Johnny said, the tightening feeling in his stomach a testimony to his own involvement with Lara. And the still undisclosed relationship with Cally.

***

"GOODNIGHT! CHEERS LIVERPOOL. REMEMBER THIS GIG IN TWENTY YEARS WHEN YOU'RE BUYING THE VIRTUAL REALITY HOLOGRAM 20TH ANNIVERSARY EDITION OF OUR ALBUM," Jamie shouted as he adjusted his red scarf and glancing over at Dominic who was stifling a smirk.

Composing himself as he made a minor adjustment to the tuning of his flame red Gretsch guitar, Dominic stamped on one of his many effects pedals. "YOU FUCKING READY FOR THIS? LIVERPOOL. I WANT TO SEE PANDEMONIUM OUT THERE! FUCKIN' PANDEMONIUM!"

As one, Jamie, Dominic and Dan leant into their mics. "SALVATION!"

And with that they burst out a caustic rendition of their biggest anthem. The song sucked the breath out of the sweat sodden crowd who were baying for more even before Dominic had finished his coruscating solo.

Having left the stage and changed his T-shirt, Jamie picked up an acoustic guitar and with the crowd thinning out to a few hundred stragglers, returned to the centre of the stage.

There, he struck up a minor chord. A sole spotlight picked him out as the lights engineer hastily realised the show wasn't quite over.

"This is a new song," Jamie announced. "And no fuckin' shouting. It's a very personal song. And any mobile phones, I'm off. This is called 'Lies'.

"There's a hole in your chest where your heart should be. Corrosion of the soul is eating you whole. Lies and lies and lies. At any price for you. Lies and lies and lies, so easy to you. Lies and lies and lies like a poison in you. Wicked lies behind pinprick eye. Lies and lies, so easy to you. Catwalk smile is just a façade, losing a life wasn't too hard. Lies and lies and lies. At any price for you. Lies and lies, so easy to you..."

His voice was a ragged yowl as he repeated the refrain of the chorus.

Followed by a beautifully cracked version of 'Long Time Dead', Jamie left the stage with a mumbled thank you.

Having left the dressing room to stand at the side of the stage, the rest of the band and Johnny hadn't said a word as they absorbed Jamie's cathartic encore.

Hugging his twin brother too him, Dom said, "Fuck me, J. No guessing who that song is about!"

"It's Lara, isn't it," Danny said with a sage nod of his head.

"Check out the brains on Einstein," Dominic said, barely able to keep his face straight. "When did you write that, bro? You kept it a bit fuckin' quiet!"

"This afternoon. In the hotel. After soundcheck," Jamie said. The relief seemed to be washing off him after the impromptu solo spot.

"Solo spots at the end of the show. I told you coming along to see Springsteen would do you good," Johnny said with a wry smile.

"She won't fuckin' like it when she hears it," Mikee said – stripped to the waist and towelling himself down, admiring his tattoos as ever.

"That's the idea," Jamie said. "Right. Now who fancies a proper beer? Get really big. Just us."

"Later. Let's work on that tune before the gear gets loaded out. The sound desk can record it for us," Dominic said as he pushed Jamie back towards the stage. "I've got a wicked fuckin' middle eight for it…"

***

The tour concluded, unsurprisingly, in Manchester.

A record breaking five consecutive nights at their hometown's Apollo Theatre. The promoters had pushed for an Arena date, but both Johnny and the band had been adamant that they wanted to reward the citizens of Manchester with a far more up close and personal show.

As Johnny milled around the backstage area, a constant stream of well-wishers and blaggers wanting to shake his hand and wish him well, he felt his phone vibrate.

Reflexively unlocking his iPhone, Johnny saw that he had mail. Glugging back his lager, he flipped open the inbox.

Lara.

A missive from Ms Bearheart herself.

His stomach tightened as he read the content.

'Hey Mr Harrison. On the road with your boys. Hope you are keeping your ass out of trouble. I know how you can be so easily led astray. You won't be surprised to find out that I've seen Jamie's new little song on YouTube. I'm so not fucking happy, Johnny. I know that songs about me. It's not even close to subtle. I'll fucking sue and drop your ass so far in the shit if that song makes it on to an album. Look, I know I hurt Jamie, but this is way out of line. Tell him to drop the song, Johnny. Or else. Love & shit & that. Lara x'

"Bitch. Fucking evil bitch," Johnny hissed to himself.

"What's up man?" shouted Danny as he walked out of the packed-to-the-rafters dressing room. Cigarette behind his ear. Shades on. His daughter cradled in one arm, nursing a beer with the other hand. Rock 'n' roll and domesticity in one Irish Mancunian package.

"Just work mither, D-Mo. Won't stop me enjoying this. Last night of the tour. Can you believe it?"

"I know. It's been fuckin' outstanding. I'm proper shagged but gimme a week off and I'll be ready to be back on it," Danny said as he kissed his daughter tenderly on her forehead. The act of fatherly devotion causing the cigarette to fall from behind his ear and bounce off Dominique's forehead onto the floor.

Scooping it up, Johnny repositioned the cigarette, and patted Danny on the cheek. "I love you man. But word to the wise. Don't let Dee see you smoking when you have little one with you!"

"No danger. The nanny's here. She looks after her when I'm playing."

"This the nannie with the and the?" Johnny asked as he made wide eyes and cupped his hands in front of his chest.

"Yeah. That's her. She's a fuckin' doll but Dee would chop my cock off if I ever went near her!"

"You reckon?" Johnny replied, as ever, loving Danny's inherent naivety.

"Anyhow. Cig and a line and we're ready to fuckin' rock the roll out of Manchester. Gonna blow the fuckin' roof off tonight. My mam and dad are here. Full family together for the first time. They are getting a show tonight…"

Making his excuses, Johnny sought the sanctuary of the promoter's office to process the thinly veiled transatlantic threat.

***

"MANCHESTER! BEST FUCKING BAND IN THE BEST FUCKING CITY IN THE WORLD! THIS HAS BEEN A SPECIAL FEW NIGHTS FOR US. I HOPE YOU'VE ENJOYED IT AS MUCH AS WE HAVE," Jamie shouted, his guitar held over his head triumphantly.

Taking the lead from his brother, Dominic, his shoulder length blond hair stuck to his face in wet tendrils, looked out across the crowd. "YOU FUCKING READY MANCHESTER? YOU READY FOR YOUR SALVATION?"

The Pavlovian response was a euphoric scream, the audience baying for the band's signature anthem.

"HERE IT IS! LAST SONG ON THE LAST NIGHT OF OUR TOUR. THIS IS ALL YOURS MANCHESTER!"

No matter how many times Johnny had heard the track, from its rehearsal room infancy to booming out of double-decker bus sized speakers at festivals, it still blew him away. And the ferocity that it was played at seemed to have risen throughout this latest tour, Dominic's playing reaching heights no-one had ever anticipated.

The psychedelic feedback faded out, and putting their instruments down, the band hugged as one before taking a bow in front of the delirious crowd.

***

Laughing softly, and sounding remarkably like his mum, Jamie smiled at Johnny. "It's been a tough one at times, but I couldn't have got through this tour without you. I love yer man. And I'll miss you when I'm gone."

"You still planning on taking off for a bit?" Johnny asked.

"Bags packed. Just a bag and my acoustic. Flight booked to Seattle tomorrow. Kurt's hometown and then travel south and see where I end up," Jamie said.

"We'll all miss you. Just don't be a stranger, eh?"

"I won't but I need some space. A break from all this."

"I know what you mean J, but let's enjoy tonight, put the tour to bed in style," Johnny said.

"You're a good man, Johnny Harrison. And it's your round…"

Chapter 65

"I don't know what to say Jamie. It. It's…" Johnny sat forward on the sofa in his apartment, and stared at the stereo, transfixed by what he had just heard. "It's fucking brilliant but wh—"

"Don't say but what. Tell me what you think of the songs," Jamie said as he paced the apartment, tapping his forefinger metronome like against his lips.

Tanned and looking the picture of health after six anonymous months in the City of Angels, Jamie had returned home having been entirely celibate, alcohol and drug free. Not that any of that triumvirate of vices had been a serious issue, but he wanted to be clean whilst he recorded what he intended to be the band's third album.

"The songs are extraordinary. The whole album works perfectly. But it's your album. It's not the band's," Johnny said almost beseechingly.

"It can be, though. I'm going to take it to them and we'll work on it together. As a band," Jamie said as he pressed playback on the Bose stereo.

***

"Hey man. I know you. You're Jamie from, err, let me get this right. From Lonely Souls. I saw you as a support in New York. Your first album. I fucking love it man!"

***

This chance conversation in a downtown Los Angeles grocery store had led to a very convivial lunch which had led to a recording studio in the Navajo desert. Which had led to Lonely Souls album number three sitting in Johnny's stereo.

"Let me get this right. You met a producer by chance who loved your album and you wrote this on your own in his studio?" Johnny asked, as he rubbed at his chin.

"Jessie Oliver. I'd never heard of him, but he was wicked. Sick studio. I'd written the songs in less than a month. No distractions and then we recorded them. He played drums and bass, I did all the guitar parts," Jamie said.

"And you think the band will re-record their parts just as they are and be happy with that?" Johnny said.

"We'll sit down. Listen to it and yeah, record it as a Lonely Souls album," Jamie said without missing a beat.

Johnny sat silent and pondered the situation. The only self-serving positive from his perspective was that the 'Lies' track was nowhere to be heard. *Every cloud and that,* he thought.

"It's brilliant, J. It feels like a classic album. They'll go fucking mental for it in America." Shaking his head at the thought of 'the numbers', Johnny returned to the pressing matter of telling the band that album three was a fait accompli having been written 8,000 miles away from Manchester…

"I knew you'd love it," Jamie said, his enthusiasm unbounded by the delicate curveball he had served up.

All Johnny could muster was another mumbled, "It's brilliant," as he thought about the multi-platinum offering he was absorbing.

"Look, I've got to go. Want to catch up with Mum and Dom. I'll leave that disc with you, yeah? I've got three more copies," Jamie said as he stood up quickly, his energy levels preternaturally high.

"Thanks man. I'll guard it with my life," Johnny said. Standing to hug Jamie, he assumed a serious tone. "You do know that this isn't going to play out as straightforward as you'd like?"

"It will. I'm sure it will," Jamie replied matter of factly.

Johnny's eyes widened at the assuredness of Jamie's statement. "I hope you're right J, I really do."

After Jamie had left his apartment, Johnny sat and crushed at his temples with his balled fists.

Mulling over the scenarios, Johnny thousand yard stared through his apartment window across the ever-evolving cityscape.

"You still recording?"

The voice was unmistakeable.

Jamie.

"Yeah dude. You just play and leave me to the twiddling. Make music Jamie."

A second voice that Johnny assumed to be Jessie – who Jamie had spoken about in non-stop glowing terms.

And then some slow minor chords played on an acoustic.

Sitting utterly spellbound for 38 minutes, Johnny listened to 11 tracks of intensely personal dark melodic wonder.

Jamie.

His acoustic.

And a smattering of piano accompaniment.

It was Jamie's *Nebraska*. A dark, introspective solo album. A fucking solo album.

"Fuck me," Johnny whistled to himself.

Not only had the lead singer of Lonely Souls just dropped a class rock album on him, he'd also thrown in a thing of fragile beauty that had left him breathless.

Pressing rewind on the stereo remote, Johnny let out a little laugh. "Well that's the cat amongst the fucking solo project pigeons…"

***

"Fuck sakes, Jamie. I've missed like you wouldn't believe and I'm made up to see you. Shit, it's the longest we've ever been apart. But this! It's your album. It's not us. It's not the fuckin' band!" Dominic said, pulling his hair back into a ponytail as he shook his head slowly.

"It can be though, bro. I want us all to work on it. Make it our album," Jamie implored.

"I need to time to take this in. Fuck, J. It's a solo album innit. That's what it is. I can't believe it. I'm fuckin' stunned."

They sat in silence and listened to the rest of the album, Dominic pulling deeply on a cigarette throughout the playback.

As the last track played to fade, Dominic looked up at his brother and smiled ruefully. "Fuck me. It's brilliant. It really is." Almost at a loss for words. "It's fuckin' brilliant. But it's not ours!"

Jamie nodded slowly trying to assuage his brother's anxieties.

"We've always written together J. Always!" Dom implored. His exasperation not evaporating quite so easily.

"Then let's make it ours. You're a miles better guitarist than I could ever hope to be. Take the guitar parts make them yours. Make it us. And Jessie isn't a patch on D-Mo and Kong. No way. It'll be us. I promise you. Listen to it. Take it with you. Live with it for a couple of weeks and then tell me we can work on it together," Jamie said. Willing his twin brother to be convinced by his pitch.

The Rock'N'The Roll. 'N That

"And what about Danny and Mikee? We keep your little secret from them for a couple of weeks? They're gagging to get back in the studio. Gagging for it. Especially D-Mo. Got to love him!"

"If you can, then yes. We do this and same as ever. It's a Lonely Souls album. Four-way split. Plus Johnny obviously," Jamie said, a smile breaking out across his face.

"Talking of Johnny. He's been seeing a fair bit of Mum," Dominic said.

"They're both consenting adults," Jamie said, a slight frown on his brow as he processed the news.

"Anyhow. I'm going to get off. Me and Eleanor are having some work done on the house. I'm gonna be honest J, I'm not happy about this but I'll listen to it and have a think, yeah?" Dominic said.

"Can't ask for any more than that. Say hiya to Eleanor. I'm off to Mum's now," Jamie said, already planning to ask her about her 'relationship' with Johnny.

***

"He was as good as I had seen him in ages. The break has done you all good. Even you!" said Cally, a flirtatious glint in her eye.

"It's tough on the road doing the rock 'n' the roll. I miss my bed too much these days," Johnny said with a warm laugh. "It's a young man's game."

"You love it. And don't ever try and tell me otherwise."

"I love it. You're right," Johnny said. "Look, there's something I want to chat to you about."

"Go on," Cally said, looking concerned. She tucked her bare feet under her and crossed her arms across her chest.

Johnny glanced down. She's even got pretty feet, he thought to himself. *Fuck. I'm not becoming one of those weird foot fetishists am I....*

"I said I would never talk to you about the band. Y'know, other than to let you know how the lads were and that."

"You did, but you can talk to me. Course you can," Cally said, her azure blue eyes squinting slightly as she furrowed her brow.

"It's Jamie. He's really sorted his shit out in America. Got a handle on his pre-gig panic attacks, seems really calm. Too calm almost. Anyhow. He's recorded an album," Johnny said.

"That's what he does. He's in a band," Cally said, deadpanning as she pulled a face at Johnny.

"Oh haha. Yes. Funnily enough I know that. He's recorded a whole album. A fucking mind-blowingly great album."

"On his own?" Cally asked.

"All on his own. Well. Him and some producer he met. But yeah. All on his own if you mean the other Lonely Souls. Did it in the desert in LA," Johnny said as tapped at the sole of his trainer.

"Very rock 'n' roll I must say," Cally said, trying to make light of the situation.

"All very LA, man," Johnny said, exaggerating the vowels in a passable West Coast American accent. "But it could be really destructive. I know that Dominic is not best pleased. The others don't know yet."

"So why tell me?" Cally asked, the soft tones in her voice so soothing to Johnny.

"Why? I suppose I just want to hear somebody say it'll all work out okay. I've just got a bad feeling. I mean, the album is stunning. As good as they have done. And that's the problem. It's Jamie's album and they'll always know that," Johnny said as he met Cally's gaze.

Every time.

Every time she looked at him, his stomach did that not-unpleasant tightening thing and his problems seemed to melt away.

"Dominic's very stubborn but he's always prepared to listen to Jamie. But I do see your point," Cally said before pursing her lips pensively.

"I just have to let them thrash this one out. I've got an opinion but it's one that gives you splinters in your arse," Johnny said.

Cally frowned at the crude expression.

"You know what I mean. Sitting on the fence and all that."

"I knew perfectly well," Cally replied.

"The album is brilliant. Could be even better after the rest of the band have worked on it. But it's never going to be totally theirs. Suppose it depends how much they want the next step and what alternatives there are."

"I don't envy you, but you just have to let it take its natural course I suppose," Cally said.

"All I can do," Johnny said with a sigh. "Fancy coming out for dinner tonight? No talk of the band. Promise."

"If you promise," Cally said before untucking her feet from beneath her and kissing Johnny softly on the mouth. "But you're paying and I'm picking the restaurant."

Chapter 66

"Who the fuck is this Jessie then?" Danny asked as he paced up and down the rehearsal room, patting his jacket pockets down for his cigarettes.

"I told you. I just bumped into the dude in a store in LA. He had his own studio and it went from there. Simple as that," Jamie said, as he watched Danny walk in concentric circles.

"It's not that simple though, J. We're a band. We're a fuckin' great band and this is just you."

Dominic remained silent as he awaited his bandmate's verdict. Sat in their familiar rehearsal room albeit with an undercurrent of tension.

"What about you, Johnny? What's your opinion? You know how to sort this shit out!" Danny said, having finally settled when he had realised he was out of cigs.

Mikee threw him a packet which he caught, taking one out before tucking it behind his ear. Then deciding he needed an instant fix of carcinogens.

"You got a light too?"

With a slight nod of his head, Mikee tossed D-Mo his Zippo. "And don't fuckin' lose it. That's the third one I've bought this year."

"Cheers Kong," Danny said as he caught the lighter and started to light up in one practiced movement.

"You can't smoke in here D-Mo!" Dominic said in a distinctly un-rock 'n' roll manner.

"Balls to that! I'm in fuckin' shock here," Danny replied as he drew deeply.

"I'll be in fuckin' shock if you set the sprinklers off and ruins all the gear. Fuckin' put it out," Dom snapped.

"Right, right. It's out," Danny said as he took one last drag before extinguishing the cigarette on his boot heel. He then produced a vaping device that looked sizable enough to bring down a light aircraft.

From behind a billow of sickly sweet-smelling vapour, Danny asked, "Go on then Johnny? What about it?"

The Rock'N'The Roll. 'N That

Leaning back against the rehearsal room wall, Johnny looked at the four expectant faces – awaiting his verdict, needing his validation again. *Time to step up Mr. Manager* he thought

Having lived with the album – and its 'hidden' acoustic partner piece – for some two weeks, Johnny was testimony to both the song's brilliance and their unit-shifting potential.

Picking his words carefully, he said, "I know this is a tricky one and I can see it from both sides."

Glancing round for a reaction, Johnny saw Jamie idly tuning his guitar with a relaxed air of calm, whilst Danny fiddled with his hair agitatedly.

"The songs are brilliant. Simple as that," Johnny said.

This afforded a quick smile to pass across Jamie's lips.

"But, it's not that simple. Regardless of royalty splits, you're a band. A really fucking tightknit band. And that's always been one of your strengths." Taking a deep breath, he ploughed on. "I think you have to take them on board but only when you've jammed them out. Put the band's stamp on them. In your studio. In your hometown. Then we sit down in a few weeks and see where we are at."

"Sounds fair," Dominic said. "D-Mo? Kong?"

"S'pose," Danny replied sulkily. "The bass parts are shite, so I know I can improve on them." He turned to Mikee, who had remained stoically quiet. "What do ya reckon Kong?"

"Same as you. I'm not happy but we have to work with them. Can't just chuck songs like that away. And as you said, I know that I can put way better drum tracks down."

Jamie nodded his head slowly, his Zen calm seemingly intact. "Let's get to work then…"

***

The relief of the night air was like an elixir to Johnny after the cloying tension of the rehearsal room. Even though the band had moved to more luxurious and roomier surroundings, the room had taken on claustrophobic qualities as their summit meeting unfurled.

Closing his eyes and leaning against his newly purchased top-of-the-range Audi A3, Johnny let the Mancunian chill seep through his shirt until he could no longer stop himself shivering against it.

Pulling out his phone, he speed-dialled Cally.

Voicemail.

"*Hiya. It went okay I guess. Yeah. Danny was most vociferous about it all funnily enough. Although Dom still seems uneasy about it all. But he's doing a good job of covering it all up. I'll see ya soon…*"

***

Like a four-stringed Scud missile, Danny flung his guitar against the plexiglass studio window. With an embarrassed skip, he sidestepped as it ricocheted back, landing at his feet, seemingly unscathed.

"IF YOU SAY, 'JESSIE SAID' ONE MORE FUCKIN' TIME!" Danny shouted through the studio mic. Bending down to retrieve the bass guitar - willing it to be intact - his heart sank yet further when the neck splintered away from the body.

"FUCK'S SAKE! LOOK WHAT YOU HAVE MADE ME DO NOW!"

"Err, I think that's a good time to call it a day," Gareth, the studio's pragmatic sound engineer said as he pushed his baseball cap back off his head and gave his receding crop a thorough scratch.

Turning the studio intercom off, Mikee entered the recording room and attempted to pacify Danny, who was sat on the floor attempting to put the pieces of his guitar together – with all the frustrations of a child with a jigsaw missing several pieces.

Back in the studio control room, Dominic winced at the scene playing out in front of him. Turning to Jamie, he said, "Go easy on him, he's onboard with all this but let him stamp his mark on it. He was going on about some nonsense that he felt like a session musician."

Jamie nodded, feeling a slight pang of guilt at his friend's irritations.

"Think on J. We're a band. This is our album. Yeah?"

***

Given the uneasy tension that had seeped into the early stages of the 're-recording' process, Johnny had kept a wide berth, letting the band resolve any differences amongst themselves.

He had taken the liberty of sending the 'new' album to the label. They had been pressuring him for some material and he had assumed a rather 'fuck it' approach and sent them the whole album.

Which had the opposite effect of his 'get them off my back' intentions…
They loved it.
Correction.
The label abso-fucking-lutely loved it. Platinum units shifting loved it. Off the scale loved it. And wanted to hear the finished product.
Yesterday.
And without any consent from anyone Johnny sent a digital folder of the 'first take' of the album down to their A & R man.
Who passed it straight on to the head of the label.
Who then demanded to come up and hear it. In person. As soon as possible.

***

With a somewhat less fraught day's recording over, the band decided to reconvene for a post-studio pint – a habit that had died out in recent weeks. They had been asked to step in as headliners at the Manchester Arena for a benefit gig as the lead singer of the original headliners was having problems checking out of The Priory.

The album was close to being completed and had multiple platinum shifting units written right through it.

"It'll crack America wide open for you," Johnny had said - to a mixed bag of a response given the album's genesis was Stateside.

Having taken group ownership of Jamie's work, the songs sounded even more extraordinary. Particularly the opening track, which had been worked into a momentum ascending behemoth – Dominic's guitar ripping through some ridiculously great percussion laid down by Mikee and Dan.

It was now Led Zep channelled through Manchester psychedelia with a quick detour to Chicago House and a stopover on Joe Strummer's Westway. The best British album that Johnny had heard in years. The centrepiece of the album was an eight-minute, psychedelic epic that begged to be played loud and live. The album was an unmistakable classic that would sell by the absolute bucket load.

"I'll jump in with you Johnny," Mikee said, as he poured his muscular frame into the black leather passenger seat of Johnny's car. The suspension gave a little as he scooted the seat back to accommodate himself.

"No bother dude. Album's sounding amazing. But you knew that," Johnny said as he cracked the window down and turned the stereo up. The outro to

'Helter Skelter' momentarily filled the car until Mikee's thumb quashed the legendary *'I've got blisters on my fingers'* moment just as Johnny was about to recite it parrot fashion.

"I need a chat, boss. Don't pull off just yet," Mikee said as he removed his iPhone from the pouched pocket on his hoodie.

Johnny turned off the ignition and took in a deep breath. The prodigiously talented drummer wasn't one to mince his words and had seemed very much at ease throughout the recent sessions. Indeed, he had been responsible for calming Danny's Mancunian-Irish frustrations.

"What's up man?" Johnny asked.

"You need to see this," Mikee said as he scrolled to the video library on his mobile.

A jumpy image filled the small screen. Once the image had stopped jumping about, Johnny saw a face reflected in a mirror.

Lara. Or at least it certainly looked like her.

Holding the phone up to the large mirror in her luxurious Manhattan hotel suite, she had captured herself naked from the waist down.

With a man between her legs.

Johnny.

The bottle green face of his prized Rolex together with his trademark Fred Perry polo shirt and dirty brown collar length hair was instantly recognisable to him.

Closing his eyes, he uttered a barely audible, "Fuck," to himself.

"It's you, isn't it boss?" Mikee asked rhetorically. Willing the answer to be no.

The image snapped off and Johnny leant forward, and repeatedly banged his head on the steering wheel.

"What the fuck man? Tell me that wasn't an ongoing thing," Mikee said, a hurt, demanding tone in his voice.

"You probably wouldn't believe me if I told you," Johnny said, feeling his world caving in on him. "And where the fuck did you get that from anyhow?"

Relaying the whole story, Johnny thought he was going to be sick when he heard that his very own 'sex tape' was being hosted on numerous porn sites in the Western world.

Lara's recording of his foolish moment of weakness had 'somehow' found its way onto the world wide web. Out there for everyone to see.

A forty-something, slightly greying no-one featuring in a leaked 'sex-tape'.

With a supermodel. *This doesn't get any more ridiculous*, Johnny thought as he struggled to compose himself.

The drummer's proclivity for all things pornographic had led to the discovery, and Johnny's dismay couldn't have been more apparent.

"This is really fuckin' bad," Mikee said. Stating the very fucking obvious.

"I know," Johnny said in a whisper. "And it won't be long before Jamie finds out about it."

"Then tell him before he does," Mikee replied stoically. "He's gonna find out. You have to tell him. Tell him what you told me." The hurt in his eyes cut Johnny to the quick. He had not just betrayed Jamie, it was the whole band's trust.

"I will," Johnny said slowly, thinking that his priority was to find out from Lara how in fuck's name this guilty secret had found its way into the public domain.

"I'll make excuses for you. You drop me off at the boozer and go and sort your shit out and decide how you are going to deal with this," Mikee said.

"Thanks man," Johnny said as he punched the drummer's watermelon sized bicep, "I will."

After he had eased himself out of the passenger seat, Mikee leaned across and 'street shook' Johnny's hand, fixing him with a well-intended glare. "Sort this."

Seeing Mikee enter the pub, Johnny again cracked the window and let the cold air rush in. He stared blankly through the windscreen feeling like he was stood in a wind tunnel being bombarded by his past and the potential wreckage of his future…

***

"But why the fuck would you record it in the first place?" Johnny asked angrily.

He had managed to contact Lara within a day of finding out about the 'leak' and was in no mood to stand on ceremony.

"If you hadn't been stupid or manipulating enough to film it, then it wouldn't be beaming world-fuckin'-wide right now would it. Fuck's sake!" Johnny rasped.

"Now hold on, Mr. High and Mighty. If you hadn't gone down on my sweet little pussy then none of this would have happened," Lara replied coyly.

"I don't believe your phone was hacked," Johnny retorted – just about resisting performing transatlantic air quotes. "And I didn't ask you to get your cunt out. I know what I did was wrong, but fuck that if you think I instigated it!"

"Tell that to Jamie. And don't use that word in front of a lady," Lara said, that goading tone again so prevalent in her voice.

"I am going to tell him. That'll be the end to your little game."

"Sure you will. Kiss goodbye to your little cash cow either way," Lara said, laughing down the phone at Johnny.

"Fuck off Lara. You horrible cunt," Johnny said coldly.

"Enjoy the journey down Johnny Harrison. 'Cos you ain't talking your ass out of this one. Ciao."

Slamming the phone down into the sofa, Johnny pinched the bridge of his nose and slumped back into the cushions. *The bitch is probably right*, he thought, *this was a lose-lose situation with Jamie and the band.*

And Cally. Who he truly loved, and he knew this could break her heart and trust in him…

The Rock'N'The Roll. 'N That

Chapter 67

As part of the 'therapy' that Jamie had undergone in LA, he had agreed that he would stop his obsessive Lara cyber searches. This had given Johnny a couple of days' grace to steel himself before he made his confession.

Forgive me Jamie, for I have sinned. Thou shalt not perform fellatio on thy lead singer's on/off supermodel girlfriend.

Even if one is off one's nut on industrial strength cocaine…

First, a summons from Cally for a coffee and some 'big news'. He had decided he had to make clear what had happened, but this felt almost harder than telling Jamie. She had to know from him though.

She had been very quiet, nothing new there – almost nervous on the phone when they had spoken, but she had said it was urgent that they met. That morning.

Surely, she can't have been browsing YouPorn searching for middle aged man punching well over his weight he thought…

Having dealt with the morning's emails – a release date for the third album had been confirmed for a month's time – Johnny showered and headed off with condemned-man-like trepidation.

"Hey lovely lady," Johnny said as Cally opened the front door to him. He kissed her on the proffered cheek and accepted her offer of a coffee.

Bringing the mugs through to the front room, Johnny looked at her. Her wavy brown hair worn over one shoulder, her gorgeous blue eyes. Perfect. As ever.

"I've got something to tell you," said Johnny as he placed his mug on the small wooden table.

"Me too. And I can't imagine your news is bigger than this. So, me first," Cally said. A smile played across her lips.

"You first," Johnny replied. Playing her game, and happy to delay his personal bombshell.

"I never expected this. You know. Us," Cally said, leaning across from her sofa and taking Johnny's hand in hers.

The Rock'N'The Roll. 'N That

He nodded his appreciation and squeezed her hand.

"Anyhow. I've checked and double checked," she said, letting out a nervous giggle. "And I'm pregnant!"

Throwing her arms around Johnny, she let out a schoolgirl on the front row at a boyband concert squeal.

Speechless. Utterly speechless.

"I don't know what to say. That's amazing," said Johnny as the maelstrom of his world sped up making him feel like an astronaut undergoing centrifugal training.

"What's your big news then?" Cally asked, her cheeks flushed red.

Stammering slightly, he said, "Oh err, it's just the new album is out in a couple of months' time and sounds unbelievable. I, err, I've got a copy in the car for you." His mouth drier than a Saharan sandstorm.

Sitting for a further hour nodding and oohing and ahhing in what he perceived to be the right places, Johnny was floundering like the first fish trying to make its maiden trek on to terra firma.

Abruptly, he then got up. "Sorry Cally, I'm running late. I've got to scoot." Hugging her into him tightly, he screwed his eyes up. "I love you. I really do. I love you both."

As he left, he heard Cally shout, "And not a word yet. As we agreed!"

Getting into the car, Johnny felt like the world was smothering him - waving and forcing a smile as Cally waved him off as she playfully patted her tummy.

And then the shit really hit the fan.

His phone pinged announcing the arrival of an email. From the label.

Sitting at the traffic lights, he opened the message.

Skim reading, he read four words that sent him reeling: *'Model ODs on Heroin'*

"Fuck me!" Johnny said to himself, utterly aghast.

Pulling over as soon as he could, he read the entire email from the band's press officer – who it appeared had taken over the vigil of Lara watch from Jamie.

A short press release from Lara's people – "*Ms Bearheart was indeed rushed to hospital after collapsing outside her apartment. An exceptionally busy workload and the stresses of her recent miscarriage have caused her to make some very poor lifestyle decisions. Some of the company that Ms Bearheart has kept of late had introduced her to certain Class A substances that she would normally have been totally opposed to and would normally have avoided at all costs. This 'Rock and Roll' lifestyle is not something she actively pursued, and she feels very much that she has been victim of extreme peer pressure to sustain certain relationships. Lara sees herself very much as a positive role model to young people, particularly young women, and completely regrets this reckless and isolated episode. Furthermore, Lara will be entering a full drug rehabilitation programme when she is well enough to leave hospital. We would ask that her privacy is respected throughout this ordeal."*

Feeling light headed, Johnny threw the car door open in order that he could grab a bottle of water from a nearby shop.

A car horn screeched as a driver had to swerve out of the path of Johnny's car door. Holding up a hand in acknowledgment, Johnny bought the water and slumped onto the pavement outside the shop with the demeanour of someone begging for change.

Even with Jamie's abstinence from digital stalking he couldn't hope to avoid these lurid headlines. Four very simple words. One very complicated situation.

And then Johnny's phone rang.

Jamie.

Bracing himself, he said, "J."

"Johnny! What the fuck's going on. There's a full-on scrape of press at my front gate, saying Lara nearly died and it's my fault! What the fuck."

"I'm on my way," was all Johnny could muster.

His day was just lurching from one headfuck to another.

Arriving at Jamie's house, there was indeed a veritable scrape of press photographers. Putting on sunglasses and putting a newspaper against the car window, Johnny was buzzed through the gates.

He was greeted by a frantic Jamie. "Thanks for coming so quick. What the fuck is going on?"

Sighing and with a slow shake of his head, he said, "Sit down J. And I'll fill you in. I've seen her statement and I know how the press will spin it."

Johnny proceeded to show Jamie the almost accusatory statement. The intent was plain for all to see. And it was obvious which way the Bearheart finger was pointing.

"Look Johnny. I did it once or twice. Smoked with her. And yeah, it was good, but it was her gear and I've never touched it since. I swear," Jamie said beseechingly.

"I believe you. 100%. But try convincing that lot if they get the bit between their teeth," Johnny said, his hand on Jamie's shoulder.

Inhaling deeply, Johnny braced himself for his own revelation.

"I loved her Johnny. I really loved her," Jamie said, his head in his hands. "I would never do or say anything to hurt her. I'm sure she loved me as well."

The Rock'N'The Roll. 'N That

Here we go, thought Johnny. *Here we fucking go.*

"Look J. Lara is many things, and I'm sure you did have something. But she's not all she seems, y'know," Johnny said, deliberating over his words meticulously.

"But that's just the side the public get to see. I saw the real her. I did!" Jamie protested.

"Do you remember when you were in London and the press were showing up wherever you went. I told you Lara was tipping the press off so she could promote her clothing brand," Johnny said.

"Yeah. It was a load of bullshit. Something or nothing. I wasn't that bothered," Jamie said as he pulled at his hair irritably.

"Well. Lara was pissed off that I told you it was all staged. She had a bit of grudge against me after that. Thought I was too protective of you and that."

"She liked you? You always seemed to get on," Jamie replied.

"Yeah well. Remember when you were stranded in Vegas after Dom's stag and I was in New York," Johnny said, fidgeting with the drawstring on his hoodie.

"Yeah?" Jamie said. A vein in his temple seemed to throb slightly.

"I met Lara at some party. Did a load of coke with her. A shitload of coke. Anyhow we went back to her hotel. I called you from there but couldn't get through. Do you remember?"

"Vaguely. I was on Dom's stag," Jamie deadpanned.

"Anyhow, I was getting ready to leave. Catch a cab back to my hotel and that…"

"What the fuck happened, Johnny?" Jamie said, standing up and starting to pace up and down his spacious front room.

"I went for a piss, came back to say my goodbyes and Lara was in her bedroom." Closing his eyes, Johnny said his next sentence very slowly. "And I went down on her."

"What the fuck do you mean? You went down on her," Jamie said, surprisingly calmly. He had now stopped pacing and was stood over Johnny.

"Jamie. I'm so sorry. So fucking sorry. She was sat there half naked. And asked me to go down on her." Squeezing his hands either side of his head, Johnny looked up at Jamie.

Who stared back blankly.

"I don't get this. She just told you to go down on her, so you did."

"Yes and no," Johnny replied meekly.

Still not raising his voice, much to Johnny's surprise. "What's that supposed to mean?"

"Yes, I did. But it wasn't straightforward. I didn't fuck her. I just left. She told me it was blackmail, so I wouldn't stick my nose in where she didn't want it."

"Unfortunate turn of phrase," Jamie said coldly.

"I know I shouldn't have done it, Jamie. I fuckin' love you man. You know that!" Johnny said, standing and opening his arms wide.

"And why the fuck are you telling me this? You could have kept it as your sordid little secret."

"It's on the internet."

"What?" Jamie replied incredulously.

"She filmed it."

Letting out a sarcastic laugh, he said, "So you're on the internet. Going down on Lara."

"She reckons she had her phone hacked," Johnny said.

"Is this some big fuckin' joke? Are the rest of the band in on this?" Jamie asked, looking around the room, half-expecting his bandmates to jump out from behind the curtains.

"It isn't. And I'm sorry. Really sorry. Ask Mikee."

"What the fuck has Mikee got to do with it?" Jamie asked, getting more bewildered by the second.

"He found it. Showed me. I told him the truth," Johnny said, desperately trying to convince Jamie of his remorse. "Lara said she would tell you if I didn't. I didn't want that. I wanted to tell you how much I regretted it."

"I can't cope with this. You. You of all people. Just go. NOW!"

"But Jamie..."

"Go," Jamie said. "Go. And don't bother coming to the gig on Saturday."

With tears in his eyes and his world spiralling out of control, Johnny left and drove through the press pack willing every one of them dead....

Chapter 68

A field day. The newspapers. Scratch that. The tabloids had absolutely gone to town with the 'story'.

'*Heroin pushing singer causes Model to OD*'
'*It's only Smack 'n' Roll, but you'll like it*'
'Rock Star & Drug pusher'
'I nearly died thanks to Jamie Thorne…'

The luridly fabricated headlines were all published on the day of the band's hometown benefit gig.

Backstage the tension was palpable. Jamie had retreated to his own dressing room and wasn't speaking. To anyone.

He hadn't soundchecked – having arrived some three hours late. Anxious mutterings were afoot, as to whether he'd play the gig.

Johnny – against Jamie's wishes – had briefed the band on the full story, although he got the distinct impression that they had all seen said homemade porn clip.

Understandably, the band had never been so solemn. Clearly, being aware of the anguish that Jamie was suffering had affected them all.

They had all read the papers. Every twisted, manipulated deceiving hateful adjective.

No-one more than Jamie himself who had spent all day pouring over every word that had been written.

He had made a two-word response via Twitter.

'*UTTER NONSENSE*'

Danny was full of righteous indignation, telling anyone that would listen that Jamie was 'innocent'. Having all refused a pre-gig press conference, Mikee made the none too thinly veiled threat that he would 'do time' if he saw a reporter anywhere near him.

And Dominic. He felt Jamie's pain worse than anyone. He had barely said a word, having spent most of the evening knocking on Jamie's dressing room door to no avail.

Nine thirty.

Showtime.

And still no indication as to whether there would be a show.

Knocking on the white wooden door, Dom said, "J. We're going on bro. We need you."

Taking to the stage, they were met with a hushed silence.

Twenty thousand open mouths. Silence as they waited for Jamie.

Will he, won't he?

It was what must have been the longest sixty seconds in the band's lives – exchanging nervous glances, willing Jamie to step forward.

And then he did.

Striding purposefully to the mic carrying an acoustic guitar. Dressed head to toe in black denim, collar popped up. Black beanie hat covering his head and shades covering his petrol blue eyes.

And no red scarf.

For the first time ever, he had taken to the stage without his habitual slash of colour.

Without looking at his bandmates, Jamie adjusted the mic stand.

You could hear the crowd audibly hold their collective breaths.

"This one seems sort of appropriate," Jamie muttered.

Ignoring the setlist, he then launched into a solo rendition of 'Lies'.

Exchanging symbiotic nods, the rest of the band followed Jamie's lead. Dominic stepping over to share the acid drenched chorus before kissing his brother on the cheek and then stepping away to launch into the most stunning of solos.

As the song finished, the crowd seemed to pause for a second before going absolutely batshit crazy. A handful of red scarves were hurled in the direction of the stage. Mobile phone cameras captured every moment.

"Thank you," Jamie said humbly.

"DON'T BELIEVE THE BULLSHIT," Danny shouted down his mic before angrily flouting all on stage regulations and lighting up.

Having dispensed with his own guitar, Jamie paced the lip of the stage for the next three songs, his vocals straining into a ragged yowl on more than one occasion.

Ignoring the setlist once again, Jamie picked up his Fender, plugged in and struck up the opening bars of 'Salvation'.

Mid-song, he jumped up on to the top of his guitar amp – balancing precariously as he watched Dominic deliver the song's familiar coda.

Leaping off just as the amp started to topple, he then drove his precious guitar neck first into the prone amplifier, which formed a macabre looking musical gravestone.

Which was feeding back wildly.

The band stuttered to a halt as Jamie, grabbing the mic in one hand, walked to the front of the stage.

Taking his shades off, he surveyed the vast arena. The towering banks of seats. The now still moshpit directly in front of him.

A hush descended over the crowd as Jamie addressed them

"I'm sorry. I can't do this anymore. I love my band." Pausing, as he looked at them all in turn, he said, "I really do. But I can't do this anymore…"

And with that he left the stage.

Walked out of the rear of the venue and jumped into a passing black cab.

As the cab pulled away and drove over the River Irwell, a mobile phone was thrown over the side of the bridge. Spinning end over end before splashing into the murky brown waters…

***

A number one album inevitably followed. The record label decided to proceed with the release despite Jamie's absence.

The hype surrounding the album was incredible. Despite no lead singer to promote the album, the sheer class of the songs and the furore and mystery engulfing the band created its own unstoppable momentum.

The Twittersphere was full of supposed sightings. None of which were corroborated.

As the months passed, Dominic retreated to his house on the hill with Eleanor and maintained a stoic silence.

Danny resumed playing the happy family man but was a seething mass of resentment as he fretted over the future of the band.

The only Lonely Soul to maintain a public persona was Mikee – who started running drum clinics for disenfranchised teenagers.

And Johnny and Cally – he spared her the ignominy of the 'sex tape' secret – made their announcement amidst muted well wishes given Jamie's disappearance.

The Rock'N'The Roll. 'N That

***

Seven months after the fateful show, Cally gave birth to the most beautiful baby girl – Poppy Anne Thorne.

Life went on. As it had to.

And everybody who cared waited and waited for word on the whereabouts of Jamie Thorne....

Chapter 69

There was not a day went by that they didn't think about Jamie.

Parenthood had come naturally to Johnny – he had settled into middle-aged parenting with a vigour that had surprised him. Cally was the most doting mother a child could wish for, although Johnny knew that every time she looked at their child, she saw Jamie – the intensity of the blue eyes was unmistakable.

Dominic had been a regular visitor – which was of huge comfort to his mother. He had taken to his new sister, but the hurt of his missing twin was never far away.

Late one lazy autumnal afternoon, Johnny was sat in the conservatory of their new family home, inducting his daughter to the delights of *The Good, The Bad and The Ugly* whilst the incessant Mancunian rain hammered therapeutically on the glass ceiling.

Hearing the now not so regular ping of his mobile phone, he tabbed through the security lock to see that he had a Twitter Direct Message.

From Jamie.

'I'm home. We need to talk…'

Wide-eyed, Johnny read and re-read the six words thirty characters message before sending his reply.

'When?'

An instant reply.

'Tonight'

***

With a hastily made excuse run by Cally, he headed off to Jamie's house – which upon arriving was totally shrouded in darkness. Seemingly still uninhabited.

Buzzing the security intercom, he whispered, "It's me."

The Rock 'N' The Roll. 'N That

A metallic *bzzzz* and the gates slowly opened.

Johnny drove through, the crunch of the gravel the only sound. He parked up and taking a deep breath, knocked on the sturdy front door.

The door had been left ajar and he stepped inside.

Acclimatising to the dark, he saw the figure of Jamie before him. The dimly lit kitchen illuminated by a handful of candles. Shadows flickered against the exposed brick walls as drafts whistled between the old window frames.

Gone was the thick brown Strummer-esque quiff, replaced by a seriously shaved crop.

He had lost weight and his once perfect cheekbones now protruded gauntly – like pieces of flint had been transplanted under the skin.

Sat at the farmhouse table, his eyes blazed like pilot lights against the charcoal semi-darkness.

Jamie broke the silence. "Been a long time."

"Hasn't it. Everybody has missed you. Every day," Johnny said quietly.

"Come and sit down. Break bread with me. We've got some catching up to do," Jamie said quietly, gesturing Johnny over. The table was empty, save a bottle of beer.

Picking up the empty bottle, he said, "Want one?"

Pulling a chair back with a piercing scrape, Johnny nodded and sat down. Grateful that the beer would assuage the excessive dry mouth he was suffering from. Hanging his parka over the back of the chair and placing his car keys, wallet and mobile phone on the table, Johnny waited for Jamie to speak first.

Offering his bottle up, Johnny reciprocated the gesture and the two bottles clinked together tunefully.

"What do you know then, Johnny?" Jamie asked.

Taking a long draw on the chilled bottle, he said, "What do I know? That you've been missed. And I'm still sorry for the part I played in that." Drinking deeply again. "You'll never know how sorry."

Shrouded in the half-light, the solitary candle behind him cast a halo like silhouette.

A real live resurrection, Johnny thought as he looked across the table at Jamie.

"The label released the album. Number one here and America. Sold by the boatload. And you didn't even have to tour it," Johnny said before letting out a wry laugh.

Ignoring Johnny's opening gambit.

"You know how much you hurt me, don't you?" Jamie said as he then produced a small white wrap and placed it on the table in front of him.

"Of course I do. I love you man and I never wanted to do anything that would hurt you. I'll never be able to apologise enough," Johnny said as he wrung his hands in contrition.

"I do believe you," Jamie said. "But you and Lara." Pausing and holding Johnny's gaze, he added, "And what about you and Mum? You've been fucking her as well."

"It's not like that," Johnny replied hastily. "Not like that at all."

"I'd known for ages. Right back to the Roses gig. Sneaking in and out of hotel rooms."

"That's not true," Johnny said, shaking the now empty bottle.

"Want another?" Jamie asked, matter of fact. Returning from the fridge, he placed them on the table together with a white dinner plate. "What's not true?"

"Me and Cally. Your mum. We haven't been sneaking around. Look, there's something I need to tell you," Johnny said.

"Let me finish first," Jamie said, wiping the back of his hand across his mouth. "Two of the people I care most about in the world. My mum and Lara. And you couldn't help yourself."

"I told you. It's not like that," Johnny protested.

"I figured you were both adults. Knew what you were getting into. But why didn't you tell me?" Jamie asked.

"There was nothing to tell at that stage. Honestly," Johnny said

"You want to know where I've been for the past year?" Jamie asked.

Nodding slightly, Johnny sat impassively, giving Jamie the floor.

"In Thailand. Living in a grass hut. Trying to figure this mess out."

Johnny shook his head slowly. "I don't know what to say," he said softly.

"Those headlines. WHAT PEOPLE WERE THINKING ABOUT ME! AND SAYING ABOUT ME!" Jamie's raised voice startled Johnny.

"The people that really mattered. The ones that loved you knew the truth, though," Johnny said, an urgent tone to his voice.

"Nice to know," Jamie said as he emptied the contents of the wrap onto the plate.

A small pile of off-white crystal powder sat in a neat mound. Jamie carved the powder into two thick parallel lines.

"You're here to break bread with me. Make the peace. Seek forgiveness," Jamie asked. "You got a note? Not had chance to get to the bank since I got home."

The Rock 'N' The Roll. 'N That

"I don't do that anymore," Johnny said, pushing the plate away. "I've not touched it in ages. Don't need it."

"C'mon Johnny. Just one. You used to love it. Digging in after gigs and that." Jamie pushed the plate back towards Johnny. "Roll a note. Just like old times."

Looking down at the rail of powder, Johnny reached for his wallet and slowly rolled a twenty-pound note into a tight straw. Offering it to Jamie. "All yours."

"You first. You're my guest remember," Jamie said. "Actually, best not. You might accidentally suck my cock…"

"No," Johnny said, pushing the plate back towards Jamie and proffering the rolled-up note.

"I've not touched anything for months. I wanted to be totally clean before I came home," Jamie said, as he too pushed the plate aside.

"Things have changed whilst you've been away. I'm pretty much clean. Don't drink much. No drugs at all. Things have changed a lot for me. That's what I'm trying to tell you. I'm a da—"

"NO. LET ME FINISH WHAT I'M TRYING TO TELL YOU," Jamie shouted as he stood up abruptly, causing his chair to topple backwards and clatter onto the slate-tiled floor.

Shoving Johnny by the shoulder. "LOOK AT ME, MAN!"

Looking up at Jamie, seeing his hurt and anger pouring out, Johnny stood up out of his chair. "Jamie, c'mon. I've come here to listen. To apologise. Again," Johnny said, as he held his hands up as if in surrender.

"DO YOU KNOW HOW MUCH I'VE BEEN HURT. BY EVERYTHING. BUT I NEVER THOUGHT YOU'D HURT ME!" Jamie said as he planted both his hands on Johnny's chest. Shoving him backwards.

Catching him off balance, Johnny caught his foot in the sleeve of his parka which had bunched up between the chair leg and the floor. Falling, he caught the back of his head against the butcher's block work surface with a sickening thud.

Dropping to the floor, unconscious, he lay perfectly still as a pool of blood haloed around his head.

Slumping to his knees, Jamie looked down, horrified at the reaction to his action.

His manager and friend lay totally motionless, save the thick flow of blood oozing from the back of his head.

"JOHNNY! FOR FUCK'S SAKE DON'T DO THIS TO ME MAN!"

Cradling Johnny's head in his arms, Jamie pushed hair back off his face. "Johnny. Johnny. Don't do this. I didn't mean to hurt you. Come on we're friends again now. All's forgiven."

Still nothing.

Holding his bloodied hands out in front of him, Jamie began to sob. Long, slow heartfelt sobs.

"C'mon Johnny. I love you man. What the fuck have I done…"

And then a mobile phone rang, snapping Jamie from his panic.

Standing and looking at the vibrating phone, the image on the caller ID screen filled him with pure horror.

Picking the phone up, he saw his mum cradling a baby with Johnny's arm around her, beaming into the camera. The name that flashed up at him was HOME. Illuminating his face in a ghostly blue. He was transfixed in shock.

The voice in his head screaming *what the fuck have I done…*

Chapter 70

For the past three weeks, the metronomic '*beep beep beep*' of the ventilator had been a constant for all visitors to the hospital room.

Jamie reunited with his mother, twin brother and two bandmates.

And meeting his half-sister for the first time.

All tempered by the medical machinations and tubes that were sustaining Johnny.

Both Jamie and Cally – as much as the demands of second-time round motherhood would allow – had kept a round the clock bedside vigil. Waiting on any slight change. Any blink or twitch that would provide some sort of hope.

"He'll be okay. I know he will," Jamie said as he held his mother's hand. "He's got to look after you and my little sister."

Brushing a finger gently against the baby's cheek, as Cally gently bounced her rhythmically on her knee. Gurgling in pleasure, flapping her tiny arms in Jamie's direction. Her petrol blue eyes wide. Blissfully unaware of the anxiety that was suffocating her mother and half-brother.

Closing her eyes, always seconds away from tears, Cally looked at Jamie, her voice a soft murmur. "You have to be right, Jamie. I can't bring Poppy up on my own. Looking at her every day as a reminder." Her voice trailed off as the stark reality again flooded her. Unable to suppress her emotions any longer, a flow of tears ran down her make-up free face.

"I know you don't want to talk about it. Her. But I had a message from Lara," Jamie said.

Cally's eyes changed from deep sorrow to venomous hatred in the flick of switch.

"She says sorry. To me. And Johnny. And she said she can never forgive herself for the lies about the pregnancy."

"That makes everything okay then?" Cally asked.

"No. No it doesn't," Jamie said with a solemn shake of his head. "And before you ask, I won't be having anything at all to do with her. Ever."

"I blame her. For all this. Everything," Cally said, her resentment never far from boiling point.

"I know," Jamie said. "I know."

The atmosphere was broken as the door opened and Dominic walked in, blond hair tied back, and sunglasses plastered to his face.

"Fuckin' wankers," Dominic said as he pulled over a chair and placed a hand on Johnny's leg.

"Dominic!" Cally scolded.

"Fuck 'em. I wish they'd piss off and give us some space. Gonna set Mikee on them next time," Dominic said, reaching over to hold his mum's hand. "Still no change?"

"Nothing," Jamie said.

"D-Mo is convinced that playing music down some headphones will wake him up," Dom said.

"Play something he hates and that'll probably do it, "Cally said as she tried to force a smile…

Chapter 71

"He'll be here," Dominic said as he pulled awkwardly at his black tie. A sharp black suit and matching Converse completed his funeral garb.

The three of them stood at the rear of the hearse, head to toe in black, sunglasses on, despite the battered and bruised Manchester sky.

The funeral director nodded at them, coughing softly to clear his throat. "We can wait another two minutes, gentlemen. But no more than that I am afraid."

"He'll be here," Dominic repeated, stared over towards the cemetery gates, willing his brother to appear.

"I'll text him," Danny said, reaching inside his suit pocket for his mobile.

"Put the fuckin' thing away," Dominic hissed. "He'll be here. I know it."

"I was only try—" Danny said.

"Sorry man. Didn't mean to snap," Dominic said as he leant forward and pulled Danny towards him, kissing him lightly on the forehead, their sunglasses clacking together.

Surreptitiously looking at his watch, the funeral director was about to speak when a black taxi cab made its way slowly towards the party, having been waved through by the security that flanked the wrought iron gates.

"I knew it," Dominic said, smiling for the first time that day.

As the cab, slowed to a stop, all eyes were on the door as it opened.

Jamie.

In an immaculate matching black suit, shirt and tie. Sunglasses on.

And his red scarf loosely hung around his neck.

Hugging all three bandmates in turn and without a word – before turning and nodding in the direction of his mum and Poppy.

"Gentlemen. If you could please slide the coffin slowly out and lift it on to your shoulders. Thank you," the funeral director said solemnly.

With a slight wobble, the coffin was raised and balanced on the inside shoulder of all four Lonely Souls.

The Rock'N'The Roll. 'N That

Taking measured steps towards the graveside, the beautifully maudlin tones of Joy Division's 'Atmosphere' began to drift across the graveyard – eliciting the first sniffles of the morning from the attendant mourners.

A guestlist that ran to some one hundred and fifty. With many more told to attend the aftershow/wake.

A humanist service had been organised – a burial at Cally's behest, with a simple headstone that would read simply: '*A good man lies here. Missed by all. Every day x*'

No speeches had been planned, the idea being that anyone with anything to say would take a moment to reflect at the wake.

As the four band members lowered the coffin, the unmistakable voice of Mick Jagger opined to the black clad gathered mourners that, '*You Can't Always Get What You Want…*'

The funeral songs had been selected by Johnny in his early twenties and intermittently chopped and changed over the years. The blasé way that he had discussed them had always irked Cally and her bloodshot eyes – concealed by large round sunglasses – let out yet more tears as the vocal refrain played out.

The coffin rocked slightly as it was lowered before resting on the freshly dug earth. Walking around the graveside to join Jamie and Dominic, the band then stood there, arms around each other's shoulders. Not a word was passed between them.

Joined by Cally – with Poppy held tightly in her arms. The baby-sized black leggings and hastily purchased black duffle coat were a heart wrenching sight – clad for a funeral but utterly oblivious to the loss and pain she would feel in later life.

The main body of mourners began to drift away – solemn nods, waves and kisses were blown at the coffin. The band stood stock still until the last of them had departed. As they broke their tight huddle, Jamie unfurled his beloved red scarf, kissed it, and let it drop onto the coffin, unable to stop tears rolling down his cheeks.

"Next album is for Johnny," Jamie said, choking back yet more tears. "I'm sorry," he whispered inaudibly.

"For Johnny," came the echoed response…

THE END. AND THAT…

A short note from the author

You've finished this book - unless you've just skipped to the notes at the back - which makes you very, very ace. THANK YOU!

With the myriad of modern distractions vying for your attention, you've bought or borrowed this book on proper papyrus or pixelated prose and invested your time into reading my words and I couldn't be more grateful.

Writing this book was a hugely enjoyable experience and subsequently got it into print and then in the hands of you wonderful readers, has made me immensely proud.

And even though it's highly likely that we've never met, I'd like to ask a favour.

If you could take a couple of minutes to nip over to Amazon and leave a review, that would be excellent. As a first-time author working with an independent publisher, reviews and internet traffic are vitally important for both of us. I'm both keen to get feedback on my endeavours and to generate web reviews which are hugely beneficial currency in terms of the ongoing success of this here novel.

Spread the word - tell people how much you enjoyed this novel!

I would also love to hear from you via all of the social medias - well the ones that I've got a grasp of I should say.

You can reach me on Twitter via @heresgilly and at my lovingly crafted website www.stevenjgillwriter.co.uk.

The website will be updated with various newsworthy items and you will be able to subscribe to a newsletter which will be sent by one of my digital carrier pigeons directly into your inbox.

Again, thank you for reading this book of mine, you've made me very happy.

Steven

The all-important thanks and acknowledgments.

I'll try not to get too emotional…

Huge thanks to -

Dave Haslam - for running his writing workshop at Folk and inspiring me to crack on with this project. The on-going encouragement was much appreciated.

Emma-Jane Unsworth - who upon reading the initial draft, encouraged me to persevere and provided some invaluable guidance and advice. Your help did make all the difference at exactly the right time. Ta Em x

Mick Peek - Much, much more than brilliant artwork! Our design meetings took on an almost 'therapy session' like quality. Your creative design ideas made me realise that all my words could become an actual book. I can't thank you enough for guiding me through my initial doubts and potential pitfalls. I'd love to think that there will be a few more covers for you to design! You're a top man Mick x

Simon Buckley - For taking a set of pictures that, as I've been told, "you'll never look better than that!" Your time and encouragement were, as always, perfectly timed and helped add a polished look to my marketing blurb. The finest and loveliest lensmith in Mancunia and beyond x

Gareth Howard and Hayley Radford at Clink Street - A book is nothing without readers. And it's even less without a publisher. Thank you for taking what was initially nothing more than a personal project and turning all my work and words into a fully formed book. The editorial process lifted it into something that I am intensely proud of. The whole experience has been quite the learning curve but one that has been thoroughly enjoyable. Thank you again for everything and here's to the next book!

Last, but resolutely not least, huge thanks to each and every one of you who supported this project and ultimately me when I was trying to get this off the ground. Without your support and backing, this would not have happened and remained tucked away gathering digital dust on my laptop.

I can't express how much this means to me and all I can say, is huge, huge thanks and I hope you have enjoyed both the book and the part you played in getting it published.

Keep on supporting whatever great art/literature/music projects that need similar backing. I guarantee, it makes a difference.

Thank you all once again.

Steven

Alphabetical list of backers for 'The Rock'n'The Roll. 'N That...'

Adrian Jones (AJ)
Aidan Jones
Alan Duffy
Alec Scriven
Alex Barley
Amanda Brown
Amanda Hewkin
Andrew Taylor
Andrew Lever
Angela Henry
Bob Brear
Charlie Bell
Chris Curson
Christopher Matthews
Claire Perry
Colin Hendrie
Daniel Taylor
David Coates
David Gill
David Chidlow
Dean Casement
Debbie Etchells
Declan Brennan
Dee Wilkie
François Cancel
Gemma Sutcliffe
Greg Thorpe

Hannah Thomas
Helen Tate
Helen Hayes
Henry Armstrong
Iain McGuire
Ian Howells
Jackie O'Malley
Jacqueline Hoepner
Jan Whiting
Jane Savvides
Jason Greenberg
Jessica Walton
Jimmy Love
John Clamp
Jon Walker
Jude Jagger
Julie Walker
Justin Rouse
Kara Leckenby
Kate Mountain
Katie Potter
Kayleigh Green
Keith Chadwick
Kelly Wild
Kirsty Ball
Laura Vaughan
Laurence Lambourn

Lisa O'Malley	Ric Michael
Mark Howard	Richard Bray
Michael Butterworth	Rob Weeden
Michael Van Zandt	Robert Jones
Michela Johnson	Ruth Turner
Mick Peek	Ruth Martin
Nichola Clark	Sam Wallis
Nick Dunn	Sarah Bates
Nicola Watson	Saul Brody
Nicole Russo	Simon Buckley
Paul Bowers	Sonya Roberts
Paul Turnbull	Stephen O'Malley
Paul Gallagher	Steve Hallam
Paul Bullock	Stuart Fraser
Paula Carville	Theresa James
Peter Weller	Tom Lloyd-Goodwin
Philip Read	Tom Smith
Philip Lovely	Warren Clarke
Philip Randles	William Borrows
Rachel Gill	